W9-AVL-568

SLAUGHTER
HOUSE
CHRONICLES

ALSO BY F. X. BIASI JR.

The Brother-in-Law

The Tanner Extraction

SLAUGHTER HOUSE
CHRONICLES

7/18/16

To: Herb
I hope this enhances
your vocation.

F. X. BIASI JR.

F. X. Biasi Jr.

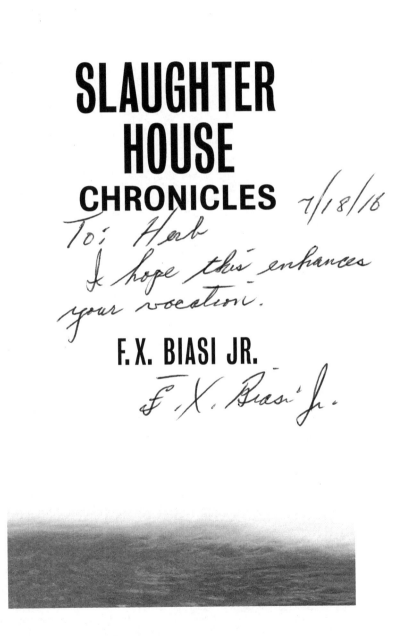

Copyright © 2016 by Francis X. Biasi Jr.

All rights reserved, including the right to reproduce this book or portions thereof in any form whatsoever without the expressed written permission of the author, except for the use of a brief quotation in a book review. For information email fxbiasijr@gmail.com

www.fxbiasijr.com

This book is a work of fiction. Names, characters, places, and incidents either are products of the author's imagination or are used fictitiously. Any resemblance to actual events or locales or persons, living or dead, is entirely coincidental.

Cover and interior design by Williams Writing, Editing & Design

ISBN 978-0-9848781-7-8

PREFACE

In 2011, when I began writing my first novel, *The Brother-In-Law,* I had no idea I would eventually complete three. At the time, all I had was a general outline about a naïve Long Island teenager who, after falling in love and marrying the daughter of a Mafia don, becomes involved in an insidious relationship with the mob.

At first I had only a vague picture of the three main characters: Bart LaRocca, the naïve teenage protagonist; Gina Nicosia, his alluring girlfriend; and Pietro Nicosia, her Mafia don father. As my thinking and writing evolved, I became enamored with character development and eventually with many of the characters. That, as much as anything else, drove the story lines of all three novels. To call what I have written a trilogy might be a stretch of the definition; however, at a minimum, it is a three-volume series featuring many of the same heroes and villains.

I believe each of the novels is interesting enough to stand on its own, and they need not be read in sequence. However, since many of the characters are prominent in all three stories, the characters and their backgrounds are relevant as the series plays out. Rather than force the reader to begin with the first book, I have provided a brief synopsis of each of the prominent crossover characters and how they fit into the series.

Bart Rock alias **Bart LaRocca, Carlos Diaz, Charles Carbone**—The protagonist in *The Brother-in-Law*, who makes a cameo appearance in *The Tanner Extraction* and plays a significant role in *Slaughter House Chronicles*. As a naïve Long Island teenager on an athletic scholarship to a Catholic prep school in Brooklyn during the late 1950s, he meets the Nicosia brothers, Al and John. Their father, Pietro, is a top lieutenant and soon to be the don of one of New York's Mafia families. Fatefully, Bart falls in love with and marries the Nicosias' younger sister, Gina.

Al Nicosia alias **Little Nicky**—Eldest son of Mafia kingpin Pietro Nicosia and brother of Bart's wife, he succeeds his father as head of one of the New York mob families. Featured in *The Brother-in-Law*.

Gina Nicosia—Youngest of the Nicosia children and devoted to her family in spite of their criminal activities, she marries Bart in 1967. Featured in *The Brother-in-Law*.

John Nicosia—Middle child of the Nicosia family and Bart's life-long friend, he avoids a life of crime, becoming a famous cardiologist in the Southwest. Featured in *The Brother-in-Law*.

Patty Jo—Bart's childhood friend, whom he introduces to John Nicosia. John and Patty Jo have a double wedding with Bart and Gina at St. Mark's in Venice. After the deaths of Gina and John, Bart and Patty Jo marry. She features in *The Brother-in-Law* and emerges as a valiant heroine in *Slaughter House Chronicles*.

David Tanner—Bart's college roommate for his first three years at the University of South Carolina. David is heir to a family fortune accumulated over two centuries of successful family businesses in Charleston. Married to Sarah, the couple have two children, **Bruce** and **Rachael**. While on a philanthropic mission to Israel in 2006, David is kidnapped and held for ransom. His kidnapping is covered in my second novel, *The Tanner Extraction,* and he has a minor role in *Slaughter House Chronicles.*

Robbie Ryan—Bart's college roommate his senior year. Robbie and Bart join the Air Force together, where Robbie becomes an F-100 pilot. During an R&R in Saigon, he introduces Bart to Major John Slaughter. John Slaughter and his family are the subjects of my third novel, *Slaughter House Chronicles.*

Sam Sardo—As a young agent assigned to the Organized Crime Task Force in New York, in *The Brother-in-Law* he attempts to convince Bart to gather evidence that would lead to Al Nicosia's arrest and conviction. In *Slaughter House Chronicles,* Sam Sardo is the director of the FBI.

John Slaughter—Retired army major general and Medal of Honor winner who meets Bart in Vietnam through Captain Robbie Ryan. The Slaughter family's epic history becomes the background for *Slaughter House Chronicles.*

Bruce Tanner—David's son, U.S. Navy SEAL, military attaché, and principal in his own private security firm. Besides his incredible physical and combat skills, he is fluent in a dozen languages. Bruce evolves into the lead protagonist in both *The Tanner Extraction* and *Slaughter House Chronicles.*

Dana Wise—FBI special agent assigned directly to the FBI director, she is a former Secret Service agent and media spokesperson for the vice president of the United States. She appears in *The Tanner Extraction* and has a prominent role in *Slaughter House Chronicles.*

Azzan Prinz and **Eitan Fein**—David Tanner's bodyguards. Former Mossad agents who served with Bruce during his embassy work in South America, they are critical resources in protecting Bart in *The Brother-in-Law* and with assisting Bruce Tanner in both *The Tanner Extraction* and *Slaughter House Chronicles.*

Isma'il Hassanat aka **Khamsin**—Son of a former Israeli Defense Force Bedouin tracker. Known by both the Israeli and Egyptian border forces as Khamsin (a desert wind blowing out of the Sinai), he was the scourge of the Sinai and Negev Deserts. In *The Tanner Extraction,* he works for a Russian international smuggling organization and plays a role in *Slaughter House Chronicles.*

Monsignor Anthony Alfano aka **Tony Alfano**—Legendary former Secret Service Agent who resigns from the Secret Service to become a Catholic priest. He becomes an intermediary with the Tanner family and Israeli authorities in *The Tanner Extraction.*

Boris Kozlov—Head of a front for one of the world's most notorious international smuggling operations, he reports directly to the former KGB general **Georgy Nikitin,** one of the world's most wanted men, in *The Tanner Extraction.* In *Slaughter House Chronicles,* Boris resurfaces to play a treacherous role.

SLAUGHTER HOUSE
CHRONICLES

CHAPTER 1

March 2014
The Slaughter Ranch, Humboldt County, California

Retired Major General John Slaughter sat on the front porch admiring the serenity and raw beauty of his ancestral ranch. Tonight he was on his second snifter of eighteen-year-old Gran Duke D'Alba brandy. Either the alcohol or subliminal memories of just how uncomfortable one could be from his four tours in Vietnam left him unfazed by the evening's mild drizzle and fifty-six-degree temperature. No matter the reason, for the last twenty-five years sitting on the front porch had been an almost nightly routine during the North Coast's short damp winters. For the last eight, his constant companion, Leo, a magnificent Rhodesian ridgeback, lay contentedly at his feet.

Normally, the seventy-four-year-old used this time before dinner to review the day's events and to plan his next day, but not this evening. He couldn't stop pondering his earlier conversation with his younger cousin and operations manager, Miles Reynolds. First, there was the issue of the pending layoffs, which he dreaded. But what really had him cogitating were Miles' last words, "There is something strange going on across the creek. "

"Like what?" Slaughter had asked.

"Since Boyer restarted the old sawmill last summer, I've

noticed there's been a constant escalation in the amount and type of traffic through their gate. Then a couple of weeks ago, I watched a crew erecting a six-foot-high, galvanized-welded fence topped with barbed wire along their side of the creek and along the highway. I thought it was strange after all these years, but I really didn't pay it much mind. Then one evening last week, while you were in San Francisco, I was riding in an ATV along the creek when suddenly I realized two armed horsemen were shadowing me from the other bank. We haven't had any problems with them in years, so why all of a sudden are they patrolling their property line? I don't know what's going on, but it makes me suspicious."

"Have you talked to anyone about this?"

"Yeah, I mentioned it to a few guys from the Rancheria who've done some logging for them. They said they have not had any work there in months. Their last gig was widening the road going to the old sawmill and expanding the clearing around it. While they were stacking the cut logs, gravel was being spread along the road. They also saw steel building materials being delivered. The guys heard a new warehouse was going to be erected. However, they also saw large steel pipe and conveyor belts delivered."

"Hmm, that's interesting. You don't need a roof and steel walls to store cut lumber. All you have to do is wrap it in plastic. I wouldn't think the pipe and conveyor belts are for lumber. Do you know who is doing the construction?"

"As far as I can tell, it's not a local contractor. It was a while ago; I'm guessing whatever they were building, it's finished by now."

"Well, Miles, if you're right, it's unlike Boyer to not be bally-hooing one of his new ventures down at the Ingomar Club, yet this is the first I've heard of it. Thanks for the heads-up."

Miles' revelation had piqued the general's curiosity. It had been years since there had been any overt animosity between the families. Two decades ago, open hostilities were the norm. A shrewd smile passed over John Slaughter's face as he recalled his bold decision to get out of the family's historical markets in commercial lumber and the beef cattle business while refocusing on outdoor furniture manufacturing, cheese production, and the breeding of endangered horses and cattle. The move meant he and the Boyers were no longer in direct competition. Since then, he and Clete Boyer Senior, the patriarch of the Boyer family, rarely crossed paths. Granted, they avoided each other as much as possible, but when they were required to be in the same place, usually at the annual Ingomar Club picnic or some prestigious civic event, they were able to muster up a smile and handshake for the sake of appearances.

As John Slaughter rolled the last sip of brandy over his palate, he wondered, *Why the barbed wire and armed patrols along his property line? What's that old coot up to after all these years of détente between us?*

CHAPTER 2

Halfway through his dinner of barbequed rib eye, baked potato, broccoli, and salad, John made up his mind. Before it got too dark, he was going to take a ride along the creek. For years after he retired, he relished that ride in the early mornings and late evenings. Usually he packed an ultralight rod and reel and a couple of his favorite lures. The thought of fishing momentarily distracted his thought process.

He smiled to himself, remembering that week shortly after he retired from the Army when he, Bart LaRocca, David Tanner, and Bob Rivett would spend the day leisurely floating down the Smith River catching salmon and trout. Then in late afternoon, they would return to this porch and drink late into the night, formulating the new business strategy for Slaughter Holdings. It was such a fruitful and exhilarating week that it prompted John to put Bart, David, and Bob on his board of directors. For ten years, every annual board meeting had been held at the Slaughter ranch and included several days of fishing and strategic assessments.

He shook his head in disbelief when he realized it had been almost fifteen years since they last had gotten together at the ranch for a board meeting. He wondered if there was still a price on Bart's head now that his Mafia brother-in-law was dead. Chiding himself for not staying in touch, he vowed, *I've got to call David Tanner tomorrow and catch up on what he and Bart have been up to.*

Sighing, John forced himself to clear his head and start thinking about his upcoming sortie along the creek. His first decision was to take one of the Morgan stallions rather than an ATV. It would be quieter and he wouldn't have to watch where he was going; his horse would do that for him. Although he no longer maintained a whole stable of saddle horses, the three he had were all powerful animals and knew their way around the property.

Just in case he too found himself shadowed by armed guards, he brought along a rod, reel, and hip waders, which he could don to pretend to be on an innocent fishing outing. However, as a precaution, he also strapped his .357 Smith & Wesson revolver around his waist and stuffed the AN/PVS-7A night-vision goggles he received as an Army retirement gift in his saddlebag. Just in case he wasn't tailed and decided to find out what was going on inside the fence, he went out to the barn to pick up a pair of six-inch diagonal cutting pliers and two feet of 22-gauge baling wire.

Walking back to the house, he remembered the new Pentax Optio WG-3 waterproof camera Miles and his wife had given him for Christmas. The camera was still in the box, but tonight seemed a good time to break it in. It took John another fifteen minutes to set up the camera and skim through the user's manual.

Around 6 p.m., with less than an hour and a half of light remaining and fog hanging over the hills on the back side of the ranch, John draped a camouflage military poncho over his still-muscled six-foot, four-inch frame and donned a dark-colored wide-brimmed rain hat. Sitting ramrod straight in the saddle, he rode out into the cold winter mist. His faithful companion Leo scampered out in front, periodically stopping to sniff and pee on his favorite trees.

In fifteen minutes he reached the creek. He slowly rode

parallel to the bank while scanning the far side for any hint of activity. Elk Creek meandered for almost fifteen miles south to north out of the hills emptying into the Van Duzen River. For most of its almost one-mile course between the two ranches, it was lined with stands of mature redwoods, cypress, and Douglas fir.

Seventy-five percent of the area's sixty-five inches of annual rainfall occurred from November through March, temporarily swelling the rivers and streams and cutting an increasingly deeper and wider swath through the soft hilly terrain. In this stretch, the creek was between thirty to fifty feet wide and had cut out a six-foot-deep gash in the forest floor. Now, in the first week of March after a relatively dry February, most of the heavy runoff had passed. Water levels were unusually low for that time of year, leaving an occasional island of sand and stones along the outside edges of the stream bed. In the center, the water was between two and three feet deep, but aided by the relatively steep decline in elevation, the current was swift.

His neighbor had done a nice job of concealing the new fence. Since it was twilight, it took the trained eye of a professional who knew what he was looking for to pick it out the square wire mesh barrier. He didn't see any armed guards patrolling the fence line, but twenty minutes later he noticed the faint glow of lights reflecting through the steadily falling mist. He hadn't been there in years, but his recollection was the sawmill could only be a couple of hundred yards from his current position. He stopped, dismounted, and listened. The cathedral-like silence of those majestic woods was disturbed by only the constant pulsation of rushing water and the occasional skittering of a nocturnal animal through the pine needles blanketing the forest floor. The fresh scent of forest and stream dominated the air.

John sat on the bank, leaning against the trunk of a huge redwood. Leo snuggled up alongside him with his head resting on his master's thigh. Puffs of condensation clouded the air each time either of them exhaled. John unknowingly shivered as the green glow created by his night-vision goggles brought back harrowing memories from his tours in Vietnam.

After a half-hour of motionless waiting and watching, the only movement he had detected from the other side of Elk Creek was two deer and a hunting owl. Fortunately, Leo was so contented all he did when he detected the deer was to lift his head and gaze in their direction.

Satisfied the patrols which had shadowed Miles were nowhere in the vicinity, John decided to venture across the creek. Remembering there used to be a fallen tree in the creek not too far upstream, he figured that would be a good place to cross. Usually, its many branches extending down into the water slowed the current enough to create a sandbar on the upstream side, making it a good place to ford without the water getting too much above his knees.

John located the fallen tree less than a hundred yards upstream. However, since the last time he was here, the dynamics of the creek's water flow had dramatically altered the stream bed. Instead of a passable sandbar, the log had driven the swift current underneath, leaving a deep black pool of swirling water on both its sides. He rode the creek for a hundred yards in both directions looking for the shallowest place where a septuagenarian who had been riddled with bullets and shrapnel more than once could cross.

Now, well into twilight, it was too dark to determine how deep the water was in the middle of the stream. Finally he found a spot where the stump of a tree was directly on the other side of the creek. No longer confident in his balance, he figured he could lasso the twelve-inch-thick trunk and use his rope to help maintain his balance over the slippery bottom and against the swift current. The only question was, could he still twirl and accurately throw the lasso that far?

After replacing his hiking boots with hip waders, he tied the laces together and strung the boots over his saddle horn. He grabbed his lasso and jumped down into the creek bed. Standing in a foot of water, he slipped one end of the rope through the small loop at the other end of his lariat, forming a two-foot noose. He then held both the rope and the noose lightly in his right hand with his index finger pointed down the rope. Coiling the rest of the lariat in his left hand, he took a deep breath, relaxed his right wrist, and began twirling the rope over his head. After three revolutions he cast the loop, extending his index finger and arm out toward his target.

It had been several years since he last used a lasso, and it showed. His first toss hardly made it to the other bank. Reeling in the rope, he chided himself for allowing his skills to deteriorate since hiring Jose to handle the animals. This time he moved deeper into the current before he placed his left foot slightly in front of the right and began twirling the lasso again. After five revolutions over his head, he let it fly. His form was much better but the loop hit the base of the stump.

Two attempts later, success! He slowly tightened the noose, testing the strength of the stump first by pulling, then by holding on and leaning his entire two hundred thirty pounds backward. Satisfied it would hold, he tightly secured the loose end around a tree on his side. He briefly turned his head toward Leo and whispered, "Meet ya on the other side."

Holding the rope chest-high, he took a deep breath then began a slow hand-over-hand foray into the current. As the water rose up around his thighs, the force of the current threatened to carry him downstream, and the algae-coated rocks on the stream bottom caused his felt waders to slip and slide. *Using the rope was a smart decision*, he thought as he struggled near midstream.

Leo waited until John was nearly across before splashing into the water a few feet upstream. Although the swift current took Leo downstream past John, his powerful legs were able to propel him to the opposite bank before his master. By the time John made it to safety and scrambled up the waist-high bank, he was exhausted. He lay on the ground catching his breath while Leo eagerly licked his face. Pulling his face away,

John chuckled and whispered, "Easy fellow, you weren't worried the old man wouldn't make it, were ya?"

It took John several minutes to catch his breath and allow his legs to recuperate before being able to get to his feet and survey his immediate vicinity. Then slowly and quietly he began moving toward the hazy illumination in the distance. Leo matched his movement step by step. The wire cutter easily cut through the galvanized fence at one of the posts. Pulling an opening between the two sections, he directed Leo through then ducked under the barbed wire himself.

Within minutes he was in sight of the floodlit clearing containing the sawmill and lumberyard. It certainly was different than the last time he was there. All he remembered was a modest clearing with a concrete slab covered by a tin roof that sheltered several band saws and a log debarker; stacks of cut and uncut lumber sat out in the open. Now, there had been added a large enclosed metal building and what appeared to a huge wood chipper. The doors to the new building were wide enough for a tractor trailer, and they were open.

John's current position made it impossible to see what was inside. He stared at the new building for a long time before he reiterated his original thought, *Why the hell do you need an enclosed warehouse in a lumberyard?*

From somewhere inside the larger structure, he could hear voices and what sounded like a forklift moving around. He was just thinking he ought to get a little closer when Leo began a low guttural growl.

John whispered, "What's the matter, boy?"

The words were hardly out of his mouth when he heard the distant rumble of an approaching vehicle. It didn't take long for a truck's headlights to penetrate the absolute blackness of the woods. Less than a minute later, he was able to make out the silhouette of a panel truck snaking it way along the forest road.

John fumbled to get his camera from around his back. By the time he had removed the camera from its pack, the yellow truck was splashing through puddles not more than fifteen feet from him. He quickly snapped two pictures, one of the cab as it passed and the other of the back license plate.

Without really thinking about it, he fell in right behind the truck, following it as it pulled up to the open doors, where John quickly slipped into the shadows behind a dumpster. When the driver stepped out of the vehicle, John recognized him as Ricky, one of Cletus Boyer Senior's nephews. Ricky captained the family's fishing fleet out of Humboldt Harbor.

While John was snapping pictures, Clete Junior and Ken Boyer emerged from inside. They exchanged high fives after Ricky shouted, "Success!" The three men retreated just inside the building, where they were shielded from John's view, but he could still make out most of what they were saying. One of the Boyer brothers asked their cousin how it went.

Ricky replied, "Fine, the sea was calm and we didn't see another vessel. We were both in and out in less than an hour. At first, when we pulled up alongside, it felt weird. It was like we were auditioning for a part in a WWII movie."

"Great," replied one of the brothers. "Back your truck up to the door and let's get the stuff unloaded. We already have orders for most of this shipment."

As Ricky hopped back into the truck, swung a U-turn, and backed up to the door, John switched his camera to video mode. When Ricky stopped the truck, the end of the truck bed was just outside the building, leaving John with a good line of sight.

Ken Boyer opened the tailgate and hopped inside. He tossed his brother a plastic bag. Cletus Junior snapped open a four-inch pocket knife, stabbed the package and dug out a sample which he tasted. A few seconds later, grinning, Clete declared, "Man, this is good stuff!"

Meanwhile Ricky retreated inside the building and returned with a forklift loaded with an empty pallet. The three men began off-loading more packages like the first one. John wasn't an expert, but it sure looked to him like two-kilo bags of cocaine.

The men filled one pallet then Ricky drove the forklift into the warehouse and returned with another empty pallet. The Boyer brothers off-loaded another pallet load of similar but smaller bags.

As soon as the three men disappeared into the warehouse, John, figuring he had recorded enough evidence, quietly began sneaking toward the creek. He had only gone a few yards when Leo emitted a low growl, stopped, and faced behind them in a defensive posture. Suddenly there came the chilling barking of big dogs. John stopped in his tracks and listened. The barking was still some distance off and coming from the woods on the other side of the clearing.

"Shit!" he mumbled to himself. Then he whispered to Leo, "We've got to get back across the creek."

Forgoing all stealth, he began the ponderous and noisy task of running through the woods in hip waders. Leo bounded a few yards behind. John located the cut in the wire mesh fence. He and Leo slipped through, but there wasn't enough time to use the extra wire he brought to reconnect the break. Instead, he made a half-assed attempt to quickly conceal the breach by simply overlapping the two sections. He figured even such a superficial effort might delay his pursuers long enough for him and Leo to make a clean getaway. However, he couldn't take the risk of another methodical rope crossing and getting caught midstream. He figured he'd have to attempt to thrash across unsupported. Worst case, even if he lost his balance and slipped into the water, he could ride the current downstream, putting additional distance between himself and his pursuers.

Reaching the creek, he looked back to see Leo bravely waiting to face the oncoming horde. Hesitating, John took a deep breath then jumped down off the bank. The instep of his right foot landed on a football-sized rock, causing his ankle joint to rotate well beyond where it was intended and sending excruciating pain rocketing through his leg and foot. His whole right side collapsed, tumbling him forward into the frigid water.

"FUCK!" John knew it was serious even before he came to

rest in eighteen inches of water. It took precious moments for the pain to somewhat subside and his survival instincts to kick in. His hip waders were filling with water. The old warrior commanded his body to respond, and after a Herculean effort he was able to stand up on his left leg. But between the water in his waders and not being able to put any weight on his right ankle, his escape looked doubtful. Drawing off decades of survival training and the numerous hopeless situations he'd experienced, he didn't panic.

He ripped off the waders, discovering that his right tibia and fibula no longer lined up. Undeterred, he tossed the boots into the current and slithered on his hands and knees behind them. His plan was to swim the approximate fifty yards downstream to the downed tree and slip under it, hiding in the branches which still hung down in the water. It was a feeble plan, but he figured he had little time before his pursuers were upon him. Considering the fact he might no longer be able to quickly scramble up the bank and mount his horse, it was the best he could come up with.

When Leo heard John's painful expletive he abandoned his defensive position and bounded down to the streambed. Sensing his master was vulnerable to their approaching pursuers, he turned to face the threat.

Numbed by the fifty-degree water and in excruciating pain, John fought to control his course in the stream's swift current. He was doing fine until he reached the eddy swirling through and under the tree. His muscles, drained by both his injury and his age, couldn't overcome the force of the current. It seized him, dragging him down under the log into the deep pool created by the vortex. Something in his instincts told him to just go with the flow and he would come out the other side.

That strategy probably would have worked except for the camera hanging over his right shoulder and diagonally crossing his chest and back like a bandoleer. As the current propelled him under the tree, a two-inch branch stub caught the strap on his back just below the shoulder blade. For several seconds he was suspended in the current with his head facing downstream and his legs upstream. His lower body was thrust from side-to-side like the spinner on a fishing lure. Desperately he attempted to wrestle free by slipping his left arm through the strap just above the camera, but the force of the current on his body had pulled the camera upward until it lodged under his armpit. The current was so strong he couldn't create enough slack in the line to slip his left arm through the strap. The futile effort was quickly draining the air out of his lungs, yet he didn't panic.

Changing tactics, he flipped his body around so his head faced upstream and his legs downstream; then he raised both his arms above his head and let the current propel him out of the strap. Miraculously, several seconds later he popped up, gasping for air, about twenty yards downstream. Suspended in three feet of water, he was disoriented and coughing up water. Dog paddling to stay afloat, he worked his way out of the swift current into shallower water and eventually touched bottom without standing up. Using his hands and arms, he pulled himself partially onto the bank but still on the Boyer side of the Elk Creek. Exhausted and disoriented, he sprawled on his back, his head out of the water, his torso half submerged while his legs bobbed in the current. It wouldn't be long before hypothermia set in, but at least the cold water somewhat numbed the pain.

■ ■ ■

In Africa, Rhodesian ridgebacks are utilized to hold lions at bay until the hunters can get close enough to issue the coup de grace. With the trademark ridge of hair standing up on his back, Leo performed the task for which his ancestors were bred. Several thundering, intimidating barks deep from within his soul stopped his less-regal canine cousins in their tracks. For several seconds it appeared to be a Mexican standoff, with the two snarling shepherds nervously pacing back and forth three feet above on the bank and Leo firmly planted on the sandbar between his master and the enemy. This scene might have lasted indefinitely except that not too far behind were two armed security guards. The two men arrived on horseback only moments after their dogs.

Ralph, the tall, wiry one, wasted no time in assessing the situation. Without hesitation, he raised his Remington 870 tactical shotgun and fired one 12-gauge round into the sand inches in front of the courageous Leo, expecting the dog to turn tail and run. The two shepherds instantly stopped pacing and stood, almost triumphantly, in place. Leo, showing no fear, instead of retreating, fiercely charged the gunman.

Nervously, with one eye glued on Leo, Ralph clumsily attempted to chamber the second round. He pulled back the fore-end to eject the spent shell, then he pushed the fore-end forward, chambering the next round. In the face of Leo's menacing charge, Ralph got careless, not waiting to pull the trigger until the 19½ inch barrel totally stopped moving. The result was that the pellets splashed harmlessly in the creek.

The second security guard, Carl, was off to the side coolly watching his partner's blundering reaction. Just as Leo sprang at his partner, Carl fired one round from his 9mm pistol. The round smashed into Leo's hind quarter. The force of the projectile spun him around, knocking him sideways back toward the creek. He plummeted onto the sandbar, rolling over several times before coming to rest in a foot of water.

The report from the shotgun blast jarred John's awareness. He rolled over on his side just in time to see Leo come to rest motionless in the creek. Aghast at Leo's fate, John struggled up on one knee, at the same time frantically groping for his weapon. Unfortunately, it had been dislodged from his holster and was now resting on the bottom of the stream.

Ralph, picking up on John's movement, dismounted. He located the gap in the fence and began cautiously heading in John's direction.

Carl, seeing the intruder groping for a weapon, fired one shot into the sand just in front of John's torso. "The next one is between your eyes," he barked.

Clearly defenseless, John raised his hands above his head and shouted, "Don't shoot, I'm unarmed."

Ralph didn't hesitate; he jumped down from the bank and charged downstream. Taking no chances, he slammed the butt of his shotgun into the side of John's head.

After the two guards dragged John up onto the sandbank, Ralph went looking for the wounded dog. To his surprise, the animal had vanished. He scrutinized the darkness for a body but found none. Thinking the current might have caught hold of the dog, he hurriedly moved along the creek bed, scanning the water and both shores. After walking along the stream for several hundred feet and finding nothing, he concluded the body had either been caught on an underwater obstruction or was already washed far downstream. Reluctantly, he gave up the search, returning back upstream to his partner and their human trespasser.

CHAPTER 3

Clete Boyer and his two sons, Clete Junior and Ken, stood alongside Carl and Ralph, looking down on the still-unconscious John Slaughter.

"He had no wallet on him, but the old coot has on dog tags identifying him as John Slaughter. Isn't that your neighbor?" Ralph asked.

"That's him." Shaking his head in amazement, Clete Senior continued, "I can't believe he still wears dog tags after all these years. And where the hell are his shoes?"

Nobody replied.

Clete stared at John for a few more seconds before he continued, "Do you think he got close enough to see anything?"

Nervously Ralph responded, "He did cut through the fence, but we can't say for sure how far he got. By the time we caught up with the dogs, he was already right here."

"Do you think he was alone?"

Ralph continued to answer the boss. "All I saw was him and the dog."

Carl finally chimed in. "I saw a single horse hitched up on the other side. It hightailed it out of here when the shooting started. I'm pretty sure it was just the old man, the dog, and the horse, Mr. Boyer."

"Okay, boys, good work. That's why I hired you, to keep

prying eyes from discovering our little operation. Did you check his pockets?"

"Yes, sir," Ralph replied. "All he had on him was a set of keys, a wire cutter, and a couple of feet of baling wire. His holster was empty, must have lost his gun in the creek."

Clete Senior seemed to ponder this for a few moments before he responded, "Okay, we can't take any chances he witnessed tonight's delivery. He's the only person I worry about; Junior can deal with anybody else. But a retired major general and a Medal of Honor winner can bring an awful lot of outside heat down on us. So now, we are going to have to make it look like the old general had a tragic accident.

"I figure his horse will wander on home and probably be discovered by either Slaughter's cowhand or that redskin general manager of his. We have to make sure the search party finds his body floating a long way downstream. We need to make it look like the old man fell or was knocked off his horse, ending up in the creek. That nasty bruise on his skull will probably make it look like he rode into a branch or hit his head when he fell. We just have to make sure that an autopsy finds water in his lungs indicating he was alive when he hit the water. Can you four make sure that happens?"

"No problem," Junior answered while the others just nodded.

While heading back to his ATV, Clete Boyer shouted over his shoulder, "After you take care of Slaughter, see if you can find that damn dog's body and bury it where it will never be found . . . and fix this fence."

"Yes, sir," the two security guards responded in unison.

Clete Junior waited for his father to start the ATV and drive off before he announced, "There's something I want to get off the old coot."

With his brother and the other two curiously watching, Junior knelt on one knee next to John's still-unconscious body. He grabbed hold of the stainless steel chain resting on the outside of the general's shirt and yanked. There was a sharp snap.

Clete stood and triumphantly held up the chain, revealing John Slaughter's metal dog tags. Smiling like a Cheshire Cat, he asked, "How many guys do you know can say they took the dog tags off a Congressional Medal of Honor winner?"

Nobody said a word in response; the other three men just stood there, their mouths gaping open at Junior's audacity.

■ ■ ■

As usual, Miles Reynolds was the first to arrive at the Slaughter house for the biweekly Friday morning staff meeting. When he pulled up to the house, he noticed the general's favorite horse saddled and grazing on the front lawn.

Up until just a few years ago, when John was still actively involved in overseeing the operations full-time, he held these biweekly meetings in the furniture factory's conference room. When he got real serious about breeding endangered horses and cattle, he decided to appoint his fifty-year-old third cousin Miles as his general manager and hold staff meetings at the ranch.

It was 7:30 a.m. when Miles arrived; he and the general would usually have a quick breakfast meeting before the other managers arrived at eight. Today's agenda would be a tough one. They would have to decide the production schedule for the factory. The long-overdue decision would most likely mean laying off forty percent of the workforce. John Slaughter hated to lay off his "family" so he had been building inventory for the last two months. He now had built up so much stock they had run out of warehouse space, and sales orders usually didn't start picking up until late March.

Even though some of the workers who would be laid off were part of Miles's extended family, he had been the one who had been pushing John for the cutbacks. Last night, John reluctantly agreed Miles was right; hours had to be reduced by forty percent until orders picked up. Today, they had to decide whether everyone went on three-day work weeks or the entire second shift got laid off. The general had indicated he intended talking to old man Boyer about temporarily taking on some of the workers in his less-seasonal businesses. That's when Miles mentioned the recent developments across the creek.

At first, when he noticed the saddled horse grazing on the front lawn, Miles' reaction was to ponder, *What's the general up to now?*

After parking in front of the large equipment barn, Miles casually walked toward the front porch, half expecting the boss to come out to greet him as he usually did. However, when the general didn't come out, Miles headed up onto the porch and knocked on the door.

No answer. He waited a few seconds then knocked again. Nothing. He tried the door; it was unlocked. He walked into the enormous, high-ceilinged open area that served as a kitchen, dining room, and great room. He looked around; not seeing the boss, he instinctively checked the large thirty-cup electric coffee pot that always sat on the marble counter top. The coffee pot had not been set up.

Strange, he thought. *That's not like John. He always has plenty of strong, hot coffee ready for these meetings.*

While he began searching the shelves in the pantry for filters and coffee, he called out, "John, you up?"

No answer. He shouted louder. Still no response. Then all at once it hit him. The horse on the front lawn fully saddled and no John; something bad must have happened. Forgetting about the coffee, he raced to the general's bedroom. Empty, bed made, cowboy boots still sitting at the foot of the chair where he always left them. Next, he checked the bathroom. Nothing.

He raced out the front door, shouting at the top of his lungs, "General, where are you?"

He first checked the equipment barn, then the horse barn. Finding nothing, he headed for the old bunkhouse which had recently been converted into two one-bedroom apartments. He really didn't expect to find anyone there. Jose, John's sole cowhand, was delivering a prize calf to Wyoming. Just as he expected, both apartments were deserted. He then scanned the corrals and the entire clearing in which the house sat. When he didn't find anything indicating the general had been there, he raced to the horse.

The animal's coat and the saddle were moist from the previous night's drizzle. John's custom-built M1 .308 Garand rifle was still in its scabbard. A canteen and hiking boots hung from the saddle horn. *That's really strange,* he thought. *Why would his boots be hanging there?*

Then he noticed the two-piece ultralight fishing rod sticking out of the saddle bag. He checked inside the bags but all that he found was a box of lures. *This is getting weirder. Assuming he took off his boots and put on waders to go fishing, why is the fishing rod still here?*

Miles stepped back, scratching his temple, just staring into the surrounding trees while exploring all possible scenarios. He was about to turn around and head back to the house when he realized the general's lariat was missing. That's when it dawned on him.

He suddenly remembered their discussion the previous afternoon. That realization sent alarm bells off in his head. *Jeez, could he have attempted to sneak over to Boyer's and . . . and what; fell in the creek . . . was intercepted by the security guards. Perhaps . . .*

He never got to complete the thought as he was interrupted by the other managers beginning to arrive. Shortly all five managers were finally on site. Miles gathered them together on the porch and explained what he had observed, but he did not share his latest fears.

"I believe the boss's horse has been out all night. It has a pretty heavy moisture coating and the saddle is sopped. I'm guessing the boss went for a ride last night and something happened. We need to get out there right now and find him. We've got three saddle horses and two ATVs. Irene, you stay here in case he shows up. The rest of us should spread out in the woods and grazing fields. I'll head upstream along the creek. Jeremy, you head downstream. Mike and Manny, you split up on the west side. I assume you've got your guns in your trucks. Bring them with you. If you spot something, and I mean anything, shoot off a round. Got it?"

Anxiously, they all looked around and nodded.

"Okay, let's get going," Miles ordered.

It was almost 9 o'clock when Miles heard a gunshot. It sounded like it came from downstream. He had been following fresh hoofprints that headed upstream along the banks of Elk Creek. Every few minutes he would call out, but up till then he found nothing. As soon as he heard the warning shot, he wasted no time in getting on the bridle path and galloping north.

When he reached his cousin Jeremy, he was kneeling next to the body of a dog. It was Leo, partially concealed in the brush. Based upon his wet, matted fur, the courageous dog apparently had crawled out of the creek, hid in the bushes, and died.

Jeremy looked up at Miles and choked out, "He's dead; shot in the hindquarters."

"Any signs the general was up this way?" Miles asked.

"No, sir. I didn't see any fresh human prints, but I really haven't done a thorough search."

"Okay," Miles said, taking out his iPhone. "Let me get a couple of photos of Leo's body, especially the gunshot wound."

After he had snapped a half-dozen photos of Leo from all angles, he turned to Jeremy and said, "Take another look around. If you find something new, fire another shot. If not, take the dog back to the house. I've been tracking what I believe is the general's trail upstream. Unless you find evidence to the contrary, I'm going to assume the dog was shot upstream and drifted down here. I'm going to head back there. If you see Mike and Manny, send them upstream to help me."

"Should I call the Boyerville police?"

"Not yet, give me some more time to follow the tracks."

Fifteen minutes later Mike and Manny joined Miles upstream. The three horsemen spread out, riding about ten yards apart.

After several minutes, Manny, who was between the other two, shouted, "Got sump'in! Looks like the boss's horse was tethered to this sapling; the nearby ground is loaded with hoofprints."

They all dismounted and walked around the area looking for more signs.

It was Mike who found it. "Here we go; I found some hoofprints headed off into the woods. By the looks of them, the horse was in full gallop. But they're not deep enough to include a rider."

"Okay, Mike, you follow the hoofprints while Manny and I scour this area."

Manny walked along the bank, first upstream fifty yards, then downstream a hundred yards. Miles jumped down into the creek bed, scrutinizing the water and sandbars on both banks looking for any clues. Twenty yards downstream Miles came across the sandbar where most of the prior evening's action took place.

He called out to Manny, "Here we go! Looks like there was a lot of action around this sandbar; there's a bunch of different boot prints plus some dog tracks."

Manny jumped down to take a look for himself. They both studied the area for a few minutes in silence.

Finally Miles asked, "What do you think?"

"I'd say there are at least four different sets of human footprints and two or three different dogs. Can't say definitely they were from last night, 'cause of the rain, but they are not too old . . . my guess, only a day or two at most. Looks like they came down from Boyer's side; I'll go up and take a look."

Miles slowly walked back upstream inspecting the bed for clues. He noticed something submerged a few feet from shore. He waded in, reached down, and pulled out one of John's hip waders. He called to Manny, and the two of them continued examining the stream until Miles found the other wader.

"This can't be a good sign," Miles fearfully mumbled.

Manny climbed back up the bank and almost immediately

shouted back, "More prints. They all lead to this one spot on the fence which seems to have been hastily repaired. Looks like some horse tracks plus tire tracks from two ATVs on the other side."

Miles joined him, and they both stood there studying their new discovery.

After a few thoughtful moments, Miles said, "Well, if he fell in and was hurt, and these guys found him, wouldn't you think we'd have heard something from the police chief by now?" Hesitating as if he was waiting for confirmation from Manny, he took off his baseball cap and scratched the back of his head. When Manny did not respond, he continued, "For now, let's assume these prints have nothing to do with whatever happened to the general, although I still think he fell in and floated downstream."

Manny looked at Miles with fear and confusion in his eyes. "Suppose they do?"

"Do what?" Miles asked abruptly.

"Do have something to do with whatever happened to the general?"

"We can't worry about that now; we just have to keep looking for him."

Manny replied with an inflection that suggested he was still contemplating his previous question, "Weren't you checking out the stream on the way here?"

Shaking his head, Miles answered, "Not as closely as I could have. We need to backtrack on foot and do a thorough job."

They had walked along the bank for fifteen minutes checking out every place they figured a body could have gotten hung up when Mike returned on an ATV. "I tracked the horse back to the house. Nothing suspicious on the way."

"Okay, we've discovered his hip waders and a lot of footprints down here but no conclusive evidence they have anything to do with what happened to the general. We're thinking maybe he fell into the creek, so we're now scouring the creek looking for any indication of that."

Manny couldn't help but ask the question they both had been avoiding. "You think he's dead?"

"Not necessarily, he could be unconscious or seriously hurt," Miles replied unconvincingly. "Let's just keep searching. Why don't you take the ATV, pick up Jeremy, and the two of you start looking downstream from where he found Leo. The two of us will work our way toward you. As much as I hate to admit it, I think it's time to put a call in to the police and make sure the boss isn't in the hospital or something."

CHAPTER 4

When the news got out General John Slaughter was missing, over fifty volunteers descended on the Slaughter ranch. Boyerville's chief of police, Clete Boyer Junior, took charge of the search and rescue operation.

After Miles explained they found some tracks along Elk Creek and that they had discovered Leo's body, the chief assigned thirty men to him in order to thoroughly scour the woods and creek up to South Fork Road. The chief also requested assistance from the Humboldt County sheriff's department. The sheriff sent Deputy Sheriff Ken Boyer to assist. Ken led the search on the Boyer side of Elk Creek, exclusively utilizing the mill's employees. With himself in the lead, Chief Boyer deployed the rest of the volunteers to search along South Fork Road and the Van Duzen River.

Suspicious of the Boyers' involvement in the general's death, Miles held back that he had fished his boss's hip waders out of the creek, although he revealed the general's dog had been found dead along the creek. What he didn't tell Chief Boyer was that Leo had been shot. He also did not reveal the footprints near the site where he found the waders. After Chief Boyer did not allow any outsiders to join the search on his father's property, Miles was more convinced than ever John Slaughter had discovered whatever strange stuff was going on at the sawmill and was killed because of it.

Three hours later Chief Boyer located Miles still searching along Elk Creek. As soon as Miles saw the chief approaching on an ATV, Miles knew the search was over.

"Miles, I'm sorry to tell you we found the general's body bobbing in an eddy at the confluence of Elk Creek and the main branch of the Van Duzen River."

Miles didn't reply. He just nodded his head while a smidgen of moisture surfaced around his eyeballs.

Chief Boyer waited several seconds before he continued, "You said you found his dog. I need to take him in as evidence and have an autopsy performed."

Miles's face showed his discomfort at the chief's statement, but what could he do? Local law enforcement had the authority to declare Leo as evidence. Besides, if the autopsy was legit, the bullet in Leo's backside should create all kinds of questions that would need answering.

"Okay," Miles reluctantly replied. "We've got him back at the house. Follow me. I'll take you to him."

■ ■ ■

Word of the gruesome discovery spread quickly among the volunteers.

An hour later, Chief Boyer made a brief announcement to a concerned gathering of local residents in front of Boyerville's administrative building confirming that one of the region's most revered sons, retired major general and Congressional Medal of Honor winner John Slaughter, had apparently drowned in a tragic accident. He also announced that an autopsy would be performed by the Humboldt County coroner's office.

To most of the residents of Humboldt County, this was the saddest day since the 1964 Christmas flood swept away a dozen towns. Late that afternoon, scores of grieving residents lined Harrison Avenue and the emergency entrance to St. Joseph's Hospital in Eureka, anxiously awaiting a glimpse of the EMS vehicle bearing the general's body.

Hoping to avoid the throng he expected at the hospital,

Coroner Nick Pain instructed the EMS driver to take them to Wier's Mortuary on 17th Street, where forensic pathologist Dr. Edward List would perform the autopsy. His maneuver was only partially successful. He was able to get the body inside before the crowd caught on to his ruse, but five minutes later the street surrounding Wier's was packed with local reporters and grieving townspeople

Realizing he was on the hot seat to determine the exact cause of General Slaughter's death, Nick had Dr. List work through the night while he observed. The morning sun was still thinking about showing itself when Dr. List finished his autopsy and declared his preliminary conclusions to the coroner. Emerging from Wier's basement, Coroner Pain was relieved to find the street finally devoid of media people and curiosity seekers. He called and woke up Chief Boyer, who agreed to meet at the coroner's office in forty-five minutes.

Before heading over to meet Chief Boyer, Pain went home, showered, and ate a big breakfast of eggs and bacon. Boyer was waiting when the coroner arrived to deliver the pathologist's preliminary report. Although they still would need the results of toxicology analysis, Coroner Nick Pain reported Dr. List was fairly certain John Slaughter's death resulted from an accidental drowning. Sure there were numerous bruises, abrasions, and cuts on his body, including a lateral malleolus fracture of his right ankle, but the doctor was convinced they were caused by a fall, probably from his horse. The most serious injury was to the side of his head, which resulted in traumatic brain injury and most likely loss of consciousness.

However, this was not the cause of his death, since there was water in his lungs indicating he was still alive when he fell in the stream. Nick speculated the numerous indentations in the contusion were most likely from hard contact with the bark of a tree, thus reinforcing the pathologist's theory of a fall from some height. The coroner's report was a relief to Chief Boyer, who, immediately after Pain left to catch some sleep, called his father to relay the good news.

While Slaughter's body was being delivered to the funeral home for the autopsy, Chief Boyer had taken Leo's body to his brother-in-law's veterinary hospital. Veterinarian Howard Reems would wait until the next day to announce the results of Leo's autopsy. In reality Dr. Reems never examined Leo's body since the chief insisted the canine's body be cremated that night. Meanwhile Chief Boyer and Coroner Pain scheduled a press conference for noon in Boyerville, where they would officially confirm the general died on his ranch at approximately 9 p.m. the previous evening in an apparent accidental drowning.

CHAPTER 5

Attorney Bob Rivett was about to enter the court room on a probate matter when he received a text message from his administrative assistant that General John Slaughter had been found dead in an apparent drowning accident. He only had fifteen minutes before his case would be heard. Not satisfied with so little information, he attempted to call Miles Reynolds. However, his call went directly to voice mail.

Immediately, he dialed information requesting the telephone number for the Boyerville Police Department. After giving him the number, the recorded message offered to connect him for a small charge. He accepted and after some clicks and five rings, a civilian employee at the police station answered. Bob asked to speak to Chief Boyer but was told the chief was unavailable.

Attorney Rivett explained who he was then attempted to learn more about the general's death. After several minutes of queries, Bob hadn't learned much more than he originally knew. He gave the employee his phone number and requested Chief Boyer call him back.

Hanging up, he checked his watch and saw he still had eight minutes before court. He decided to call David Tanner to inform him of the general's death.

"David, it's Bob Rivett."

"Bob, you old codger; how you doin'? God, how long has it been . . . two or three years?"

"Three years, I think. The last time we all got together was the 2012 board meeting at your place in Seville."

"That's right. I can't believe it has really been that long. So, how's the general doing?"

"That's why I'm calling; I have some sad news." The words seemed to catch in his throat, and he hesitated.

Not waiting for Bob to continue, David Tanner apprehensively replied, "Don't tell me."

"Afraid so, David; I just heard on the news he was in some kind of an accident and was discovered floating in Elk Creek. It's all pretty sketchy right now; I've left messages for both his general manager, Miles, and the local police chief attempting to get more information."

David Tanner, always a man of action, responded immediately, "If you want, I can pick you up tomorrow morning with my plane and we can fly up there together."

"I don't think that's necessary. There is no need for you to come out here. I'll arrange for a charter to fly me up to Eureka this evening, and I have all the paperwork necessary to take charge of his arrangements. Since his wishes were that he be buried at Arlington National, we'll be headed in your direction. If you want, you can send out one of your planes to fly his remains back to Washington, DC. In the meantime, I'll make arrangements for some type of viewing and memorial service in Eureka within the next few days. As soon as I get a schedule worked out I'll call you back with the specifics. Okay?"

"All right, that makes sense to me. Just let me know when you need one of my planes out there to transport his casket to DC. You know, John was one of my favorite people; anything you need, just give me a shout."

"Just one more thing. David, you'll let our other fishing buddy know what's happened?"

"Sure. You are aware he is back in the States permanently?"

"No, when did this happen?"

"About a year ago, not too long after his first wife's brother died in prison."

"I hadn't heard that Al Nicosia died," Bob said. "John never mentioned it. So Bart figures he's safe now?"

"He's not one hundred percent certain, but there is nobody left to pay the bounty; all the other old-timers are either dead or dribbling down their chins, and the young wise guys are just elated they no longer have pay homage to the old bastard.

"Anyway, Bart decided to accept the government's offer of a new identity for himself and his new wife, Patty Jo, and return to the States. It's not very imaginative, but he now goes by Bart Rock with matching Social Security identification and birth certificate."

"Interesting," Bob mused. "Over the years on our fishing trips and from the general I had picked up some sketchy details of Bart's issues with his brother-in-law, but apparently there is a whole lot more I don't know about Bart's saga."

"So you never read the novel *Family*?"

"No, I'm not a big fiction reader."

"Well, you ought to. Some of it is sensationalized and the author used some literary license, but it does a pretty good job of chronicling Bart's desperate struggle with his first wife's Mafia connections."

"Well, guess what just moved up on my reading list."

There was a moment of silence between the two before David said, "All right then, I'll be waiting for you to call back with the details."

"Yeah, like I said, I should have them worked out something late tomorrow."

■ ■ ■

Miles Reynolds and his wife were soberly driving back from delivering the general's burial suit to the funeral director.

"You're sure, Miles?"

"I'm telling you, Anne, this was no accident. Why else would Chief Boyer claim Leo was killed protecting the general from a bear or a mountain lion when it is clear from these pictures on my cell phone there were no claw or teeth marks anywhere on his body? The only blood is where the bullet penetrated his rump. Not only that, Manny and I scoured the creek where we believe the general went in; other than boot, hoof, and dog prints, there were no other wild animal prints. It's just a half-assed attempt to validate John being bucked off when his horse was spooked, knocking him unconscious and resulting in his drowning in the creek.

"Perhaps something or somebody did spook the general's horse and Leo attempted to protect his master, but it wasn't any bear or mountain lion. Whatever happened, I'm willing to bet Boyer's people were involved."

"So what are you going to do about it?" Anne asked.

"Nothin'. If there is one thing we've learned over the last hundred and fifty years, it's that we can't go up against the white man alone; and right now, I don't know anyone we can trust."

CHAPTER 6

It was the best-attended wake and memorial service anyone in Humboldt County could remember. The lines at Weir's Funeral Home still extended out the door and down the front sidewalk at 8 p.m., when the general's wake was scheduled to end. Bob Rivett convinced old man Weir to keep the doors open till after 10:00 p.m. At nine o'clock the next morning, St. Alban's Episcopal Church in Arcata was overflowing for John Slaughter's memorial service. Later that afternoon, the general's casket was loaded on David Tanner's Gulfstream G-650 at Arcata-Eureka Airport for the five-hour flight to Ronald Reagan Airport in Washington, DC.

The *Washington Post* ran an obituary on Major General John Slaughter which included the citation for the Medal of Honor he was awarded during the Vietnam War:

> For conspicuous acts of courage and boldness in action at the risk of his own life above and beyond the call of duty. Captain Slaughter's company was ordered to extricate a supply convoy from enemy attack. Moving through the dense jungle to aid the besieged unit, his company encountered a strong enemy force occupying well-concealed defensive positions, and the company's leading element quickly sustained several casualties. Captain Slaughter immediately ran forward to the

scene of the most intense action to direct the company's efforts. Deploying one platoon on the flank, he led the other two platoons in an attack on the enemy in the face of intense fire. During this action both radio operators accompanying him were wounded. At grave risk to himself, he defied the enemy's murderous fire, and helped the wounded operators to a position where they could receive medical care. As he moved forward again, the enemy neutralized one of his machine gun crews. Seizing the weapon, he charged forward firing the machine gun, shouting orders, and rallying his men, thus maintaining the momentum of the attack. Under increasingly heavy enemy fire, he ordered his assistant to take cover and, alone, Captain Slaughter continued to advance, firing the machine gun until the wounded had been evacuated and the attack in this area could be resumed. When movement on the other flank was halted by the enemy's fanatical defense, Captain Slaughter moved to personally direct this critical phase of the battle. Leading the renewed effort, he was blown off his feet and wounded by an enemy mortar shell. Despite his painful wounds he refused medical aid and persevered in the forefront of the attack on the enemy's position. He led the assault on several enemy gun emplacements. He then directed close-in air support to bomb enemy positions only yards from his own position, thus totally eliminating the enemy assault and saving the convoy. His outstanding personal leadership under intense enemy fire inspired his men to heroic efforts and was instrumental in the ultimate success of the operation. Captain Slaughter's magnificent courage, selfless concern for his men, and professional skill reflect the utmost credit upon himself and the U.S. Army.

The cherry blossoms were in full bloom on a clear blustery spring morning at Arlington National Cemetery when John Slaughter was put to rest in a military ceremony. In attendance, besides numerous Army dignitaries, were twenty-two men who had served with him during his four tours in Vietnam. Following the playing of "Taps," Army Chief of Staff General Marvin Lee presented the tricornered flag to U.S. Air Force Chief Master Sergeant Victor McCoy, believed to be Slaughter's closest surviving relative.

In the background, three older men solemnly waited to introduce themselves to Sergeant McCoy. Bob Rivett waited for McCoy to extricate himself from the numerous people anxious to pay their final respects to John and to tell his nephew what a great soldier the general had been. After the actual ceremony had been over for almost twenty minutes, Victor was finally alone and slowly making his way to his rental car when Attorney Rivett and his two companions approached the six-foot, five-inch chief master sergeant.

"Excuse me, Sergeant McCoy," Bob said, "I would like to introduce myself and these two gentlemen to you. We were all good friends of your uncle; I'm Bob Rivett, his attorney. I was the one who sent you the telegram informing you of the general's passing and I also coordinated today's arrangements with the Army."

At first while he studied these three "old men," Victor appeared annoyed by the interruption. His first thought was, *How many more of my uncle's Army buddies am I going to have to listen to?* His face betrayed his irritation.

Adorned in his best three-piece lawyer's suit, Rivett ignored the slight. Nodding to the tall distinguished man on his right, Bob Rivett continued, "This is David Tanner. David has been a friend and business associate of your uncle's ever since John retired from the Army." Then, looking around as if to make sure no one was nearby listening, he said in a soft voice, "This other gentleman, Bart Rock, knew your uncle in Vietnam. Your uncle picked all three of us to serve as outside directors of Slaughter Holdings for the last twenty-five years."

Victor scrunched his eyebrows, looking skeptically at the three interlopers. "Okay . . . nice to meet you all . . . I think."

Then he seemed to reflect for a few moments before he continued dismissively, "Look, I haven't seen my uncle in more than ten years and I haven't been to the Slaughter house in over twenty. I'm not sure there is anything we have to talk about."

"We are aware of your relationship with your uncle, and I'm sorry, Victor, I didn't mean to come across so mysteriously . . . the reason we are here is because we all made a promise to your uncle that if anything happened to him, we would make ourselves available to you."

Rivett paused for a moment, allowing McCoy the opportunity to reflect on his last statement. When he continued, his tone exuded sincerity. "Look, even though you and your uncle have not been close for a long time, he followed your Air Force career and was extremely proud of your accomplishments. So much so that he believed you could carry on the family legacy."

"Family legacy! What the hell does that mean?"

Bob laughed. "Well, if you'll indulge us we'll be happy to enlighten you. Perhaps we should find a more comfortable place to talk. How about it?"

"I guess . . . you have some place in mind?"

"Yeah, David has a condo not too far from here; we can go there."

"Fine, where is it?"

"It's the Watergate West Building. If you'd like, I'll ride with you and show you the way."

Victor chuckled sarcastically. "Watergate . . . how appropriate for a mysterious meeting. Okay, Mr. Rivett, let's get this over with."

Fifteen minutes later the four men were sitting in David Tanner's sixth-floor living room drinking Bloody Marys and admiring the panoramic view of the Potomac.

"Nice place, Mr. Tanner. So, who really are you guys and what do you want?"

The general's three friends exchanged consenting glances before the lawyer replied, "Still skeptical, huh? Let me see if I can put your mind to rest. I'll get right to the point. I've been your uncle's attorney ever since he retired from the Army. As I said, I also happen to be on the board of directors for Slaughter Holdings and I am the executor of his estate, but what I am most proud of is that I have been his friend and close confidant for twenty-five years. As the executor of John Slaughter's estate, I've come to inform you that he made you his primary heir." Reaching into his briefcase, Bob pulled out a copy of the general's will and handed it to Vic.

Vic only glanced at the papers before asking, "His heir, what does that mean?"

"That means, Sergeant, you are now a very rich man."

Victor's mouth dropped open, and his left eye squinted as his head went slightly askew. After a few seconds it looked as if he was going to say something, but nothing came out. Finally recovering, he managed to ask, "How rich?"

"Well," Rivett replied, beaming, "there is approximately three million in cash and investments. The property and livestock are worth somewhere in the same neighborhood, and the furniture and cheese businesses are worth another couple of million."

"You're shitting me!"

"I shit you not. You really are one of the richest chief master sergeants in the Air Force."

Shaking his head and wearing a confounded look, Victor muttered, "I guess . . . but what am I going to do with those businesses and assets?"

Rivett rose from his chair and with his best fatherly inflection replied, "That's why we're here, Victor. All three of us, as directors of Slaughter Holdings, have a responsibility to provide the new owner with an in-depth understanding of the company and to assist in the transition of its management." The attorney paused for a moment in order to allow Victor to absorb what he had said. "However, perhaps even more important is our personal responsibility as his friends. You see, we've promised John we would help you understand what options you have and, once you decide what you want to do, provide you with whatever assistance you need to achieve your objectives."

Bart spoke up. "I believe you and I have a lot in common, Victor. It seems we've both spent much of our lives running away from our past and who we are. Unfortunately, for me, it's too late to recapture my heritage; but for you . . . you're still young. There aren't any insurmountable obstacles preventing you from reclaiming your heritage."

"What are you talking about? I can't just pick up and move back to California. First of all, I'm still in the Air Force, and second, why would I want to?"

David Tanner asked, "So, Vic, how many more years do you plan on staying in the Air Force?"

"I need eight more years before I get to thirty years."

"What's the difference between the twenty-two years you've already put in and thirty?"

"Duh . . . about three thousand dollars a month in retirement pay."

"Okay, that's $36,000 a year. Bob, do you have any idea how much his uncle was making a year on his businesses and investments?"

"Well, not exactly, but I believe it was in excess of three hundred and fifty grand a year."

Victor's jaw dropped, and Tanner used the younger man's astonishment to drive home his point. "That's ten years of extra retirement pay every year!"

It was Bob Rivett who spoke next. "That's right, but in all honesty, that's not your only option to achieve incredible financial security. You could liquidate everything and probably net over five million, which, if invested conservatively, could return the same three hundred and fifty thousand dollars a year without ever touching the principal." Bob hesitated for effect. "But therein lies the reason why your uncle asked us to assist you. You see, those businesses employ around fifty people. They're mostly Native Americans, and many of them are your distant cousins. Chances are, a new owner would probably close down the Humboldt County operations and consolidate them elsewhere, leaving fifty people without work." Rivett stopped, again allowing his words to sink in.

Victor scrutinized the three men finally settling back on Bob. "What the hell do I know about running those kinds of businesses? I've been an airman since I was eighteen years old! Besides, I never had a head for finance."

"Your uncle had that all figured out," Bob replied. "He has a general manager to run the day-to-day stuff and a management team which is extremely competent. In fact, over the last few years, he has not had too much input into the day-to-day routine operations. He was pretty much concerned just with finance and strategic decisions. He's been planning this whole transition for well over a decade, then several years ago in a board of directors' meeting at David's place in Spain he solicited our involvement."

Vic was shaking his head back and forth. Showing his agitation, he erupted, "I don't believe this!"

Then his voice jumped up several octaves as he scoffed, "My great-uncle, who I haven't seen since he forced me to enlist twenty-two years ago, worked this thing out without even consulting me—"

Rivett quickly cut him off before he reached a full tirade. "Calm down. First of all, he didn't 'work it out,' as you call it. He simply laid out a flexible plan. It's up to you, with our help . . . if you choose to use it . . . to work it out. Secondly, I was under the impression he didn't 'force you' to enlist; it was your only option in exchange for not being prosecuted for assault."

Rivett's last statement had an instant sobering effect on Vic, but he still remained defiant. "Yeah, yeah . . . I guess that is one way to look at it." He acerbically added, "Just how are you three supposed to help me?"

Ignoring the younger man's derisiveness, his uncle's attorney replied, "Good question. First of all, no matter what you decide, we are only here to provide you with whatever you ask us for. We are not here to impose your uncle's demands on you. We are here as advisors and only at your wishes. That said, we believe we can bring a lot of expertise to the table and you would be wise to use us.

"For example, David is one of the most successful real estate investors and developers in the country and has access to the capital markets. Bart has thirty years of operations finance experience and can either run the business temporarily or tutor you. Me, I can handle any legal issues. Just like we did for the general, we can assist you with the strategic planning.

"Now, if you should decide to give owning these businesses a try, Bart will virtually move in with you in Boyerville and act as your mentor for as long as it takes for you to feel confident enough to be on your own. Even if you decide to sell the operations either immediately or after spending time with Bart, we will assist in their liquidation. How's that sound?"

"Incredible! Not just incredible that he made this arrangement, but incredible he thought I would be interested."

It was Attorney Rivett's turn to smile. "No, actually he didn't think you would, that's why he made a list of potential investors and put feelers out to the most likely ones in order to gauge their level of interest. Based on the reaction he received, you could probably sell it all within six months. The only thing he requested was that you attempt to avoid selling the businesses and the ranch to the Boyers."

"Ah, the Slaughters' old nemesis. Why am I not surprised his last wish was that the Boyers never get their filthy paws on any of the family assets? Well, you can all rest easy; I have no love for them either."

Attorney Rivett walked behind Victor's chair and put his hands on the sergeant's shoulders. "Look, I'm sure this is a lot to absorb, especially on the day of John's burial; you don't have to decide anything right now. Go home, talk to your wife, then call me in a few days. When you think you're ready, we can discuss your options in more detail. In the meantime, as executor of the estate and until the will clears probate, I've asked Bart to camp out in Boyerville to act as temporary CEO of Slaughter Holdings. Are you okay with that?"

Vic looked up and over his shoulder at Bob. "I'm fine with that. In fact, now I'm anxious to get Bart's opinion of the condition of the enterprise. Bart, how long do you think it will take for you to get a good feel for the operations?"

Everybody turned toward Bart, anticipating his response. "A week, maybe two. Why do you ask?"

"I think I'd like to talk to you after you've had a chance to make a first-hand assessment of what it will take for a rookie like me to get up to speed."

"That sounds like a smart idea," Bob replied, smiling. "So, when Bart's comfortable, he'll send you something in writing. In the meantime, here are our business cards. Should you have questions don't hesitate to call any of us."

"I have just one thing I need clarification on. I'm guessing my uncle never married or had children; is that correct?"

Bart spoke up. "I don't believe he ever got married, but I do know he was engaged to an Australian army nurse during one of his tours in Vietnam."

Bob Rivett seconded Bart's answer. "He never mentioned to me that he ever got married or had children, and from a legal perspective, in the last twenty-five years nothing has ever come up on either situation."

Turning to Bart, Vic asked, "What do you know about the engagement? When was it and what ever happened to the girl?"

"I think it was 1970 or '71. I was an Air Force captain safely stationed near Saigon; your uncle was an Army major with the dangerous assignment of escorting supply caravans through hostile territory. Coincidentally, one of my former college roommates, an Air Force pilot, Captain Robbie Ryan, had saved John's ass a couple of times by bombing the shit out of Vietcong forces that had your uncle's battalion pinned down and about to be overrun. As thanks for Robbie's accurate and timely delivery of Armageddon on the enemy, Major Slaughter treated Robbie to R&R in Saigon. Since I was close by in Tan Son Nhut Air Base, Robbie convinced John to drag me along. Anyway, after a day or two sampling the delights of the big city we decided to head down to the coast and spend a relaxing couple of days at a beach resort about eighty kilometers southeast of Saigon that was popular with servicemen. There also happened to be an Australian medical detachment stationed there. We were hardly there an hour when your uncle starts charming an Australian nurse. The two of them hit it off immediately, and they soon disappeared for the whole weekend. On the way back to Saigon, Robbie and I could tell that John was hopelessly smitten. Robbie later told me that John and, I think her name was Lieutenant Wynn, met regularly either in Saigon or at the resort. Shortly after I got back to the States, Robbie wrote me in a letter that John and Lieutenant Wynn were engaged."

"So, what happened that they didn't get married?"

"I'm really not sure. John, Robbie, and I lost contact. It wasn't until twenty years later that I learned of Robbie's death as a civilian in Vietnam after the war. That's when I tracked John down. I found him retired and living in Eureka. He hadn't known about Robbie's death either.

"While we were shooting the shit over the phone, I mentioned something about always wanting to salmon fish in the Pacific Northwest, and he jumped all over it, inviting me out to Eureka for what he called a week of heavy-duty fishing. We had a great time that week and vowed to make it an annual event. Several years later I brought David here along, and he added Bob. Eventually, he asked us to help him with strategic planning.

"Oops, I guess I got carried away. Getting back to your uncle's engagement, on one of our fishing trips, I asked John about Lieutenant Wynn, and he immediately got all sullen and muttered that breaking off their engagement was the hardest decision he ever made. When I asked him why he did it, he mumbled something about their long-term objectives being different, and he immediately changed the subject."

Attorney Rivett cut in. "Actually, I believe I can add something to the story. Shortly after he hired me as his lawyer, he asked me to discreetly attempt to track down Lieutenant Jill Wynn. It took me a few months, but I finally located her married to a rancher in Queensland and the mother of three children."

"What was my uncle's reaction to the news?"

"He smiled and said, 'She got what she dreamed of . . . good for her.' We never talked about it again."

Victor shook his head and smiled. "Yup, I can see him saying that." Then standing up, he continued, "I guess we're done, huh?"

Attorney Rivett smiled. "Sounds like it," he said. "Call us if you think of something else."

"Will do," Vic replied as he reached out to shake Rivett's hand.

CHAPTER 7

Bart hadn't written an enterprise evaluation and recommendations in fifteen years, but once he got started at Slaughter Holdings, it was like riding a bicycle. Within ten days he had FedExed a five-page analysis with a short bullet list of recommendations to Chief Master Sergeant Victor Slaughter at Hurlburt Field.

During his career, Bart had a reputation for being able to synthesize complex issues into precise, easily understandable concepts. His report to Victor was no exception. After studying Bart's report, even a man with only a high school education who had spent his whole adult life exclusively in the military discovered he was able to broadly comprehend the key operating and financial principles surrounding Slaughter Holdings. In addition, he was able to achieve a significant degree of confidence that his Air Force leadership training along with Bart's mentoring and the strong management team already in place would likely provide him with sufficient skills to maintain Slaughter Holdings as a profitable enterprise.

All he had left to do was to convince his wife Tanya and their three adopted children to move to Northern California. Of course, even after that was accomplished, there would still be the issue of Tanya's Air Force career. Although he could retire immediately, Tanya was fourteen months short of her twenty-year anniversary and she was overdue for reassignment.

With little time left, they expected she would receive orders for Afghanistan or one of the other air bases in the Middle East.

By mid-May, Victor had convinced his family that moving to California's North Coast on a two-hundred-acre ranch would be an exciting adventure. Even if Tanya received overseas orders, it would only be for a year or less until she could retire. In the meantime, Vic himself would retire so he and the children could begin settling into their new home in California.

Now excited about his post-military career, Chief Master Sergeant Victor McCoy put in his retirement papers effective July 31st, exactly twenty-two years after he first enlisted. Tanya finally received her orders on July 18th. Just as they had feared, she was to report to her new squadron at Pope Field for deployment to Al Udeid Air Base in Qatar by September 7th.

■ ■ ■

Clete Boyer Senior generally only called his eldest son when he wanted something. This time was no exception. "Junior, were you able to find out anything about this consultant they've got over there at Slaughter's?"

"A little bit, Pop; rumor has it he was hired by the general's estate to evaluate the business and the assets. Speculation is the heirs want to sell it all off."

"Well, that's good news. Were you also able to determine who the heirs are?"

"No, I checked with Probate, but nothing had been filed yet."

"What about the consultant, what do you know about him?" his father asked.

"His name is Bart Rock. I had Ken pull a routine traffic stop on him to get a look at his driver's license. He's sixty-five years old and has a Colorado driver's license. He's had a room at the Carter House in Eureka. Uncle Bernie ran a credit check on him. Before last year, there is no record of Bart Rock ever having credit. No credit cards, no mortgage, no car loans, no nothing. It's weird, it's like the guy landed on the planet last year. Anyway, his occupation is listed as financial consultant."

"Well, son, this guy sounds interesting. I'll have to meet this Bart Rock, especially if he's involved in the liquidation. I'd sure like to get that Slaughter property back in the family."

"Be careful, Pop, I'm concerned about this guy surfacing out of nowhere. It almost looks as if he might be some kind of undercover cop."

"Or perhaps, Junior, he's in witness protection."

"Damn, that's a thought! I'd like to get his fingerprints run through IAFIS."

"That's a good idea. In the meantime, I'd really like to meet this guy. You wouldn't happen to know where he eats dinner?"

Irritated, Junior replied, "What do I look like, Pop, his concierge?"

His father retaliated for Junior's smart-ass remark with that demeaning tone of voice Clete Junior had loathed since he was old enough to remember. "All right, Junior, I forgot you're only this dinky town's police chief. I'll check with someone who's plugged into what's going on in the big city."

Pissed, Chief Boyer slammed down the phone without saying good-bye to his father.

CHAPTER 8

Bart was sitting alone people-watching at the impressive blond oak bar in the 301 Restaurant. He was nursing a glass of Envy 2011 Cabernet Sauvignon when Clete Boyer Senior sauntered in and approached the bar. The newcomer nodded and smiled at Bart just as he would to any stranger. Then he casually took the stool right next to him. The barmaid, a shapely fortyish woman with purplish-red hair and a four-inch seahorse tattoo visible on her neck, hurried over. "Evening, Mr. Boyer, what can I get you?"

Bart was surprised and curious at the barmaid's mention of "Mr. Boyer." He gave the newcomer a quick once-over.

Boyer noticed Bart's interest at the same time he responded, "Tequila, Shirley."

"You want the salt and lime tonight?"

"Not unless you're going to try to pour me the cheap stuff."

Shirley's face turned almost the same color as her hair. "Noooo . . . Mr. Boyer, I never pour you anything but top shelf."

"Okay then, no salt and lime needed."

Bart chuckled just loud enough for Boyer to hear.

Reacting to Bart's amusement at the banter, Clete swiveled on his stool to face him. He quickly eyed the man up and down, noticing his attire was casual but expensive-looking, "You're new in town, aren't you?"

"Yup," Bart replied as he swiveled on his stool. Holding out his hand he continued, "Bart Rock, Mr. Boyer. I've heard a lot about you. I have to admit, I would never have guessed who you are if Shirley had not said your name."

"Why's that, Mr. Rock?"

"Well, for one thing, you dress so unassumingly."

Boyer chuckled, but said nothing as Shirley returned. She set Clete's shot down in front of him without saying a word. Clete quickly swiveled back, picked up his glass while announcing, just before throwing back his head and dumping the shot into his mouth, "First one today."

He then swiveled back, facing Bart, and asked, "So, you've heard of me, have you? Was any of it good?"

"Well, do you consider being referred to as a shrewd businessman good?"

"Depends on who's doing the referring."

"That would be John Slaughter's attorney, Bob Rivett."

"Well, then I'll take it as a compliment." Still playing it coy, he asked, "How do you know Rivett?"

"He's the one who hired me."

Still acting like he hadn't planned the meeting, Boyer replied, "Oh, you must be the financial consultant out at Slaughter Holdings."

"The one and only," Bart replied with a grin.

"So, what do you think?"

"Think about what, the need for salt and lime with a shot of top-shelf tequila?"

"You play it close to the vest, don't you? No problem, I respect that. If you're considering selling off Slaughter's assets, I'd like first crack at them . . . especially the ranch."

"I'll bet you would."

"What does that mean, Rock?" Clete shot back with a hint of insecurity.

"Nothing, Mr. Boyer; just that I understand most of Slaughter's assets would fit nicely into your portfolio."

Boyer stared at Bart with an expression indicating he was itching to respond but he never did.

Bart held Boyer's eye, smiling.

Both men held their gaze until Boyer looked down at his watch and in more of a boast than a simple fact announced, "Oops, gotta go. I've have a meeting with the mayor in fifteen minutes." After quickly chug-a-lugging the rest of his drink he reached into his pants pocket, pulling out a wad of bills secured by a rubber band. He made a production of peeling off two Jeffersons and tossing them on the bar. He then turned back to Bart, grinning "Nice to meet you, Mr.—eh, can I call you Bart?"

Bart didn't respond immediately. Boyer's performance with the roll of large bills evoked memories of his Mafia brother-in-law, Little Nicky. Suddenly he noticed Clete was staring at him with a curious look on his face. "Eh . . . sure, call me anything you like. Just don't call me after 10 p.m."

Boyer snickered as he held out his hand. "Okay then, Bart." He emphasized the B. "See you around town. Don't forget; if you're selling, I'm buying."

Bart firmly took hold of Boyer's outstretched hand but did not reply. As he did with all his handshakes, the seventy-five-year-old patriarch of the Boyer clan attempted to intimidate with the force of his grip. At the point where most other men flinched, Rock surprised him by matching his clasp while still sporting a confident smile.

The show of machismo lasted for a full five seconds before Boyer broke it off and silently turned to leave the bar.

■ ■ ■

On the Baja Peninsula, eight hundred miles south of Eureka, his employer and host refilled Captain Stefan Marinov's gold-rimmed tumbler with another two fingers of Don Julio Tequila Real and watched with admiration as his guest threw it down in one gulp.

With only a slight hint of a Spanish accent, Teodoro Sanchez Felix said in English, "I've lost count, Captain, but was that your fifth or sixth shot?"

Shrugging, Marinov replied, "Who counts?"

"You're right, but perhaps it would be a good idea for you to tell me about your voyage before you're too drunk to remember it."

Captain Marinov sneered then methodically took a long swig of water before he arrogantly replied in his heavy Eastern-European accented English, "It will take a lot more than a few shots of Mexican liquor to affect my memory, Don Felix." He paused while he smiled broadly, displaying his apparent lack of routine dental hygiene.

His Mexican host frowned while he contemplated his recent hire. *What a classless pig. It's a wonder he ever made it to the rank of captain.*

Still sober enough to recognize Don Felix's sudden displeasure, the captain cringed. It wouldn't be wise to piss off his new boss. He wasn't called "El Tiburon" or "The Shark" for nothing. Quickly backpedaling, he attempted to get back in the Mexican's good graces.

"We made the whole run without being detected. The rendezvous and transfer off the coast came off as planned. The installation of those two new German diesel-electric engines along with stripping it of all the unnecessary military gear and weapons allowed us to average almost seventeen knots submerged. Now that I've run the course once, next time, barring bad seas around Flat Iron Rock, we should be able to complete the round trip in less than five days. You would never know this boat is almost sixty years old and hadn't left dry dock in almost fifteen years."

"That's wonderful, Captain. How did the new sonar work?"

"Oh, I forgot; that was the best surprise of all. I can't believe how much the technology has changed. Its range is double what I am used to, and the new engine and drive gears are far quieter than the originals. Unless they are specifically looking for us, the Americans will never know we're running up their coast."

"Great! Now tell me about your crew; do you trust them?"

"Absolutely, I handpicked each of them for this job. Every one of them served under me in the Bulgarian navy. There are no drug addicts. Even though they all like their beer and rakia while on shore leave, they've proved to me they will keep their mouths shut and maintain a low profile."

"That's good; what's the old naval adage, 'loose lips sink ships'?"

Snickering, Captain Marinov replied, "That only applies to the English and American sailors, who everyone knows can't hold their liquor."

Both men laughed hardily at the expense of their loathed Anglo foes.

Don Felix poured another tumbler of tequila into his guest's glass before announcing, "I have a surprise for your crew." He hesitated while Marinov drained the contents of his glass. When the captain was finished, he resumed, "After you left with the first shipment, I had my chef scour the Internet for authentic Balkan cuisine. Although some of the provisions he ordered still haven't arrived from Europe, when you sail off tomorrow you'll have two pallets of ingredients and packaged goods. I believe your cook will be able to make the crew feel like they're just cruising in the Black Sea while fully contented with his traditional Bulgarian meals."

Still attempting to ensure he was on El Tiburon's good side, the captain held up his empty glass, declaring, "That's wonderful, Don Felix. You truly are a considerate employer."

Now amused by his Bulgarian guest's alcohol capacity and curious about the extent of his other vices, El Tiburon poured out two more glasses of tequila. "You know, Captain, you don't have to stay in town tonight. I have plenty of room here at the ranch and you might find my women a lot more appealing than the ones in the local bars. Like you, I also handpick my employees."

Getting up from his chair, the Bulgarian showed no signs of being the slightest bit tipsy until he spoke, or was it just his Eastern European accent? "I think I'll take you up on the offer."

"Good!" Don Felix replied. Smiling, he held up his tumbler, "To a long and profitable relationship."

The two men clinked their glasses together and quickly tossed down one last shot before El Tiburon called to have the girls sent up to the main house.

CHAPTER 9

It was August 6th, and they were now in a hurry. Tanya only had a month of leave left before she had to report to Pope Field. Victor had just turned off Highway 36 onto Riverfront Road and was exceeding the speed limit by nine miles per hour. He wasn't technically driving recklessly, but given there were no guardrails on this stretch of Riverfront Road with its numerous hairpin turns and switchbacks, he was pushing his luck.

They thought they had given themselves plenty of time to make the 2,800-mile drive from Hurlburt Field on the Florida Panhandle to Boyerville, California, but the original plan did not include a detour through Las Vegas nor losing a half day along the Redwood Highway gawking at two-thousand-year-old trees in the Avenue of Giants. Even after Victor capitulated to Tanya and the kids' incessant pleading to see Vegas, he never envisioned stopping for two whole days and nights. Once they had checked into their adjoining rooms at the Mandalay, he realized they all needed some breathing room for a few days.

Before they started their cross-country adventure, their 2014 Chevy Suburban seemed like a huge vehicle; but after three long days and some 1,700 miles it felt like the five of them had been crammed into a Volkswagen Beetle. The three children were particularly testy with each other, and even the normally patient Tanya was beginning to show signs of irritation. So they dallied longer than anticipated to reenergize and to get off of each others' nerves.

Now, the moving van was due to arrive at the house tomorrow. He knew Tanya would want to vacuum, dust, mop, and probably even wash the inside of all the kitchen cabinets before their household goods were unpacked.

This would be Tanya's first glimpse of the Slaughter family's estate. Sullenly he mentally chided himself for being so secretive about his family. Since he and Tanya had fallen in love nine years earlier, Victor had not shared a lot of his childhood with the love of his life, and he wondered how big a mistake that was going to turn out to be.

Even while he was attempting to convince Tanya to move to Eureka, deep down he was not even sure what effect his troubled past would have on him. Perhaps if he had been more open with her he would have had the opportunity to come to grips with his life before the Air Force. Well, in less than twenty minutes they would turn onto the long dirt road leading to what his mother used to refer to as "the slaughterhouse." Then, he had no doubt, a whole host of suppressed memories and emotions would flood his mind.

Subconsciously, he pursed his lips as some memories apparently weren't going to wait for the turnoff. His mother . . . what a piece of work she was. Even though it was thirty years ago, he still remembered it like it was yesterday. The "slut," as his grandma occasionally referred her, would leave him sleeping under an itchy horse blanket in the backseat of his deceased grandfather's rusty old 1970 Imperial while she hung out in Tillie's Roadhouse. He shuddered as he could almost hear her edgy admonition upon her return, usually with some fetid loudmouth, "You stay under that blanket and shut up. If I hear one peep out of you, I'll lock you up in the trunk until tomorrow morning."

Shivering at the thought, he attempted to drive out these dreadful memories; however, almost instantly a new nightmarish recollection burst into in to his head. *God, I was always so hungry back then. It felt as if there was something in my stomach gnawing to get out.* He could see himself scrambling into the stinky, cockroach-invested dumpster behind Tillie's looking for scraps of food, and the recollection actually made him feel nauseous.

He sighed, and Tanya noticed. "What's the matter?" she asked.

Forcing a meager smile, he replied, "Nothin'. It's just been a long time."

Tanya attempted to add some wisdom to his remark. "I guess. Twenty-two years is a . . ."

He only heard the first few words before his mind zoned out, off and racing again. This time he was focused on the days the "slut" would dump him off at Grandma Drusilla's and disappear for days. Although she was the antithesis of his mother, she was another piece of work in her own right. An incredibly religious woman, she believed the Bible and prayer held the answer to all life's trials and tribulations.

As an innocent eight-year-old, he couldn't figure out why Grandma would go ballistic whenever he would tell her his mother lost another wrestling match to some man in the front seat of the Imperial. For years after his mother had run off, Drusilla would cringe whenever he asked why she left or who his father was; then she would respond in annoyance, "Someday you can ask your mother those questions."

Finally, after she calmed down, she would read to him for hours from the Bible. When she got tired of reading, she'd make him get down on his knees and pray for his mother's salvation. When he was fourteen, after one of those marathon sessions he finally came to grips with the fact his mother was never coming back. Shattered by the realization, he ran away, telling himself he was going to find her. But deep down in his soul he knew it was just an excuse to get away from the old bag.

He was shaking his head in disbelief at his early childhood memories when he noticed the flashing red-and-blue lights behind him.

"Shit," he muttered, not loud enough for the kids in the back seat to hear him. He anxiously checked the speedometer.

"What's the matter?" Tanya asked.

"Cop, but we're okay. I'm only going eight miles over the speed limit."

She turned to look behind them. "His lights are flashing. Do you think he wants you to pull over?"

Just then the cop gave two short chirps with his siren.

"Maybe it's the welcoming committee," Victor said with an uneasy laugh as he searched for a safe spot to pull off the winding road. It took another quarter mile before he was able to find a fishermen's turnoff big enough for both vehicles to pull into.

CHAPTER 10

Victor watched through his rearview mirror as the officer appeared to be working the computer on his dashboard, apparently plugging in the Florida license plate number and waiting for feedback. After what seemed like an eternity but in reality was only ninety seconds, the officer opened his door and got out of the vehicle. He was big, wide at the shoulders and thirty pounds overweight. Leaving his door open, he stood looking at Victor's Suburban while he blocked the sun's reflection off his bald head by ceremoniously putting on a brown, wide-brimmed sheriff's hat. He then adjusted his gun belt and sauntered toward the Suburban.

"You better get the registration out of the glove box, Tanya. I've got a feeling this isn't a social visit."

"You don't think he's going to write you up for going eight miles per hour over the speed limit?"

"I don't know, but why else would he bother to stop us on this dangerous stretch of road?"

As the officer confidently strolled toward the Suburban, he unclipped the leather strap securing his gun to its holster. Stopping three feet from the driver's door with his hand on his weapon, he gestured for Victor to roll down his window. Victor complied. The deputy removed his mirrored aviator-style sunglasses, revealing bloodshot eyes perched above conspicuous periorbital dark circles. The officer sort of squatted in order to get a good look around the inside of the vehicle. His eyes narrowed as they moved through the vehicle, observing the diverse makeup of its occupants.

Forged by years of commanding men, the driver appeared unintimidated. He stared straight back at the officer with a look that insinuated, "This is a bullshit stop."

The lawman scrutinized the Caucasian driver. He was about his age and, judging by how far his seat was set back, was well over six feet tall. Based upon the size of his head and shoulders, he wasn't just long, he was also impressively brawny.

In the passenger seat sat the blackest women he had ever encountered, not that he got to meet a lot of African-Americans on the North Coast. Yet, in spite of his inherent and cultivated prejudices, he found her features extremely appealing. She had shiny jet-black hair layered with subtle red bangs. If she was wearing lipstick, it must have been close to her natural color. But it was her sultry eyes defiantly peering at him that instantly made him feel uneasy. He quickly directed his attention to the backseat, where more surprises awaited.

Sitting in the middle was a young Asian girl who seemed to be cowering against a gangly, black, adolescent female whose caramel-colored skin tone suggested she could be the offspring of the couple up front. The vehicle's final occupant was a red-haired, wide-eyed white boy sitting behind the driver with an inquisitive look radiating from his face.

Without even attempting to mask his scorn, the grinning deputy exclaimed, "Well, what have we here—a United Nations delegation?"

Ah shit, Victor thought. *I guess the bigotry hasn't changed much in the last twenty-two years.* Seeing no advantage in responding, he just smiled at the deputy, but Tanya wasn't as passive.

Before enlisting in the Air Force, Tanya had been the victim of her own "parade of horrible." Like Vic, she did not know who her father was, and her birth mother wallowed in drugs and alcohol until Tanya was taken away by Child Protective

Services at the age of three. She bounced around between group and foster homes where she was subjected to cruel and sometimes physically abusive treatment. After languishing in this nightmare for over six years, she was finally placed with a loving biracial couple in Charlotte, North Carolina.

But even with that salvation, she discovered a new kind of suffering. Biracial families were not that common in the 1990s, especially in the South. Now she had to learn how to deal with name-calling and bullying in school. As a result, she developed several unique skills for dealing with bigots and bullies. By the time she was a teenager, Tanya was no longer intimidated, either physically or intellectually, by anything or anyone. That quickly became obvious to any potential antagonists. As a result, few people messed with her more than once.

Ducking her head and leaning forward so she could look into the eyes of the smart-ass deputy sheriff, she smiled and replied, "Are you referring to the fact that you just stopped a southern redneck with his nigger bitch and a rainbow coalition of snot-nosed kids?"

The deputy's mouth dropped open, and you could have knocked him over with a feather.

Victor, thinking his wife was being dangerously hostile, snapped his head in her direction. He had every intention of chiding her until he saw the devilish smirk on her face. Instantly he realized, instead of being antagonistic, it was just her perverse way of satirizing the deputy's insulting "United Nations delegation" remark.

Turning back toward the deputy, he could see her retort had worked as the deputy's mouth still hung open and there was a faraway look in his eyes. Unable to control himself, Vic began to snicker. It took the deputy a full five seconds to recover before sternly commanding, "License and registration."

Victor was ready with both and offered them through the open window. As the deputy reached for the identification, Victor noticed the white lettering on his black name tag, Deputy Sheriff K. Boyer.

Deputy Sheriff Boyer accepted the two pieces of identification, turned, and hastily retreated back to his squad car.

Victor glanced over at Tanya. "Cute!"

"Well . . . I didn't like the way he said 'United Nations delegation.' What did he think; we were too dumb to understand his inference?"

From the back seat, fifteen-year-old Cindy chimed in, "I never heard you use the n-word before, Mom."

"You better get used to it, sweetie. Given your complexion, I'm guessing it won't be the last time you hear it in this neck of the woods."

Chuckling, Victor replied, "Wasn't it obvious that he was happy to see our cultural diversity?"

"Sure he was," Tanya replied with sarcasm dripping from every word. "Now he is going to come back and tell us he's glad we wandered through his jurisdiction and offer to escort us to a nice motel where we can comfortably spend the night."

"I'm more interested as to whether he recognizes who I am and how he reacts when he does."

"What's that all about?" Tanya asked.

"Later, darling," Victor replied, flashing an uneasy smile.

■ ■ ■

Back in his cruiser, Deputy Sheriff Ken Boyer was on his cell phone with his brother, who asked, "Are you sure, Ken?"

"I don't know, Junior; you tell me. It says right here on his license and registration, Victor McCoy, DOB 1974; same year as you. There's also a sticker on the windshield from some Air Force base."

"So, just as we figured, he must be one of the heirs. They're probably headed to the Slaughter place right now."

"What do you want me to do, Junior?"

"Nothing, maybe he's not here to stay. After all, he does have a career in the military. Perhaps he'll be more interested in selling the old place than the general was. I'm sure Pop wouldn't want us to piss him off until we know what his intentions are."

"Okay, I'll just give him back his license and registration and tell him to drive carefully."

"Yeah, do that, Ken, but also tell him you only stopped him because you saw the out-of-state plate and didn't know if he realized how treacherous that highway is, especially after it gets dark."

"Will do, Chief."

"Er . . . hold on a second . . . you know what; belay that thought. It can't hurt to acknowledge you know who he is, that I'm chief of police and you're my brother. That ought to get him thinking. See if you can find out if they're staying at the Slaughter place tonight. If not, try to get them to reveal where they are lodging. Wherever it is, I'd like to stop by tomorrow and welcome my old friend Vic back to town."

"You're shitting me, Junior. He's not gonna want to see you. It was because of you Pop ran him out of town."

"Maybe not, but he could also think it was the best thing that ever happened to him."

"Yeah, right."

"Just do it, Ken, then call me back and tell me what his reaction is."

"Ten-four, Chief."

CHAPTER 11

"Here's your license and registration back, Mr. McCoy. I pulled you over because I noticed the out-of-state plates and didn't know if you realized what a treacherous stretch of road this can be . . . especially after it gets dark."

"Well, thank you, Deputy, we're only going another couple of miles. Say, aren't you Clete Junior's little brother Ken?"

Deputy Boyer proved he was cleverer than his older brother thought by playing dumb. "You must mean younger brother since I'm bigger than he is. So, you know my brother, the chief of police in Boyerville?"

"I didn't even know Boyerville now has its own police force. So, Junior is the chief. Isn't that something . . . sure, I even remember you, Ken. You followed your brother around like a puppy dog. Does he still treat you like you're his personal slave?"

Ken laughed. "He tries, but I don't let him get away with that as much as I used to. That's one of the reasons I work for the county instead of my brother."

Vic sized Ken up and down before he chuckled and replied, "Yeah, I can tell you're your own man."

"So, I just figured out who you are . . . you're Vic McCoy, one of the Slaughter kin. Man, you sure filled out too. I remember you as a tall drink of water. Wow, it looks like you've been pumping some iron."

"Air Force Special Operations requires you stay in shape."

"Special Ops, hum . . . impressive. You on leave?"

"Not any more. I'm retired as of last week."

"Get out of here . . . retired, as young as you are. Aren't you afraid you'll get bored?"

"Uncle John never did and I plan on picking up where he left off."

"So, you'll be moving up here?"

"Yup, moving van shows up tomorrow."

"Well then, neighbor, aren't you going to introduce me to your family?"

"Sure, Ken; this is my wife, Tanya, and in the back are our children. Cindy's is on the right, she's the oldest, Billy's on the left and he is next oldest, and the youngest is Yo in the middle."

Deputy Boyer leaned into the driver's window to get a good look at the family. When he did, Vic caught a whiff of stale beer and the remnants of onion from Ken's hamburger lunch at the Eel River Brewing Company in Fortuna. Vic turned his nose away from the window but when the deputy started talking, it didn't help.

"Welcome to redwood country. I bet you kids have never seen anything like these giant redwoods down in Florida."

Feeling empowered by her mother's earlier wisecrack, fifteen-year-old Cindy responded, "Nope, I bet there is going to be a lot of things out here us hillbillies never experienced before."

Vic's head and shoulders swiveled around to the back seat, and he shot his adopted daughter a killer look.

Tanya, realizing she had started something that might get ugly, quickly injected in a more amiable tone, "Yeah, we can't wait to have the time to explore the wonders of the North Coast."

"Well, you'll never run out of new things to see and places to go. This is one of the most incredible places on the planet. Say, Vic, how about I give you an escort out to the old place?"

"You don't have to go out of your way, Deputy. I'm sure I can still find my way."

"It's no trouble. That's the least I can do for an old friend of the family." Clearly in an attempt to impress the kids, Deputy Ken Boyer exclaimed, "Come on, I'll lead with the lights flashing." Then shouting over his shoulder while he walked toward his car, he said something that made Vic cringe. "Wait till I tell Junior you're back in town. I bet he's gonna wanna come straight out to say hello."

"Great," Vic muttered just loud enough for his family to hear.

After Vic had pulled back on the highway three car-lengths behind the deputy, Tanya remarked, "So, that went well, don't you think?"

"Surprisingly, but I had this strange feeling he knew who I was long before he came back to the car. In fact, my sense is the whole thing was an act. Unless things have drastically changed in the last couple of decades, a Boyer wouldn't be as enthusiastic to see a McCoy or Slaughter as he seemed to be."

"Why's that?" Tanya asked anxiously.

"I'll fill you in later."

Tanya lightly punched Vic in the arm. "What have you gotten us into, my love?"

"Nothing we can't handle. We will just have to be vigilant until I figure out exactly where I stand with the Boyers after all these years. My uncle John must have gotten along with them well enough to stay here for over twenty-five years."

"So darling, I'm guessing there are a few things you need to tell me about your early years in redwood country."

"There sure are . . . there sure are," Vic solemnly declared.

■ ■ ■

The two vehicles wound their way for another ten minutes through stands of redwoods and past tiny houses with sagging roofs and peeling paint while Vic negotiated a dozen or so hairpin turns. When Deputy Boyer pulled off onto the shoulder just past a gravel drive, Victor announced to his family, "We're here!"

Turning off the pavement, he slowly maneuvered the Suburban over a narrow wooden bridge crossing the small creek which had been meandering alongside the highway; then they bounced over the cattle grates separating two twenty-foot-tall cedar totem poles. The hand-carved totems were adorned with the painted figures of various animals.

"Those totems are new." He seemed to be reflecting on something for a few seconds before he continued, "Welcome to the Slaughter place; it's somewhere between a ranch and a forest preserve."

"Can we stop and look at all the animals on those poles?" twelve-year-old Billy asked.

"Sure, we're in no hurry now that we're here."

Vic pulled over just inside the totems and everyone got out. As they did, Deputy Boyer beeped his horn and waved before squealing back onto the highway. Meanwhile, the always-energetic Billy raced to one of the poles.

Running his hands over the painted face of a coyote, he said, "Wow! Look at all these animals. There is a bear and a wolf, and look up top; there's an eagle with a fish in his talons. I've never seen a real totem pole before, they're cool. Who did this?"

"I don't know," Vic replied.

"The colors are stunning," Tanya added. "These weren't here when you lived here?"

"Nope, there was just a large cedar tree on either side of the cattle grate."

"Are there Indians here?" shy nine-year-old Yo asked with a hint of alarm in her voice.

"Yes, there are. There are lots of Indians around here; in fact you're looking at one."

Yo looked around nervously, and Billy excitedly shouted, "Where?"

"Me," Vic said proudly. "My great-grandmother was a full-blooded Wiyot Indian. That makes me at least one-sixteenth Native American."

"Cool!" Billy exclaimed.

"You never told me that," Tanya said skeptically.

"Would it have made a difference if I did?"

"No, but I would have been a little more careful when I laced our watermelon with vodka."

"Bigot," Vic shot back with a smile on his face.

The two youngest kids quizzically looked at Cindy, hoping she could shed some light on their mother's comment. Cindy got the watermelon part but the vodka thing eluded her. She contorted her mouth and eyebrows to indicate, *It beats me.*

Vic, noticing the kids' reactions, decided it wasn't the right time and place to continue this kibitzing so he declared, "Come on, let's get to the house and I'll tell you as much about the Slaughter-McCoy family tree as I know."

The gravel road soon gave way to two tire ruts with scraggly clumps of grass between them. They drove through a wide meadow of grass and wildflowers. In the distance they could make out a few scattered cattle and horses feeding on the lush vegetation. Five hundred yards later they passed through a grove of eighty-year-old redwoods.

"These redwoods are babies compared to some of the ones near the back of the ranch," Vic announced. "Over a hundred years ago all the original trees along the road were cut down to be sold for lumber and to make way for hundreds of cattle to graze here. After they paved the highway, my great-grandfather planted these in order to block the view of the house from the road. Near the back of the property there are still some original trees as much as eight hundred years old and with trunks as wide as this truck."

"Cool," Billy exclaimed. "When can we go see them?"

"Not today," Tanya declared. "We have lots to do before the moving truck gets here."

In less than a minute their vehicle began to emerge from the stand of juvenile redwoods.

"Whoa, that's not the way I remember it!" Vic exclaimed, stopping the car to stare at the golden two-story timber and log house with its cheery ocean-blue roof panels.

All three children gasped, and Tanya couldn't control herself,

"You've got to be kidding me, the place is awesome! So this is where you grew up?"

"Not exactly," Vic replied. Then he sort of mumbled to himself, "Score one more for the general."

While everyone gawked at the inviting house, Vic continued, "When I lived here it was a low single-story ranch with ugly weathered log siding and with moss blanketing the roof. With only a few small windows it had kind of a bunker look, and the inside was dark and dank.

"I actually only spent a couple of years living here. I hated the place; it always seemed dismal and cold just like my grandmother. Frankly, between its looks and my witchy grandmother, the place scared the hell out of me. I'm guessing my mother felt the same way or why else would she refer to it as 'the slaughterhouse' instead of home?" Vic hesitated as he continued to drink in the new ambiance. Finally, he announced, "Amazingly, it no longer has that same feel. It looks like Uncle John cut the roof off and put in those huge windows to let more light into the main floor, then added a second floor above the back bedrooms. Replacing the old cedar roof with those blue steel panels really adds life to the place. That's also a whole new portico and front entrance. Even the porch roof seems to have been raised to let more light in the front windows."

"Wow, there's a corral full of horses over by that big barn!" Cindy exclaimed. Then as an afterthought she said, "I wonder what all those cars are doing parked next to the barn?"

Her father whipped his head around to the barn and just stared for a few seconds before replying, "I don't know, it seems we may have some company."

"What's that smell?" Yo asked, holding her nose.

Tanya laughed. "What do you think it is?"

"Yuck," Cindy responded. "I bet it's animal poop!"

Just then the front door opened, and a troupe of approximately ten people emptied out under the portico.

"Who are those people?" Tanya asked apprehensively.

"I have no idea . . . wait a minute, I think I recognize one of them from when I was a kid."

Vic took his foot off the brake, and the Suburban began creeping toward the front entrance. He stopped just under the overhang while the crowd eagerly waited on the porch. For a few seconds the whole scene went on pause.

Finally, Vic opened his door and got out; Tanya followed. The children, apprehensive, remained frozen in the backseat. The new owner of the Slaughter ranch walked around the front of the car and took hold of his wife's hand.

"Hello," he said to the short, stocky, dark-skinned middle-aged man he thought he recognized. "We've met, haven't we?"

"Yes sir, Mr. McCoy. My name is Miles Reynolds, I'm your distant cousin, and you might recall I was working here for the general before you enlisted. On behalf of the rest of the relatives, friends, and employees of the Slaughter family, I want to welcome you and your family to Humboldt County. Unfortunately, since we only found out yesterday you were arriving today, we didn't have time to arrange for a more suitable celebration. Regardless, we were all thrilled you've decided to come live at the ranch and continue to operate Slaughter Holdings."

"Well, thank you for your warm welcome. My wife, Tanya, and our children are happy to be here. Come on out, kids, and meet your new family and friends."

Both back doors opened and the three children timidly left the safety of the Suburban. They sheepishly hovered around their parents.

A pudgy, dark, middle-aged woman standing beside Miles broke the impasse by stepping forward, smiling. "I'm Anne, Miles' wife. All of us here today are members of either the Wiyot or Yurok tribes and are related to your great-grandmother. We all also work for one of the Slaughter enterprises. The general was a wonderful man whom we all respected and admired, not just because he was a great hero during the Vietnam War and a successful businessman after he retired, but also because he never forgot he was one of us. We are still saddened by his untimely death, yet we look forward to our new relationship with you and your family. We pledge our full support to you and your family."

"Thank you, Anne. That was quite a speech; I am touched by your devotion to my uncle and your pledge to me and my family. To be honest, I felt no love for this place and came very close to selling it. However, when I found out who one of the potential buyers was . . . well, I couldn't bring myself to do it."

At that moment, broad smiles passed over all the faces in the crowd and someone from the back shouted, "Was it the Boyers?"

"Since it didn't happen, let's not discuss it," Victor replied. He moved forward and began shaking hands while he talked, "Thank you, all of you. If there was still any doubt in my mind that we did the right thing by coming here, this welcome surely ended it. I look forward to getting to know each and every one of you. Now let's go inside so my family can see their new home."

Tanya followed her husband's lead and began moving through the crowd shaking hands with the men and hugging the women. Their parents' actions seemed to alleviate the children's initial shyness, and they too began warming up to their new relatives and neighbors. By the time the family had reached the oversized front door, everyone was smiling and laughing as if they had known each other for years.

On the way in, Vic turned to Miles. "Where's Rock?"

"He went down to Sacramento to meet with Mr. Rivett and to pick up his wife at the airport. He said he'd be back sometime tomorrow evening."

"Where's he been staying while he was here?"

"So far a hotel in Eureka, but now he's rented a place in town for him and his wife."

Standing in the entrance foyer, the Boyer family was in awe at the incredible panorama of robust redwood. At both ends of the structure, two large trapezoid windows bathed the entire cathedral-ceilinged main floor in the brilliance of the afternoon summer sun. Except for the slate foyer and marble counter tops, every surface was either varnished or natural redwood. The floor boards were six-inch natural planking. Four shiny massive support columns held up one impressive crossbeam running the entire length of the house. The walls were paneled in one-foot-wide vertical planking and were strategically adorned with photographs and paintings of nature and wildlife.

The open main level was divided into one large great room off to their right. An open staircase, positioned just to the right of the foyer, led to a second-floor balcony. In the center of the main level was a dining area containing one ten-foot rectangular oak table surrounded by eight high-back chairs. A granite counter top fronted by two tree-limb barstools separated the dining area from a large kitchen, while the staircase delineated it from the great room.

It was obvious the general and his interior decorator, if he had one, intended the décor to accentuate his masculinity. A large three-piece curved dark leather sectional faced a massive floor-to-ceiling stone fireplace adorned with a mantle honed from a piece of weathered driftwood. On either side of the sectional were two handmade wooden end tables. A coffee table made from a four-inch-thick slab of redwood separated the couch from the fireplace and sat on an eight-by-eleven Whiskey River Turquoise area rug. Off to either side were leather recliners. Artificial light was provided by four recessed floodlights surrounding a fan with extra long blades and four additional hanging lights.

The kitchen was rustic with oak cabinets, stainless steel appliances, a cutting-board-topped island, and a stone alcove in which the stove sat. At the far end of the kitchen was a hall leading to a half bath and the master suite.

Billy was the first to react with as much of an exclamation as a question. "This is really our new home!"

"So, I guess you kids like it?" Vic responded.

Bubbling over, Cindy intuitively headed for the staircase. "I'll tell you after I see my room." Yo scampered after her.

Looking at Tanya, Vic prodded, "How about you, sweetheart?"

"It's rich, yet light and airy. Everything is done with quality materials, but it sure has a masculine flavor," she replied.

Anne, her head nodding injected, "You got that right."

Vic chuckled. "I get the masculine part, but let me tell you, you should have seen the place before Uncle John had it renovated. It was downright gloomy, especially with all the stuffed animal heads peering down from the walls."

"Well, maybe some curtains in the kitchen and place mats along with a centerpiece on the dining room table will tone down the masculinity. Let's go see the master bedroom. I bet that really needs a woman's touch."

CHAPTER 12

"I had a military policeman I know at Beale Air Force Base ask around. He found out McCoy's wife is an Air Force master sergeant still on active duty and scheduled to be deployed to the Middle East."

"That's interesting, Junior; it probably means McCoy is really committed to staying for a while," the patriarch of the family, Clete Boyer Senior, replied. "So what's this Rock character doing here? I originally thought he was here to either run the place or separate out the assets for sale."

"He still could be here to run it for McCoy; after all, Pop, what does a military guy know about horses, cattle, and manufacturing?"

Clete Senior laughed out loud. "That's what I said about his uncle twenty-five years ago. Regardless, Junior, we should pop on over there tomorrow and see if Victor McCoy still holds a grudge for what we did to him."

■ ■ ■

It was pretty late by the time everyone had eaten from the mountain of food brought by the welcoming party. Miles and Anne were helping Vic and Tanya put away the last of the dishes, and the kids were already fast asleep in their new bedrooms.

Tanya had been waiting to ask this question since their

encounter with Deputy Sheriff Boyer earlier that afternoon.
"So, who's going to tell me all about this Slaughter-Boyer thing?"

Vic looked over at Miles, whose eyes sheepishly shifted
down to his hands. Anne seemed to be ready to say something
when Vic chimed in, "Okay, I'll do it, but I may need Miles'
and Anne's help. They've been around the general a lot more
than I have, and I'm sure they've heard a lot of stories from
the old-timers over the years."

Vic hesitated while he took a deep breath. "What I am about
to tell you I heard from my grandmother. It's probably somewhat slanted by decades of animosity between the families,
but all I can do is tell it the way I heard it.

"Sometime in the 1850s, Gordon Slaughter, my great-great-
great-grandfather, met Abel Boyer in San Francisco. They
teamed up to buy two hundred head of cattle in Placerville and
drive them up here. Once here, they sold enough cattle so each
of them could purchase some acreage. Then they evenly split
up the rest of the herd. Grandma didn't tell me why, but she
alluded to the fact their parting was not amicable and resulted
in years of animosity between the two families."

Vic noticed that Miles was smiling. "So Miles," he asked,
"Can you add more specifics to my story?"

"Later, you're doing fine for now."

"Okay . . . so, Gordon and his wife had two children, Gordon Junior and Abigail. Sometime in the 1870s both families
either lost or sold their ranches. Gordon then worked for
one of the big dairymen over in Ferndale. By the mid-1890s,
Gordon Junior owned a cheese factory and store in Ferndale
while Abigail had run off with a traveling salesman never to
be heard from again.

"Meanwhile, Abel Boyer's first wife gave him a son and a
daughter. She died and he quickly remarried. After many years,
his second wife finally gave him another son. Grandma could
only remember the name of the youngest, Aaron. Eventually,
Aaron worked as a lumberjack all around the North Coast. By
1900 he had worked his way up in the logging company to be

foreman. One day the owner of the operation was accidently killed when a log broke away from a crew and rolled down a hill, flattening the tent the owner used for his office with him still inside. That paved the way for Aaron to marry the owner's daughter and take over the business."

Anne, no wallflower, spoke up with venom in her voice. "The way I heard it, it was no accident. Boyer had designs on his boss's daughter, but he knew the man would never let him marry his daughter. Boyer ordered his men to roll that tree down the hill, knowing it would flatten the tent and everything in it. "

Tanya immediately reacted with suspicion. "How do you know that, Anne? It was over a hundred years ago."

Not quite backpedaling, Anne replied, "Well, I can't prove it, but it was common knowledge Aaron had his sights set on the daughter and the owner intended to send his daughter back East to some finishing school. I can say with a high degree of certainty that, within days of the accident, two of the three men on the crew were also killed in suspicious accidents. The third, a Yurok Indian, told my grandfather he was getting out of town because he believed Boyer was going to kill him for what he knew. Shortly after he confided in my grandfather, he disappeared; nobody ever heard from him again. To add icing to the cake, this would not be the last time one of Boyer's rivals was eliminated in a tragic accidents."

Still not convinced, Tanya rolled her eyes before she said to Vic, "Okay, let's get back to the Slaughters' history."

"Okay," Vic replied, "Enos Slaughter, my great-grandfather born in 1898, was Gordon Junior's only child. Both his parents died of natural causes before he turned sixteen. Gordon's attorney used the proceeds from the sale of the cheese factory and the store to pay for Enos to attend boarding school in San Francisco. By the time the United States got into WWI, Enos was in his second year at the University of California in Berkley. Naïvely enamored with the Army after seeing the numerous propaganda posters hanging around campus, he enlisted and fought valiantly enough in Europe to receive a battlefield commission. After the war, he had no desire to finish his studies. He was anxious to get home and make his fortune in the lumber business. Aaron Boyer owned the biggest and most successful lumber business in Northern California, but he wouldn't hire Enos because of some old feud between the families. Eventually, Enos found work as a logging foreman for one of Boyer's smaller competitors.

"After Aaron's first wife died in the influenza pandemic in 1918, the word was he turned into a mean, hard-drinking gambler whom everyone despised in spite of his money and influence. One winter night in 1921, Enos and Aaron were engaged in a jacks-or-better poker game at one of the saloons in Eureka. Aaron was having an incredible run of luck. Luck, combined with his usual grandiose betting, had run everyone out of the game except Enos.

"That was just the way Aaron liked it, one-on-one with someone he would relish giving a good thrashing to. All of a sudden, Boyer's luck changed and Enos started winning hand after hand. The more money Boyer lost, the more he drank. Soon, almost all the money on the table, over $1,500, was either in the pot or sitting in front of Enos. Boyer was dealt a pair of jacks, an ace, a seven, and a five. Slaughter had a pair of tens, a jack, an eight, and a deuce. It was Slaughter's bet; with only a pair of tens, he had to pass. Boyer bet his last hundred on his pair of jacks. Slaughter, with his pair of tens, called. Boyer discarded three cards and drew three nines, but he had no cash left. Slaughter also discarded three cards but he never looked at his new draw."

Miles interrupted, "As I heard it, by then everybody in the saloon was huddled around the card table or hanging over the balcony itching to see the most-hated man in town get his ass kicked at poker by this young upstart."

Vic laughed then continued, "Since Slaughter was apparently not able to open with a pair of jacks or better, the much older and experienced Boyer was sure his full house of nines over jacks was a winner. Fortified by too much alcohol and being a natural show-off, Aaron boasted, 'I'll put up all my property west of Elk Creek against everything you've got on your side.'

"Apparently my great-grandfather was getting uncomfortable with where this was headed, so he responded, 'Don't be ridiculous, Mr. Boyer, the lumber alone is worth five times what I've got here.'

"Now really agitated and insulted, Boyer responded with venom dripping off each word, 'Just like a gutless Slaughter. Scared of losing tonight's windfall, you little punk?'

"Now it was my great-grandfather's turn to come back with a toxic dig. 'No sir, I just don't want to take advantage of an old drunk.'

"That really pissed Boyer off. 'You little son-of-a-bitch!" he shouted. 'Either put up or shut up.'

"*Screw it,* Enos thought, *I tried to talk some sense into him.* 'Okay, old man. Somebody give Boyer a piece of paper and a pen so he can write up his bet and throw it in the pot.'

"Everybody in the room watched in silence as Aaron Boyer wrote his bet on a piece of paper supplied by the saloon's owner. When he had finished and tossed his pledge in the pot, Enos pushed his stack of money into the middle. Suddenly, there was a loud cheer and thunderous clapping."

Miles interrupted, "Let me tell this part, Vic. It gives me a rush every time I tell it."

"Okay, Miles, it's your floor."

With the biggest grin you ever saw, Miles relayed the story just as it was told to him by his grandfather. "Boyer flips over his cards and says with the utmost contempt, 'Read it and weep, asshole . . . full house, three nines and a pair of jacks!'

"At first there were murmurs, then a hush fell over the saloon as Enos studied his opponent's cards. With a hint of admiration, Enos said, 'Nice draw!' Then, deadpan, he began slowly turning over his cards; a ten, another ten, a five, another five. At this point he hesitated for a moment, looked Boyer in the eye, and without looking down turned over the last card. The handful of men circling the table erupted in excitement while those unable to see the cards pressed in closer. Somebody finally shouted, 'Full house, tens over fives! The lucky son-of-a-bitch did it!'

"It was pandemonium; people were slapping Enos on the back while he raked in his winnings and stuffed Boyer's note in his shirt pocket. Just so it's clear, that note was for this piece of property we're standing on. Anyway, Aaron slinked out of the saloon a totally dejected and beaten man."

"This is a true story? He really never looked at his draw?" Tanya asked incredulously.

"Of course," Anne replied. "It's too incredible to be made up, and we've all heard the same story told for as long as anyone can remember."

"So that's why there's all this animosity between the Slaughters and the Boyers?"

"Hell no" was Mile's instant retort. "That just solidified the feud that started in the 1860s between Gordon and Abel."

"And what was that all about?" Vic asked.

"Some other time; I don't think this is the right time to go into that story."

Vic nodded his acceptance, but the curiosity was showing all over his face. "Okay . . . anyway, I can testify to at least another seventy years of conflict culminating with me having to enlist in the Air Force or go to jail for assaulting Clete Junior."

Tanya's mouth dropped, and Vic instantly regretted springing his hidden past on her so abruptly. "It's not like it sounds, honey. I was just defending myself. Look, I think this is enough for tonight, perhaps we can continue this in the morning."

"Sure, cause me to have a sleepless night," Tanya barked, clearly disturbed by Vic's revelation.

Anne, sensing the younger couple needed to talk about this in private, poked Miles with her elbow. "Come on, we have to get home and get some sleep. After all, we have to be back here tomorrow morning to help you unpack when the moving van arrives."

"That's another thing," Tanya replied. "This place is already incredibly furnished; I have no idea where we are going to put our stuff."

"Don't worry about it, Tanya," Anne replied. "We'll find a place for anything you don't need. We'll be back tomorrow morning around eight to help you get settled. We'll show you around some of the outbuildings. There's probably enough space in them to hold whatever you don't want in here."

CHAPTER 13

Miles and Anne were the first to arrive promptly at 8 a.m. The whole McCoy family was already up and dressed. Almost before they said their greetings, two more pickups arrived loaded with lumber.

Miles was beaming like a Cheshire Cat as he announced, "We thought the kids might need something to keep them occupied so we brought out one of your uncle's favorite products. He designed it himself and it has been one of our best sellers. This model is the top of the line, and I'm sure your children will have many hours of fun on it."

"What is it? What is it?" Billy shouted while jumping up and down like a kangaroo.

"It's called the Sierra, and it is a play set that includes three swings, a rope ladder, a trapeze bar, a rock wall, and a slide. It's topped with an enclosed tree house."

"Wow!" Billy and Yo exclaimed simultaneously.

"Are they going to set it up for us?" Billy asked.

"They sure are, young man," Miles replied with a grin. "You want to hang around and watch the guys put it together?"

Billy was the only one to respond affirmatively, but the girls didn't follow the adults into the house.

Once inside, Tanya asked, "Coffee?" as she headed for the general's thirty-cup pot.

"Sure," Miles and Anne replied.

While she was filling up two more cups, she said, "I made a full pot, so there should be enough for the movers and the guys outside."

In between sips of her black coffee, Anne asked, "So, have you had a chance to look around and decide which furniture you want to keep?"

Victor chuckled. "Besides our bed and the kids' beds and furniture, we're happy with everything the way it is. All of Uncle John's stuff is first class. Don't get us wrong, our furniture isn't junk, but it can't hold a candle to my uncle's stuff."

"Yeah, all the tables, chairs, and cabinets were handmade for him at his factory from old-growth redwood and cedar. He also had the leather couches and chairs custom-made by a guy near Portland. I'm sure he paid a fortune for them."

"So, what are we going to do with the stuff we don't need?" Tanya asked.

Anne didn't hesitate. "Well, some of it will probably work pretty well in the two bunkhouse apartments out back. The leftovers we could stretch-wrap and store in the barn or . . . you could donate it to some needy Native American families."

Tanya gave Vic a quick glance. He nodded.

"We like the thought of donating it," Tanya said with a smile.

"Good," Miles replied. "Anything you don't want in here can be temporarily stored in the bunkhouse apartments until we have a chance to sort it all out."

"Sounds good," answered Vic.

▪ ▪ ▪

The moving van arrived twenty minutes later. Bart, accompanied by his wife, Patty Jo, showed up in time to help with the unpacking of boxes.

As was generally the case, the unpacking of household goods fell on the wife and could be extremely hectic. Fortunately, Tanya's NCO training proved extremely helpful. She was able to quickly and efficiently make decisions on where items should go, and her ability to delegate expedited the whole tedious effort. While she focused on the kitchen, she was able to use Anne and Patty Jo in the bathrooms and linen closets. She had the men setting up the bedrooms and carting off boxes as they were emptied. Meanwhile, the children hung around outside anxiously watching their play set being put together.

Around noon, Miles called in a lunch order to Pizza King in Fontana. He then had one of the workers from the factory pick it up and deliver it to the ranch. By 1:30, the movers had finished unloading, everyone had eaten lunch, and the adults were watching the kids play on their newly assembled outdoor playset.

Only minutes after the moving van left they were startled by two new vehicles barreling up the dirt drive.

"Damn!" Miles exclaimed. "That's Clete Junior in the police cruiser and old man Boyer in the black Escalade."

No one spoke as the two vehicles bounced over the dirt drive, throwing up a blanket of dust. As soon as both vehicles skidded to a stop only a few yards from where they were sitting, one of the men who had set up the play set turned to Miles and announced, "If you don't need us anymore, we ought to head back to the factory."

Miles, wishing he had an excuse to avoid facing the two most-hated men in the county, responded, "Yeah, why don't you guys do that. We can handle it from here."

While the two men were making a beeline to their vehicles Vic muttered, just loud enough for everyone to hear, "I wish I could cut out without having to meet these two assholes." Then, reluctantly, he started walking toward the Boyers.

As he approached, Vic was amazed how, in spite of Clete Senior's seventy-plus years, he and Junior had virtually the same bounce to their step. In fact, meeting them for the first time, some people might think they were brothers. To the average-size man, both Boyers would be imposing figures. Junior was an inch or two taller than his father. However, both men were built like brick shithouses.

Clete Senior was dressed in jeans, a checkered flannel shirt, and cowboy boots. His age was elusive, muted by a neatly trimmed salt and pepper goatee, and the black Stetson hat he wore hid his thinning gray hair. But the feature that captured your attention was his slate-gray eyes, which seemed to bore right into you until you flinched.

Junior stood six foot two and outweighed his father by twenty pounds. He was impeccably dressed in his uniform. There was a perfect crease down the front of his tan trousers. Pinned to the pocket of his starched shirt was a gold badge, and his left sleeve was adorned with the colorful patch of the Boyerville Police Department. His black, low-cut duty boots were spit-shined, and his gold belt buckle looked like it had been recently polished. Even more than the uniform, Junior's intimidation factor was the black .45 caliber Glock 41 hanging from his utility belt.

Unlike his father, Chief Boyer was clean-shaven. Although he was wearing a brown Smokey the Bear hat, Vic guessed he shaved his head since there were no visible sideburns or neck hair.

Both men had to look up into Vic's eyes.

It was Clete Senior who spoke first as he gave Vic the once-over. "Damn, Victor, Ken was right, you do have an imposing presence. Twenty years in the Air Force seems to have served you well. I wouldn't have recognized you if we had bumped into each other on the street."

"Hello, Mr. Boyer," Vic said with a hint of amusement, "and you, too, Chief Boyer; to what do I owe this honor?"

The police chief, looking offended, replied, "Didn't Ken tell you I wanted to stop by for a friendly chat?"

"He mentioned something like that, but I didn't think it would be this soon."

Clete Senior spoke up. "Well, Victor, when Junior told me you were here, I couldn't wait to come over to welcome you back home."

Now sporting a scornful smirk and with sarcasm oozing off

every word, Vic responded, "Jeez, Mr. Boyer, is that because we parted on such good terms?"

"Easy boy," Clete Senior replied. "That was a long time ago and an unfortunate misunderstanding. A lot of water has gone under the bridge since then. Over the years your uncle and I developed a cordial relationship. I was deeply saddened by his unfortunate accident."

In the brief silence that followed, out of the corner of his eye Vic noticed Miles cringe, but he didn't have time to reflect on the possible implications.

Clete Senior continued, "Besides, as I said earlier, it looks like the result of our little misunderstanding worked out quite well for you." Then he abruptly changed the subject, directing his attention to Tanya. "I already know Mr. Rock, but aren't you going to introduce me to your lovely family?"

Victor McCoy glared at the two Boyers for a long time before he grudgingly responded, "Sure, Mr. Boyer, it has been a long time, and you are right. The result of our little misunderstanding, as you call it, did work out quite well for me. I'm willing to let bygones be bygones, if you guys are."

Nodding his head and holding his hand out to shake, Clete Senior replied, "Good."

Vic accepted the old man's hand, and they exchanged a hearty shake which Boyer seemed to hang on to a little too long. When he finally extricated himself, Vic offered his hand to Clete Junior, adding, "Looks like things worked out pretty good for you too, *Chief*."

The police chief's handshake was limp and damp, which didn't surprise Vic. He said, "Okay, let's introduce you around."

At best, the visit of the Boyers could be described as awkward. It was obvious Vic and Junior were still ambivalent about burying the hatchet, and in spite of Clete Senior initiating the introduction to Vic's family, neither Boyer displayed any genuine interested in Tanya, the children, or Patty Jo and Anne.

Sensing their insincerity and already feeling uncomfortable

around these two men, Tanya immediately announced she and the kids needed to go inside and finish setting up their bedrooms. Patty Jo and Anne exchanged glances before Anne volunteered, "We'll come in and help."

After the ladies had gone back inside and the men were alone, Clete Senior reiterated his condolences for the general's death. Then, for a second time, he went on to refer to it as an "unfortunate accident." Whereupon Junior, sounding as if the entire incident had a devastating emotional impact on him personally, proceeded to describe the "urgent massive search effort" he organized which successfully located the body. He went on to detail the coroner's examination report that found the general had sustained a severe blow to the head which probably rendered him unconscious. However, the cause of death was listed as accidental drowning. Then Junior asserted his theory of what happened. Based upon a veterinarian's assessment of Leo's remains discovered by Mile's men, the canine had apparently been mauled by a large predator.

Hearing this, Miles sucked in a deep breath loud enough for everyone to take notice. Junior shot Miles an evil look but continued unabashed to his conclusion that John was most likely thrown from his horse when the animal was spooked by either a black bear or a mountain lion.

This time, Miles's jaw tightened and his face went flush. Clete Senior misinterpreted Miles's reaction. Thinking it was grief driving the Indian's reactions, the old man began to extol Leo's courage for selflessly defending his master.

At this point, Miles lost it. Angrily mumbling something unintelligible, he suddenly jumped up, and without looking back, he bolted toward the bunkhouse.

While everyone watched Miles stomp off, only Clete Junior had the audacity to comment, "I wonder what's got under his saddle?"

"Yeah," Bart injected. "I've had the opportunity to talk to him and a lot of the employees of Slaughter Holdings. I can tell you that John Slaughter was like a father to many of them.

His death and the uncertainty of what was going to happen with their jobs has had a very chilling effect on their lives."

Ten minutes later, as the Boyers were heading back out the driveway, Vic turned to Bart and asked, "Do you really think Miles' reaction was only remorse and fear for his job?"

"I doubt it," Bart replied. "I'm willing to bet it had something to do with the Boyers' explanation of what happened to your uncle. Let's go find out."

They found Miles around the back of the bunkhouse, frantically puffing on a cigarette with the hired cowhand, Jose.

"I didn't know you smoked," Bart said.

"I don't," Miles replied, "but I had to do something to calm down after I heard that bullshit."

"What bullshit was that?" Vic asked as Jose quietly slipped away.

"I know you were just a kid when you lived here for any length of time, but you really don't buy that shit either of them had any regrets John Slaughter was dead, do you?"

"Not really," Vic replied. "That's it? You're upset at their hypocrisy?"

"No, that just got me revved up. What really pissed me off was the bullshit about the large predator. You want to know how I know it was bullshit? God knows, I've been itching to tell this to somebody I can trust ever since that day."

Eyebrows raised, Vic replied, "Sure, first, let me get us three more beers."

Following a long heavy sigh, Miles responded, "Better make it a six-pack; this is going to take awhile."

CHAPTER 14

During the last several months, Miles had re-examined details of the whole incident in his head many times. Now, for the first time, he was able to unburden himself to two men he believed he could trust and who perhaps could even help him expose what he believed to be a cover-up. Exactly what was being covered up, he wasn't sure. All he knew for sure was that only a few hours before the general drowned in Elk Creek, he had alerted him that something strange was happening on the Boyer side. Maybe it was a coincidence, but then what was motivating Chief Boyer to declare that Leo was mauled by a wild animal? Miles even had photographic evidence there were no claw or teeth marks on the carcass. But there was a bullet wound.

He spent almost an hour expounding on the events leading up to his realization John was missing, the search, and the actions of Chief Boyer immediately prior to and following the discovery of the body. When he explained the part about Jeremy discovering Leo's body, Miles showed them the cell phone photos he had taken. Vic and Bart were mesmerized by Miles' account. They hardly asked a question or commented throughout the whole story.

Finally, when he sensed Miles was done, Bart asked, "Did you ever go looking for John's gun in the creek?"

"No," Miles stated with a hint of curiosity. "What good would that do?"

"Well," Bart countered, "maybe nothing. Right now, it's just one more loose end. Suppose we find it and see that it's been fired. Maybe John shot Leo then committed suicide."

Miles was pissed. "Christ!" he bellowed. "I thought you said you were his long-time friend. If you think he was capable of shooting his dog much less taking his own life, you don't know him at all."

"Easy, Miles, I'm not saying that's what happened. It's just one possible scenario. In mysteries like this, it's best to explore every possible angle."

Frustrated, Miles plowed forward. "All right, I get that . . . however; let me just go through this by the numbers. *One,* for years, there have been persistent rumors the Boyers have been buying up marijuana from all the small growers in the area. *Two,* I saw armed guards patrolling on the far side of Elk Creek. *Three,* why would you need armed guards patrolling a lumber mill? *Four,* I told John about the patrols only hours before he was discovered in the creek. *Lastly,* why make up a bullshit story about Leo attempting to fend off a ferocious animal attack when it was obvious he was shot?"

Miles stopped momentarily to catch his breath before asking, "Vic, are you buying what I'm suggesting?"

"I don't know; I'm still overwhelmed by what you're implying . . . the Boyers or one of their employees killed my uncle for trespassing or discovering an illegal marijuana factory at the sawmill?"

"That's exactly what he's claiming," Bart responded.

Vic was shaking his head. "Look, nobody is more cognizant than me that the Boyers are capable of twisting the truth. After all, it was me who twenty-two years ago was forced to leave town or face jail time for defending myself against our current chief of police. So, yeah, I don't trust what the bastards say . . . but murder. That's quite a stretch."

Miles interrupted, "I'm thinking—" He let out a truncated laugh. "—now might be the appropriate time to unravel for you this whole feud between the Slaughters and the Boyers. When I'm done, I'm confident you're going to understand how I know the Boyers are capable of anything, even murder."

Vic and Bart exchanged eager expressions while Miles, drawing a deep breath, collected his thoughts.

After a prolonged pause, he began, "Long before your great-grandfather Enos won this land in the card game, a nasty disagreement put the Boyers and Slaughters at odds. To my knowledge, neither family has talked about it publicly in over a hundred years."

Looking around as if to make sure no one else was listening, Miles almost whispered, "It is Wiyot folklore that the feud began with the massacres in 1860."

Bart leaned forward at full attention. "What massacres?"

"You've heard about these?" Miles asked, staring at Vic.

"I don't remember ever learning about it in school."

"I'm not surprised. It's not something the white establishment likes to acknowledge. Even your grandmother who was half Native refused to talk about it. However, the massacre was well-documented historically and was reported in San Francisco and New York by the young American writer Bret Harte. At the time, Harte was working as a printer's helper and assistant editor at a local newspaper."

Miles sucked in another long deep breath, and his voice got real somber. "Around George Washington's birthday in 1860, a group of white men belonging to the Humboldt Volunteers first attacked and killed over fifty Wiyot who were sleeping during a week of celebrating their annual world renewal ceremony in the Tuluwat Village on Indian Island. Most of the men, as was their custom, had left the island that night to gather food for the next day. As a result, mostly women, children, and old men were slaughtered. The massacre on Indian Island was followed by similar attacks on villages all along the

Eel River. In total, over two hundred of our ancestors were killed, virtually destroying our culture.

"You're probably wondering what this has to do with the feud, aren't you?"

"Yeah," Vic replied, perplexed.

"Okay, just so you know, there isn't any written confirmation of what I'm going to tell you. It is just family folklore that's been passed down from one generation to another. Your uncle was told about it by his grandmother, but even he almost never talked about it.

"At one time, your great-great-great grandfather, Gordon Slaughter, and one of the Boyers' ancestors by the name of Abel were partners. They were also both members of a volunteer militia group called the Humboldt Volunteers. On the night before the massacre on Indian Island, Gordon pleaded for the volunteers not to attack the Wiyot. When his pleas failed, he and one other unnamed man refused to accompany the raiding party. As a result, they were both ostracized, resulting in years of personal harassment.

"At the forefront of the harassment was his former partner, Abel Boyer, and Abel's brother. On the one-year anniversary of the massacre, Gordon's barn suspiciously caught fire and burned to the ground. He rebuilt it, but on the second anniversary, the same thing strangely occurred. By the third anniversary, Gordon was ready, lying in wait with a rifle. Sure enough, around midnight, two men came skulking out of the woods headed for Gordon's barn. He waited until they lit a torch then he fired, wounding one of the men in the leg. Both men fled, with one of them having to be carried along by the other. Although he could have, Gordon never fired a second shot, in hopes one was enough to discourage anyone from harassing him again. The two intruders were never identified and Gordon didn't file a report with the sheriff. However, the next time anyone saw Abel Boyer, he was hobbling along on a crutch and for the rest of his life he walked with a limp. A few months later, Gordon sold his ranch and all his animals, relocating to Ferndale, where he built a modest house and worked on one of the Russ family's dairies.

"As far as anyone knows, there don't seem to be any further incidents until Enos showed up in town as the foreman of a competing logging company. However, based upon the reported dialogue between the two during that infamous card game, they both seemed aware of the bad blood between their ancestors. After he won the land from Aaron, Enos quit his foreman job and started up a competing logging and sawmill operation.

"Unlike old Aaron Boyer, Enos was friendly with the local tribes and went out of his way to hire Indians in his operations. On the other hand, Aaron tried everything in his power to legally run the Indians off their land while Enos attempted to thwart those efforts. Several times, Enos even went so far as to file countersuits on the tribes' behalf. More than once he took the train all the way to Washington, DC, to plead their case before the Bureau of Indian Affairs.

"Enos's actions really pissed old Aaron off, but when Enos married a Wiyot woman and built the original log house on the land he won, the feud got real nasty. Boyer was so livid, he moved his family into town, which was then called Lumberton, and he shut down the sawmill so that he would have no need to come out this way. He also vowed that one day he would own this property again. It wasn't until the 1980s when your uncle took over Slaughter Holdings and decided to get out of the logging and timber business that they started the mill back up. From then until that night in February, Clete Senior and your uncle seemed to have reached some kind of a détente.

"But back to Enos and Aaron. They continued to have minor confrontations. Aaron Boyer had a reputation as a barroom brawler, but he had met his match with the much younger Enos. When I was growing up, stories about the fist fights those two used to get into on Saturday nights were my favorite part of family gatherings. One story has it that Boyer even pulled a gun on your unarmed great-grandfather and would have shot him if the bartender hadn't smashed a bottle over Aaron's head.

"I forgot to mention, they say the reason Aaron Boyer was such a mean son-of-a-bitch and a brawler was because his first wife and daughter died during the influenza epidemic in 1918. Before then, he wasn't any worse than a lot of the other loggers of that era. For ten years after their deaths, he was the most malicious man in the county. Finally, he got himself a much younger mail-order bride and they had a son, Alfred. For a while after Alfred was born, they say old Aaron became half-civil."

"I don't recall hearing about an Alfred Boyer," Vic said.

"You'll probably understand why as the story goes on. So, about the same time Alfred was born, your great-grandmother, whom we called Spring Rain, conceived a child, your grandmother, Drusilla born in 1932. Your uncle John was born six years later. The Boyers also had two more children, Clete Senior, born the same year as your uncle John, and two years later Bernie. Aaron Boyer was almost sixty by the time Bernie was born."

Surprised, Vic exclaimed, "Spring Rain! I never heard my great-grandmother called that. I only met her a few times; I don't think she lived here on the ranch."

"Yeah, here's where the story and the feud really gets complicated." Miles popped another can of beer before he continued, "Your great-grandfather died in a hunting accident in 1948, and Spring Rain hired a general manager to run their very successful Slaughter lumber and sawmill businesses. Meanwhile, Alfred Boyer and your grandmother had become teenage lovers. They planned on running away together as soon as Drusilla graduated from high school. Somehow, Aaron found out about their romance and went ballistic. He forbade Alfred from seeing 'that half-breed' Drusilla. He was adamant he was not going to let his family's blood be contaminated by some 'Injun.'

"However, the passion of youth was too overwhelming; within a few months they were secretly meeting again. When they thought they had been discovered, Alfred took one of his father's pickups, and the two of them ran off to San Francisco. After a few days in the big city, they decided to drive over to Nevada and get married.

"When Aaron found out they had run off together, he was furious. He hired a private investigator to track them down. The investigator caught up with them at a motel in South Lake Tahoe the night before they had planned on marrying. Since both Alfred and Drusilla were now over eighteen years old, there wasn't much Aaron could do to force them back home . . . except file a stolen vehicle report, which is exactly what he did. Armed with a copy of the police report, the private investigator went to South Lake Tahoe police and had the couple arrested and returned, under his supervision, to town. Incidentally, by then Lumberton had been renamed Boyerville.

"That old man was a real prick; the only way he would agree to drop the stolen vehicle charges against both of them was if Alfred enlisted in the Marines, which he did. That ought to sound familiar to you. Anyway, by then, Aaron was in his seventies. The lovers figured he'd probably be dead by the time Alfred got out of the service and then nothing could stop them from getting married. Their gamble seemed to have paid off when Aaron died of a heart attack in 1950. The only problem was, the Korean War had gotten in their way. In 1951, less than a month before he was scheduled to be discharged, Alfred was killed.

"After Alfred's father refused to let his son marry her because she was half Indian, Drusilla's attitude toward her mother seemed to change. Drusilla would tell Spring Rain she hated her and the Indian blood that ran through her veins. She would angrily implore her mother to go back to the reservation where she belonged. This really hurt Spring Rain; so, in 1956 when John went off to West Point, she put all of Slaughter Holdings into a trust for Drusilla and John. Then Spring Rain moved back with her Wiyot family on what is now the Table Bluff Reservation.

"The trust was to be run for the next ten years by the man Spring Rain had hired as general manager eight years earlier and who, ironically, Drusilla would eventually marry, William McCoy."

Bart, visibly moved, couldn't contain his emotion. "Oh, what a heartbreaking story."

Nodding his head up and down, Vic countered, "Well, now at least I'm beginning to understand why Grandma was such a cantankerous old bitch."

"No," Miles injected emphatically, "that's only part of the reason. For years after she married William and your mother Pricilla was born, Drusilla was extremely happy and content. She even reconciled with her mother, although Spring Rain never moved back on the ranch. Then in 1970 when your mother, who we all called Prissy, was twelve years old, William was killed in a car accident and things started going offtrack again for Drusilla."

Miles hesitated, took a sip of beer, then continued, "She found God and your mother got rebellious. If your grandmother ever thought she hated her mother, that was nothing compared to the way Prissy felt about her mother. From the time she was thirteen until she disappeared in 1985, she did everything she could to wreak emotional pain on your grandmother. Besides sleeping with every pair of pants that showed any interest in her, she was a drunk and a drug addict. She was arrested numerous times for petty theft, and worst of all, she exposed you to all those things. But the real killer for your grandmother was when Prissy got pregnant with you and she didn't know or refused to reveal who the father was.

"After you were born, Drusilla tried to get legal custody of you, but in those days, the courts were reluctant to take a child away from its mother. What the court saw appeared to be a sober and loving mother doing her best to provide for her child. She was living in welfare housing and getting a monthly check and food stamps. Theoretically, she could put a roof over your head and have enough money to feed you.

The problem was . . . she would spend most of her check and trade her food stamps for drugs and alcohol. Meanwhile, you spent as much time in the backseat of your grandfather's old Chrysler as you did in the low-income apartment."

"Yeah, I have vivid memories of the Chrysler," Vic said with just a hint of anger.

Glancing over at Bart, he continued, "Some of my earliest memories are of my mother covering me with a blanket in the backseat while she and some dude played WrestleMania in the front seat or on the hood."

Bart's mouth dropped, but he didn't say anything. Vic noted Bart's reaction before he continued, "Hell, it wasn't much better when she left me with my grandmother; just different. Drusilla believed that my salvation would only be achieved if I prayed on my knees for hours on end and was beaten with a strap every time I repeated one of the words I had heard from my mother and her boyfriends. It got especially bad after my mother dropped me on her porch and disappeared. By the time I was fourteen, I had enough, so I ran away."

Bart was flabbergasted, but he managed to ask, "Where the hell did you go?"

"Oakland . . . I stole fifty dollars out of my grandmother's purse and hitched a ride over to Redding with a truck driver. From there I jumped on a freight train down to Roseville, near Sacramento. I then hitched a ride into the Bay Area. Hell, I was so dumb I got out in Oakland thinking it was San Francisco."

Shaking his head from side to side, Bart said, "Incredible!"

Vic laughed. "What's incredible was that I actually survived my time in Oakland. First, I hooked up with a gang of runaways like myself. We ate by pilfering from stores and rolling drunks; we slept in abandoned buildings. After about a year, I graduated to an up-and-coming street gang. Over the months, the gang got bolder and bolder, infringing into other gangs' territories. Near the end, we were heavily into selling drugs and constantly involved in turf wars. There were drive-bys and shootouts almost every week, and the cops were starting to crack down. I did some things that I really regret although I never killed anybody."

"I never heard about this," Miles said with sadness.

"That's because I never told anybody, although I think Uncle John had some inkling I was into some bad stuff."

"What made you get out?" Bart asked.

"Fear," Vic said without hesitation. He took a deep breath then continued, "Me and another gang member were sent on a run to pick up some guns over in San Francisco. While we were gone, the police raided the gang's hangout, where a vicious gun battle ensued. Four of our members, including our leader, were killed, as were two cops. Since two cops were killed, the police went looking for the rest of the gang members. Me and the other guy who were sent to pick up the guns were the only ones to escape capture. Frankly, I panicked. I hid out in Berkeley for a few days then hitchhiked my way back here."

"Man, you were lucky," Bart said with conviction.

"Tell me; and my luck didn't stop there. While I was gone, Grandma had completely lost it. She wound up being committed to a mental institution. Shortly thereafter, my uncle John retired from the Army and came home to run things. He took me in and never asked one question as to where I had been or what I had done. That was the best two years of my young life. He was the father I never had, a teacher and a friend. If it hadn't been for him, I would never have straightened out."

"Did you . . . straighten out? I seem to recall Miles saying you had to enlist in order to avert being prosecuted for assault."

Chuckling, Vic responded, "There was that, but I can honestly say I was framed. I just told this story to Tanya after you guys left last night.

"Clete Junior and I didn't like each other very much. He was the big football hero and I was the bastard half-breed. He had lots of friends and I was an outsider. He had spent his whole life up here as a redneck and I had just done two years down in the city being a hoody. He and his friends were always trying to harass me. Since I was bigger than all of them and knew how to act tough, they pretty much stopped at name-calling.

"Finally, on the last day of high school, Junior decided to find out if I was as tough as I looked. Behind the stands on the football field, and with him watching at a safe distance, he got three of his buddies to confront me. At first, I told them I didn't want any trouble, but that only egged them on. One of them pushed me and I backed off. That was probably the worst thing I could have done with these bullies. Feeling more confident, the three jerks surrounded me while Junior moseyed over. One of them grabbed me from behind while the other two moved in from the side. Junior picked up the pace and came in for a frontal assault.

"Out of options, I reached up over my shoulders and grabbed the guy on my back by his shirt, while at the same time throwing my upper body forward. The guy went flying over my head and crashed into Junior feet first. I quickly pivoted and kicked the guy on my left in the nuts. The fourth had a baseball bat and hit me on the arm, but by then my adrenaline was really pumping. I didn't even feel the blow. I body-slammed him, knocking him over into one of the stand supports. I then went after Boyer, who was up and trying to decide whether to attack or run. I never gave him the option. I hit him with a punch to the gut that doubled him over, and then I followed with an uppercut, fracturing his cheek and breaking his nose. Game over. The other three took off."

With admiration Bart said, "That's what usually happens when you stand up to bullies."

"Yeah, well; it didn't quite work out in my favor. A teacher happened to show up when I was standing over Boyer shouting, 'Come on, get up. I'm not finished with you yet, shithead!'

"I tried to tell him, the principal, and the sheriff's deputy that four of them had jumped me, but they wouldn't listen to me. Besides, all the other bystanders swore the bastard half-breed had attacked Boyer. So the evidence wasn't in my favor."

At this point, Vic sucked in a deep breath and slowly blew it out with puffed-up cheeks. Shaking his head again like he was reliving the nightmare, he continued, "Uncle John argued my case first with the sheriff and then with Clete Senior, but the Boyers wouldn't back down and drop the charges. To this day, I have no idea what Uncle John said, but he took Clete Senior outside into the parking lot. When they came back, Boyer told the sheriff that he would drop the charges if I enlisted in the military. I didn't want to do it, but Uncle John gave me this look that sent shivers up and down my spine. I reluctantly agreed.

"Afterwards, he told me he believed my version and he was proud of the way I handled myself. Then he asked, 'So what were you going to do after you graduated?' I never answered him.

"Actually, I had given it some thought and had decided, if I couldn't come up with anything better before the end of the summer, I would enlist in the Air Force. In fact, I had already talked to an Air Force recruiter who had come to the school. I had even brought home a brochure. I'm guessing Uncle John had seen the pamphlet on my dresser."

Both Miles and Bart laughed before Miles said, "I'm guessing you're right."

"You know," Bart began very seriously, "there are a few patterns or perhaps coincidences I picked up from both your stories."

"Like what?" Vic asked.

"You might think I'm an alarmist or at best a conspiracy theorist, but there seems to be a pattern of Slaughter males becoming the victims of tragic accidents."

There was a moment of weighty silence until Miles spoke up in an agitated voice. "That rumor has always swirled around the local Native American community. It's uncanny, every time we think we have a champion, he seems to have a tragic accident. There's never been any proof of foul play, but there are quite a few suspicious coincidences."

Leaning toward Miles, Vic anxiously asked, "Like what?"

"Well, the hunter that accidently shot and killed Enos eventually became Boyer's mill foreman." Without hesitating, Miles continued and his pace sped up. "Then, I know for a fact the day after your grandfather was killed in the automobile accident, Aaron bought himself a brand-new pickup truck even though the old one was less than a year old. Mix that with the fact it was reported your grandfather's vehicle appeared to have been sideswiped by a red vehicle, which just happened to be the color of Boyer's old pickup." He hesitated again, then added, "Makes you wonder, doesn't it?"

With a sardonic smile, Bart presented one of his favorite adages. "I remember this from the first James Bond novel I ever read. It was so long ago I no longer remember which book it was, but I'll never forget it. It goes something like this, 'The first time is happenstance, the second time is coincidence, and the third time is enemy action.' I believe we are into the enemy action phase of this Boyer-Slaughter connection."

Vic, sitting in a redwood lawn chair, leaned forward, propping his right elbow on his left knee and resting his chin on his knuckles like Rodin's *Thinker*. He exclaimed, "Damn, if any of this true, what the hell can we do to prove it?"

"Who knows," Miles replied, shaking his head. "I've been trying to figure it out for the last few months. Most people believe the Boyers have the mayor and county sheriff in their pockets. That, along with Junior being the law in this town, makes it's a pretty good bet they have enough political clout to overpower anyone or anything getting in their way. The one exception was your uncle. His status as a retired general and Medal of Honor recipient scared most opponents off, and that even seemed to include Clete Senior."

Bart abruptly stood up and began slowly pacing the lawn while reflectively stroking under his chin. Miles and Vic anxiously watched in expectation of some revelation coming out of the consultant. They weren't disappointed. Just as abruptly as he started pacing he stopped, turned in their direction, and announced, "If we are going to try to do anything, we are going to need some specialized assistance."

Vic's face blazed with determination, "What do you mean *IF?*" he asked loudly.

"Good," Bart acknowledged. "I know it's been a while, but I think we should start by scouring the creek for John's gun and any other evidence."

"You know," Miles said, "talking about other evidence, did I fail to mention the general's dog tags weren't around his neck when they found him?"

Vic, surprised, blurted out, "He still wore his dog tags!"

"I don't believe he ever took them off. It probably never dawned on him that he could remove them," Miles responded. "It's possible they were washed off by the current or snapped off by something in the creek."

CHAPTER 15

Armed with the one-hundred-fifty-year history of Slaughter-Boyer hostilities, Vic felt obligated to provide Tanya with an understanding of the potential gravity of their situation. By 2 a.m., after hours of Tanya sitting in bed with her legs crossed and listening intently, her only reaction had been to shake her head from side to side in disbelief, muttering, "I don't believe this" or "You've got to be kidding me."

When Vic finally finished with the recent events surrounding his uncle's death, Tanya asked, "What are we going to do?"

"We plan on dragging the creek for Uncle John's gun or any other evidence; other than that, nothing. Anyway, I was thinking maybe you and the kids ought to go visit your parents for a week or so."

"No way! We just got here and I only have a few weeks left before I have to report. I have no intention of spending them in North Carolina without you."

"Look, Tanya, I don't know where this is going to lead, but given the history, it might get pretty nasty. I really don't like the thought of you and the kids being exposed to that kind of danger."

Tanya stewed for a few moments before replying with a determined look in her eyes, "I doubt they're in any danger; messing with children would be a dumb move. Besides, you and I aren't exactly pacifists. I'll clean my guns tomorrow and we'll have a long talk with the kids about being vigilant and not straying too far from the house until school starts in a few weeks. This might just be a good lesson for them to learn . . . not to cower to bullies."

"So, are we going to tell them exactly what's going on?"

Making a sour face, Tanya replied, "Nooo, we'll just say there have been some weird things going on and until we figure it all out we want them to be wary."

Massaging his lower lip with his thumb and index finger, Vic stared at his wife for a long time before he replied, "All right, but if there are any signs of hostilities, I'm going to get you and the kids out of here. I don't care where to just as long as it's out of this county."

"We'll see," Tanya replied with a hint of insolence.

■ ■ ■

It was midafternoon two days later before the three men began searching the creek in the area where Miles had discovered John's hip waders and the numerous footprints. Miles had brought along three clam rakes, and the men each staked out a ten-yard section to scrape. The creek bottom was strewn with stones and rocks that were constantly getting hung up in the prongs, making progress slow and torturous. After two hours of futile raking, they had come up with nothing but blisters on their hands. Vic suggested they stop for the day and figure out a more suitable method of searching the stream.

Back at the house, Tanya was in the background fixing dinner while the guys were sitting at the kitchen counter sipping on Negra Modelos.

After listening to them for several minutes, she interrupted their brainstorming. "Why don't you rent an underwater metal detector and buy some cheap diving masks?"

Then without waiting for a reaction, she nonchalantly returned to her dinner preparations.

The men sat speechless for a moment, absorbing the simplicity of her wisdom. Finally, Bart said, "I can pick them both up on my way out here tomorrow morning."

Apologetically, Miles responded, "I can't make it tomorrow morning. I have something important to do at the plant. I should be able to get back out in the afternoon. Can you guys work it without me?"

"No problem," Vic replied.

CHAPTER 16

Just like he envisioned his ancestors had done, fifteen-year-old Allie Reynolds was fishing off the rocks among the many cracks and crevices along Flatiron Rock's north shore. This would be his first of four nights alone on this small island, and he was already hungry and lonely.

When his buddies dropped him off on this fourteen-acre rock a couple of hundred yards offshore from Trinidad State Park, he thought this was going to be a great adventure; now, eight hours later, he wasn't so sure. His earlier forays around the island for lunch only resulted in him gathering a few meager mussels while risking being bashed against the rocks by the unrelenting waves. Ever since lunch, he had been fishing with no luck, and he was getting desperate. With the setting sun the wind had picked up, and the temperature was dropping fast. He tried maintaining his spirits by telling himself if the others were able to do it, so could he.

Suddenly, he spotted a crab scurrying across a small stretch of sandy bottom in between the rocks just a few yards away. Again defying the danger of the waves and the sixty-degree ocean, he dropped his line and slowly worked his way around the jagged basalt impediments between him and his prey. *No way,* he thought, *was this tasty morsel going to hang around long enough for me to catch it.*

To Allie's surprise and delight, it stopped its dash. Allie

was now standing on the sand up to his waist in water, only a few feet away from his dinner. For an instant it seemed as if the incessant swells faltered. Taking a deep breath, he dove at the creature. It attempted to scamper out of danger, but Allie drove his hands into the sandy bottom, propelling himself after his dinner.

His surge paid off as he caught the fleeing crab by one of its back legs. Surfacing with a triumphant gasp, he held a large Dungeness crab high above his head. Just then the resurgent surf crashed into his chest, swallowing him up to his chin. With Herculean effort, Allie was able to maintain his footing and avoid being swept into the nearby rocks or losing his prey. Now, all he had to do was make it back on shore. The crab, desperate to secure his freedom, furiously twisted its body attempting to clamp one of its claws onto his captor. That would surely convince the predator he wasn't worth the risk of injury. However, Allie, stumbling over the sharp rocks and shells, made it back to shore with his catch still furiously contorting in his grip.

He was so proud of his feat, he felt compelled to share it with someone, but first he had to get his wet clothes off. Hastily dashing back to the crude shelter he had constructed of drift wood, he secured his catch by placing a rock on its back. Ripping off his shirt and jeans, he wrapped himself in a blanket. Shivering, he wrung out his clothes as best he could then stretched them out on a large boulder. Fumbling through his backpack with one hand, he located his cell phone.

Technically, besides the clothes on his back, the rules of the initiation dictated he only bring six survival articles with him: two gallons of water, a knife, a fishing line and hook, a cigarette lighter, a, flashlight, and a wool blanket. Allie, however, couldn't bear to be out of contact with his girlfriend for several hours, much less four days. Knowing his buddies would search his pockets and backpack, he taped his smartphone under his armpit. He had texted her when he was initially dropped off;

then once more earlier in the afternoon to tell her he missed her; this time he sent her a photo of his catch.

Almost immediately, she replied praising his success and telling him what a great warrior she had as a boyfriend.

Flatiron Rock is one of a handful of a wildlife habitat islands off Trinidad State Park managed by the Bureau of Land Management in partnership with Cher-Ae Heights Indian Community of the Trinidad Rancheria. It is not open to the public. Wildlife enthusiasts with binoculars can view the island and its many seabirds from Trinidad Memorial Lighthouse. In order not to be discovered, Allie had been warned to stay on the west side of the island and not to build a fire. He was not a big fan of raw seafood, but he had no choice. By the time he got a fire going, it would be dark and a flickering fire might be seen from the mainland. Perhaps it was the situation or his effort to secure it, but from the first bite, Allie thought the fresh-caught raw crab tasted better than any he had eaten cooked.

The sun was just barely balancing on the horizon when above the sound of crashing waves Allie heard the unmistakable call of geese. A small colony of non-breeding Aleutian cackling geese circled and began gliding in for a landing on the crest of a ridge near the island's southern corner. This cousin of the larger Canadian geese used these offshore islands as a safe nighttime roost while flying at dawn to the mainland to feed.

Now if I could just catch one of those, he mused, *I'd be set for the next couple of days. Except I couldn't stomach eating one of them raw; tomorrow during daylight I'd have to risk making a fire. Perhaps if there is a morning marine layer, nobody will notice a little smoke. But first, I have to catch one.*

Grimacing, he reluctantly slipped back into his still-wet clothes. Shivering again, he rummaged along the shore for a straight piece of driftwood which he could fashion into a spear. To his delight, he actually found an old broom handle. Using his knife, he whittled one end into a point. Hunched low and moving deliberately, he proceeded up the ever-darkening slope to where the geese had settled in for the night.

When the sun had finally disappeared beyond the horizon and all that remained was a pinkish-red glow, he turned on his flashlight. Meticulously, Allie continued up the slope toward the south crest. He decided that his best chance of success was to outflank the birds and come at them from higher ground. Swiftly and quietly he continued to work his way to the cliff that marked the southwest face of the island. To his confusion, he began noticing a strange glow seeping up over the edge of the cliff. Bewildered, he hastened to the edge of the cliff.

Forty feet below, floodlights from two vessels illuminated a small protected cove. At first he couldn't believe his eyes; one of the vessels appeared to be a submarine. The other was clearly Ricky Boyer's thirty-six-foot fishing boat, the *Yaht Zee*. *What's the Navy doing here . . . at night . . . with Ricky? I wonder if they're making a movie. Wow, I've got to get a picture of this, no one will believe me.*

Allie began clicking off pictures while a troop of non-uniformed sailors transferred packages from the sub to the *Yaht Zee*. He had taken about five photos when someone below spotted Allie's flashlight, which was still turned on and dangling from its strap around his wrist. The man began shouting and pointing. Almost immediately, a bullet ricocheted off the cliff face just below Allie's feet. Instantly dropping to his stomach, he fumbled to shut off the flashlight. Realizing he was momentarily safe, he lay on his stomach thinking, *Whatever is going on down there can't be good if they're so quick to shoot. I better find a place to hide.*

Down on the *Yaht Zee*, Ricky Boyer was livid. "Who the fuck is that?" he shouted. "This island is supposed to be deserted."

Desperately, Ricky scanned the sheer rock walls searching for a way for his men to climb up. It became quickly apparent there was no easy way up. Frustrated, he began urgently shouting orders. "Lower the dinghy and two of you get around to the other side before he can get away. I want whoever that is captured. As soon as we finish loading this stuff, I'll swing around to the other side of the island."

Allie carefully peered over the edge just as two men jumped into a fourteen-foot skiff, fired up its small outboard motor, and sped out of the cove. *Shit! I need to get off this rock and fast.* He moved as quickly as he could in the darkness, reaching the water on the eastern side before the skiff was in sight. Prior to jumping into the waves, Allie stopped long enough to text three photos to his girlfriend. Then he dove into the water and began frantically swimming the quarter mile to shore.

By the time Ricky was able to make his way out of the cove and around to the other side of Flatiron Rock, his men had scoured the barren landscape with a powerful searchlight, concluding their quarry had probably fled into the sea. Frantic to apprehend whoever it was, Ricky swung the *Yaht Zee* away from the island and toward the stretch of water separating it from the mainland. Meanwhile, the skiff had raced toward shore and begun a slow trolling back toward Castle Rock. Ricky, in the yacht, methodically crisscrossed the water, making his way toward shore.

Allie, an excellent swimmer, tried eluding his pursuers by diving under, changing direction while attempting to surface for air out of their powerful beams. At one point he even succeeded in hiding beneath the *Yaht Zee*'s hull, but he couldn't keep up with the zigzagging vessel. The next time he surfaced, both their floodlights pinpointed the desperate swimmer at virtually the same time. The interloper was halfway to the beach.

The *Yaht Zee* finally maneuvered close enough for one of the crew to reach out and snare Allie in the shoulder. Allie screamed in pain as the barbed point rammed into his left pectoral muscle and lodged under his scapula. The pain was so excruciating he passed out long before he was hauled, like a tuna, into the boat.

Ricky frisked the unconscious teenager, finding only a pocketknife and his cell phone, which was now fried beyond repair by the water. "What are we going to do with him?" one of the crew asked.

Breaking into a devious smile, Ricky replied, "I think we'll let Captain Marinov drop him off on his way back to Mexico."

CHAPTER 17

Bart arrived at the ranch around ten; he and Vic were at the creek by 10:30. Although they had both read the metal detector's directions before they left the house, this would be the first time either of them had used one.

Bart put on the headphones, turned on the equipment, then threw a handful of coins among the sand and rocks lining the creek. It didn't take long for him to discover the most effective speed and arc for the wand. Within minutes he had located all the coins. He began meticulously working the area in ten-yard quadrants across the crystal-clear stream while Vic, donning a snorkel mask, searched underwater in the deep dark pools.

Just before lunch, Bart was about to quit after only locating a handful of rusty metal screws, bolts, and two horseshoes when suddenly the locator's beeper started screaming and the indicator needle jumped to over eighty. Groping among the rocks, he felt the very distinctive profile of a handgun. Pulling it up, it became immediately apparent by its still-pristine condition that the weapon had not been submerged for very long.

As soon as Vic surfaced Bart called out, "I've found a gun!"

Vic hustled upstream in knee-deep water to where Bart was drying his discovery with his shirt. Vic immediately recognized it as a Smith & Wesson .357 revolver, the same make and model Miles had told them John usually carried in his holster. Inspecting it further, they easily determined it was still fully loaded.

Vic couldn't contain his excitement. "We'll have to verify the serial number, but I'm willing to bet it was Uncle John's!"

"You want to continue to look?" Bart asked.

"Yeah, I want to at least finish checking around that partially submerged tree trunk."

"Okay," Bart replied. "I suspect the revolver wasn't carried too far from where he lost it, but perhaps there is some lighter stuff further downstream. I think I'll scan on the other side of the tree."

Bart was walking along the bank with the detector still on while the business end dangled a few inches from the ground. Suddenly, it began beeping. He stopped and ran the wand over the spot. To his surprise he picked up a strong signal over a two-foot wide area. Sifting through the mud and pebbles, he located a pellet, then several others. By the time the metal detector stopped beeping, he had uncovered seven buckshot and one bullet. It was an interesting find, its significance unknown.

About the same time Bart was studying his find of pellets, Vic surfaced, shouting, "I just found a camera hung up on a tree limb! It doesn't look like it's been there very long either."

Vic waded out of the stream, joining Bart on the bank. They both stood there looking at the green-and-black Pentax camera.

"Turn it on," Bart suggested.

Vic hit the on button. Instantly, the lens popped out of the front and its three-inch LCD screen sprang to life.

Surprised and excited, Vic shouted, "Damn, it still works!"

He played around with the camera's buttons until he found the playback mode. A video erupted on the screen; its picture was dark and had been taken from a considerable distance, making details impossible to distinguish on its small screen.

"Let's take it back to the house and load the memory card into my laptop," Vic suggested with a hint of anticipation.

■ ■ ■

Vic was sitting at John's desk while Bart hovered over his shoulder. They had just finished viewing the photos and videos from the camera.

"What do you think?" Vic asked

"You're assuming it's your uncle's."

"Yeah, who else's could it be?"

"Don't know, but did you notice the date on the pictures?"

"No, I was too busy trying to make out the faces in the photos. Why, what was it?"

"It was 04.03.2014."

"That can't be, that's a month after my uncle died."

"I know, maybe it's not his camera."

"Who else's could it be and how did it get in the stream practically right next to where we found his gun? Perhaps he just screwed up the date when he set up the camera. Regardless, one thing is clear to me; it was Junior and Ken unloading what looks like cocaine bags from a truck. Unfortunately, I didn't recognize the driver or where the pictures were taken, but I'm willing to bet it's at the sawmill."

"Is Miles coming by today?" Bart asked.

"He should be here soon, and maybe he'll know if this could be my uncle's camera. He'll probably be able to tell us where the pictures were taken and who the third guy is. Meanwhile, let me bounce something off you."

"Okay," Bart responded.

Vic began, "I told Tanya the whole Slaughter-Boyer story last night. I then suggested she take the kids to her parents' place in North Carolina for their safety. Predictably, she said she wasn't leaving here until it was time for her to report." Vic got a real serious look on his face before he continued, "I think I already know the answer to this question but I wanted to get your take on it . . . just how much danger do you think we're in?"

Bart straightened up and took a few steps toward the

window before he turned and answered, "Depends. If we could somehow prove this is John's camera and we have pictures of them unloading street drugs on the night he died, it would sure indicate the Boyers had a motive for killing him. It would be almost impossible to then turn the evidence over to local law enforcement without the Boyers getting wind of it. Given what we've learned about them the last few days, I suspect they'd stop at nothing to eliminate the threat.

"On the other hand, right now, we've got nothing. We don't even know if it's John's camera or what's in the bags . . . not to mention the problem with the dates."

"Yeah, that's kind of the way I see it too."

CHAPTER 18

While they waited for Miles to arrive, Bart wandered out back to make a call to David Tanner.

David immediately recognized his old college roommate's cell phone number and enthusiastically answered, "Hey old buddy, how goes it?"

"Very different from what we anticipated," Bart responded somberly.

Picking up on Bart's subdued tone, David asked, "What's the matter?"

"It's complicated, David; let me try to sum it up in a couple of sentences. We may have found evidence that leads us to believe John's death may not have been an accident."

"What makes you think that?"

"Vic and I believe we've discovered John's camera submerged in Elk Creek. It contains photos and videos of an apparent drug operation on the adjacent ranch. This along with what we recently learned from Miles concerning a Hatfield-and-McCoy type feud that's been going on for over a hundred and fifty years between the Slaughters and a family named Boyer."

"Hmmm, that's a lot to absorb and one hell of a hypothesis."

When Bart didn't immediately respond, David Tanner continued, "Boyer, that's the rich obnoxious family with the sawmill on the other side of Elk Creek, isn't it?"

"You got it."

"Let me see if I interpreted your awful metaphors correctly. John's death may not be an accident; instead it may be the result of him uncovering an illegal drug operation run by the family with whom the Slaughters have a long-standing feud. Did I get that right?"

"Essentially, that's our preliminary theory, but there's a little more to it than that."

"Okay, how good's your evidence?"

"From a strict legal standpoint, it's got holes in it big enough to drive a truck through. On the other hand, my gut tells me John's death was not an accident and the Boyers are hiding something."

"Like what?"

"Well, for one thing, they're perpetuating a story that on the night he drowned John's dog was killed by a large carnivore while attempting to protect John. In contrast, Miles has a picture of a bullet hole in the dog's rump. Now you tell me, why would they make up a story like that if something fishy wasn't going on?"

"Okay, sounds like more digging is required. What can I do?"

"What's Bruce up to these days?"

"He's got a couple of corporate security gigs going, but they're no big deal. You want him to come out there and give you a hand?"

"Well, we could use some professional protection, especially if the Boyers discover we've been snooping around and may have found something."

"Okay, what are your next steps?"

"Try to prove the camera is John's and the photos on it show the Boyers unloading illegal drugs on their property. Those facts would give them a clear motive for killing him. By the way, did I mention that the Boyerville police chief and one of Humboldt County's deputy sheriffs belong to that rich obnoxious family?"

David let out a sardonic chuckle. "That explains why you're not going directly to the cops with your suspicions."

"Yep, history would indicate these people can become pretty ruthless when cornered. That's where Bruce's expertise might come in handy, at least until we have enough evidence to kick this up to the state or federal level."

"That's probably a judicious course of action. I believe I can arrange to have the cavalry out there sometime tomorrow."

■ ■ ■

When Miles arrived late in the afternoon, the first thing Vic showed him was the camera. "We found this in the creek. Any chance this was John's?"

"Definitely, it's the same model I gave him for Christmas. In fact, just before you arrived, when Anne and I were cleaning out his stuff, I was surprised I didn't come across it somewhere. Are there any pictures on it?"

"Oh yeah, I've got them uploaded to my computer. Come take a look."

After looking at the photographs and videos, Miles was fuming. "I knew those sons-of-bitches were up to something illegal. The guy driving the truck is Bernie's son, Ricky. He runs their fleet of fishing and charter boats. This gives us a motive for them killing the general."

"Maybe," Vic replied reluctantly. "The problem is the dates on the photos are the month after my uncle's death."

Shaking his head, Miles replied, "That can't be, those dates must be wrong."

"We agree," Bart replied. "Unless we can figure out why the dates are wrong, we can't connect these photos to the night he was killed. On the other hand, we can't let that stop us from continuing to investigate. Perhaps we can find enough other evidence so we don't need these photos."

"Like what?" Miles asked.

Smiling, Bart replied, "Illegal drug operations need to launder a lot of cash, which usually requires access to an unscrupulous banker." Bart paused, letting the thought sink in before he continued, "Tell me about Bernie. He's Clete Senior's younger brother, right? Doesn't he run Lumbermen's Savings and Loan?"

"Yeah, it's more like he owns it. Do you know him?" Miles asked.

"Never met him, but I did some checking on the bank. I was curious as to why John never used a local bank, preferring to do business with Chase and Wells Fargo."

"What did you discover?" Vic asked.

"Other than the fact it's a small regional bank and is privately held, nothing really. I just figured since, as a private bank, they are not required to report to the Securities Exchange Commission, John shied away. Now that I understand some of the dynamics between the families, it makes total sense he'd do business elsewhere. I'm thinking it's worth having somebody take a closer look at Lumbermen's."

Bart took his cell phone out of his rear pocket and hit the speed dial for David Tanner.

David picked up in two rings. "What, you've solved the whole thing already?"

"Funny, Tanner. Hey, haven't you been looking to buy a private bank?"

"No, what makes you ask that?"

Bart ignored David's question. "Sure you are, why don't you have your corporate acquisition people take a look at a small private regional bank up this way called Lumbermen's Savings and Loan. It's run by one of the Boyers."

David chuckled. "I suppose I should send you the report?"

"Gee, that would be nice."

"This wouldn't have anything to do with laundering of drug money, would it?"

"One can only hope. Listen, I was thinking, maybe it would be good if you came along with Bruce and we avoid meeting here at the ranch. I'll get us a meeting room at the Holiday Inn Express at the Arcata-Eureka Airport. I'll pick you up at the terminal if you will text me your arrival time a couple of hours before you expect to land."

"What's going through your Machiavellian mind, Bart?"

"I'd like the opportunity to lay out the whole picture for you and possibly concoct a plan before we spring the A-Team on the opposition."

"Okay, we can do that."

CHAPTER 19

The hour drive on Highways 36 and 101 between Boyerville and Arcata-Eureka Airport parallels the Eel River and Humboldt Bay while passing through the cities of Eureka and Arcata. On the days when the bay is not obscured by a marine layer or a winter storm, it is an incredibly beautiful drive. This morning was clear with a light breeze off the bay and temperatures in the low 60s. Vic was cruising along at five miles per hour above the speed limit while Bart soaked up the scenery.

"What happened to Miles today?" Bart asked as they sped past the turnoff to Miles' place.

"He called first thing this morning saying he was on a search party and didn't know how long it would take."

"Search party! What's that all about?"

"It seems his nephew went off alone on a camping trip and is late coming back. When some of his buddies went to check on him, he was nowhere to be found."

"Jeez!" Bart exclaimed. "I hope they find him and he's okay."

"Yeah, me too. I told Miles to call us later this morning if they still needed more volunteers later today."

Vic and Bart drove along in silence, relishing the serenity of a calm Humboldt Bay and the full-bodied flavor of the Starbucks coffees Vic had picked up on his way through Fortuna.

As they approached downtown Arcata, Vic broke the silence. "So, how did Patty Jo like the house you rented?"

"Given the limited choices of furnished places to rent month-to-month, she's satisfied. The good part is everything we need is only a couple of blocks away."

"I don't understand why you didn't want to stay in one of the bunkhouse units. There's still plenty of room in there for the two of you."

"I thought about it. Given what's going on now, I'm glad we left it open."

"What do you mean?"

"Well, if we need some reinforcements, it's better that they stay on property."

"Funny you should mention that. I brought Tanya up to speed on what we've found and what we are doing today. She sort of freaked out. Now she's thinking maybe she and the kids ought to get out of here for a few weeks." Vic gave Bart a quick glance and chuckled uncomfortably. "You know what she said when I told her not to worry, that you might be bringing in the A-Team?"

"No, what did she say?"

"I hope you won't take this as too much of an insult . . . her words were, 'The A-Team, what's that stand for, the Alzheimer's Team?'"

Bart laughed so long and hard he could hardly catch his breath. Finally, after several minutes he was able to compose himself.

"I can see why both of you might think that. I'm confident you'll find we can muster up more youthful resources than David and me. I'll have Patty Jo stop by this morning; I believe she'll be able to alleviate some of Tanya's concern. Meanwhile, I'm sure after you've meet David's son Bruce, your perspective will also change."

Bart dialed Patty Jo's cell phone. She picked up on the fifth ring. "Hey babe," she answered, "you calling for directions?"

"Funny . . . no, I'm not. I'm going to put you on the speaker so Vic can hear you."

"Good morning, Vic," Patty Jo said.

"Good morning to you, too, Patty Jo," Vic replied.

"We need a favor," Bart said. "Vic filled Tanya in on the potential for danger and told her we were going to the airport this morning to pick up reinforcements. Based upon her reaction, I think she's got the impression all I can muster up are a couple of old, washed-up executives who will probably pee in their pants when faced with a bunch of guys pointing guns at us."

Patty Jo let out an unladylike snort. "Hell, you might do that without a confrontation."

"You know what I mean; she needs to have some confidence this is not the first time we have been threatened with violence. Then you might describe for her the kind of world-class protection the Tanners can bring to the party . . . capisci?"

"I can do that, but don't you think there is a risk she'll freak out when she finds out our background?"

"I'm sure you can smooth that over, but if it does, so be it."

After Bart hung up, Vic said, "So?"

"So . . . what?" Bart responded.

"So, are you going to tell *me* just who the hell you guys are?"

Bart laughed. "Yeah, I was going to wait till we were with the Tanners so you could hear the whole story all at once. Now that the cat is out of the bag, I might as well save some time by filling you in on me and Patty Jo. Just remember, you won't have the complete picture until we've had a chance to meet with David and Bruce."

A crafty smile unfolded across Bart's mouth and his eyes twinkled. "Have you read the novel *Family* by Chuck Stanfield?"

"You mean the story about a guy who marries into a Mafia family?"

"That's the one; so you've read it?"

"Yeah, who hasn't? It was a bestseller during Little Nicky's trial."

"Well, my real name was Bart LaRocca."

"You're kidding!"

"Dead serious; and Patty Jo was married to the other brother, John, who was able to get away from the family."

"Holy shit! That means David Tanner was the college roommate."

"That's right, one of them anyway. The other roommate, Robbie, introduced me to your uncle John in Vietnam. I had Stanfield change John's last name in the book so as to not tarnish his Medal of Honor legacy."

"I don't believe this; I'm riding with the guy who threw acid on Little Nicky's balls!"

"Yeah, but that was a long time ago."

"Is there still a hit out on you?"

"Doubt it; all the old guys are either dead or drooling in their pasta. But I did change my last name as a precautionary measure."

"So, you and Patty Jo did get married after all. I always wondered how that turned out."

Bart smiled. "We have so much in common, even though neither of us will ever feel the same passion for each other as we did for Gina and John. We do love each other and since we've been about five years old have always enjoyed being together."

Bart let Vic process this new information before he continued, "Now besides a bunch of aging action heroes, today you are going to meet David's son, Bruce. Bruce is about your age and, like you, recently retired from the military. He was a Navy SEAL and from what I've heard has a reputation as some kind of a superhero."

Vic glanced over at Bart with a quick quizzical expression, then, as if a light went off in his head, he exclaimed, "Lieutenant Colonel Bruce Tanner! I've worked with him on a couple of missions. Oh, this is getting eerie."

"What do you mean?" Bart asked.

"Well, it's like . . . what do they call it . . . six degrees of separation."

Bart patted Vic on the shoulder. "I don't know if I buy that we are all just six steps removed from everyone else in the world. What I can tell you is David and I can muster up a boatload of robust resources when we need them. You'll probably find that out before we head back to the ranch this afternoon."

CHAPTER 20

The city of Eureka is the county seat for Humboldt County. Arcata-Eureka Airport sits fifteen miles north of the city. The airport has two asphalt runways perfect for small jets like Tanner's Gulfstream G280. The small terminal was jammed with passengers and greeters waiting for the morning United Express flight from San Francisco. Since it was a nice warm morning, Bart and Vic avoided the crowd by waiting just outside the fence that separates the tarmac from the parking lot.

Tanner's Gulfstream taxied to a parking spot well left of the terminal and almost directly in front of Bart and Vic. David's long-time head of security, Azzan Prinz, was the first to emerge onto the portable jet stairs. He performed a methodical scan of the terminal area, quickly spotting Bart. He said something over his shoulder then descended the steps. David followed close behind with Bruce next. That was all Bart expected this morning so he was surprised when Bruce's girlfriend, Dana Wise, appeared. He was even more amazed when David's other security guard, Eitan Fein, brought up the rear.

Bart nudged Vic with his elbow. "It looks like David didn't take any chances. He brought everybody." Waving to the new arrivals, Bart added, "I assume you recognized David. That's Bruce following his father down the steps. The gorgeous blonde is Bruce's fiancée, Dana Wise. She's a former Secret Service agent and currently a special assistant to the

FBI director. The other two are David's security detail, both former Mossad agents."

"Wow!" Vic exclaimed, "that's a lot of firepower. Do you think they are all here to stay awhile?"

"I don't know, we will have to wait and see. Let's go meet them."

David was the first one through the door. Holding out his hand, he broke into a broad smile when he saw Vic. "Victor, nice to see you again. I just wish it was a social visit."

Vic responded to David's outstretched hand by clasping it with both his hands. "Thank you, David. Now I can understand why my uncle held you and Bruce in such high regard. You said you'd help and . . . here you are."

"Well, let's just figure out exactly how we can assist . . . So, let me do the introductions. This is Dana, Azzan, and Eitan. Bruce is inside getting a rental car. He figured it would be better if they had their own transportation."

Picking up on the word *they* David asked, "Who-all's staying?"

"I was thinking at least Bruce and Eitan, but let's not finalize that until after we've all had a chance to assess the situation."

Ten minutes later Bruce emerged from the terminal shaking his head and holding a set of keys. "I never heard of Honk Car Rental, but my administrative assistant discovered it was the only one in town renting SUVs." Then recognizing Vic, he broke out into a broad smile. "Sergeant Vic McCoy, I remember your briefing like it was yesterday. You and your Air Force spotters sure had your shit together. That was one of the smoothest missions I ever took part in."

"Yeah, well, Commander, you Navy guys pulled it off just like it was planned. But now we're both just civilians."

"Yup, although occasionally I still put my ass on the line for Uncle Sam. Fortunately, the pay is a hell of a lot better now."

Smiling shrewdly, Vic replied, "So I hear; we'll have to talk about that after we've cleaned this up." Vic continued, "So, who's coming with me?"

"Why don't you and Azzan go with them, Dad," Bruce replied.

"Sounds good to me," David responded. "Is that okay with you, Vic?"

"That would be great."

As they were walking to Vic's Suburban, Bart asked David, "How'd you get Sardo to let you borrow Dana?"

"Easy, I just told him you needed her and that if we came up with anything, the FBI could have the credit."

Bart let out a quiet chuckle, and Vic asked, "Who's Sardo?"

Again, Bart snickered before he answered, "Sam Sardo, he was the assistant U.S. attorney to whom I turned over the evidence that finally put Little Nicky away. He's now the director of the FBI."

"Six degrees of separation," Vic proclaimed with a wide grin on his face.

■ ■ ■

After setting up in a conference room at the Holiday Inn Express, Vic began laying out the likely scenario of what transpired on the night the general died. He then detailed the next day's events just as Miles had relayed it to them. Finally, he had everyone gather around his laptop so he could show them the enlarged photos and video. There weren't many questions until he was finished, when Dana asked, "Are we certain the pictures and video were taken at the Boyers' sawmill?"

Vic glanced over at Bart before answering, "No, Miles indicated the two buildings clearly visible in the pictures are not ones he remembers from the old sawmill operation. However, the word is they've recently completed some new construction on site."

"We're not as concerned about verifying location as we are about the date stamp on the photos and video. We can always figure out a way to get a look at the sawmill but take a look at the date and time on each photo."

He pointed to the date stamp at the top of one photo then

paged through several other photos. "See, it clearly says 04.03.2014. We checked the cameras settings, and it's set up for the classic civilian format of month/day/year, which would indicate these pictures were taken on April 3, 2014. My uncle died on March 4, 2014, or 03.04.2014."

"So this couldn't be his camera," Dana declared.

"Well," Vic responded, "Miles gave him the exact same camera for Christmas and we have the empty box it came in. So, though it's not proof it was my uncle's, it's the same make and model. Here's what I'm thinking happened. Uncle John took the camera out of the box for the first time that night to use on his foray over to the sawmill. He was in hurry to set it up, which you have to do before it will allow you to take any pictures. In his haste, when he set the date he got confused. Look at the time stamp on this photo. It's 21:04, not 9:04 p.m. That's the military time format he used for virtually his whole adult life. So, when he set the date, he didn't realize he picked the civilian month/day/year format. Then, out of habit, he set it using the military format of day/month/year or 04.03.2014 . . . does that make sense?"

No one said anything for a few seconds, then Dana spoke up. "Okay, everything you say makes sense, but the problem is in order for me to get a search warrant we are going to have to find some other evidence."

Bruce jumped in. "No problem, we can start by doing what Vic suggested . . . getting on site to verify the pictures were taken at the Boyers' operation."

"Right," Bart said, "that probably should be the first thing we do. Vic, I think now you should give them a blow-by-blow account of the history between your family and the Boyers. They need to understand some of the history between the families and how it may have played into this whole situation."

It took Vic, with Bart's occasional augmentation, almost an hour to go through the six-generation history. This time, there were numerous interruptions.

When Vic was finally finished, David was the first to comment. "I agree with Bart, it can't be a coincidence that so many Slaughter patriarchs just happened to die in mysterious accidents. I believe you and your family will be in real danger once they find out we are investigating. I'm thinking both Azzan and Eitan should stay, along with Bruce. Bruce, what are your thoughts?"

"Oh, without question. In fact, I think I'd like to bring in some additional talent."

"Whoa!" Vic replied loudly. "Wouldn't the influx of a whole hoard of new faces tip them off we're sniffing around their garbage?"

It was Bart who spoke up first. "Hell yeah, that's the idea. We want to make them nervous; that way maybe they'll make a mistake or do something stupid."

Vic frowned. "Like what?"

"Well, given what you told us their track record is, it's likely they'll come after us," Bruce answered in a somber tone.

Vic slowly panned the room, looking for somebody to cut in and tell him Bruce was joking, but all the other faces had dead-serious expressions.

Sensing Vic's trepidation, Bart decided he'd throw it all out on the table so they could judge Vic's reaction. "Look, Vic, we haven't talked about this as a group, but I think I understand what the others are thinking. First, we should make an incursion onto the property in order to verify those pictures are showing illegal drugs being delivered to the Boyers' sawmill.

"Second, where there are illegal drugs, there is lots of cash needing laundering, and most likely that means Lumbermen's Bank is how they're washing it. That's evidence the Feds would really get excited about, so we should figure out how to get into the bank's records.

"Third, finding out if the operation crosses state lines might give the Feds another reason to come on board.

"Finally, we have to uncover some evidence John was killed because he discovered the Boyers' drug operation.

"So, with all that going on, it will be nearly impossible not to tip our hand. However, once we have those four things nailed down, we can turn it over to Dana for the FBI to investigate. Once the FBI is involved, Dana will assure your family is protected. In the meantime, we need to have sufficient resources to repel anything they throw at us."

"Actually," Vic replied, "all I really care about is proving the last point."

Cocking her head to the side and pursing her lips, Dana replied, "Understood, but unless we can link his murder to a federal offense, the FBI won't have jurisdiction."

Victor had his right elbow on the table with his cheek leaning on the back of his fingers. As soon as Dana finished her statement, Vic began running his knuckles across his stubble, deep in thought. Finally, he responded, "Tell me how all this is going to work and how we are going to keep my family safe."

Bart was the first to answer. "Well, I'm thinking we do have to get Tanya and the kids out of here. I would like to propose David fly Patty Jo, Tanya, and the kids to my place in Colorado on his way home tonight. Nobody will think to look for them in Evergreen. Beyond that, I haven't a clue."

Bruce spoke up. "Colorado is probably safe, but I'd like to have a couple of bodyguards camp out at your place, Bart."

"That's fine with me; there is plenty of room," Bart replied. "What are your thoughts, Vic?"

"I'm apprehensive but don't see any other alternative. Based on my talk with Tanya last night, I think she'll be relieved. I'll call her right now and tell her to pack up and head over here. I assume Patty Jo can pick them up in your car. Then you can drive it back."

"That works," Bart replied. "After you've called, we should send out for some lunch and lay out a game plan."

CHAPTER 21

Bart ordered subs from the Hole in the Wall sandwich shop. While they waited for their lunch to be delivered, they began bouncing ideas off each other.

Bart looked at David Tanner and asked, "What do you think about bringing in Mike Musgrave to help us sort out Lumbermen's role in the money laundering?"

Dana interrupted before David could answer. "Who's he?"

"I'm surprised you haven't heard of him," Bart responded. "He's an old golfing buddy from Charlotte. David and I went to Hilton Head with him on a couple of golf outings. He spent twenty years with the Secret Service on the Treasury side, where he was a legendary money-laundering expert. He finished out his government career with the DEA. He's retired now but still doing consulting for most of the major banks."

When Bart was finished with his answer, David finally responded, "I think that would be a great idea. My guys weren't able to come up with much except that Lumbermen's real owners are buried under layers of corporate sleight of hand."

"If he agrees to help, I'd like to work with him," Dana enthusiastically replied. "I'd like to pick up some of what he knows about money laundering."

"Good," Bart responded, "then I'll call him to see if he's available." Glancing at Vic, Bart said, "I might have to ply him with a small consulting fee. I assume Slaughter Holdings can accommodate that."

Vic started to reply but David interrupted him, "I got this. I owe your uncle a few big favors he would never let me repay."

"That's not necessary," Vic responded. "You just coming out here on such short notice is repayment enough."

Grinning, Bart said, "You guys can work that out. Meanwhile, I'll call Mike and give him your number, Dana."

Bruce quickly jumped in. "If we're done with that issue, I was just thinking. Since Ricky was the one delivering the drugs and he runs their fishing fleet, doesn't it make sense they're bringing it in by sea?"

"It would, except there really isn't any commercial cargo being received at Humboldt Bay docks," responded Bart.

"Actually, I wasn't thinking it was being smuggled in as commercial cargo. I thought it was more likely they were rendezvousing offshore with another vessel. Maybe even outside the twelve-mile limit."

They all knew Vic's head was in the game when he offered, "Or maybe it's an air drop. Whatever it is, there's no question in my mind that Ricky is making the pickup."

"Now that's a good theory, but how are we going to prove it? It's pretty hard to tail a boat without being seen," Bart countered.

Bruce never hesitated. "By the same token, there has to be an awful lot of private fishing boats along the North Coast, making it risky to attempt a drop in broad daylight. I'd say it is more likely they'd do it at night."

Vic concurred. "That would fit with the video of Ricky delivering the goods after dark."

"Agreed," Bruce replied. "Perhaps we should just monitor their fishing fleet looking for one that is out at night. Then, if we identify one, we can hide a GPS tracker on its hull."

"Then what?" Vic asked.

"Depends," Bruce replied. "At first, we'll just monitor its activity. Maybe we can figure out a pattern. If we're lucky, we'll be able to figure out their schedule and rendezvous point, or perhaps we'll just have to follow it."

Vic responded, "But that could take a while. Why don't we figure out if Ricky always uses the same boat? If so, just slap a monitor on it straightaway. "

"That's a good idea, Vic," Bart offered. "I bet Miles can tell us if Ricky has a favorite vessel."

Having just identified two positive actions, the group became silent, feeling pretty confident with their progress. After a short period of silence, Dana cut in, "The general wasn't cremated, was he?"

"No," Vic replied curiously. "Why do you ask?"

"I was thinking," Dana responded. "Maybe we can put some pressure on the Boyers by having another autopsy done on John's body. "

"How do we do that?" Vic asked.

"Oh, it's pretty easy, especially since the body is no longer in the local law enforcement's jurisdiction. You, as his sole surviving relative, can have one done privately or perhaps we can get another legal entity interested."

David responded, "It will take too long to get another jurisdiction involved. I know someone we could hire and get it done as soon as we can get the body exhumed."

"Who would that be?" Bart asked.

"Have you ever heard of Dr. Peter Lambert, the former Dade County coroner?"

"Isn't he the one who proved that famous rock star from the seventies didn't commit suicide?" Dana answered.

Vic looked puzzled. "But if we do it privately, especially in the DC area, how does that pressure the Boyers? In fact, how will they ever know about it?"

"You will sign an authorization having the Humboldt County coroner send Peter the results of his autopsy," Dana replied.

"You think that will work?" Vic asked.

"Who knows? If the Boyers are as influential as we think, the coroner will be anxious to inform them someone else is looking at the case. Then, who knows what their reaction will be. Besides, we might just learn something contradicting the local coroner's conclusions," Dana answered convincingly.

Vic, nodding his head and smiling, said, "I really like that idea. Let's do it! Too bad they had Leo cremated, I would love to see that autopsy redone."

"All right," Bart said enthusiastically. "Sounds like we have a plan to get started on all fronts. Perhaps we should explore what other additional resources we may need, especially more protection."

Both Vic and Bruce had some ideas for additional muscle from their retired Air Force Special Ops and Navy SEAL buddies. They both made calls arranging for two guys in Evergreen and a half-dozen others for the Slaughter ranch.

CHAPTER 22

After watching David's plane take off, Vic put his arm around Bart's shoulder and said, "I really appreciate you and Patty Jo offering to host Tanya and the kids until we sort this stuff out. Patty Jo was already talking about all the cool day trips she was planning for them. I've gotta say when your A-Team decides to do something, no grass grows under their feet."

Bart snickered. "Yeah, well, we've all been around the block a few times and don't like to wait for things to come to us. We are used to making things happen."

Vic was about to say something when his phone rang. It was Miles. Vic put the call on the speaker. "How'd the search go, Miles?"

"Not good. When are you guys going to be back?"

"About an hour. Why, what's up?"

"I really don't want to talk about it on the phone. Can you stop by my place on your way home?"

"Sure; we'll have a few friends with us. Is that okay?"

"That's fine; we'll probably need some reinforcements."

Vic gave Bart a quizzical look before he said good-bye to Miles and hung up.

"What do you think that was all about?" Vic asked.

"I don't know, but it doesn't sound good. I'll tell Bruce we're going to take a detour on the way to the ranch."

■ ■ ■

As the three vehicles drove down the long gravel driveway in Blue Lake, Miles was impatiently pacing back and forth on the front porch with his brother. Both men carried shotguns. You could almost see some of the anxiety drain from Miles' body when Vic and Bart got out of their vehicles. He jumped off the porch, hurrying to greet them. His brother slowly followed.

Miles appeared distressed. "Am I glad to see you. You remember my brother, Jim, from the other day. I can't tell you how worried we've been."

"Hey, Jim," Vic said. Bart nodded a greeting then introduced Bruce, Azzan, and Eitan.

Vic, Bart, Bruce, Azzan, and Eitan formed a semicircle in front of Miles,

"What's going on?" Vic asked with profound concern.

"Come inside; I want you to meet somebody."

Inside Miles' cozy three-bedroom house, Anne and Fern, Jim's wife, were sitting on a leather couch next to an attractive teenage girl. Vic introduced the three new faces to everybody.

After they shook hands, Miles said, "I would like for you to meet Willow. She's a good friend of Jim's boy, Allie."

Willow interrupted. "I'm his girlfriend," she announced with determination enveloped in a hint of anxiety.

"Right, his girlfriend," Miles corrected himself. "Anyway, my nephew Allie is the one we were searching for today."

"How long has he been missing?" Bruce asked.

"His buddies dropped him off on Flat Iron Rock four days ago. Willow was the last one to hear from him that same evening."

"Flat Iron Rock?" Vic quizzically repeated. "Why would he be dropped off on that tiny barren island?"

"It's some misguided teenage myth," Miles replied with just a hint of exasperation. "Let me give you some background. About ten years ago, a group of the Wiyot boys on the high school cross-country team came to the conclusion that our ancestors used to have some kind of rite of passage into manhood. This ordeal included spending four nights alone on Flatiron Rock with a minimum of provisions. No one knows how they came up with this idea since there is nothing in our tribal folklore to substantiate it. Anyway, for the last ten years, any of the Wiyot boys wanting to be accepted on the varsity team were strongly badgered into undergoing this initiation. There was nothing more important to Allie than to become a member of the cross-country team and to run the mile in spring track. In spite of Willow's begging him not to take on the challenge, Allie was vehement he was not going to wimp out.

"So his buddies dropped him off on Flatiron Rock. All he was supposed to bring along were two gallons of water, a knife, fishing gear, a lighter, and a flashlight. However, Willow convinced him to sneak his cell phone along so they could stay in contact. He sent her a couple of text messages the first afternoon. Then another message around dinner time with a photo of a crab he had caught and was going to eat for dinner. The last message she received from him was exactly at 8:37 p.m. It was three pictures . . . Willow, show these gentlemen the photos Allie sent you."

Willow reached into her purse and pulled out her phone, tapped the screen a few times, then passed around the phone for everyone to view. After they all viewed the first photo without comment, Willow hit the screen again and a new picture popped up. It was again passed around in silence. Finally, Willow brought up the last picture.

When they were done, Bart nodded his head and pursed his lips. "Can I assume that's one of Boyer's fishing vessels?"

"Yep," Miles answered.

"Jeez!" Bart exclaimed. "Allie must have stumbled right into the middle of one of the Boyer's drug drops."

Bruce followed, "They're getting the stuff up from Mexico smuggled in a submarine. Ingenious! I would never have guessed that. I heard rumors the cartels were using submersibles in the Caribbean, but I am amazed they are actually doing it in the Pacific."

"Why's that?" Bart asked.

"Well, there is virtually no place to hide a sub on this coast. The coastline along the Gulf of Mexico is lined with rivers and dense overhanging tropical foliage. It's easy to hide a sub there. On the rocky, desert Pacific coast all the way from San Francisco down past Baja, a submarine would stand out like a pink elephant on blacktop."

Dana took the phone from Willow and scanned the photos one more time before she addressed Miles. "How can we be sure the fishing boat is one of Boyer's?"

"Willow, will you zoom in on the stern for us," Miles replied.

Willow swiped the screen until all that showed was the back of the vessel. She then held it up for all to see.

Miles triumphantly announced, "See, it's the *Yaht Zee,* one of Boyer's fishing fleet."

Dana gave Willow a look of concern as she said, "So, he was due back this morning and never showed?"

"That's right," Willow replied, sniffling. "His buddies went out to get him as soon as the sun came up, but he wasn't on the island."

"Weren't you worried when you didn't hear from him after the first night?" Dana asked sympathetically.

"Sure I was," Willow responded, a little more composed. "I tried to call him dozens of times but I only got his voice mail. I didn't know what to do. I couldn't talk to his friends 'cause then they'd know he brought his phone." Willow let out a forlorn sigh.

Heading off Willow before she could lose it, Anne quickly said, "When they went to pick him up and he wasn't there, they called Willow to find out if somehow he left early or whether she had heard from him."

Then Miles jumped in. "That's when she called Jim and

Fern, and they called me. At first we didn't want to inform the authorities because Flatiron Rock has restricted access. After Willow showed me the pictures, I knew it was too dangerous to go to them with Ken Boyer being one of the deputy sheriffs. So I put together our own search team. We've searched up and down the coast for fifteen miles without finding a trace of Allie. Frankly, besides worrying for Allie's safety, I'm also concerned for Willow. If they've got Allie, they also have his phone. Once they discover the photos he sent Willow, they'll come looking for the evidence."

"You're absolutely correct," Bruce responded. "On the other hand, we just can't let the search stop here. Let's think about this, it's been four days. Since they haven't come after Willow yet, it's a good bet they don't know she has the photos. I say we file a missing persons report and give them the real reason you didn't initially go to the authorities. Meanwhile, we can take some precautions to protect Willow. She can stay right here; I can have a security team here tomorrow. Meanwhile, Azzan and Eitan will keep watch. How's that sound?"

Turning to Jim and Fern, Miles asked, "What do you guys think?"

Fern instantly replied, "As far as I'm concerned, it's up to Willow. She's the one in danger."

Willow looked around the room sheepishly. "We can't stop looking for Allie." She hesitated then with more conviction continued, "If going to the police is our best chance of finding him, we have to do it. We don't have to tell them about the pictures . . . do we?"

"No, not yet," Bruce replied. Then with a warm smile he tried to reassure her, "Don't worry. We'll keep you safe even if we have to sneak you out of town."

That was Vic's cue to tell them about his family. "Tanya and the kids are gone. We sent them to a safe house earlier today."

"You think it's that bad, huh?" Anne asked.

"Not sure," Vic replied, shrugging. "It's just a precaution."

CHAPTER 23

Bruce left his vehicle with Azzan while he rode with Bart. Bart stopped at his rental house to pick up a few days' worth of clothes and personal items before heading out to the ranch.

Later that evening, while they quietly sat at the kitchen table eating leftover fried chicken and drinking beer, Bruce spoke up. "As upset and pissed as I am with this whole Allie thing, it actually helps to focus our efforts."

"How's that?" asked Vic.

"Well, first we now know exactly how they're getting the drugs from Mexico. Plus, Azzan and Eitan being on watch at Miles' means we should probably forgo infiltrating the Boyers' sawmill tonight."

"I concur on not going in at night," Vic replied. "I was just thinking . . . a nighttime excursion might not be the best tactic anyway. Given what happened to the general, you'd have to figure the guards are on hyperalert at night. Daytime might be another story. With trucks coming and going, plus all the workers around the sawmill, security has to be more lax, especially with the use of dogs. It would be pretty hard for the dogs to sort out our scent from all that other stuff. I would be surprised if the dogs aren't caged while the mill is operating."

Bruce smiled. "McCoy, I think you've hit on something. Bart, let's have you drop Vic and me off near the lumber mill's entrance early tomorrow morning. We'll stake out and see if we can figure a way to go right through the front door."

■ ■ ■

It was just barely light when Bart, driving his rented Yukon, approached Boyer's sawmill entrance.

"Well, what have we here?" Bart remarked to Bruce and Vic, who were out of the sight of anyone scrutinizing the vehicle from a distance. To avoid being spotted, Vic had folded down the backseats of the Yukon. He and Bruce were lying on their stomachs as Bart passed in front of the gate.

"Besides the new perimeter fence, that looks like a brand-new gate and guard shack . . . so much for you two just waltzing up the driveway."

Bruce snickered and Vic sarcastically muttered, "Damn, foiled again."

Bart slowed to a crawl as they passed the gate. "It looks like there are two guards inside the shack."

As Bart drove past the shack a single guard, his automatic weapon clearly visible, stepped outside and gave the SUV a look designed to discourage any malingerers. Bart reacted like any normal passerby would on seeing the armed guard; he sped up. Over his shoulder he said, "That was no standard rent-a-cop. He's got an AR-15 slung over his shoulder. I thought those type of weapons were illegal in California."

"They are," Bruce replied. "There are ways around the ban, including the local cops ignoring it."

Vic gave Bruce an impatient expression. Bruce nodded back; then he said to Bart, "Drive up the road a quarter of a mile or so and let us out. We'll call you when we are ready to be picked up."

"What are you going to do?" Bart asked.

"Reconnaissance," Bruce replied.

Vic and Bruce started getting their gear ready. They were well-prepared. They both wore jungle fatigues and face camouflage. Each carried silenced side arms, combat knives, binoculars, two liters of water, and power bars. Bruce had a wire cutter in his back pocket. Vic cradled what Bruce had called "the equalizer" when he took it out of the case.

"How did you get your hands on an MSR with a NATO barrel?" Vic had asked when he first saw it back at the ranch.

"I told you, I still do some government work. You know how to use it?"

"I have some familiarity with it. At one time or another I've trained with just about every type of sniper rifle in the arsenal . . . but it's been a few years."

▪ ▪ ▪

Four-tenths of a mile from the sawmill entrance, Bart finally rounded a bend where the dirt shoulder was wide enough for him to pull off the pavement. "Get ready!" he announced, "I'm gonna let you out just ahead."

He stopped just long enough for both men to slip out the rear passenger side door and disappear quietly into the underbrush. By the time Bart pulled back on the pavement, they had totally vanished. Bart continued driving for another fifteen minutes before he turned around, heading back toward the Slaughter ranch. As he approached the gatehouse, the guard was still at his post. This time, the sentry seemed to tense up when he saw the Yukon approach. Perhaps he recognized the vehicle and driver as having recently passed heading in the opposite direction and was suspicious. Maintaining the speed limit, Bart casually smiled and waved to the man as he drove passed.

Bruce and Vic slid down the embankment leading to the dry runoff ditch running alongside the highway. Concealing themselves in the scraggly weeds and bushes, they waited as several vehicles drove by. When it was absolutely quiet except for the chirping of birds, they scrambled up the other side of the ditch. Picking their way around a series of leafy bushes and through a stand of scrub pine trees, they found themselves directly in front of the fence and totally invisible to any passing motorists.

Bruce was poised to cut through the welded steel mesh fence when Vic grabbed his hand.

"Hold it!" Vic ordered. "I think that's a fiber-optic sensing cable running along the middle of the fence."

Bruce froze. "Shit," he murmured. "Now what?" he asked, but not expecting Vic to supply the answer.

Both men sat down leaning against trees while pondering their dilemma.

Finally, after several minutes, Bruce exhaled loudly before declaring, "Well, unless you have a better idea, we are just going to have to go right through the gate."

Vic cocked his head, giving Bruce a perplexed look. "And just how do you propose we accomplish that?"

Bruce smiled. "I'm guessing trucks are going to eventually start passing through that gate. We'll just have to hitch a ride on one."

"Sounds like fun," Vic cynically replied.

■ ■ ■

Retracing their steps, they headed back to the road. Crossing over, they climbed up the incline on the other side where they would again be concealed by trees and bushes. Slowly and quietly they worked their way back, finding an excellent viewing perch directly across and fifty feet above the intimidating black-clad sentry patrolling the gate.

At approximately 7:45 the gate was raised to allow a fire-engine-red Pathfinder to enter. The SUV parked off to the side of the entrance. The first guard was quickly joined from inside the guard shack by his equally sinister-looking partner. Both men stood facing the Pathfinder while four unimpressive rent-a-cops in gray uniforms piled out.

"Shift change," Bruce whispered.

The six men exchanged short stoic greetings then the rent-a-cops headed for the shack while the two going off shift waited behind the guard shack. Minutes later two white Ford 4x4 pickups came barreling down the drive from deep inside the property. They skidded to a halt alongside the two men in black. Both men hopped into the backseat of the first vehicle. As the two white pickups pulled out onto the highway, Bruce and Vic observed four more men riding in the second vehicle. Caged in the second pickup's bed were two vicious-looking German shepherds barking their heads off.

Vic gave Bruce a concerned look. "Eight guys on the night shift! The two that were on the gate looked like trained mercenaries. That's some pretty heavy firepower for a sawmill."

Bruce responded with a solemn, "Ya think."

As soon as the night crew pulled out, a day-shift guard took up a position on either side of the entrance. The other two disappeared into the shack.

A few minutes before 8 a.m., workers in a wide assortment of older, beat-up vehicles began arriving at the entrance. The gate was raised by one of the inside guards. Uncontested, vehicles barely slowed as they sped through the open gate. Occasionally one of the workers would wave to the security detail. After the last of approximately fifteen vehicles entered, the gate was lowered again.

Fifteen minutes later, a loaded log truck pulled up, stopping just outside the gate. While the barrier was being raised, a second truck loaded with wood chips arrived. Again, no security checks were conducted and after the first two trucks were let in, the gate remained open with the two guards standing on either side of the entrance while the other two remained hidden inside the shack.

Vic and Bruce watched as long flatbeds hauling huge logs and dump trucks containing wood or bark chips began entering at uneven intervals. A half-hour later, the first truck returned, apparently after dumping its load at the mill. The second truck soon followed.

After watching the irregular pattern for almost an hour,

Bruce had seen enough. "So, what do you think; are we ready to hop in the back of one of those dump trucks?"

"You think one of them might stop and pick us up?" Vic sarcastically asked.

Ignoring Vic's mockery, Bruce suggested, "Suppose we push a couple of small boulders out on the road and see what happens."

Vic's eyes widened. "That might work."

"Let's head back to that last curve in the road. One of us can hang back until he sees a dump truck coming then signal the other to push the boulders out on the road. Hopefully, the driver will see them in time and stop. Once he does, we can climb in from the back and bury ourselves in the wood chips."

"Suppose it's a log truck instead of a dump truck?" Vic asked.

"Then we let him clear the road and go on. We just keep rock rolling until we get a dump truck."

"Okay," Vic replied. "Just one question."

"Yeah?"

Vic was studying the fence with his binoculars and never looked away as he said, "Once we're satisfied this is the place on John's video, how are we going to get back out?"

"Anyway we can," Bruce replied, chuckling.

"Is that a typical Navy extraction plan?"

"Never . . . let's get going."

"Not yet," Vic replied. "I've got an idea. Take a look through your binoculars at the fence on both sides of the gate."

Bruce did as Vic suggested. "Okay; what am I looking for?"

"Locate the fiber-optic cable."

"Got it."

"Notice how at the last post it dives straight for the ground."

"Oh yeah. So what?"

"Look at the other side of the driveway, it does the same thing. Buried under the ground on one side should be a start sensor and on the other side an end sensor. The start sensor sends a signal out through the fiber-optic cable around the entire perimeter of the fence to the end sensor which transmits it back. The returned signal is monitored and analyzed by a controller for disturbances." Vic let that sink in before he continued, "Let's find out what they do when there is a disturbance."

"Okay, like how?"

"Why don't you go back down the road a ways and disturb the fence then find a place to hide."

"I can do that," Bruce replied.

Seven minutes later, a shout came from inside the guard shack. One of the guards from inside hustled out with two shotguns, tossed the extra to one of the other guards, and the two of them headed for the Pathfinder, which peeled out the gate speeding in Bruce's direction. The gate was immediately lowered and one of the remaining guards alertly stood in front of the shack with his gun drawn.

Vic could see a second guard standing behind the front window monitoring a row of computer screens. Trucks started backing up on both sides of the gate. Ten minutes later, Vic watched as the Pathfinder crept back toward the entrance, matching the pace of a guard who was slowly walking along the outside of the fence line. When the Pathfinder reached the end of the traffic jam, its driver gave the thumbs-up sign to his cohort blocking the entrance.

Seconds later, the gate was raised and the flow of trucks resumed. The guard who had been walking the fence line returned to the shack. He and the guard doing the computer monitoring had a brief discussion, which Vic could not make out, then the two men turned and disappeared to the back of the building.

That was exactly what Vic was hoping they would do. He was smiling when Bruce stealthily showed up next to him.

"Learn anything?" Bruce asked.

"I'll have to do one more check later, but I think I've figured out how we are going to get back out."

Bruce nodded then asked, "Can we go now?"

"Let's do it," Vic said confidently.

■ ■ ■

They picked a spot just beyond a curve where the slope was moderate and lined with rocks and trees. Bruce helped Vic roll three decent-sized rocks to the shoulder a hundred feet into the straightaway. He then proceeded around the corner and down into the ditch on the far side of the road. It didn't take more than a few minutes before Bruce gave Vic the signal. Vic rolled the three basketball-sized rocks out into the road and scrambled back up behind a bush. This was their lucky day; a dump truck came barreling toward Bruce's position. The driver slowed as he went into the curve. As soon as he started straightening out again, he saw the obstructions in his path. He slammed on the brakes, causing the hulking truck to screech to a halt just a few feet short of calamity.

Bruce was out of the ditch and chasing after the truck as soon as it passed. Seconds later, Vic was out of hiding and dashing for the passenger side of the truck. Focused on the obstacles blocking the road, the driver never noticed the two men racing for the back of his vehicle. Vic and Bruce both leaped up, grabbing the rim of the dump bed while simultaneously planting a foot on the bottom side rail. In one motion, they propelled their bodies over the side and onto the pile of chips. They were buried in chips before the driver rolled the three boulders off the road and returned to the cab.

At the gate, the guards never wavered in their laxness, allowing the dump truck to bounce on through. Bruce was thinking as the gatehouse slowly disappeared behind them, *Fortunate for us, amateurs by day and professional mercenaries by night.*

The truck bounced over the uneven gravel road and through stands of redwood and cypress trees. Bruce and Vic took turns peering over the side, looking for signs of the mill.

Bruce, still partially buried by chips, thought he felt

something smooth and slick under his knee. Rummaging around beneath his leg, he discovered a black plastic garbage bag. Locating the top of the bag he undid the pull-ties. The bag was packed with leaves. Pulling out a handful, he wasn't surprised when they turned out to be dried cannabis leaves.

Vic was the first to sense they were nearing their destination. Not knowing how soon the chips would be dumped, he motioned to Bruce it was time to bail out. In order to avoid being seen by the driver, they climbed over the rear gate. Using the bottom rail as a foothold, they hung on waiting for the right moment to jump. When the vehicle slowed for a curve, they jumped and disappeared into the woods undetected. Vic made a beeline for a fallen redwood where they could conceal themselves from the road to consider their next move.

Crouched behind the log, Bruce held up a handful of leaves and jokingly asked, "Got any rolling paper?"

They could hear the grinding and screeching of equipment and could smell fresh-cut lumber, but they weren't yet in sight of the mill.

Bruce, now a little more serious, said, "I suggest we work our way through the trees paralleling the road until we are able to get a good look at the layout."

It took them another five minutes of quietly weaving themselves between trees before they reached the edge of a clearing buzzing with activity. A half-dozen trucks were lined up waiting to be unloaded. Beyond the queuing trucks was the old covered sawmill with its half-century-old debarking and sawing machines. Off to the side was a relatively green painted production line composed of several large hoppers connected by conveyor belts. Behind both operations was a large metal building with open truck doors.

It was now ten o'clock in the morning and the place was at full throttle. The smell of fresh-cut timber overwhelmed the still summer air. An orchestra of machinery played its dreadful symphony. Trucks were coming and going, logs were being debarked and cut, chips and bark were being moved around by backhoes, and a bevy of rough-looking men, throwbacks to a bygone era, were working their butts off.

Bruce and Vic watched a backhoe dump natural-colored wood chips into a front-end hopper which fed them into a rotating drum. Coming out the other end of the drum were black-colored chips. These newly colored chips dropped onto an incline conveyor belt which whizzed them approximately fifty feet, finally dropping them in a huge pile. Another backhoe moved the chips to one of four different colored piles.

Breaking their silence, Vic whispered, "That chip-coloring equipment and warehouse-type building look brand-new. I'm betting that's what all the construction activity Miles mentioned was all about."

"You're probably right," Bruce replied, "but I'm curious . . . why an enclosed steel building. It wouldn't seem these types of products require protection from the elements."

"You've got a good point, Bruce. Perhaps we should sneak inside that building and find out what's really going on."

"Good idea, let's work our way around the back and see if we can get a better look," Bruce replied.

They quietly backed deeper into the trees and began working their way around to the other side of the clearing. Hidden by the trees and brush, the two intruders reached their destination undetected. Crouching behind the rotting stump of a once massive pine tree, they watched with interest as a burly worker ran a wide web of clear stretch film around the perimeter of a pallet stacked with bags of colored mulch. He then loaded the pallet on a flatbed truck with the forklift. When the bed was full, the forklift operator presented the truck driver with shipping documents.

Bruce and Vic stayed hidden until the truck pulled away and the forklift operator drove toward the mulch piles, where he exchanged his forklift for a front-end loader. He then proceeded to scoop up a bucketload of colored mulch, delivering it into the building through a door on the opposite end. He repeated the delivery several times, then parked the backhoe next to the forklift before dismounting and heading toward a row of three port-o-johns.

"You think there is anyone else is in the building?" Vic asked.

"Don't know," Bruce replied, "but I think I'll go find out."

"How are you going to do that?"

"I'm going to walk right in the back doors." He then stripped off his camouflaged top, revealing a black T-shirt. "You stay here and keep me covered," he directed. "I think I can pretty much handle myself with these yahoos but you never know."

Sarcastically, Vic shot back, "I don't know, that yahoo driving the forklift looked pretty tough."

Bruce made a funny face before he turned to walk off. Vic grabbed his arm. "Shouldn't you wipe that face paint off?"

Bruce didn't respond, but he pulled out a red-checkered bandana and began vigorously scrubbing his face. When he thought he was done he turned to Vic. "How's that?"

"Here, give me that rag," Vic replied, reaching for the bandana. Vic finished Bruce's cleanup then stuffed the soiled cloth in his pocket.

Grinning, Bruce strolled toward the building. As he reached the open back doors, he stopped to survey the inside of the building. He quickly determined it was unoccupied.

Entering the building, he could see one side wall lined with pallets of bagged mulch while the other side contained a packaging line and conveyor belts. Cautiously, he wandered further inside.

Pretty harmless, he thought.

The packaging line intrigued him. It had a front-end hopper where apparently the colored mulch was dumped before it was distributed on a short conveyor belt which led to a bagging machine. Suspended above the machine on an unwind stand was a large roll of printed polyethylene film. Bruce visualized how the bag was formed then stuffed with mulch before it was finally sealed. The finished bag of mulch then dropped on another conveyor belt. At the end of that belt a half-stacked pallet was waiting to be completed. The brand name on the bags was Great Northwest. The labeling identified the product as classic black landscape mulch.

Funny, he thought as he looked down on the unfinished stack, *why is there a gap right in the middle?*

Bruce continued to study the pallet, attempting to figure out why they would leave a one-foot square void in the center. Out of curiosity, he leaned over the outside row and peered down into the hole. The bottom two layers appeared fully stacked but the next four had a gap in the middle.

He shook his head. *Really strange! I wonder if any of the finished pallets fit the same pattern.* Walking across the aisle, he examined a full pallet of black mulch. *No gap,* he thought.

He then removed the center bag off the top layer. The center was filled, except not by a bag of Great Northwest mulch. Instead it was stuffed with clear plastic bags filled with a fine white powder. He guessed each bag contained two kilos of cocaine.

He quickly checked several more completed black mulch pallets. They too contained center cavities loaded with bags of the white substance.

Moving to a pallet of red mulch he went through the same exercise. This time the cavity was stuffed with clear bags of a chunky hazy crystalline substance which he guessed was crystal meth. He wasn't surprised when he then checked a pallet of brown mulch and found the center filled with half-gallon ziplock bags of weed.

Pretty smart; who'd think to stop and search a truckload of mulch. Shaking his head and smiling in admiration, he thought, *They even have their products color coded.*

At about the same moment, outside the building Vic noticed the forklift driver coming out of the port-o-john and returning to his forklift. He watched as the man drove to a small metal building perhaps twenty feet wide and fifteen feet deep. The man jumped down to unlock a double door, then maneuvered the forklift inside. A few moments later he backed out with a pallet of small plastic bags which looked similar to the ones in the general's video. The forklift then headed in the direction of the large building.

Should I warn Bruce? Nah, he insisted he could take care of himself. I'll just position myself so I can have a view of what transpires. Vic moved to a position where he had a clear view of both Bruce and anyone coming through the far door. Then he readied his sniper rifle.

Bruce was mildly surprised when the sound of a forklift interrupted his train of thought. When he saw what it was carrying, he was mildly excited. *Oh! Here comes a resupply of goodies,* he mused, smiling.

It took several seconds for the driver to discover the interloper. At first he didn't make much of it, but then he seemed to realize he didn't recognize the man milling around pallets of brown mulch.

Acting like he belonged, Bruce casually waved to the driver. The six-foot-four, 250-pound worker stopped a few yards away and slowly extracted himself from his machine. "Who the fuck are you and how'd you get in here?"

"OSHA," Bruce answered, having to look up into the taller man's eyes.

Using his left hand, Bruce slowly reached for his wallet in his back pocket. He flipped it open, revealing his retired Navy ID. The driver never even looked down at Bruce's offering.

Bruce quickly closed the wallet and asked authoritatively, "Where is your hard hat?"

The driver started to say something, but Bruce hit him just above his left eye with a vicious right cross. The man's eyes rolled back in his head, and he started to fall backward. Bruce reached out, grabbing him by the shirt, and slowly lowered him to the concrete floor.

Bruce looked around for something with which he could tie him up. Locating several feet of plastic strapping and an oily rag in a trash bin, he hog-tied the unconscious driver, stuffed the rag in his mouth, and dragged him behind a stack of pallets. Bruce poked a hole in one of the bags on the forklift and squeezed out a smidgen to taste. Just as he suspected, it was cocaine.

Smiling at the success of their mission so far, he gave the inside of the building one last look before heading for the back exit. He was almost outside when he stopped, turned around and headed back toward the forklift. Bruce stopped next to the piece of machinery, and reached up and removed a clip board. He briefly flipped through the attached paperwork, scanning each page and memorizing the ship-to and bill-to names and addresses. He then returned it to the forklift and casually walked out the back door.

CHAPTER 24

Anxious to make their getaway before the forklift driver was discovered, Bruce and Vic hightailed it back into the woods. They ran as fast as they dared while zigzagging between trees and hurtling obstacles. Reaching a concealed spot just fifty yards short of the guard shack, they stopped to rest and plot their next move.

There did not appear to be any unusual activity around the guard shack, indicating their foray had not yet been discovered.

"Okay, what now?" Bruce asked as they caught their breaths.

"Give me a minute," Vic replied, peering through binoculars.

Handing Bruce the binoculars, he suggested, "Take a look at the back of the shack."

Vic gave Bruce a few seconds to study the building before he said, "See that small pipe coming out of the ground then disappearing halfway up the wall?"

"Yeah?" Bruce replied quizzically.

"I believe it shields the optical wire coming from the fence. I noticed after the guards came back from investigating your fence-line interruption, they disappeared into the back of the shack, where I believe they reset the controls. If I'm correct, the control box should be mounted on the inside of the wall just above or below where the pipe goes through. If we take out the control box, all their monitoring equipment will go black. They won't be able to figure out if or where there's a breach in the fence."

"And how are we going to take out the control box?"

"I'm going to pump a couple of rounds through that cheap plywood structure and into the back of the controller."

"Suppose you're wrong about the location of the control box?"

Pointing across the street, Vic responded, "Well, I'm also going take out that transformer hanging on the telephone pole across the street. Notice the electric line comes into the shack from that same pole. Taking out both the source of their power and the controller should pretty much assure they're blind to our escape."

"Why take out both, shouldn't blowing the transformer alone do the job?"

"Not if they have a battery backup."

"So, let me make sure I understand the situation. If you take out the transformer but miss the controller and they have battery backup, we're toast."

"That's about it."

"Wonderful," Bruce responded with a smidgen of sarcasm. "One way or the other, shouldn't we first call Bart to pick us up someplace?"

"Good idea."

Bart agreed to meet them at the same spot where he dropped them off as quickly as he could get there.

Minutes later, they watched as Vic's Suburban raced past the entrance. They waited two minutes before Vic put a round from the silenced rifle into the transformer. The transformer exploded like a small bomb, sending a rain of sparks down on the parched grass along the side of the road. The two sentries at the gate instinctively hit the ground, their weapons poised to fire as soon as they could identify the threat. It was only seconds until they realized there was no real danger except for the smoldering grass ignited by the rain of sparks. Relieved, they scrambled to their feet and were soon joined by one of their compatriots from inside the shack.

Recognizing they had to act quickly before the burgeoning brush fire raced up the hillside and began consuming the abundant brushwood, one of the guards shouted, "We've got to put that out . . . fast!"

A second guard dashed into the guard shack and quickly emerged with a shovel, a rake, and a large piece of canvas. Distributing the tools to the other two, he raced across the road with the others closely following. While the three sentries were occupied in a frantic effort to extinguish the ever-growing blaze, Vic, in rapid succession, pumped five bullets into the back of the guard shack, each neatly spaced within a three-foot square above and below the point where the sensing wire ran through the wall.

Seconds later the remaining guard emerged from the shack shouting, "The battery backup must not have cut in; we've lost the whole system. We're blind!"

Vic proudly whispered, "Good guess, eh!"

Bruce smiled. "Yeah, but shouldn't we go now, or are you too enamored of your handiwork?"

There was no need for Vic to respond. They quietly disappeared deeper into the trees, heading for their rendezvous point with Bart. Several minutes later, they cut through the perimeter fence, racing to where Bart was anxiously waiting off the side of the road.

Bart had just turned into the Slaughter ranch's driveway when they heard the furious shrieking of sirens barreling toward them. Two Boyerville police cars, a fire truck, and an EMS vehicle zipped past the Slaughter driveway in a close caravan heading toward the Boyer place. Moments later the irritating blare of sirens ceased.

■ ■ ■

"I think we've made a lot of progress since we last saw you in Eureka," Bruce announced as he looked at Dana's herky-jerky image on Skype. "I sent a couple of photos to your cell phone. You're not going to believe this. They're smuggling the narcotics up from Mexico in what looks to me like an old whiskey-class Russian submarine. Tragically, the photos were taken by Miles' nephew, who's gone missing and we fear may have been killed for witnessing the delivery. Before he disappeared, he managed to send the photos to his girlfriend. We have the girlfriend in a safe house with Azzan and Eitan watching over her. Tomorrow a couple of ex-Special Forces guys I know will arrive and take over her protection."

Dana didn't respond for a few seconds, then she replied, "Anything you want me to do about the boy?"

"Yeah, the boy's parents have informed the county sheriff of his disappearance. Perhaps you can check to see if the sheriff put out an all-points bulletin on an Allie Reynolds. Also, would you have somebody monitor for reports of an unidentified body being discovered along the coast."

"Will do . . . I did get the sub photos a few minutes ago. I was curious as to where they were taken, who took them, and how you got your hands on them. Anyway, I've already forwarded them to Bob Hoffman at the CIA, asking him for his take on the sub."

"Good work! You can tell Bob they were taken at Flat Iron Rock just north of Eureka. The other vessel belongs to one of the real power-broker families in this part of the country by the name of Boyer. Then ask him if he can locate where they could possibly hide the sub without being noticed along the west coast of Mexico. It would seem that even in a country as corrupt as Mexico, you can't just dock a Cold War sub in Ensenada harbor without setting off some kind of alarm bells. Frankly, I'm at a loss to recollect anywhere north of Cabo where you could hide something like that between runs."

"Why does it have to be north of Cabo?"

"It doesn't; there are two other choices. One would be around the Cape and into the Gulf of California, perhaps parking it near Sinaloa. However, that would virtually double the round-trip distance and significantly increase the risk of being observed. The gulf is crawling with scientific, ecological, and tourist traffic. I doubt smugglers would be anxious to assume the additional chance of being observed.

"The other possibility is south of Puerto Vallarta. It's not a high-traffic area like the gulf, and there are quite a few hiding places along that stretch of coast. On the other hand, it's a long haul. No, I'm convinced it's most likely a good distance north of Cabo, but I'm at a loss as to how they are hiding it."

"Okay, anything else?"

"We verified the location of the photos on John's camera. Miles was right, they were taken at the Boyers' sawmill. We also stumbled upon how they're distributing the drugs from here. By the way, we found cocaine, meth, and marijuana. It's really quite brilliant how they're doing it. The coke and meth come from Mexico in the submarine; dump trucks loaded with mulch, bark, or woodchips haul the pot, probably locally grown. Then they have this slick operation where they color and package the mulch, bark, and chips. The drugs are hidden in a cavity in the center of each pallet of bagged product. Get this; the color of the product actually determines which drug is concealed on the pallet; black for coke, red for meth, and brown for cannabis."

Dana had been so quiet, Bruce asked, "You still there?"

"Yeah, I'm just so amazed at this operation, I'm speechless."

Bruce let out a hearty laugh. "Well, I'm not even finished yet. So they load these pallets on a truck and ship them out. We witnessed one flatbed going out this morning. I took a peek at the bill of lading. It was making three deliveries in Nevada, one to Silver City Sand and Gravel in Reno and the other two in Vegas, De Scalzo Building Supplies and Desert Landscape & Supply. I'm guessing this isn't the only state Boyer services, but that was the only truck leaving while we were there."

"Should I give the DEA a tip on these three?"

"Not yet, I don't want the Boyers so spooked they shut down."

"That's fine but I can't hold off for too long . . . it's been a productive twenty-four hours, hasn't it?"

"I guess so. How'd it go on your end?"

"We got the exhumation order and Dr. Lambert talked to the Humboldt County coroner. The guy was not all that excited about having his work reviewed by Lambert. However, he had no choice except to overnight Peter the files. Less than a half-hour later, Lambert received a call from the Boyerville police chief asking him why he was reviewing the coroner's report."

"What did he tell him?"

"He told him he wasn't sure but he guessed it had something to do with a large life insurance policy containing a double indemnity clause. Peter thought the chief was skeptical of his explanation."

"He's probably right; especially after the chief learned their perimeter was breached today. It looks like our attempt to up the temperature is working."

"How'd they discover someone breached their security?"

Bruce laughed. "Seems in order to make our escape, it was necessary for me to get physical with one of Boyer's employees. Then Vic was required to discharge his weapon in order to interrupt their security system. Fortunately, no one was seriously hurt."

"Maybe not, but now at least one guy can probably identify you as his assailant. Maybe you should stay out of sight for a few days."

"You worried, sweetheart?"

"I'm not worried, but I suspect the Boyers are. Who knows what the local police might do? And the FBI can't get involved without tipping our hand."

"Okay, babe, I'll play it cool a little while longer."

"Good . . . Oh by the way, your father sent his buddy Mike Musgrave the file on Lumbermen's Savings and Loan. It didn't take Mike long to call me to say he discovered Lumbermen's outsources their information technology operation to a consulting firm out of Nevada, Infotech.

"Infotech just happens to be run by Kevin Mulrooney. It seems Mike has run across Mulrooney twice before, once in the early nineties while he was investigating the Rhode Island savings and loan crisis, then again about ten years later in a New York case. The first time, Mulrooney could not be directly tied to any illegal activities. However, in 2002 he became the sacrificial lamb in a money laundering scheme at a Manhattan bank. He pleaded guilty and served four years.

"The terms of his release prohibit him from ever working in a financial institution again. That fact alone would give us grounds to have Treasury agents go in there. On the other hand, given Mike's history with the guy, it might be quicker if we could get Mulrooney to turn on his employer. Who knows what this guy might be willing to give up rather than do more time."

"Sounds like a good idea. Do you think Mike would play along?"

"Definitely! He sounded bored with what he is doing now."

"Then let's give it a shot."

Oozing with enthusiasm, Dana replied, "Okay, assuming Mike's on board, he and I will be out there tomorrow afternoon. I'll text you a photo of Mulrooney. It's a few years old, but it should do. Perhaps you can put a tail on him so that when we arrive we can shake him up right away. I can't wait to see the look on his face when he sees Mike again."

"That sounds like a good job for Bart," Bruce replied, looking over his shoulder at Bart and grinning.

CHAPTER 25

"Our Mexican business partner woke me up at 5:30 this morning; he's worried and wanted to know about the incident at the mill. How the hell did he find that out so fast?"

"I don't know, Pop. We've got a half-dozen illegals working at the mill and a couple more on Ricky's boats. Frankly, I'm concerned, too. Three surprises in one day makes me wonder."

"Tell me what you're thinking, Junior."

"First the county coroner gets a call saying the family is having Slaughter's body exhumed for a second autopsy. Then we have this incident at the sawmill. Just before I came out here, I got word the FBI was asking about the missing persons report on that Indian kid Ricky nabbed spying on them. Frankly, I'm wondering if Vic and some of the general's old friends aren't behind it all."

"But it wasn't McCoy who coldcocked Big Ed at the sawmill."

"No, but the guy was about the same age and looked ex-military."

"So you're thinking if Vic is suspicious enough to request another autopsy then it's likely he had one of his buddies snooping around our operation."

Junior gave his father a somber look. "You saw Miles' reaction the other day when you brought up the theory about the dog getting mauled defending Slaughter from some wild animal. After all, it was he and his guys who found the dog. He's not stupid, he knows the dog's only visible injury was from a bullet. It wouldn't surprise me if that little shit was the one planting these seeds in Vic's head."

"Listen, I've got to fly down to Cabo this afternoon and face Don Felix. I just can't tell him we know nothing. So, if that's what you think, as the law in this town, you should stop by the Slaughter place and try to figure out what Vic is up to."

"How do you suppose I do that?"

"I don't know; you're supposed to be a skilled interrogator. Inform him about the break-in then give him a description of the guy who punched out Big Ed. Ask him if the guy sounds familiar or whether he's seen anything suspicious lately. Hell, come right out and ask him what's prompting the second autopsy. Maybe if you come straight at him, you'll catch him off-guard and he'll let something slip."

"I don't know, Pop. There's still quite a bit of friction between us. There's no telling how he'll react. Perhaps I ought to have Ken do it."

"No way! It's in your jurisdiction. You do it," the old man demanded. "Perhaps that little bit of tension between you and Vic might just cause him to show his hand."

■ ■ ■

At 8:30 the next morning Vic was busy frying up eggs and bacon while Bruce was sitting at the dining room table scrutinizing satellite images Bob Hoffman had just emailed him.

"Well, that didn't take him long," Bart announced as he walked back into the kitchen from the front porch. "Here comes Chief Boyer up the driveway now."

Vic glanced over his right shoulder at Bruce. "Perhaps you should stay out of sight while he's here. They've probably got a pretty good description of you from the forklift operator."

Bruce nodded, packed up his laptop, and headed out the back door for the bunkhouse.

"Let's meet that son-of-a-bitch outside. I can't stand the

thought of him in my uncle's house," Vic snarled like a pissed-off Rottweiler.

Bart corrected him. "It's your house now."

"You know what I mean."

"I do, and I feel the same way."

Grabbing an extra cup of coffee, Vic led Bart outside and down the front steps in order to cut off Chief Boyer before he could get too close to the house. Mustering up all the pleasantness he could, Vic approached Junior with a smile.

"Good morning, Clete." Holding out the extra cup, he continued, "You're just in time for a cup of freshly made coffee. I assume you drink it black."

Junior was startled by Vic's affable greeting and couldn't prevent the surprise from showing on his face. He quickly recovered, transitioning into his most congenial demeanor.

"Good morning to you, Victor and you too . . . eh, it's Bart, isn't it?"

Bart simply nodded, but Chief Boyer wasn't even watching. He was too anxious to get off on a good footing with Vic this morning. Sporting a broad smile while reaching out to accept the cup, he attempted to sweet-talk Vic.

"I was just thinking how good another cup of coffee would taste, and lo and behold, here you come to save the day. Thanks."

He took a quick sip then abruptly turned his attention to Bart, continuing his friendly tone. "Good to see you again, Mr. Rock. How are you enjoying your stay in Eureka?"

"I love it up here, Sheriff. The air is so fresh and the people are incredibly friendly."

Chief Boyer scrutinized Bart's face briefly for any hint of sarcasm before he glanced back at Vic. "How are your wife and kids liking it here?"

Vic pondered whether he should reveal the fact they were gone. He quickly concluded there was no sense in being deceptive. If Junior didn't already know they were gone, it wouldn't take long for him to figure it out. "They are out of town for a few days. One last fling before school starts."

"Where are they off to, San Francisco?"

What the hell, Vic thought. "Yeah, how'd you guess?"

Smiling, Chief Boyer arrogantly responded, "After all, I am a trained investigator."

"I'd guess!" Bart responded, feigning admiration.

A slight smirk passed over the lawman's mouth just before he transitioned to a more professional tone. "Say, have you heard that we had an intruder over at the sawmill yesterday?"

"No, but we did hear a whole bunch of sirens yesterday just after lunch."

"That would be about the time we discovered the breach in our security fence. But by then, whoever it was had gotten away."

"Any ideas why someone would want to invade a sawmill," Vic asked with as much innocence as he could simulate, but his choice of the word *invade* exposed his mockery.

The police chief was not used to such a sardonic response, so he had to rein in his irritation and gather his thoughts before answering. "We think it was a competitor. We've recently launched a new venture, producing landscape mulch. We are the first forward-integrated lumber company in the northwest to produce our own colored mulch. That gives us a distinct cost advantage over the competition, and we are starting to take market share away from some of the big national distributors. We're guessing it was one of them spying on us. At any rate, one of our employees discovered the breach and was brutally attacked. Apparently, that confrontation was enough to scare the spies off, but not before they started a brush fire to cover their escape."

"That must be unsettling. How's the guy who got slugged; was anyone else hurt?" Bart asked somberly.

The chief gave Bart a strange look then continued, "We were lucky. One black eye was the only injury, but it could have been a lot worse if the fire had gotten out of control."

Chief Boyer seemed to be examining their reaction before he continued, "So the reason I am telling you all this is because we want to identify these intruders and I was wondering if you could help."

Again, the chief seemed to be waiting for a reaction, but Vic and Bart remained stoic.

He continued, "The intruder was about your age, Vic, approximately six-foot, three-inches tall, well-built with sandy-colored hair. Our guy who was attacked indicated the guy seemed to have a military air about him. You haven't seen anybody fitting that description, have you?"

Should I? Vic wondered. *Oh, what the hell; we want to make them uncomfortable.* "Actually, I have, a couple of my Air Force buddies came in last night. They'll be staying here on the ranch, but neither one is over six foot tall. You want me to round them up so your guy can take a look?"

While Clete Jr. appeared to be stunned by Vic's announcement, Bart shot Vic a perplexed look indicating, *Where the hell are you going with this?*

Finally overcoming his surprise, Junior responded, "Eh . . . th . . . that won't be necessary. I'll take your word they don't fit the description and arrived after the incident."

"Okay," Vic replied, "it's your choice." Quickly changing direction, he asked, "Say, Sheriff, any word on that Native American kid who went missing?"

"I assume you're referring to Allie Reynolds." Not waiting for a reply, he continued, "No, we've got nothing except we've been unable to locate his girlfriend. There's some thought the two of them ran off together."

"You do know Allie is Miles' nephew?"

"Yeah, the sheriff talked to the boy's parents and to Miles when they filed the missing persons report. They have some cockamamie idea somebody harmed the kid. We've talked to all his friends; they claim he was alone on the island. So how could anyone harm him? It's more likely he tried to swim back to shore and drowned, or he and his girlfriend ran off together."

"I'm not trying to imply everything isn't being done to find the boy, Clete, but couldn't there be two other possibilities?

The first being the Coast Guard caught him on a restricted sanctuary and they have him in custody. Although, if they do, I suspect his family would have been informed. Then the second possibility is that someone else showed up on the island after his buddies dropped him off and that somebody is responsible for his disappearance."

"Of course, anything is possible, but the county sheriff's people have scoured the island, finding no evidence anyone other than Allie has been on the island recently."

Vic held out his hand to shake with the police chief. "All right, so be it. Well, good luck finding your intruder and the boy."

Chief Boyer responded with his hand, but his grasp lacked sincerity and his mind seemed to be elsewhere.

CHAPTER 26

"I'm worried, Pop. McCoy is definitely up to something. He claims his wife and kids went on a trip to San Francisco and he told me some of his Air Force buddies are in town last night. I had Ken do some checking at the airport. No military types arrived by plane yesterday. However, the day before, a private plane landed with five passengers: a sophisticated older man, a hot chick, and three guys who could be ex-military. The plane is registered to a huge real estate company, Tanner International Development. One of the men, Bruce Tanner, rented an SUV. The group was seen being met by two men who match McCoy's and Rock's descriptions. My contacts at the airport reported half of them left in the rented SUV and the other half with the two men who met them."

Feeling pretty good about his intelligence work, Junior couldn't help but take a poke at his father's constant digs of his police work. "In spite of my mediocre detective skills—" He paused to make sure the old man caught his sarcasm. "—I also learned they spent most of the day at the Holiday Inn Express in a conference room Rock rented."

Clete Senior did pick up on his son's jab, and a momentary smirk grudgingly warped his lips.

Satisfied he had gotten his point across, Junior, a little more confident than before, continued, "Get this, only the old man and the woman got back on the plane, but they were joined by two other women and three children. I'm guessing it was Vic's family plus Rock's wife that boarded the plane."

His confidence peaking, Junior smugly added, "The pilot filed a flight plan for Palm Beach with a stopover in Denver. You'll recall I had already learned that Rock is from Colorado. I think we can assume Rock's wife is hosting Vic's wife and kids at his place."

"Good work, son."

"Oh, I'm not done yet, Dad. The name of the guy who rented an SUV was Bruce Tanner. Ken is running a check on Tanner as we speak.

"Incidentally, Ken tells me there's a rumor going around the county that the Indian kid was kidnapped by a submarine which he took photos of and texted to his girlfriend. Apparently, she's scared somebody is going to come after the pictures and consequently she's hiding out."

"Okay, I agree, McCoy and Rock are definitely up to something. I'm not convinced yet it has anything to do with the break-in at the mill. It could just be Rock has convinced Vic to begin shopping around for a buyer. Hell, that's what I'd do. Given the Slaughters' connections at the Rancheria , they may even be working to package a deal with the Indians to develop a big-time resort/casino complex. Wouldn't that be a coup? However, I'm more concerned about the Indian girlfriend and those pictures, assuming they really do exist." Then in more of a statement than a question, the old man continued, "Perhaps it time for us to put some additional Xenophon resources in play."

"To do what, Pop?"

"First off, I think I'll call Claude at Xenophon Headquarters in DC and see if they're interested in a 24/7 contract. We don't need anyone snooping around the mill again and obviously the daytime rent-a-cops are useless."

"Those ex-black-ops guys are expensive. Do you really think that's necessary?"

"Why not, the cost is mouse nuts compared to the investment we have in this operation. Besides, the one successful breach at the mill occurred during daylight hours. You saw how professionally the two Xenophon guys, Ralph and Carl, intercepted and neutralized the general. That whole sequence of events convinced me we can trust them to discreetly handle any assignment. I'm sure Xenophon would be able to supply us with all the resources we need to protect our investment."

"What else are you thinking?" Junior asked.

"I'm thinking we need to buy us some leverage."

"Like what?"

"We need to find both McCoy's wife and kids and that Indian kid's girlfriend."

"Jeez, Pop, I hope you're not contemplating what I think you are."

"Where are your balls, son? If you're skittish about this, you just need to get me two things; I'll arrange for any dirty work."

Apprehensive, Junior asked, "What do you need?"

With his eyes almost boring a hole through his son, the old man spat out, "It's WE, Junior. Do you get that?" Emphasizing the plural again he continued, "WE, not just me . . . need a couple of trump cards. See if you can get your brother to locate this girlfriend and if you still have Rock's home address in Colorado. I'll have someone from Xenophon find out if that's where McCoy's family is hiding out. Can you do those two simple things or do I have to farm that out, too?"

Humiliated again, Junior stormed off without responding.

■ ■ ■

"Claude, it's Clete Boyer Senior."

"Hello, Mr. Boyer, how are things going? I hope our services are still satisfactory."

"Very satisfactory; in fact, I'd like to expand our agreement."

"Fantastic. What are we talking about?"

"First, I'm sure you heard we had a break-in yesterday during the day shift."

"Yes, I did see the report. Was anything important compromised?"

"We're still not sure, but we don't want to take any more chances with the rent-a-cops. We'd like you to take over 24/7. Are you interested?"

"Absolutely. We can start first thing in the morning with the same hourly rate."

"Good. I also have a couple of other slightly more hazardous assignments in mind. Is your organization interested in those, too?"

"Absolutely, Mr. Boyer. I'm assuming it might be similar in nature to the one in March."

"Similar but more proactive than reactive. Is there a way we can discreetly discuss what I have in mind?"

"Face-to-face discussions are always the best way to insure confidentiality and to negotiate the fees for these kinds of activities. Unfortunately, I'm leaving for Iraq this afternoon. Can it wait until I get back, say in a couple of days?"

"Not really, we might be in imminent risk here. I want to move on both these operations in the next twenty-four to forty-eight hours."

"Okay then; how do you feel about dealing with Carl?"

"Based upon the way he handled the problem in March, I'd be glad to deal with him directly."

"Good, I'll plan on swinging by California on my way back from the Middle East to get an update. In the meantime, Carl and I will be in contact via encrypted emails."

■ ■ ■

Clete Boyer Senior drank heavily on the two-hour flight in the chartered Cessna Citation Jet. Up till now, he always looked forward to these business trips to San Jose del Cabo to meet with the head of the Tijuana cartel. Of course, it helped that after they completed their business he would get to screw his brains out with Carmelita. But this was the second time in less than six months Don Felix had to summon him because of a problem. Don Felix didn't like problems.

Suddenly, it dawned on him; it was probably Carmelita's

cousin Pedro who informed the don about this latest problem. At Carmelita's urging he had hired her cousin to work at the mill. He always figured Don Felix only provided her to him in order to ply him for information. He hadn't dawned on him at the time, but obviously Pedro was Don Felix's plant in his operation. He probably wasn't even Carmelita's cousin. Now he wondered if the whore would even be at the condo this time, and that made him even more sullen.

Don Felix was already waiting for Clete Senior when he arrived at the 4,000-square-foot golf course villa he bought with cash several years earlier. For the first time since Don Felix introduced her to Clete, Carmelita was not sunbathing in the nude out on the veranda.

Much to his surprise, the don seemed to be in a good mood as he greeted him. "Welcome back, my friend, how long has it been?" Then answering his own question, he continued, "March, wasn't it?"

"That would be about right," Clete replied.

"It's been a very profitable four months, hasn't it?"

"Sure has," Clete replied enthusiastically. He was beginning to feel better about this meeting.

"It's been so good, I don't want to overreact to some of the things I hear about your security becoming somewhat lax."

He seemed to pause, waiting for his American partner to respond. When Clete said nothing, Don Felix continued. "So, would you indulge me by giving me a sense of what's been happening and how you're dealing with it?"

"Certainly, you have a right to know about serious problems when they occur. You can be assured, when they do, we take care of them expeditiously."

Deciding to let this prick know he didn't totally have his head up his ass, he began, "I am assuming Pedro has fully briefed you on both incidents and you understand the risks."

Smiling at Clete's rare audacity, the don responded, "Yes, Pedro has been quite informative on the security breach at the mill. However, he was a little sketchy concerning the situation with the submarine photographs. Incidentally, your nephew's quick decision with the boy was admirable. I also concede your track record has been exemplary, so let's not belabor the past. What are you doing to remedy these most recent threats?"

"Even though both of these incidents only surfaced in the last twenty-four hours, I have already been in contact with Xenophon to immediately take over security 24/7 and to embark on two operations which should mitigate both threats."

"Tell me your plans."

"Please understand, we are still gathering intelligence and have not completely worked out the details."

"I understand, as you said, it's been less than twenty-four hours."

"I'm glad you recognize many of the details are still fluid. Given what we now know, here is what we are thinking. Xenophon has adequate resources and has agreed to take on both projects although it will cost me a small fortune. Both efforts will be synchronized to kick off at 3 a.m. tomorrow even though they will occur almost fifteen hundred miles apart.

"The most important objective is to verify if there are photos of the sub unloading its cargo onto my nephew's boat. Assuming there actually are photos, we are fairly certain they exist only on the girlfriend's cell phone, and we mean to keep it that way. On the flight down here, my sons informed me they believe the girl is hiding at her uncle's farm a few miles south of Eureka."

"Let me just clarify one point, Clete. If a photo does not exist, how would anyone even know to suggest there was a sub in the area?"

"Good point, I've made the same observation, and we haven't heard about any other witnesses on Flat Iron Rock. At any rate, Xenophon is prepared to deal with either situation. The simplest being we confiscate the phone and put the fear of God into the girl and her family. However, it's more likely there will be the need for a tragic fire in which the whole family perishes."

"I assume with your law enforcement connections, an accident will not get too much scrutiny."

"You're correct; we've been dealing with Indian problems for over a century and haven't been burnt yet." In between sinister chuckles, Clete Boyer Senior managed to exclaim, "Oops, did I say burnt?"

"Okay, it's risky. I think you've thought it out and have the resources to pull it off. What about the other operation?"

"Actually, that one should be a cakewalk. We're only dealing with a couple of women and children. They're hiding fifteen miles west of Denver." Then grinning and puffing his chest out in satisfaction, Clete continued smugly, "Slaughter sent them there believing we'd never find them but *my boys* are good."

Clete paused for a second waiting for a response from the don, but the drug lord didn't react. Without showing his disappointment, he continued, "I'm still not sure what McCoy's game is, but once we have his wife and kids, I think he can be convinced to back off."

"What makes you think he hasn't provided additional protection for his family?"

"Yeah, he could have done that, but it makes no difference. Xenophon's operatives are all Special Ops people. I'm sure they could handle a few ex-Air Force NCOs."

"Perhaps you're right, but I'd like to propose an alternative and it won't cost you a dime."

Liking the price, Clete replied, "What do you have in mind?"

"I have some people in Arizona with considerable experience in abductions. I can have them up there tomorrow morning."

Even though Clete Boyer was generally more comfortable handling his own problems, he did not want to insult the don plus he was anxious to end this discussion in hopes of getting in a quickie with Carmelita. "That's very kind of you to offer your resources, and I accept. I'll have Junior email you the address. You will synchronize it for 3 a.m. tomorrow night, right?"

"Absolutely, we should talk tomorrow afternoon and confirm everything is a go. Now, I suppose you'd like to spend some time with Carmelita; she should be here any minute."

That sealed the deal, the trip was now officially a success.

That all changed when, two hours later, Junior called, informing him Bruce Tanner was a retired U.S. Navy SEAL who now ran his own private military contracting company and was mostly likely the one who KOed Big Ed.

CHAPTER 27

Bart inspected the photo of Kevin Mulrooney Dana had texted to Bruce. "I've seen this guy," Bart declared. "He's a regular at the 301 Restaurant; sometimes he eats a late dinner at the bar. I kind of got the sense he might have something going with the barmaid Shirley."

"So, you're thinking of using Shirley to set up Mulrooney?"

"Sort of, she probably will know whether he is coming in tonight. I'll be waiting for her at the bar when her shift starts. I think she starts around five. I'll get there early and have a drink in front of me before she comes on."

"Then you'll just charm her into finding out what Mulrooney's plans are for the evening?"

Flashing a devious smile, Bart replied, "Something like that."

■ ■ ■

Bart was the only customer at the bar when Shirley came on shift. He was nursing a glass of Glennhawk 2009 Diablo Royale and waiting for his appetizer to arrive. She greeted the day-shift bartender and they counted out the cash drawer. When they were done, her male predecessor nodded his head toward Bruce and announced, "The gentleman at the end of the bar has been waiting for an order of raw oysters. Before I take off, I'll run by the kitchen and see if it's ready."

Shirley recognized Bart as a frequent customer over the

last few months. She slowly moved in his direction, smiling. "Other than waiting for the oysters, are you doing okay?"

"Just peachy," Bart replied.

"I haven't heard that saying in quite some time. Well, if you need anything—" She turned her head from one end of the empty bar to the other. "—it looks like I can provide you with personal service for the time being."

"Now that's even better than peachy," he responded with a lecherous inflection in his voice and Groucho Marx raised eyebrows.

Shirley, thinking the old guy was cute, chuckled.

Two minutes later, the off-duty bartender returned, announcing, "Sorry, they still haven't shucked them." Then he turned around and left.

"Assholes!" Shirley muttered under her breath. Turning toward Bart she said, "If you're okay with your drink for a few minutes, I'll head back to the kitchen and scare up your oysters."

Impressed with her initiative, Bart replied, "I'm fine."

Shirley returned a few minutes later with a bucket of oysters on ice, an oyster knife, and several plates. Holding the shells in a bar towel, she expertly shucked a dozen in less than two minutes, piling them on the plate and adding two slices of lemon. "Cocktail or hot sauce?" she asked.

"Both," Bart replied. "You sure are a good shucker."

She giggled at the customer's likely double entendre, and readily played along. "Ought to be; I started shucking for my dad when I was about eight years old." Having fun with the word play she continued, "Almost lopped off a couple of appendages before I was ten."

"Yours or his?" Bart asked playfully.

"Whichever," she answered before breaking into a naughty-sounding chuckle.

Thinking it might be time to end this racy dialogue, Bart attempted to ask a serious question. "You eat them yourself?"

Rolling her eyes, Shirley mischievously replied, "Are you asking about the appendages or the mollusks?"

Now curious to see how far she'd take this, Bart left the door wide open for her to come back with another witticism. "Either."

"I can do clams but not oysters," she responded a little more seriously.

Relieved their crafty word game seemed to be over, Bart decided to solidify their rapport. "As good as you are, they ought to have you do all the shucking right here at the bar. Maybe even give you one of those stainless steel bins filled with ice. Clams and oysters are one of those things that most people don't think about ordering, but if they were sitting right out in plain view, I'd bet you'd sell a lot more."

"Tell me about it," Shirley replied, shrugging. "I've already proposed that to management, but the chef is a control freak and won't have any part of it."

"Well, I'm going to make that suggestion to the manager. Can you point him out to me when you see him?"

"Sure, but he doesn't usually show up till after eight. Are you going to be around that long?"

That was his opening! All he had to do was bait the hook. "Probably not. However, I could come back around the time you get off," Bart replied with an impish grin.

Shirley stared at Bart with a quizzical look, apparently trying to decide if the "old man" figured it was all right to hit on her because of their earlier racy banter.

Then she took the bait, although she managed to mask her consternation. "Hey, customers are always encouraged to come back, but I'm thinking maybe you had more than a late drink in mind. If that was your intention, you should know my boyfriend will be in about nine and he's the jealous type."

Reeling her in, he said, "That wouldn't be Mr. Mulrooney, would it?"

She was momentarily floored but quickly recovered, "So, you know Kevin . . . I suppose he put you up to hitting on me?"

"No, I've never formally met him. I've just watched the two of you here a couple of nights and made a wild guess. So, he's coming in tonight, huh?"

Now aggravated, Shirley brusquely replied, "That's none of your business, old man," then turned away, walking hastily to the cash register and ceremoniously returning with Bart's check.

Bart quietly finished his oysters and wine, glanced at the check, and left a hundred-dollar bill under his wine glass before he started walking out. As he passed a glaring Shirley, he said, "I'm sorry if I offended you."

Shirley ignored his apology by turning her back on him then picking up a bar rag before walking over to clear away his soiled place setting and glass. She flinched when she spotted the hundred, then snapped her head around toward the brash old man and shook her head in bewilderment.

CHAPTER 28

Since it opened several years earlier, 301 had become the meeting place for the town's late crowd of high-powered businesspeople. Shortly before 9 p.m., Mike Musgrave, looking like the consummate banker in a gray pinstriped suit, starched white button-down shirt, and red tie, entered the 301. He headed straight for the bar while Dana waited in the FBI pool car she had just driven up from the Sacramento field office.

The near end of the bar was crowded with regulars occupied in boisterous and animated conversations. Shirley was busy punching bar orders into the point-of-sale computer cash register. Mulrooney had not yet arrived, so Mike planted himself on the last stool at the far end, leaving himself with his back to a large plate glass window. Bart's observation had been that Mulrooney liked to sit on the last stool.

When Shirley finally spotted the handsome middle-aged gentleman at the end of the bar, she scurried over to take his order. On the way over, she subconsciously straightened out her apron and pushed her bleached-blonde hair back behind her ears. "Welcome to the 301. What's your poison tonight?"

Seeing her name tag, Mike said, "Hey, Shirley, I think I'll start with a gin and tonic with a twist of lime. Make it on the rocks in a tall glass."

"Coming right up," Shirley replied as she smiled and did an about-face.

Mike slapped a twenty on the bar so Shirley would see it when she returned with his drink.

She was back in two minutes. "Want to run a tab, hon?"

"Sure, doll, I'm waiting for somebody. God knows how long he'll be." Mike left the twenty sitting on the bar.

Ten minutes later Mulrooney walked in the front door and made a beeline for the bar. He smiled and waved to Shirley before he saw the man in "his" seat. Momentarily hesitating, he scanned the bar before he settled on a spot two stools away from Mike. He was hardly off his feet when he did a double take of the man in his seat.

At that moment Shirley showed up. "The usual, Kevin?"

Visibly shaken, it took Mulrooney a few seconds to suppress his alarm and arrive at a quick decision. "Eh . . . hold it for now, Shirley, I think I left my wallet at the office."

He stood, turned and took four steps toward the front door before he realized there was a woman blocking his path and flashing her FBI credentials.

Before anyone else at the bar had a chance to see them, she flipped the leather badge holder shut and in a friendly voice said, "Hi Kevin, you're probably right. It's too noisy in the bar to conduct our business. Fortunately, I've reserved a table in the dining room where we can have some privacy."

Kevin Mulrooney's eyes momentarily had that "deer in the headlight" look while he frantically scanned the room looking for an escape route. Suddenly, he felt the presence of another individual, only inches from his back. He was still attempting to process his situation when softly into his right ear he heard, "Don't even think about it. You're already looking at twenty-five years to life."

Instantly, all the vigor went out of Mulrooney; his shoulders slumped noticeably and his eyes went vacant. He robotically followed the female FBI agent to a small table in a dark corner of the dining room.

Dana sat next to their quarry with Mike directly across.

Mike didn't wait very long to begin. "I'm assuming by your reaction you remember me. In case you've forgotten from where, I'm Mike Musgrave, from Rhode Island back in '91 and New York in '02." Brian's facial expression imparted a sense of defeat as Mike continued, "That's right; I'm the one who put you away for four years. This time, unless you agree to cooperate with us, you'll probably spend the rest of your life behind bars."

Kevin was still reeling when Dana waved off a waiter who was heading for their table. Then she compounded Mulrooney's fears. "We're not just talking about your violating the terms of your parole and complicity in Lumbermen's money-laundering schemes, this time it's also about the murders of John Slaughter and Allie Reynolds."

"MURDER!" Mulrooney gasped in horror as he involuntarily lurched forward. Frantic, his eyes raced around the room and he fought to compose himself. Finally, in desperation, he sucked in a deep breath before almost whispering, "I didn't have anything to do with murdering anyone."

"Knowing you the way I do, Kevin, I believe you," Musgrave replied. "In fact, if I didn't, you'd already be in handcuffs."

Sensing a spark of hope, Mulrooney pleaded, "What do you want?"

"The Boyers and whoever their partners are," Dana responded.

Tiny droplets of sweat appeared on Mulrooney's temples, slowly trickling down the edge of his sideburns. "You know they'll kill me," he grimly announced.

It was his turn to hesitate for effect while his eyes flittered between his two captors. When he began again, his whole demeanor exuded sincerity. "I'll help you. I'll tell you everything I know. I'll even give you copies of all the records. In return, I'll need protection, and I can't go back to jail."

"The protection is not a problem," Dana replied. "We'll see about jail. Just start talking."

"No, not here; besides, before I talk, I want a deal . . . in writing . . . I want full immunity from prosecution and witness protection."

Since this wasn't even an official investigation yet, Dana was reluctant to commit to a deal. Mike, with nothing to lose, jumped right in. "Okay, we'll have your deal tomorrow afternoon. Meet us four o'clock tomorrow at the Holiday Inn Express out at the airport. For your sake, you better bring us something we don't already know."

"No worries; I'll have plenty of good stuff for you," Mulrooney replied with a sense of relief.

Mike gave Dana a quick nod, and they both stood up and walked out of the restaurant.

As soon as they were outside, Dana looked back over her shoulder to make sure no one was behind them. "What was that all about? You know we don't have the authority to offer him a deal. Hell, you don't even work for any law enforcement agency, and I'm sure not going to stick my neck out for this slimeball."

Mike chuckled. "Hold that thought while I buy us some insurance. Keep an eye out; it wouldn't be good to get caught at this."

Baffled, Dana instantly shot back, "Caught at what, Mike?"

Not waiting to explain, Mike responded as he walked away, "I'll explain later. Just pop the trunk of the car and signal me if anyone is coming."

Dana hit the remote and the trunk on her FBI Ford sedan clicked open just as Mike arrived at the back of their vehicle. He opened it the rest of the way and rummaged through his luggage for a few seconds before he came out with a black box slightly larger than a pack of cigarettes. Quickly he slammed the trunk shut and headed for a beat-up white GMC Yukon sitting all alone at the end of the parking lot. He checked the license plate before stopping at the rear passenger door. He gave Dana one last glance, and she responded with two thumbs up. Grinning, he squatted alongside the rear tire for about fifteen seconds before re-emerging. Brushing dirt off his knees, he flashed Dana a smile before proceeding to their vehicle.

Back in the pool car a mildly edgy Dana chided Mike, "I'm guessing that was an unauthorized GPS tracking device you illegally attached to the underside of his vehicle. Why are we taking that big a risk when we are going to meet him again tomorrow?"

"He's running," Mike said authoritatively while he punched an icon on his iPhone.

"How do you know that?" Dana instantly shot back.

Mike was still punching stuff into his phone as he spoke. "He doesn't want to go back to prison, and he really doesn't trust us to give him total immunity. So, as far as he's concerned, he has no choice but to run. Besides, if he was serious, he would have demanded his lawyer have the opportunity to review the immunity agreement before he gave us anything."

Dana was still pondering Mike's deduction when he interrupted her. "Okay, got the signal. Let's pull around the corner and wait for him to drive off."

■ ■ ■

Kevin Mulrooney sat anxiously at the table for five minutes after the two G-men left. He was mentally going over his contingency plan for just such an encounter when Shirley showed up alongside him. Her sudden appearance nudged him out of deep thought.

"Your friends didn't stay long," she said quizzically.

Looking up, he gave her an uneasy smile. "Yeah, cheap bastards; they didn't even buy me a drink. What say we go back to the bar and you pour me a double Jack Daniels?"

"What about your wallet?"

It took him a few seconds to relate to her question and his eyes betrayed his confusion. "Oh," he finally said while he was getting up, "it was in my coat pocket all along."

Shirley could tell something was wrong, but she dared not pursue it any further for now. She figured he'd eventually tell her; after all, he always did unburden himself after they'd had sex.

The bar was still busy so Shirley barely had time to deliver Kevin his whiskey before another customer motioned for a refill. Kevin didn't waste any time throwing down his double shot in one gulp. He had to wait a couple of minutes before he was able to hail her for another. After delivering his second double, she said, "I'm not closing tonight; you want to hang around till eleven?"

"No," he replied, "I've got something to do."

"Should I stop by your place after I get off?"

"No, not tonight; I'll come by your apartment around midnight."

That's peculiar, she thought as she headed back down the other end to wait on other customers. *He hates my place.*

Kevin, again preoccupied with his escape plan, hardly noticed she'd slipped away. Finally, after several minutes, he was convinced he had it all worked out. After guzzling the second shot, he threw twenty-five dollars on the bar and left with only a cursory wave to Shirley.

As a precaution to make sure he wasn't being watched, Kevin did a walk around the parking lot and along the adjacent street. Not seeing a tail, he headed for his SUV, smiling to himself while thinking how naïve those federal agents were to believe he'd just hang around until tomorrow.

CHAPTER 29

"I've been thinking," Dana said, as they sat in the car four blocks down and on a side street waiting for the tracker to tell them Kevin was on the move. "If this guy is desperate enough to run away from federal agents, what other impulsive measures do you think he'll try to employ?"

"If I'm right, this won't be impulsive; he has a well-designed escape plan. If that fails, his next best option is to try to re-negotiate a deal by claiming to have details we won't get anywhere else."

"Okay, makes sense, but suppose he doesn't run and shows up tomorrow with his lawyer?"

"It might be helpful between now and then for you to have a talk with your boss."

"I was afraid of that," Dana sullenly replied.

Just then Mike's cell phone beeped. He glanced at the screen before declaring, "That's it . . . he's on the move."

"You know," Dana said as she slowly pulled away from the curb, "if he is running, unless he has a private plane waiting at the airport, he's probably going to have to get on I-5 at some point. It might be a good idea to hang back and not intercept him until after he leaves Humboldt County, where we'll have a shot at keeping the news of his detention from reaching the Boyers."

"Good idea; now do you understand why I am taking the risk with the tracker?"

"Yeah, Mike, but it doesn't make me any less nervous."

Mike chuckled.

■ ■ ■

In 1996, California became the first state to establish a medical marijuana program. Over the next fifteen years, various legal rulings and new bills expanded the boundaries for growing, selling, and possessing quantities of cannabis. As a result, legal indoor growers sprouted up all over California's North Coast in an area comprising Mendocino, Humboldt, and Trinity counties. Since it was no longer necessary to purchase pot illicitly, the market for illegal marijuana virtually dried up. By 2009, illegal growers who had been getting $200 per pound for their product could hardly give it away as customers shifted their purchases to the state's legal dispensaries.

There was still a street market for people who couldn't (or wouldn't) get a prescription, but Clete Boyer was the first to realize this latent source of marijuana could be harnessed by someone who had the infrastructure to provide an efficient distribution network to neighboring states. Using his wholesale lumber supply distribution network as the delivery mechanism, Clete was able to provide dependable deliveries to drug kingpins not just in California but also in Oregon, Washington, Idaho, and Nevada. The result was a limited but profitable business generating mounds of cash. By early 2010, Boyer was sitting on almost two million in cash and in desperate need of a way to wash it.

Fortunately, his father, Aaron, always the opportunist, became a local hero in 1936 when he purchased the failing local bank, Lumbermen's Savings and Loan. After Aaron died, Clete's younger brother, Bernie, ran the private bank. Clete wanted to use the bank to launder the cash, but Bernie, though he was intrigued by the prospect, knew he didn't have the skills or experience to pull it off without getting caught by the Feds.

Like most of the Boyers over the years, Bernie wasn't completely deterred by the risk. He diligently began researching old money-laundering cases in order to learn how it was done. That was until he saw an old article in the Sunday *New York Times* stating the infamous Manhattan Bank money launderer, Kevin Mulrooney, had been released from prison. Mulrooney was just the kind of ingenious fraudster the Boyers needed to wash their illegal gains through Lumbermen's. Bernie hired a private investigator to track down Mulrooney. The private eye located Kevin in Orlando working as a finance manager at a timeshare resort. Boyer arranged for Mulrooney to meet him in Las Vegas, where he offered the ex-banker a job at Lumbermen's. However, Mulrooney, having just completed four years behind bars, was not anxious to plunge headfirst into another illegal scheme.

A year later, Kevin was able to get himself transferred to his company's newest timeshare development in Reno. He had only been in Reno for a few months when one Friday night at the Peppermill Resort he found himself playing blackjack at the same high-stakes table as Bernie Boyer. At first, neither man recognized the other, but they both were winning and slowly developed a friendly banter.

Eventually, one of Kevin's remarks unlocked Bernie's memory. "Kevin Mulrooney!" Bernie exclaimed in surprise. "Of course, how could I forget. We discussed a job opportunity about a year ago. How's it going?"

Scratching behind his ear, Kevin squinted at Bernie while the mechanical shuffler was mixing the three decks. He had received only one other job offer besides the timeshare sales position so he quickly put two and two together. "Sure, I remember you; you're the banker from Northern California. Did you ever find anybody to fill that position?"

"Why, are you interested?"

"No, just curious."

"Well, we are still looking. We just haven't been able to find anybody matching your unique set of skills."

Bernie hesitated while the cards were being dealt. He had sixteen and the dealer had a jack showing. He took a hit and was dealt a jack. He made a funny face as the dealer swept up Bernie's busted hand and ante.

Bernie gave Kevin a sincere look and said, "We should talk again; we both might have a different perspective now."

Mulrooney didn't respond as he motioned for the dealer to hit his thirteen. He smiled when the dealer turned up an eight. He continued to watch as the dealer flipped over his hole card, exposing a deuce. Someone at the table mumbled, "Hope there's a face card coming up."

The smug dealer turned over a nine. Kevin slapped his hand on the table but didn't utter anything.

While the dealer was clearing up the cards, Kevin looked up at Bernie. "You staying here?"

"Yup, and you?"

"I'm living here now; I have a condo just east of town."

They both put down their next bets, and their attention waned as the dealer began flipping over cards again. It was their last serious conversation of the night.

Ten o'clock the next morning, Bernie was packing his carry-on luggage when the phone rang in his room. "Hello?" he answered inquisitively since it was still too early for his ride to have arrived.

"Mr. Boyer," the voice on the other end began, "this is Kevin Mulrooney. Can we meet someplace and talk?"

"Sure. It will have to be soon, I'm heading for the airport in an hour."

"How are you getting to the airport?"

"The resort's limo."

"Suppose I meet you at your hotel in . . . say thirty minutes and I drive you to the airport?"

"That works for me. I'll be in the café having breakfast."

■ ■ ■

The café at the Peppermill was jammed. All the tables around

Bernie's were filled when Kevin walked in and sat down across from the banker. "Thanks for agreeing to meet me this morning, Mr. Boyer."

"Please, Kevin, call me Bernie."

"Okay, Bernie; I was thinking about the last time we met and the opportunity you presented. At the time, I really hadn't thought about doing anything like that again. It seemed too risky. However, since then I've had some ideas which could alleviate much of the risk. If I were to get into something like this again, it would have to be totally under my terms. Understood?"

Cautiously, Bernie replied, "Oooookay . . . like what terms?"

"Before we even go there, I need to know about your CFO. What's his role in this and can we trust him?"

"Our CFO is Alvin Aires, he's my wife's sister's boy. He wanted to do this on his own, but I wasn't going to put my future in the hands of an amateur. He'll be glad to have a professional mentoring him."

A broad smile bloomed on Kevin's face. "Oh, that's even better. All right, here's the deal. I'll come in as a consultant for one year training Alvin to take it over."

Bernie was nodding as Kevin continued, "I'm assuming you're already sitting on a pile of cash, right?"

Boastfully, Bernie quickly scanned the nearby tables to make sure no one was getting too nosey then he whispered, "Yeah . . . it's got to be close to $2 million."

Kevin's face lit up. "Good, you're going to need it. First, you're going to pay me $100K up front, next you and your brother are going to buy up as many cash-producing businesses as you can find . . . pizza joints, cheap gas stations, bars, restaurants, convenience stores, massage parlors, nail salons, and every kind of vending machine including electronic tellers. You can't have too many legal cash-producing businesses. You might even consider buying some property for cash in Central America. Getting the picture?"

Bernie nodded, and Mulrooney continued, "We're only

going to do two things: first, you're going to use cash to buy these assets; second, we are going to start blending your tainted cash with the proceeds from these businesses. Granted, the legit ones will have to pay more income tax, but that's a small price to pay to wash away your ongoing windfall. Then, when I'm convinced Alvin can handle it, I'll disappear with an additional half-mil. Does this sound okay with you?"

"Yeah, but I'll have to run this by my brother Clete. I'll have an answer in a few days."

"Good, let's head out to catch your plane; we can talk some more on the way."

CHAPTER 30

"Well, how about that," Mike exclaimed, "looks like he stopped behind the bank. Wonder what he's up to? Let's give him a minute then drive by to make sure his car is still parked in the lot."

They passed by the parking lot just in time to see Mulrooney close and lock the bank's glass door behind him and disappear up the stairs leading to the executive offices.

"Let's drive around the block, I can't imagine he'll be long," Mike said.

After three trips around, Kevin still hadn't emerged. "I'm going to park around the corner and wait," Dana declared. "We can pick him up again once he's back on 101."

It was after 11 p.m. when his vehicle started moving again. "I don't think he's headed for the highway," Mike announced. "It looks like he's headed south on J Street. Turn left at the corner, we'll run parallel with him on Meridian Street."

Ten streets later, Kevin turned right on 4th Street, drove a few blocks, then stopped in another parking lot. This time it was in front of a run-down apartment building.

"I'll bet this is Shirley's place," Dana observed. "Mulrooney lives in a single-family house just outside of town. I'm going to park across the street and saunter on over so I can check the names on the mail boxes."

"You want me to come along?"

"No, that would be too conspicuous; anyway, I'm armed. I can handle this alone."

"Okay, Wonder Woman, do your stuff."

Mike watched as Dana made her way to the lobby of a 1970s-style wooden, two-story building in desperate need of a paint job. The main door was not locked; Dana walked right in. She was back out in less than ten seconds. Sliding back into the driver's seat, she announced, "There's a Shirley Schneer living in apartment 1A. You think that's his girlfriend?"

Mike let out a loud puff followed by a sour look before he responded, "The barmaid was definitely named Shirley. We better get comfortable."

"You think he's here for the night?" Dana asked.

"Who knows? It could just be a farewell quickie. Let's give him an hour and see what happens."

Forty-five minutes later Kevin with Shirley hanging all over him appeared in the lobby. She was wearing nothing but a pink baby-doll top and her hair was all disheveled. From their parking spot across the street they watched the couple kiss and embrace.

Mike bemoaned, "Damn, I didn't need to witness that. I haven't seen my wife in a month. She's been in Dallas helping our youngest daughter take care of our new twin grand-daughters. "

Mike's personal revelation surprised Dana even though the scene evoked provocative memories of her last night with Bruce. Shaking off the stimulation, she nonchalantly asked, "How many kids do you have?"

"Two girls, both a two-hour plane ride away."

Just then Mulrooney and Shirley decided they had had enough and broke off their clench. Mulrooney said something then turned and headed out the door. Shirley followed him a few steps outside before stopping and yelling something. Kevin turned, said something back then continued . . . not for his SUV but for a blue, beat-up Saturn. "Shit," Mike murmured, "he really stopped by to switch vehicles."

"I guess we'll just have to trust the tailing skills they taught me at Wonder Women School."

"Yeah; meanwhile, keep an eye on which way he heads, I'm going to run over and retrieve the GPS from his SUV."

Mike was back in less than thirty seconds and Mulrooney's taillights were still visible. Dana sped after the Saturn. She was able to skillfully fall in a safe distance behind. After Mulrooney turned on Highway 101, it was easier for her to blend in among the northbound traffic. Their quarry turned off the highway onto Northcrest Drive and drove a few blocks before pulling up to the entrance of a self-storage facility. Kevin rolled down his window, punched a code into a keyboard, and waited for the security gate to slide open.

Dana was coasting past while Kevin was punching in the access code. "Don't stop," Mike said, "just slow down to a crawl. I'm going to hop out and see if I can get in before the gate closes."

The fifty-five-year-old former Treasury agent lost his balance as he jumped out of the moving vehicle. Falling on his right elbow, he tore the right pants leg at the knee and the sleeve of his $600 Michael Kors suit. Blood stained his pants. Undeterred, he popped up and dashed for the slowly closing opening. He was able to squeeze through with only inches to spare. The Saturn was parked outside the third building and Mulrooney was nowhere in sight. Mike headed straight for the vehicle, placing the GPS tracker in the right rear wheel well. He then retreated to the far side of the building closest to the gate and waited.

Kevin Mulrooney took less than fifteen minutes to return with a large suitcase and a stainless steel briefcase. Mike chuckled to himself thinking, *Did I have him pegged or what?*

Once out the gate, the Saturn turned in the direction of Highway 101 while Mike Musgrave slipped out just before it closed. He scanned up and down the street looking for Dana. A few seconds later, she flashed her headlights. She was sitting directly across the street in the parking lot of an auto body shop.

Mike dashed across the street and jumped in the car. He was hardly settled when Dana asked in jest, "How you feeling after bouncing off the pavement like that?"

Ignoring her teasing tone, Mike responded earnestly, "I'm fine, just a little bloody and embarrassed; not to mention I ruined my favorite suit."

"Well, if it's any consolation, I'm impressed with your prediction he would run. You might not be as nimble as you used to be, but your instincts are still well-honed."

"Yeah, and I always thought the mind was the first thing to go."

"You didn't bust your iPhone, did you?" Dana asked, only half kidding.

"Nope, I verified the signal while I was waiting for him to come out." Checking the screen on his phone, he declared, "In fact, I've got him again on 101 headed north."

Still in a playful mood, Dana challenged Musgrave, "I'll bet you a ten-spot he's going to make a beeline for the Oregon border."

"You're not going to sucker me into that bet," Mike responded. "I'm seventy-five percent certain he's headed for Canada. The only question in my mind is whether he'll cut off on 199 and swing over to I-5 or stay on 101 all the way up the coast? Heading over to I-5 would be the fastest way to the border as long as he can control his girlfriend's old jalopy at night on 199's twists and turns."

"Well, if he's hoping to cross the Canadian border before we figure out he's not showing for the meeting, he's got to take the shortest route."

"I'm with you. How are you about navigating 199 at night?"

"Looking forward to it. Speeding around pitch-black curves with thousand-foot drop-offs is another class at Wonder Women School. I'm more worried whether you can handle it."

"Bring it on; I can take anything Wonder Woman can dish out."

CHAPTER 31

"You really think they are going to try something tonight?" Bart asked.

"No, but I wouldn't put it past them," Bruce replied. "It can't hurt to set up surveillance. After all, we did bring in reinforcements as a precaution."

"I agree with Bruce," Victor commented. "You saw the look on Junior's face. He's pissed, but more than anything, he's worried now that I told him I sent my family away and some of my buddies have stopped by."

"Yeah," Bruce added, "it makes sense, if they were contemplating something, they'll likely do it soon rather than later. They don't have to wait for any help; as we witnessed, they already have some pretty heavy hitters on their payroll. Why not use those high-priced mercenaries for a preemptive strike."

"Okay, I'm convinced. What can I do?" Bart asked.

Turning his head away from Bart, Bruce gave Victor a mischievous wink. "Ah, why don't you go to bed early and rest up; tomorrow might be a busy day."

Bart's face turned scarlet and his tone was acerbic. "Stick it! You guys aren't putting me out to pasture yet."

"Jeez, Bart, don't get your balls in an uproar; I was just kidding."

"I know; so was I. However, I will be glad to stay warm in

here cradling my shotgun while you guys lie around on wet ground freezing *your* balls off."

Then, breaking out in a mischievous grin, he added, "However, if you'd like, I'll keep a pot of hot coffee on for you."

All of a sudden Bruce got real serious. "Actually, Bart, if they strike, Boyer's storm troopers could be coming from any direction. How do you feel about functioning as our command and control center?"

Bruce could immediately tell by Bart's expression he was interested but wary so he didn't wait for a reply. "You'd be using two really neat high-tech systems we've brought along with us. The first is a thermal imaging night-vision camera, the FLIR TS32r Pro Scout. The other system is a Sonetics four-person wireless communications system. Used together, these two surveillance tools should give us a distinct advantage over any intruders. The only catch is our lives may depend on you learning how to operate both of these in the next couple of hours."

Bart's apprehension continued to dominate his facial expression while his eyes flashed back and forth between Bruce and Vic until he asked, "How complicated are these things?"

"Don't look so worried, Eitan is an expert and an excellent teacher. He'll have you proficient in both systems before you know it. Meanwhile, Vic and I need to find a place where you and a sniper will have a 360-degree panoramic view of the ranch. Any ideas, Vic?"

"Not off the top of my head, but let's take a walk outside."

Walking around the property, they reached the conclusion that the barn loft provided the best view of the ranch but would only provide a 180-degree panorama unless one was constantly running back and forth between the two loft doors at either end. Vic finally said, "We could station Bart at one door and the sniper at the other, but if the bad guys come from more than one direction at the same time, they'd be like a one-armed paperhanger."

Vic hesitated while he carefully inspected the barn one more time. After a few anxious seconds he announced, "Well, it looks like we are just going to have to build a temporary stand up on the roof."

"I agree," Bruce replied. "Didn't I see a four-by-eight piece of three-quarter-inch plywood in the barn with a bunch of four-by-four posts?"

"I believe you did," Vic acknowledged.

"Good! Suppose we nail a four-by-four leg to each corner of a sheet. Assuming we cut the legs at the correct length and at the appropriate angle, we might be able to balance the plywood on the peak. The legs should act as outriggers to prevent the platform from teetering."

"Interesting thought," Vic replied. "Let's give it a try."

It took them almost an hour to get the measurements of the legs right, to cut them, and to safely balance their platform on the barn roof. It was close quarters, but the three-quarter-inch sheet of plywood was just rigid enough to hold Bart's weight along with all his electronic gear and a former Air Force sniper.

After they had Bart and the sniper all set up, Vic and Bruce concealed themselves in the trees on the south side of the barn approximately two hundred yards away. Azzan and Eitan did the same on the north side. The final man set up on the ground just inside the doors to the barn. Each team and the man inside the barn were in constant contact with Bart via the wireless communications equipment. Bruce, Vic, Azzan, and Eitan each had on night-vision goggles.

Bart used the thermal imaging camera to pinpoint each team and then tested their wireless communications. They were ready for action before 11 p.m.; all they had left to do was wait for the anticipated intruders.

■ ■ ■

Mulrooney took the 199 exit headed for I-5 and Grants Pass, Oregon. Dana had already arranged for assistance from the Portland FBI office. As soon as Mulrooney took the 199 turn-off, Dana called the duty officer, who dispatched a two-man team from Portland for the interception. A short time later,

Dana received a call from Special Agent John Penn stating the Oregon state police would actually make the stop.

In a pitch-black section of Interstate 5 a few desolate miles south of Canyonville, Oregon, Dana picked up the flashing red-and-blue lights from almost a mile away. Two state police cruisers and an FBI SUV had the blue Saturn with California plates sandwiched between them off on the shoulder. Special Agent Penn and another agent were standing on the passenger side of their vehicle talking to two troopers while Mulrooney, looking dejected, was handcuffed in the backseat.

Special Agent Penn didn't wait for Dana to get out of her vehicle before heading in her direction. He intercepted her before she got within earshot of the troopers. Attempting to conceal the uneasiness he was feeling about the traffic stop and detention, Penn smiled as he greeted Dana and Mike. "Nice night for a ride in the country, isn't it?"

Dana extended her hand to shake Penn's. "Sure is, Special Agent Penn. Let me introduce you to former Treasury Agent Mike Musgrave. Mike's been working for us as a consultant on this case."

While the three exchanged handshakes, Penn got right to business. "So, since I'm still in the dark myself, I wasn't able to explain to the troopers why we requested they pull the citizen over and detain him until you arrived. Would you like to fill me in now?"

Dana pursed her lips. "Sorry for keeping you in the dark, Penn. At this point, we've identified Mulrooney as a person-of-interest in a potential national security issue. We are not yet sure of the exact nature of the threat, but the whole thing is complicated by our suspicion that some Northern California law enforcement officials may have been compromised. For that reason, I'd like to keep a lid on this for now. You think this can be arranged?"

Special Agent Penn's consternation showed on his face, but he didn't hesitate to respond. "Depends. What do you want to do with Mulrooney now?"

"I'd like to find a place close by to go through his personals and interrogate him without actually logging him in anywhere."

"There's a state police district headquarters facility about thirty miles south of here in Central Point."

"That's perfect. How can we get access?"

"We'll have to get on the phone with the area commander. He's going to want to know what this is all about."

"Yeah, I'd be surprised if he didn't. I'm prepared to tell him the same thing I just told you. So we can call him right now."

Penn used his cell phone to dial the district commander. "Captain, this is Special Agent Penn again. Wonder if you can accommodate another favor?"

"Depends, Penn. What do you need?"

"I'm going to turn you over to FBI Special Agent Dana Wise from Washington, DC; she's the one who is actually making the request. Okay?"

The captain didn't respond immediately. "So you're not in charge, Agent Penn?"

"That's an affirmative, Captain Reed."

"Interesting . . . put her on."

Dana smiled at Penn as she took his cell phone. "Hello, Captain Reed, I'm actually a special assistant to Director Sardo." Dana paused, giving her revelation time to sink in. "The director would be grateful if you would allow me to use your Central Point facility for a few hours to interrogate this suspect. At this point the only information I am authorized to release to you is that we believe the subject is potentially a national security risk."

"Really," the captain replied with just a smidgen of doubt in his voice. The phone went silent while he considered his options.

Dana gave him several seconds before she asked, "Are you still there, Captain Reed?"

Ignoring her question, he replied, "I'll meet you at Central Point."

"Great, thank you, Captain. You won't regret this."

"We'll see," he replied skeptically.

While everyone's eyes were fixed on Dana, Mike, unnoticed, stealthily made his way to the Saturn to retrieve the GPS tracking device.

A half-hour later, Dana and Mike were sitting in a room at the Central Point command office going through Mulrooney's personal effects while he was locked in an interrogation room.

"We've hit the jackpot," Mike said. "He's carrying at least a hundred grand in cash, a list of offshore bank accounts, and two fake passports. I'm betting this portable hard drive is intended to be some kind of an insurance policy, but he never figured he'd be caught with it in his possession. I can't wait to access it."

"Yeah, me too. Let's go in and see if he'll give us a verbal preview of what we can expect."

When Dana and Mike entered the interrogation room, Mulrooney was desperately attempting to hide his panic. "I suppose your original offer of complete immunity is off the table now."

Mike chuckled and Dana scowled. Mulrooney could easily guess who was going to be the bad cop. Looking at Musgrave, he said, "I know a lot more than you'll find on that hard drive. If . . ."

Dana cut him off. "We don't have time to play your games, Mulrooney. You're looking at the death penalty for two murders; I need a complete confession right now before I even consider talking to you about a deal."

Mulrooney gave Mike a pleading look but his old nemesis remained stone-faced. "Okay . . . okay, the only thing on the hard drive is the history of the Boyers' money laundering but it doesn't contain any information about their partners."

Kevin paused while scrutinizing Mike's and Dana's faces for any sign he had struck a chord. Unable to detect anything, he decided to up the ante. "But I can give you the names and details of how the real big boys of international money laundering and smuggling operate. I'm talking about Mexican,

Guatemalan, and Bulgarian cartels and their connections to Middle Eastern terrorist groups. I can even provide you with the names of countless complicit government officials from dozens of countries. What I know will make the Boyers' activities look like chopped liver."

"So you say, Kevin. I'll tell you what, my partner here is going to load your external hard drive up on his computer and start taking notes. In the meantime, you're going to begin telling me everything. When we're done, I'm going to compare what you've told me to what Mike learns. Assuming you actually do have some information not on the drive, you might just avoid the death penalty."

While Mike left the room, Dana took a small tape recorder out of her purse, turned it on and put it on the table in front of Mulrooney. "Start talking," she commanded.

Over the next two hours, Mulrooney was true to his word, revealing names and invaluable details on drug smuggling, money laundering, and offshore political corruption along with critical details into the financing channels of a half-dozen terrorist groups. Unfortunately, he claimed to be unable to reveal anything about the general's death or Allie's disappearance.

After comparing Mike's notes from the hard drive to Dana's tape of Kevin's disclosures, there was one piece of digital information Dana wanted to pursue further. Returning to the interrogation room where Kevin was being held, she accusingly asked, "What are you holding back on Xenophon?"

"Nothing, they're just one of the security firms hired to protect the Boyers' properties. Bernie once mentioned Xenophon is a big-time outfit with government contracts all over the world."

"Were they guarding the sawmill on the night John Slaughter died?"

"Sure, they were contracted a month or two before that."

"I think you're holding something back," Dana said, her eyes boring into Mulrooney's.

Clearly intimidated, Kevin stared at his hands and picked

at his thumbnail with the opposite index finger. After a long pause he pursed his lips together before he reluctantly admitted, "There is one thing that may be important." Then he paused again.

"Are you going to tell me?" Dana asked in an impatient tone.

Still hesitant, Mulrooney sighed before he said in almost a hushed tone, "Shortly after the general's death Bernie made a large cash payment to at least three Xenophon employees."

Dana pressed him further. "Is that it?"

This time, Kevin's distress was jacked up another notch and he briefly stuttered. "Th . . . th . . . th . . . ere's something else going down because today Bernie told me to set aside one million in cash for the end of the week when the head of Xenophon would be coming to pick it up."

"If you want any break at all, tell us what they're up to," Dana advised him.

"I told you all I know. You don't think these people confide all their shit in me . . . do you?"

"Bullshit, Kevin, maybe you don't know the exact details as to what's going to happen, but you're smart enough to make an educated guess. I'll tell you what, I'm going to go see what else Mike has gleaned from your hard drive and when I come back you better have something for me on the Boyers' plans."

Dana let Mulrooney stew for fifteen minutes before she returned to the interrogation room along with Mike Musgrave. Kevin could tell just by the look on both their faces that he was cooked.

Mike started in first. "You lied to us, Kevin, there are enough links and threads on that hard drive to give us all the same information you verbally gave to Dana."

Dana cut in. "That means the deal is off and unless you can give us something new, not only are we going to charge you as being an accessory to murder after the fact, we are going to charge you as a co-conspirator to whatever is going down tonight."

"Whoa!" Mulrooney howled. "I really don't know what

they're up to, all I heard was there was supposed to be some kind of synchronized thing at 3 a.m. in Colorado and Rohnerville."

Dana's jaw dropped. She gave a quick glance at her watch. "Shit!" she muttered loud enough for everyone to hear then bolted out of the room with Musgrave trailing right behind her. "What's up?" Mike asked as he trailed Dana down the hall; she didn't answer as she had already hit Bruce's speed dial number on her phone and was waiting for him to pick up. She let it ring until it went into his voice mail. "Bruce, they're going after Tanya and the kids at Bart's and the girlfriend at Miles' place. Both assaults are planned for 3 a.m."

After she hung up, she turned to Mike. "You stay here with Special Agent Penn. Fill him in and see if the two of you can get some more out of this scumbag. I've got to get back to Eureka."

"That's a long drive; you'll never get back in time."

"I don't plan on driving. I saw a state police helicopter out back. I'm going to talk Captain Reed into having one of his guys fly me down there. I've got forty-five minutes."

Dana had already given Captain Reed an overview of the situation including her concerns about the Humboldt County sheriff. Now, desperate for his cooperation, she briefly filled him on what they had just learned. In spite of what she had told him, he refused to let one of his choppers penetrate California air space without at least notifying the California state police. Dana pleaded with him, but he remained steadfast. Frustrated, she woke up Director Sardo. Quickly she described both perilous situations and her frustration with the Oregon captain's position. After he promised to immediately dispatch agents to both sites, he assured her he'd get Captain Reed's cooperation.

Within ten minutes, two FBI helicopters were dispatched from Sacramento to Rohnerville. Each chopper contained a three-man SWAT team. Two SUVs containing a total of eight agents were also racing from Denver to Evergreen.

While she was waiting for her boss's assistance, Dana called David Tanner, who provided her with both Bart's home phone number in Evergreen and his cell phone number. Both of her calls went to voice mail, where she left urgent messages.

The commissioner of the California Highway Patrol was pissed when his private telephone woke him up from a deep sleep. Ripping the phone off its receiver, he was about to give the caller a piece of his mind when the voice on the other end declared, "Tom, this is Sam Sardo; sorry to wake you at this hour, but it couldn't wait till the morning."

The voice of the FBI director, whom he had known for years, shook Tom out of his ugly mood. His voice still gravelly, he responded, "So I'm guessing this isn't a social call, Tom."

"Unfortunately, no . . . I need your help on an extremely serious situation. I've just ordered a SWAT team from Sacramento to Eureka in helicopters to hopefully prevent an attack on a federal witness. Unfortunately, based upon some of the evidence we have, the local law enforcement organizations may have been compromised. Although we don't suspect any of your guys are involved, we can't take a chance the locals are monitoring your communications. As an urgent matter of life and death, I'm requesting you let our guys handle the initial contact. Unfortunately, they may not be able to get up there from Sacramento in time. That leaves us with the only other federal resource with a chance of getting there in time just over the border in Oregon. I'm requesting you authorize an Oregon state police helicopter to cross over to your jurisdiction with one of my people on board. Will you do that, Sam?"

After a brief hesitation, the commissioner responded, "Absolutely, Tom! Is there anything else we can do to assist?"

"I would appreciate if you could keep a lid on this until we can get our boots on the ground."

"That might be risky if one of my units stumbles across what appears to be a chaotic situation."

"I know, Tom, but at this point, I don't think we have any other choice."

"Okay, if you're that sure, I'll go along. I assume I can expect a heads-up with some additional details as soon as the situation stabilizes?"

"You've got my word; I'll personally give you a call."

Thirty seconds later, Captain Reed got a call from the director, and Dana was in the air in less than ten minutes.

■ ■ ■

It wasn't until 2:30 that Bruce realized he had left his phone on the kitchen table, and he was anxious to find out how Dana and Mike had made out with Mulrooney. Rather than leave his partner alone in the woods, he radioed Bart, asking him to call her for an update.

Almost as soon as her phone started to vibrate, Dana realized the number on the screen was Bart's cell phone. She never even let him even start talking. "Bart, where's Bruce?"

"He's on surveillance in the woods, we're expecting some kind of an assault tonight by the Boyers."

"Which woods?" Dana urgently asked.

"Slaughter's."

With anxiety seeping through her voice Dana abruptly cut in, "Wrong place! They're going after the girlfriend at Miles' place and after Tanya and the kids at yours!"

"Holy shit!" Bart uttered, but again Dana cut in.

"Both are scheduled for 3 a.m., you have less than twenty-five minutes to get ready. I'm on my way in a helicopter with an ETA of 3:15. I have reinforcements headed to both places. I think they're close enough to your Evergreen house to get there in time, but they're probably not going to make it to Miles'. You guys got to get over there."

"Have you called Tanya or Patty Jo?" Bart asked apprehensively.

"Tried but got no answer. As soon as I hang up, I'll try your home phone again. David is attempting to call Patty Jo's cell phone. Vic should try Tanya's."

CHAPTER 32

With the windows of her third-floor bedroom wide open, the mountain air at eight thousand feet had plunged the temperature to nearly sixty degrees. Tanya was lying in bed with the sheets pulled up to her neck, attempting to avoid braving the chill in order to shut the windows. Meanwhile she was bemoaning the prospect of not seeing Vic and the kids for almost a year. For the umpteenth time, she rolled over on her side to check the alarm clock sitting on the night stand.

"Two forty-five," she mumbled under her breath. "No sense lying here. Might as well get up and close the windows then go down and keep Joe company."

Joe and his partner downstairs, Rich, were Vic and Tanya's friends from the Air Force. They were both still young, having retired before their thirty-eighth birthdays as air police NCOs. Over six feet tall and around two hundred pounds, they were skilled in martial arts and knew how to handle multiple weapons.

Joe, bundled up in a gray hooded sweatshirt, was on the last few minutes of his watch when Tanya joined him on the side deck.

"Can't sleep?" Joe asked.

"Just trying to get my body used to ungodly hours before I deploy," she replied jokingly. "Can I get you something to drink?"

"A cup of hot tea would be nice."

"Okay, I'll heat up some water."

At that moment, four diminutive Mexican intruders clad in black and wearing ski masks were methodically working their way downhill from the highway toward Bart's back deck. They were instructed to begin the assault at 3 a.m., but their Tijuana handler had failed to mention it was supposed to be 3 a.m. Pacific time; they were an hour early.

The house sat on the south side of a mountain some thirty feet above Aspen Drive and two hundred yards below Highway 74. The driveway off Aspen Drive was a curved uphill concrete slab over one hundred feet long. The back deck was almost twenty feet higher than the front garage doors.

There were twenty steps on the L-shaped staircase leading up from the garage level to the front door. In the back, one set of three outside steps led to both decks. The house had four entrances, one through the garage to a large game room and spare bedroom suite off to the far side. The front door, at the top of the staircase, led to a hallway on the main level. To the right was the laundry room, a full bath, and a large office. In the center of the hall, two staircases converged, one from downstairs and the other leading to the third floor with four more bedrooms. Except for the laundry room and bathroom, the whole main level was done in dark hardwood floors. Off to the left of the main entrance was a large combination great room, kitchen, and dining area. Gigantic pine support beams and posts held up the twenty-foot-high cedar ceiling. Except for the four two-foot-diameter supports, the entire front-facing great room overlooked a magnificent mountain meadow through large tinted windows. On the far end of the kitchen a normal-size glass door opened up on to the side deck. A sliding glass door in the dining area led to the back deck. Both deck areas were connected.

The kettle was just beginning to whistle when Tanya began walking back to the side deck to ask Joe how he liked his tea. Just as she reached the glass door, Joe's body flopped to the deck a few feet on the other side of the door. A dark liquid began seeping out onto the deck boards from under his head. Tanya froze. Her first thought was to rush out on to the deck to help Joe. Then her training and motherly instincts kicked in. She made an abrupt U-turn, sprinting for the staircase that split the modern three-story house in half. In spite of her primal fear for her children, she knew she couldn't protect them alone, she needed to first warn Rick downstairs. Jumping down all six steps, she almost slammed into the wall.

Rich was in the bathroom dousing his face with cold water. He heard Tanya's thump as she landed on the slate floor. Alarmed, he immediately assumed a defensive position.

"We're under attack!" Tanya shouted. "Joe's been shot. I'm going up to protect the kids and Patty Jo."

Tanya turned and sprinted back to the staircase, bounding three at a time up the steps to the third floor. Reaching the top, she first woke the three kids as quickly and quietly as she could. She then herded them into the master bedroom. Patty Jo was still fast asleep. Shaking her, Tanya's voice was full of urgency. "Patty Jo, get up, we're under attack . . . take the kids into the bathroom and lock the door."

Patty Jo was out of bed and instantly alert as Tanya sprinted back to her bedroom in a desperate attempt to quickly locate and load her weapon.

While Tanya was rummaging through her luggage for her quick access pistol safe, Rich had carefully made it upstairs to the kitchen. After catching a brief glimpse of Joe's lifeless body on the side deck, he assumed a defensive position in the kitchen, crouched between the island counter and the kitchen sink. He had an excellent line of fire at anyone attempting to assault the kitchen from either the side door or the sliding glass doors leading from the deck.

After Patty Jo ushered the three children into the bathroom she had them lock the door and sit in the tub while she hurriedly returned to her bedroom. Dashing into the walk-in closet, she located the shotgun Bart always kept hidden there.

Finding it, she groped around the sweater shelf for the box of shells.

■ ■ ■

Surveying the large room beyond the counters, Rich felt as if he was in a fishbowl, with floor-to-ceiling windows facing out the front of the house and glass doors on two sides. After seeing Joe's body, the first thing he did was push the kitchen table and all six chairs up against the back sliding glass door. Anyone attempting to enter from that direction would likely be momentarily hampered by the obstacles.

Meanwhile, after retrieving and loading her weapon, Tanya positioned herself on the third-floor landing. She was lying on her stomach out of sight from anyone on the second floor. Training her Beretta M9 between the railing's wooden support spindles, she thought, *They're not getting up three steps without eating my lead.* The staircase leading between floors was two-tiered. It began directly below Tanya's position with six steps leading to an intermediate landing four feet below and directly in front of her. Then the staircase did a 180-degree turn before six more steps led to the third floor. Moonlight streaming in through a large window on the landing gave her all the light she needed.

Patty Jo crouched behind the bed diagonally opposite the door. She rested her left elbow and forearm on the top of the mattress, providing a stable support for the 12-guage Winchester 101 over-under double-barreled shotgun. She and her first husband, John Nicosia, had been avid trap shooters, so Patty Jo knew how to shoot. The only question in her mind was what her reaction would be when the target was another human being.

■ ■ ■

Simultaneously, deck chairs crashed through both glass doors, immediately followed by the sound of a grenade bouncing along the wood floor. Rich had anticipated this possibility and had stuffed his ears with pieces of paper towels and opened one of the cabinets under the counter pulling out the pots. As soon as he heard the clanking of the grenade on the wood floor he thrust his upper body into the cabinet, closed his eyes and covered his ears with his hands. It was a flashbang grenade, and its detonation occurred on the far side of the large family room behind a leather couch. Between the couch and his precautions, Rich was able to quickly recover from the concussion.

He had already resumed a shooting position before the first dark-clad assailant attempted to breach the back sliding door by pushing the table and chairs out of his way. He never made it inside as Rich put the first round into his side and the second into his neck. Before he had a chance to turn and face the side entrance, a second invader leaped through the broken glass, firing wildly in Rich's direction. The slugs harmlessly whizzed over his head into the sink counter. Before Rich could get off a shot, the shooter rolled out of his field of vision. While he was focused on the second intruder, a third gunmen burst through the back door and pumped three bullets into Rich's back.

The Rocks' next-door neighbor, Jerry Blasé, an airlines pilot, was getting ready to drive to Denver International Airport for his 6:00 commute to American Airline's Dallas hub when he heard the first grenade and saw a momentary flash out his bathroom window. Immediately he ran to his back deck, where he heard several gunshots and saw the muzzle flashes. Without hesitation, he quickly ran back inside to dial 911.

The three remaining gunmen methodically searched the two lower levels of the house. Finding no one, they huddled at the base of the steps leading to the third floor. Tanya had not expected the first flashbang grenade, but the gunmen's lower level search had provided her sufficient time to recover her senses before one of the gunmen began slowly ascending the staircase. He hugged the inside wall and hesitated at each step. When he stopped on the third step Tanya had a clean shot. She fired once; the Parabellum projectile entered his face just below his nose on a downward trajectory, smashed through the roof of his mouth and out the back of his neck after severing his spinal cord between C4 and C5. His body crumpled and rolled partially back down the staircase. His surprised companions pulled him by his legs off the steps and regrouped. Their mission was to take Tanya and the children hostage, but that was before they had lost two of their companions.

As the assault team's leader stood looking at their second casualty, he contemplated aborting the mission, but the prospect of now splitting their bonus only two ways incited his confidence. Besides, failure was not an option the cartel's leadership accepted. If they could not pull off the kidnapping, his instructions were to kill everyone in the house. Suddenly, it dawned on him one of his dead partners had another grenade. He frisked the body lying at his feet, finding nothing. Quickly moving back into the kitchen he located the body of the other slain intruder, recovering the extra grenade. Returning to the base of the stairs, he instructed his remaining partner to attempt to distract Tanya by firing through the ceiling. The tactic worked, forcing Tanya to roll sideways across the floor. At that same instant the leader pulled the pin and flipped the last flashbang grenade up over the landing. Luck was in Tanya's favor; the grenade flew through the bathroom door directly behind where she had been positioned. It bounced off the ceramic floor, rolling behind the toilet bowl before it detonated. Tanya heard it bounce off the floor. Her reaction was instant, closing her eyes and covering her head and ears with her hands and forearms. The concussion was still enough to momentarily stun her. Downstairs and shielded from the blast, the two assailants hardly hesitated before rushing up the stairs. They were on top of Tanya before she had a chance to recover. She was still lying motionless on her stomach when the leader, in retaliation for his dead companions, kicked her in her right side then, for good measure, in the face. While the leader was occupied neutralizing Tanya, the second assailant did a quick sweep of the three bedrooms with open doors finding them empty. Standing in front of the last closed door, he received a nod from his leader before kicking in the door and busting into the room. The leader stood in astonishment as instantaneously there was a loud blast and his partner was lifted off his feet. The Mexican's body bounced off the door jamb before tumbling to the floor like a rag doll. The impact sent his handgun tumbling to the floor, landing unnoticed less than a foot from Tanya's left side.

Momentarily, the last assailant's instinct compelled him to dive into the room with his gun blazing, but he quickly realized that would be an unnecessary risk. After all, he did have their primary target lying unconscious at his feet. If he couldn't kidnap the whole family, the mother would have to suffice. Just as he began to turn in the mother's direction, to his surprise she moved. In the split second it took his brain to register what was happening, Tanya had snatched up the dead gunman's weapon with her left hand, raised it, and fired upward. The projectile hit him in the underside of his forearm, shattering his ulna and causing him to be incapable of holding on to his gun. He gasped in pain but had the sense to hurl himself down the stairs just as Tanya's second shot whizzed past his ear. When he hit the middle landing his head bounced off the wall, denting the wallboard. Though he was momentarily stunned, fear somehow gave him the capacity to ignore the blow to his head and the searing pain from his broken arm. Instinctively, he rolled down the final three steps into the foyer, stumbled to his feet and sprinted out the front door just as police sirens screamed in the distance.

He staggered down the outside stairs leading to the driveway, where he prayed his only remaining associate would be waiting in their getaway vehicle.

CHAPTER 33

At 2:45 a.m., Clete Junior and Deputy Sheriff Ken Boyer were standing in a remote corner of Redwood Acres Fairgrounds on the east side of Eureka. Clete had driven to the fairgrounds in his personal pickup while Ken, who was still on-duty, sat in his patrol car.

Clete was fidgety while Ken was downright nervous. "Look, Ken, I don't like this any more than you do, but the stakes are too high. Right now, it's only a rumor the kid was kidnapped by a submarine. If his girlfriend really does have pictures of the *Yaht Zee* and the sub, we'll all be up shit creek. This diversion is the best way to keep the rest of the sheriff's department from interrupting the Xenophon boys."

"I know, Junior; it's not the assault or creating this diversion that's got me nervous, it's you shooting at my car. Do I really have to be sitting in it when you do it? Suppose you hit me?"

"Christ, Ken!" his brother shouted. "What do you think, I'm some kind of an amateur? Besides, if you're not sitting in the driver's seat, there will be glass all over it instead of on you."

Although Ken wasn't convinced glass on the seat would ever be noticed, he scowled at his brother. "Oh fuck it; let's get this over with."

Ken got back in his patrol car and Junior walked about a hundred feet away before he turned, raised his twenty-two rifle, and began firing. He put two bullets into the passenger side windshield and three rounds into the front grill.

When he was finished he walked back to the patrol car to check on his brother. Ken was sitting motionless just staring at the two holes in his windshield.

"You okay, Ken?" his brother asked, chuckling.

It took Ken several seconds to respond sourly, "I'm fine. That's the first time I've ever been shot at. I actually felt one of the bullets whizz by my ear. I hope you're satisfied, I've got glass all over me."

Attempting to prevent himself from laughing at his younger brother's distress, Junior suggested, "We ought to get moving; why don't you wait two minutes for me to get out of here before you call it in."

"Okay," Ken replied halfheartedly.

Junior leaned over into the open window with his forearms resting on the window frame. "Are you sure you're going to be okay?"

Shaking his head as if to snap himself out of a trance, Ken turned his head toward his brother and said, "You better get going."

Two minutes later Deputy Sheriff Ken Boyer called in on his car radio, "Shots fired at the fairgrounds; in pursuit of two suspects on foot heading toward Ryan Creek."

That call would occupy the Humboldt County Sheriff's Department's attention for almost an hour until they received their first call of shots fired fifteen miles south in rural Tompkins Hill.

■ ■ ■

Bart was frantic as he yelled into the speaker, "We're wrong, they're not coming here, they're going after Tanya and the kids in Colorado and Willow at Miles' place!"

There was a moment of dead air before Bruce responded with a sense of urgency in his voice, "Everyone meet at the barn ASAP. Bart, bring all that gear with you and pack it in the back of Vic's SUV. How much time do we have?"

"Maybe twenty minutes."

Vic tried to get Tanya while Bart dialed both Patty Jo's cell and his home phone number. All the calls went to voice mail. Meanwhile, Bruce called one of his guys, Bill, at Miles'. "You've got some nasty visitors coming at 3 a.m. I expect they're professionals and will come in force. We're on our way but we'll probably be late to the party."

"We'll be ready" was Bill's calm reply.

While their gear was being loaded in the Suburban, Bruce began barking orders. "Vic, you, me and Bart will take your SUV; I'll drive while you and Bart keep trying to contact Tanya and Patty Jo. Azzan, you take the rest of the guys in the rental."

Ten minutes later they were speeding bumper to bumper down Highway 36. In the backseat, Bart swore the right side of the vehicle was off the ground when Bruce made the sharp right corner at Hydesville. "Jeez, Bruce!" he shouted. "We won't do anybody any good if you roll this thing or hit a tree."

Vic swiveled in the front passenger seat, giving Bart the evil eye just as his cell phone began playing the Air Force theme song. The screen displayed his wife's cell phone number. "It's Tanya," he announced with relief.

While Bruce continued at breakneck speed, Vic answered his phone. "Hi babe, we've . . ."

A voice, not Tanya's, cut him off, "It's Patty Jo . . . there's been an attack . . . it's all over . . . the police and FBI are here now . . . we're all alive . . . the kids are fine . . . Tanya got a few bruises, but she'll be okay."

"Thank God!" Vic blurted out then relayed the good news to the rest of the team.

"Let me talk to Tanya," he said into the phone.

"She can't talk right now," Patty Jo replied. "The EMS people are loading her in the ambulance for a trip down to a nearby military hospital. Like I said, she's sustained a few bruises, but

I don't think they are serious. You really need to talk to the children; they've been extremely brave but could use some consoling. I'm going to give Cindy the phone; ask Bart to call me on my cell."

While Vic was talking to his children, Bart called Patty Jo.

"Hey," she answered.

"What happened?" he asked.

Struggling to control her agitation, Patty Jo began, "It was kind of confusing. I think there were at least four assailants. The first I was aware anything was wrong was when Tanya came running into the room with the kids ordering me to hide in the bathroom with them. After I locked them in the bathroom, I ran to the closet to get your shotgun; then I hid on the side of the bed. I recall lots of gunshots and a couple of explosions, then one of the attackers kicked in the bedroom door."

She hesitated and took a deep breath before she began again but in a much different, somber tone. "Joe and Rich are dead, so are three of the attackers."

Again she stopped and when she started her voice changed again; now she sounded more composed. "I blew him away . . . I pulled the trigger just like he was a clay pigeon. When I saw the blood and stuff splatter I felt a kind of elation. I think now I finally might understand how you felt after you dumped the acid on Al."

Bart was stunned; he didn't know what to say. Finally, after what seemed like minutes but was actually just seconds, he replied, "I'm glad you are all okay. Vic and I will be there as soon as we can. Right now, we believe there will be a second attack at Miles' place that we've got to attend to. I'll call you back in an hour or so, okay?"

"Damn!" Patty Jo replied. "Now I've got to worry about you too! Be careful, honey . . . I've got to go too. The FBI wants to drive me and the children to the hospital to be with Tanya."

Bart waited for Vic to end his conversation with the children before telling them what Patty Jo had revealed. Vic, already shaken, cursed when he learned about Joe and Rich.

Bruce didn't let him dwell on it for too long. "All right," he said into the microphone for everyone in both vehicles to hear, "same teams as back at Vic's. First thing we have to do is use the thermal imaging to figure out what we're up against. Then we'll fan out. Bart and Ron, just like back at the ranch, you'll track the action with the imaging equipment and keep us up to speed via the headsets. I'm guessing these guys are equipped with NVGs too, so our only advantage will be the big-picture view from Bart."

CHAPTER 34

Twenty years earlier, when Miles was promoted to operations manager of Slaughter Holdings, he and Anne purchased the fifty-acre farm along the Eel River with credit. The land was flat with only half the acreage cleared of trees. The house was a typical 1930s wooden frame farmhouse with two bedrooms, a kitchen, small dining area, and one full bathroom. A large propane tank sat about fifty feet to the left of the house and supplied their heat and cooking fuel. A porch ran across the entire front. There were several outlying buildings, a barn, and an old outhouse now used by Anne to store her gardening tools and supplies.

Due to their careers, they never really had the time to operate it as they had originally planned. Currently, they had fifteen head of cattle, two horses, some chickens, and a few sheep and goats. Each year Miles would till two acres so Anne could have her vegetable garden.

■ ■ ■

Two critical elements of successful clandestine operations are surveillance and planning. Due to the last-minute timing of Clete Boyer's decision to go after Vic's family and Allie's girlfriend, little pre-planning could be accomplished and only limited surveillance was possible. However, both assault teams were able to have eyes on their targets an hour before the raids were scheduled. But the planning would have to be done on the fly.

In both cases, the surveillance and initial contact worked as planned. However, in Evergreen, the assault team could not have anticipated that Tanya's insomnia would result in their attack being discovered and that after dispatching the two bodyguards the women would not just capitulate.

At Miles' farm, Ralph was on surveillance just off Grizzly Creek Road an hour before the scheduled assault. It didn't take him long to locate the sniper positioned behind bales of hay in the opening to the hayloft. During his watch, he did not pick up any lights or movement in the house.

With their headlights off and shielded by the trees bordering the front property line, the rest of the assault team arrived in two vehicles ten minutes early. Ralph's observations identified only one immediate threat which they could easily neutralize with their own sniper.

In a similar twist of fate to the events in Evergreen, they had no way of anticipating that the sentry in the barn would receive a call warning him of the imminent attack at the exact moment the rest of the team arrived.

The leader, Carl, received his final report from Ralph over two-way radio. "Other than one sentry up in the hayloft, there's been no movement. I'm guessing there is another guard in the house, but he hasn't moved."

"Okay," Carl directed, "I'm sending Tom to join you, it looks like only two hundred and fifty yards to the barn from where you are; he should be able to easily make the shot to take out the guy in the loft. We'll hang back in the vehicles ready to haul ass for the house as soon as we hear Tom's shot."

When Tom had made his way to Ralph's position, he dialed in the hayloft on his night scope. He scrutinized the opening for a long time before he turned to Ralph, whispering, "There's nobody up there."

"What are you talking about? I've been watching him for almost an hour. He hasn't left that spot."

"What can I tell you, he's not there now? Here, you look for yourself."

Ralph took the sniper rifle and looked through the scope. He examined the hayloft then panned the entire barn and house. "You're right, he's nowhere to be found. Maybe he's just taking a piss. Let's wait a few minutes before we tell Carl."

They waited, and waited some more; finally Carl crept up behind them. "What's up? We were supposed to go five minutes ago."

"He's not there. We can't find him anywhere," Tom sheepishly replied.

"Any other movement?"

"No, it's dead; nothing has changed except for the guy in the loft. I'm guessing he nodded off behind the bales," Ralph said with confidence.

"Okay, you're probably right. Let's get back to the vehicles and hit this place."

Three minutes later two GMC Yukons skidded off Grizzly Creek Road into Miles' long, unpaved, bumpy private drive. Still running dark, the eight heavily armed mercenaries believed their night-vision goggles would provide them with the ultimate advantage against their outgunned foe.

▪ ▪ ▪

As soon as Bill hung up from Bruce's ominous warning, he stealthily backed away from the bales of hay, climbed down the wooden ladder, and burst out the back door at full stride, crossing the two hundred feet between the barn and the rear kitchen door of the house in less than eight seconds. Fortuitously, Bill's sprint across the open ground to the house coincided exactly with Ralph's momentary briefing of Tom.

As ex-Navy SEALS, both Bill and his partner Frank were light sleepers. Frank actually was awakened by Bill's footfalls before he got within ten feet of the kitchen door. By the time Bill yanked open the screen door, Frank's automatic pistol was trained on the doorway. Bill had already yanked open the screen door and his hand was on the inside door's knob before he remembered the safe signal, three rapid hard knocks followed by two soft.

Frank relaxed somewhat but kept his pistol trained on the door until he heard Bill's unmistakable New York accent. "It's me, Frank . . . I'm comin' in."

"Enter," Frank replied gruffly.

Calming himself, Bill proceeded to relay the sketchy details of his call from Bruce. When he was finished Frank checked his watch. "Eight minutes; that means they're probably at the front gate. No time to get in the cars and skedaddle. You keep an eye out and I'll wake up the others," Frank commanded.

He woke up Miles and his wife first. "Don't turn on the light, we've got trouble."

Miles listened intently to Frank's news, then calmly suggested, "Maybe we can sneak out the back and head down to the slough. I have a rowboat hidden in the bushes which we can take to the river then row upstream to Fontana."

After waking up his brother and his wife, they woke Willow. When all seven met at the back door, Miles announced, "It's about two hundred yards to the slough; if we can keep the house between us and the driveway we just might be able to reach the slough undetected."

They were out the back door and across the open field before the assailants began their attack. Frank and Bill hung back at the edge of the bushes lining the slough while Miles located his boat. It was late summer and the water in the slough was not deep enough to float the boat with seven passengers. "We can walk alongside till it's deep enough to hold all of us, that shouldn't be too far," Miles suggested.

"You go," Bill ordered, "Frank and I will stay here and hold them off till reinforcements arrive. We'll catch up with you later in town."

Miles' facial expression appeared to indicate he wanted to argue but when he noticed Bill's eyes staring at the three women, he apparently thought better of it.

Bill and Frank were taking up positions approximately fifty yards apart when the two SUVs blasted into the driveway. By then, the boat with its five passengers onboard was already in deep enough water for Miles and his brother to begin rowing for their lives. Frank and Bill dispersed in the bushes, lying in wait for the inevitable search.

CHAPTER 35

Carl was surprised when the two charging vehicles made it all the way to the front porch without being blasted by bullets. Following a thorough search of the house, the barn, and a small shed, his fears were confirmed; somehow in the last ten or fifteen minutes their quarry had vanished.

Two pickups and an SUV were still sitting in front of the barn, so he was pretty sure they had fled on foot. If somehow they became aware of the pending assault, it was unlikely they would have headed for the main road; besides, if they had, Ralph would have spotted them. There appeared to be only two choices, either they fled out the back toward the trees running along the river or to one of the neighboring farmhouses. His gut told him they'd head for the river, not wanting to involve any of their innocent neighbors.

Carl surveyed the landscape with his NVGs; it was as flat as a pancake with no place to hide except a line of scrub bushes beginning a few hundred yards behind the house and running directly into the trees along the river.

"Okay," he ordered, "let's spread out and do a sweep on both sides of those bushes. In all likelihood they made it to those bushes. We need to try to cut them off before they make it to the river. We have the advantage with the NVGs while they're groping around in the dark. And for Christ's sake, try not to shoot one another."

Scrutinizing the open field, under the hazy glare of a half-moon, Bill and Frank could barely make out the silhouettes of the eight men slowly advancing on a path that would lead them to their position. Two of the stalkers flared out in a loop that would bring them to the back side of the slough. The remaining six continued straight for them. Realizing they were about to be sandwiched between two advancing columns, Frank crept back to where he was in Bill's sight and got his attention with a coyote howl. Using hand signals, Frank instructed Bill to take care of the two men headed behind them and he'd deal with the six in front.

Bill waited to fire until his two targets were parallel to him and no more than fifty feet away. He emptied a full clip of 9mm Lugers from his CMMG Mk9LE on the two targets, permanently taking both of them out of action. He quickly changed clips and retreated back to the other side of the slough. Before Frank had an opportunity for a good shot, Bill's deadly salvo caught everyone by surprise. Almost instantly, his six targets hit the ground and commenced indiscriminately raking the bushes with automatic weapons fire. The good news was now they only had to worry about six attackers; the bad news was their location was no longer in doubt to an enemy with the advantage of night-vision goggles.

They quickly realized that, in spite of their cover, the only way they could return fire without being picked off was to randomly change positions after every salvo. The downside to this strategy was that while they were changing positions, the assailants were able to advance. On the plus side, this unpredictable tactic prevented the assault team from becoming too bold in their charge, especially after Bill got lucky when he caught one of the assailants in mid charge and wounded the man in the shoulder. But by then, both defenders were running low on ammunition and Frank's vision had been impaired by flying splinters after a volley ripped into a nearby bush, spraying fragments of wood and bark into his face and neck. It was starting to look desperate for the two defenders until out of the darkness two new bouncing shafts of light penetrated the blackness.

■ ■ ■

From their position at the head of the drive, Bart, with Bruce looking over his shoulder, scanned Miles' farm with the thermal imaging camera while the others anxiously listened to the staccato sounds of automatic weapons fire off in the distance.

"Looks like ten subjects, two are in the bushes caught in a cross fire. There are eight attackers surrounding them out in the field," Bart observed loud enough for the whole team to hear.

Bruce enhanced Bart's observation. "Our guys are pinned down. It also looks like two of the eight in the field aren't moving and their heat profile is much lower than the rest. Let's hope they're not any of our people. Let's try to divert some attention from Bill and Frank. We'll drive in dark until we get past the house or until we're sure they've spotted us. Then Azzan and I will punch on the headlights. It looks like they have on NVGs; the sudden burst of lights should blow their optic nerves long enough for us to gain the advantage. As soon as we hit the lights, you guys jump out. Azzan and I will attempt to hold their attention by continuing to barrel straight at them. Hopefully that will give you guys additional time to move in and maybe take out a few more targets.

"I'll take the right side of the bushes. Azzan, you take the left. Remember we'll only have a few seconds before they'll be blasting the vehicles; so old buddy, stay low until you bail out . . . understood?"

"Don't worry about me," Azzan replied, smiling. "I don't plan on dying in a rented SUV."

"Just two more things," Bruce instructed, "I'd like to take at least one of them alive and Bart, you're staying here so you can keep us updated over the com system on what you see through the camera."

▪ ▪ ▪

The assailant caught a flicker of movement out of the corner of his night-vision goggles. It took a few seconds to focus on what he had glimpsed. From the direction of the farmhouse, there appeared to be two large dark objects barreling straight toward him. Turning to verify his suspicions, he immediately recognized the objects as SUVs. He broadcast into his microphone to warn his comrades. "We've got company! Two vehicles coming from the house!"

The heads of all five remaining attackers swiveled around to catch a glimpse of the new threat. At almost that exact instant Bruce and Azzan flipped on their headlights. The unexpected blast of illumination coming through their NVGs instantly blinded them. They never saw the vehicle doors open and five black-clad invaders spring out. Out of desperation, they fired blindly in the direction of the charging vehicles. Bruce's tactics gave his guys all the advantage they needed. Within seconds, three more Xenophon combatants were either killed or so seriously wounded they were out of the fight. Their remaining comrades soon realized they were caught between their original targets and the newly arrived reinforcements.

Bruce, disregarding his own safety, did not bail out of his SUV in spite of the numerous rounds peppering his vehicle. Undaunted and desperate to learn the fate of Miles and his family, he drove straight into the slough. Crashing into the bushes he came to rest in the muck less than twenty feet from Frank who, lying on his back pulling splinters out of his face, never witnessed the glorious turn of events. Bill, on the other hand, watched with glee as the cavalry instantly turned the course of the battle. Not just satisfied to become a spectator, he used the opportunity to take out one of the foe before rushing to locate Frank. Bruce was hardly out his door when Bill arrived.

"I haven't heard any firing from Frank for a while. I think he's been hit."

While the fighting raged on in the field, Bill called out, "Frank, where are you?"

"Over here" came the immediate reply only yards away. "I can't see."

"It's okay," Bruce responded over the sound of gunfire. "We'll find you."

"Is that you, Bruce?" Frank responded. "It sure took you long enough to get here."

Ignoring Frank's dig, Bruce asked Bill, "Where's Miles and his family?"

"Probably in Fontana by now; the old codger had a boat tucked away in this slough. They were long gone before the enemy discovered we had bolted."

At that moment, Bruce's cell phone began vibrating in his pocket. It was Dana. He answered immediately as calmly as if he was sitting in Starbucks having a grande latte. "Hey, babe, what's up?"

"Are you all right?"she responded, slightly taken aback by his casual demeanor.

"We're good. Miles and his family got away before the action started. Frank and Bill hung back and did a fine job of holding off the assailants until we got here. There are still a few of Boyer's mercenaries holding out, and it might take some time to root them out."

"Maybe we can help," Dana replied. "Two FBI choppers are only a few minutes away, but you should be able to hear my rotors any second now."

"Great, but it's a little confusing down here. I hope they don't confuse my guys for the enemy."

"Give me an overview of the situation and I'll try to direct the action."

"All right; right now we've got the enemy sandwiched between three of us in the bushes and six of our guys out in the field. As best I can tell, there were only three of them left but based upon the continuing barrage of firing, they're not about to surrender. I'd like to take them alive for interrogation; so, perhaps it might be enough for you and your FBI reinforcements to hover over the field shining those choppers' high-powered search lights down on them. What do you think?"

"It's worth a try. I'm in contact with the SWAT team; I'll give them the layout and tell them the plan. Anything else?"

"Just one more thing; we've got one of our guys injured, and a bunch of the bad guys either dead or injured. We're gonna need a whole bunch of EMS vehicles."

"Understood."

Seconds later, the unmistakable sound of helicopter blades reverberated through the night sky. Immediately, shafts of blinding light flashed randomly across the field, resulting in a momentary cessation of hostilities.

From an Oregon state police helicopter hovering above them, Dana's voice boomed over a loudspeaker. "This is the FBI, everyone on both sides, put down your weapons and come out with your hands in the air." Within seconds, the two Sacramento-based FBI choppers arrived on scene. Heavily armed SWAT team members could be seen poised in the open doors, their weapons ready to open up at the first hostile response.

There wasn't even a hesitation on the part of the three remaining Xenophon troops as they almost instantly threw down their weapons and stood with their hands in the air. Bruce and his men did the same.

It was over; now came the hard part, obtaining enough evidence to put the Boyers away for a long time and facing all the ramifications from the tragedy in Evergreen.

CHAPTER 36

The rented Gulfstream was streaking across the morning sky at 42,000 feet; it was scheduled to arrive at Colorado Springs Airport slightly after noon. Upon landing, a limo would be waiting to drive Vic and Bart to Fort Carson Army Hospital. Bruce planned on renting a car for the hour trip up to Evergreen, where he would meet with Director Sardo at Bart's house.

Since the early morning firefight on Miles' farm, Vic had been nervously awaiting each of Patty Jo's frequent updates. Tanya had suffered three broken ribs, a bruised and swollen kidney, plus multiple hairline fractures to her cheek. Given the extensive but non-life-threatening nature of her injuries, she had been lucid enough to demand to be transported to Fort Carson Military Hospital, where subsequent follow-up attacks would be unlikely. Patty Jo and the children followed in her car with a Colorado state police escort.

Director Sardo wasted no time after Dana's call from Oregon. He was on site in Evergreen before 7 a.m. Since none of the dead attackers carried identification, all agents had to go on was the observation that the three dead assailants appeared to be Hispanic. The two fleeing kidnappers initially eluded capture by traveling on back roads. Hours later they arrived in Fort Collins via a circuitous route. They had no way of knowing Patty Jo's neighbor, Jerry Blasé, was able to give a description and partial license plate number of their vehicle.

By mid-morning, the wounded kidnap leader's arm was swollen to twice its original size and was causing him excruciating pain. Desperate for medications, the two fleeing gunmen attempted to rob a drugstore in Fort Collins. Alerted by the store's silent alarm, a Fort Collins police cruiser, already on high alert as a result of the APB, responded to the scene just in time to witness the getaway vehicle speeding away.

It was immediately apparent this was a similar vehicle to the one identified in the APB. The officer gave chase and was soon joined by two other police cruisers. Shots were exchanged during a high-speed chase through light traffic. On North College Avenue where it skirted the southwest corner of Terry Lake, it seemed as if every law enforcement vehicle in the state pounced on the suspects like a pride of lions on a fleeing wildebeest. One state police SUV smashed into the suspects' vehicle, sending it careening into a telephone pole. Neither fugitive was wearing a seat belt, resulting in their receiving critical injuries from the high-speed impact.

Back in Eureka, Dana quickly obtained arrest warrants for Clete Senior, his two sons, his brother, and his brother's son. With the assistance of both Treasury and ATF resources, she obtained and was executing search warrants for all of Boyer Industries' many facilities and each of the family members' personal residences, along with the Xenophon employees' Eureka motel rooms and their corporate headquarters in Arlington, Virginia.

Director Sardo was on his cell phone when Bruce arrived. While the director continued to talk on his phone, an agent escorted Bruce through the house, briefing him on the evidence they were able to gather so far. Although all the bodies had been removed, the ghostly chalk outlines and dried blood pools left no doubt this had been a vicious firefight. The kitchen and family room were riddled with bullet holes and saturated with semi-dried blood, as was the staircase. Most of the windows on the main floor had been shattered, allowing fresh mountain air to circulate, yet the house still had a smoky, fetid smell about it. The upstairs hall and wall surrounding the entrance to the master bedroom was caked with blood and clumps of human tissue. A forensics team was attempting to confirm the horrific details provided by Tanya and Patty Jo.

During his two decades in the military, Bruce had been involved in numerous firefights and witnessed the brutal deaths of both friend and foe, yet he never was affected like this. Everything seemed a little hazy, almost as if it were a dream, except that sick feeling in his stomach which was threatening to erupt up his esophagus. Every instinct he had screamed, *"GET OUT OF HERE!"* But he couldn't leave; he needed to understand what had happened, even if for no other reason than to provide Vic and Bart with details of how terrifying it must have been for their families and how courageous Tanya's and Patty Jo's actions were.

Sardo caught up with Bruce in the master bedroom while he was standing beside the bed staring at the powder burns on the cream-colored bedspread and attempting to reconstruct, in his own mind, Patty Jo's thoughts and emotions as the intruder kicked down the door.

Bruce's face beamed with pride as he acknowledged the director's presence. "These have to be the two gutsiest women I've ever known," he said. "They both must have realized their two professional bodyguards had been killed, so they knew they weren't dealing with amateurs; yet they didn't panic, they held their ground and calmly blew away their attackers."

"No kidding." The director added, "When my agents arrived, the two of them were barricaded in the bedroom with the children; their weapons poised to take out anyone who attempted to enter. That was in spite of the fact Tanya had been pretty severely beaten up."

"What about the kids?" Bruce asked.

"They were scared but not hysterical; they seemed to be more concerned about their mother's injuries than about the killers coming back."

"Talking about the killers, I just heard on the radio the last two were apprehended in Fort Collins."

"Yup, the state and local police did a nice job of intercepting them. Their vehicle smashed head on into a telephone pole at high speed; it's doubtful either of them will live long enough to give us any information." Director Sardo hesitated for a moment then continued, "I'm sorry about your guys. The one who was killed on the porch never knew what hit him, and the one behind the kitchen sink must have put up one hell of a fight."

"Thank you for that, but actually I'd never met either Joe or Rich; they were actually Vic's former Air Force buddies from Colorado Springs."

"You know, Bruce, at first it bothered me that we didn't get here in time. Based upon Mulrooney's information, both attacks were supposed to happen at 3:00 a.m. Pacific time, yet this one was an hour early. At this point, we can only speculate as to why they didn't come off simultaneously. It was either that nobody told the guys in Colorado that it was supposed to happen at 3 a.m. Pacific Time or they somehow got screwed up with the time zones since during Standard Time, Arizona and Colorado are both on Mountain Time but Arizona does not switch to Daylight Savings Time. Assuming Mulrooney's understanding was correct, without that screw-up, we probably would have been able to prevent this slaughter."

"So, what do we know about these guys?"

"Unlike the crew in Eureka, it is unlikely they are Xenophon contract employees. We believe they may be members of one of the Mexican cartels, but they had no identification on them and their vehicle was stolen in Denver. We've provided photographs to the head of the Southwest Border Initiative, and we'll just have to wait to see if any of them can be identified. Even then, we might not be able to link them to a specific gang since some of these guys change affiliations as the power struggle shifts . . . but there is some other news."

"Tell me it's good."

"Not really, let's just say it's worthy of note . . . first, the Coast Guard has recovered a body off Catalina Island that appears to be that of a young man or boy. There is not much left of the features so we'll have to wait for dental records to determine if it's our missing young Wiyot youth."

"Damn, I was hoping Miles' nephew was in hiding someplace. Anything else?"

"Yeah, David's coroner buddy, Dr. Lambert, confirmed that John suffered from a broken ankle, probably from a fall, and that his death was the result of drowning in water consistent with a stream or lake. There was, however, the issue of the bruise on the side of his head. The original coroner classified it as to have occurred during the fall by hitting his head on a tree or log. Well, Lambert says that it actually the result of a blow from the butt of a rife. Quantico has matched the distinctive markings to a specific brand and model, a Remington 870 tactical shotgun. We're currently doing a thorough search of all the Boyer properties plus the Xenophon employees' rooms looking for a match. We may not be able to charge someone with first-degree murder in the general's death, but we might be able to get them on a lesser charge of second degree or manslaughter."

"That sounds good, Director. How's Mike Musgrave doing with the data files?"

"He's been working with Treasury to decipher the files. Between the electronic trail and Mulrooney's statements, there appears to be enough information to link the Boyers and Lumbermen's Bank to a massive international money-laundering network, but it's probably going to take several months before the whole thing is sorted out."

CHAPTER 37

Vic and Bart were apprehensive about what was happening at the hospital. Patty Jo's last call, shortly after they were airborne, indicated the doctors had delayed any decision on whether to operate on Tanya's face. In the meantime, she had been moved to a private room with twenty-four-hour security and was sleeping under a mild sedative.

Since her condition was not critical, the children, under Patty Jo's supervision, were allowed to wait in Tanya's room. Over the last couple of days in Colorado, Patty Jo had come to know each of the children quite well, and they seemed to react to her as they would a grandmother. Patty Jo's assessment of the children's emotional state pretty much mirrored what the FBI director had told Bruce, that they seemed to be more concerned about their mother than about the ordeal they had just been through.

Following Patty Jo's brief update, Vic talked to each of the children, but during his conversation with the eldest, Cindy, he got the impression she was suppressing her actual feelings. He concluded that Cindy was in a fragile state but was bravely masking her emotions so as to not upset her brother and sister. On the other hand, the two youngest were extremely anxious to chat with him.

Based upon his brief conversations with the kids, he concurred with Patty Jo on Billy and Yo. It seemed clear to him that they had not yet focused on how close they had actually come to being kidnapped or butchered. Yo's only concerns were whether her mother would still have to go away for a year and how long would it be before he got there. Billy, on the other hand, seemed to be processing the events of the previous night like it had just been another violent video game. He didn't seem to make the real-world connection between the bloodshed and his and his sisters' perilous situation.

When Vic and Bart finally arrived outside Tanya's room, their IDs were checked by the two MPs guarding the door. Before entering, they peered through the small window on the door. It was a fairly large room. Besides Tanya's bed and all the paraphernalia hooked up to her, the room contained a couch and two lounge chairs. Tanya appeared to still be sleeping. Yo and Patty Jo were squeezed into one of the chairs, engrossed in a children's book. Billy was sitting in the other chair watching cartoons on television while Cindy was curled up on the couch, fast asleep.

Vic slowly and quietly opened the door. He was hardly in the room when Yo saw him and screeched, "DADDY!" She instantly jumped up, dashing into her father's arms. Once she was safely wrapped in his strong embrace, the little girl leaned her head back and chided, "What took you so long?"

Vic, as much for his own comfort as for Yo's, replied, "It's okay, baby, everything will be all right. All the bad guys have been caught and I'm here to stay."

Billy was equally as excited to see his father, but his reaction was totally different.

"I saw two dead guys. Mrs. Rock told us to cover our eyes and not look but I sneaked a peak. There was blood and stuff all over the floor and walls. Those bad guys messed with the wrong girls."

Billy's pronouncement verified Vic's suspicions that his son did not yet appreciate the difference between a video game and reality, but now was not the appropriate time to set him straight. Holding Yo in one arm, he reached out with his other and said to Billy, "Come here and give me a hug, tough guy."

Cindy woke when Yo shouted "Daddy," but her reaction was subdued. She just slowly sat up, exhibiting just a hint of a meager smile.

Initially, Patty Jo's only reaction was a deep sigh of relief followed by her own tight-lipped smile. Then when she and Bart were finally embracing, he could feel her trembling in his arms. He kissed her on the forehead then squeezed her firmly while whispering in her ear, "You can let it go now."

But she still couldn't, not in front of the children. Later, when they were alone in their hotel room, she would break down and blubber for five minutes. It was the first time she had cried since her first husband, John Nicosia, died.

After a few minutes, Vic was able to get a closeup look at his wife. Although much of her face was masked with bandages, the swelling and discoloration was still clearly noticeable.

While he was staring at Tanya, Patty Jo wandered to his side and in a very quiet voice said, "She was incredibly calm and focused when the assault began. So much so, initially, when she woke me with the kids I didn't take her announcement we were being attacked seriously. It wasn't until she ordered me to take the kids in the bathroom and lock the door and I heard the first shots that I knew we were in a grave situation. She must have taken quite a jolt from the concussion grenade and later when that bastard kicked her; yet, as soon as he was gone she managed to immediately rush into the bedroom to check on me and the kids. It wasn't until the EMTs forced her to lie down that she even acknowledged she was injured."

"That doesn't surprise me," Vic replied. "She's always been an incredible woman. Not just because she's military, but because she had the guts to initially adopt Cindy as a single mother on active duty."

To their complete surprise, Tanya's raspy voice chimed in, with her barely moving her lips and mouth, "And a good shot, too."

Surprised, Vic exploded into a hearty laugh and reached out to clasp her hand. "Thank God you're okay. I would have never forgiven myself for not being there had you been seriously hurt."

Grimacing through clenched teeth she managed to jokingly mock him, "What, a smashed face and broken ribs is not serious enough for you?"

Turning her face to Bart, she painfully added, "Patty Jo tells me you once had the unpleasant experience of getting the crap kicked out of you too."

"Yeah, I had almost identical injuries as yours. Did she also tell you I eventually got my revenge?"

Trying to force a smile but failing, she slurred, "I read the book." She then hesitated and took a deep breath before continuing, "Patty Jo is an incredible woman herself. You have no idea how astonished I and my heavy-footed friend were when his partner was blown out the bedroom door. She's the real reason he bolted; he didn't want to face whoever was waiting in the bedroom."

Fearing any further details would upset the kids, Vic tried to give Tanya a hand signal warning her not to pursue the gory details any further, but she just gave him a quizzical look.

Patty Jo picked up on their nonverbal interaction. Placing her hands on Billy and Yo's shoulders, she said, "I wouldn't worry about these guys. They've pretty much figured it out from the bits and pieces they've heard; plus, Billy hasn't been shy about describing what he saw on the way out. Besides, they're proud as hell at their mother's bravery. Isn't that right, children?"

"Yes," they all responded, but Vic knew that eventually all of them would be haunted by the brutal images from the previous night.

CHAPTER 38

TV news trucks lined the road like food venders at a street festival, so Director Sardo and Bruce Tanner, in order to escape the revolting aftermath of the gun battle and remain out of view of the media, retreated to the back deck. They were getting an update on the capture of the last two attackers from a Colorado state police captain when Dana called on the director's phone.

Before she had a chance to begin providing him with an update of the latest results from Eureka, he interrupted, "I'm with Bruce, we've just finished our walk-through of the house. Hold up a second while I put you on the speaker phone so he can hear this too."

"Hey Dana," Bruce announced after Sardo pushed the speaker key.

"Hi, Bruce . . . I was just starting to tell the director, besides the stuff Mike's been able to pull off Mulrooney's hard drive, we've hit the jackpot with the search warrants.

"Let me start with the most exciting discovery of all. We recovered and put into evidence a Remington 870 tactical shotgun belonging to one of the Xenophon security guards named Ralph Dunn. We thought its stock carvings were similar to the ones Doctor Lambert identified on the side of the general's head. After we confronted Ralph with that evidence and informed him he was going to be charged with the general's murder, he folded like a wet pizza box. He gave up his partner Carl, Clete Senior and Junior, plus Ken as all being involved in the general's death. He even went so far as to claim Junior was the one who held John's head underwater until he drowned. Then, Ralph claimed, Junior tore off the general's dog tags in his final act of triumph. Later, we confirmed Ralph's allegations by locating the dog tags in Junior's desk drawer at the Boyerville Police Department."

"Are you telling me we've got Junior for the first-degree murder of John Slaughter?"

"Oh, there's no question he did it, and his father and brother were accomplices. The only problem is, when the news of the Xenophon debacle at Miles' place was broadcast over the police radio, they all took off. This morning Junior's body was discovered in a motel room near Crescent City. Apparently, he blew his brains out. We haven't been able to locate the father and brother. We have their photographs distributed all over the West, and they are about to make it on all the major networks' news programs."

Bruce seemed sullen. "Based upon what Vic told me about Junior, it doesn't surprise me he'd not want to face prosecution, but I doubt his father and brother would do the same."

"Yeah," Dana responded, "we think the old man and Ken ran off and left Junior to face the music alone. That's why he offed himself." Without hesitating she continued, "Back to the good news; when we confronted the nephew Ricky with the photos of his boat and crew off-loading the drugs from the submarine, he admitted the boy spotted them and they chased the kid down while he was swimming for shore. But he claims the kid was alive when they turned him over to the captain of the sub, a Bulgarian named Marinov."

"Wow! Did we ever get dental confirmation the body that was found floating off Catalina was that of Allie?"

"Not yet, but there was a handmade bead bracelet on the boy's wrist that is similar to one his girlfriend gave him."

"Damn," Bruce proclaimed. "I was really hoping he was still alive and being held captive in Mexico."

"Oh, that reminds me, confirming Mulrooney's other allegations, Mike and the Treasury boys have been able to trace a good piece of the money-laundering operation back to Mexico. Lumbermen's Bank was apparently only a minor player as far as the actual washing of cash. The really big players included banks in Texas, Mexico, Honduras, several Caribbean islands, the Middle East, and Bulgaria. It was an incredibly complicated operation that used real estate and development companies in Florida and Eastern Europe. Not only did they launder cash from drug and weapons smuggling, but they also hid stolen money for terrorists and payoffs for corrupt politicians and dictators. As you would expect, many of these illegal transactions were run through shell companies. Here is the really interesting thing, although we're not sure exactly how it fits. Dozens of these shell companies were all set up by one law firm in Panama which no one has ever heard of before, Hawksworth, Costa and Petrovich."

"So, are you guys thinking there is a connection between the Eastern European banks and the Soviet-era sub?"

"We're working on that right now. There is some thought at CIA that Captain Marinov is the nephew of a former deputy director in the Bulgarian military intelligence service and someone the current government has been trying to prove is behind a lot of the country's rampant corruption."

"Good work. Man, you and Mike played this Mulrooney thing perfectly; who would have guessed squeezing that slimeball would have caused so many things to fall in place? By the way, have we identified which one of the Mexican cartels was supplying the cocaine and meth to the Boyers?"

"Yeah, it's the Tijuana group headed by Teodoro Sanchez Felix. Ricky confirmed his uncle had a relationship with Felix, and Bob Hoffman's people comparing satellite images from two years ago to last week located what looks like a Soviet-style sub base just south of Ensenada, Mexico. They then went back and looked at images from last year and were able to identify the construction of a concrete cover along the cliffs of a small cove between two prominent outcroppings."

"What would we do without satellite images and guys like Bob and his people to interpret them? So, DEA and the Mexicans are going to raid the place?"

"DEA hasn't told the Mexicans yet."

Director Sardo cut in for the first time. "What are they waiting for?"

"You, sir."

"Me, why me? It's not FBI's call."

"Apparently it's not DEA's either."

Sardo hesitated for a few moments while he absorbed yet another national law enforcement conundrum. "Is there something you're not telling me, Wise?"

"Yes, sir."

"Do you want me to call you back alone on a secure line?"

"That's an affirmative, sir."

CHAPTER 39

Vic and the kids had connecting rooms at the IHG Army Hotel on Fort Carson; it was close to Evans Army Hospital and provided the gate security of a U.S. military installation. Tanya would probably only spend another day in the hospital, but her doctors requested she convalesce for another week nearby. Doctors hoped by then her swelling would have subsided enough for them to make a decision on how much surgery was necessary.

Bruce planned on spending one night at the hotel on Fort Carson so he hopefully could talk to Tanya before he and Vic met with Joe's and Rich's families.

Bart and Patty Jo elected to get a room at the Garden of the Gods Club and Resort in Colorado Springs, where David Tanner was booked.

Although Vic had taken adjoining rooms at the hotel with the intention the children could have their own beds to sleep in, Billy and Yo refused to leave their father's side. While the two youngest obviously required the physical security and protection of their father, Cindy was distant. Originally, when Vic first arrived, she appeared to be sleeping peacefully. However, as the day wore on he noticed she became edgy and remote, hunkering down alone in the adjoining room. Around 9 p.m., after Billy and Yo were soundly sleeping, Vic checked in on

Cindy. She was lying on the bed staring at the television. A Disney adolescent sitcom was flashing on the tube, but she had the sound on mute with a blank look in her eyes. When she realized her father was standing in the doorway, she gave him a brief, halfhearted smile then quickly looked away.

"Hey, baby, how are you doing?" Vic asked.

She turned back toward him, replying halfheartedly, "I'm good." Yet her eyes betrayed her desperation.

Sensing his daughter was going to need a little coaxing before she would open up, Vic shut the door behind him. Walking slowly toward her, he gave her a verbal nudge. "Scary stuff, huh?"

She still didn't reply, but her eyes told him he had hit a chord. Father and adopted daughter stared at each other for a long time before Cindy asked, "What happened to Joe and Rich . . . they're dead, aren't they?"

Vic moved in closer to his daughter, sat on the edge of the bed, and clasped her hand. "Yes, honey. They were both killed putting up a heroic effort defending all of you."

While Cindy looked to be staring right through her father, she said with a real sense of sadness, "They told me they served with you in Afghanistan."

"That's correct, they were both brave men. We had a lot of close calls together. I only wish I had been there when they really needed me."

"I'm glad you weren't" was her instant response.

Surprised by his daughter's enigmatic response and anxious to get her to fully open up, he replied, "Why's that?"

This time, she looked him intently in the eyes, answering with conviction, "Because you would have been down in the kitchen with them and probably be dead now, too."

Moved by his daughter's response, Vic felt an overwhelming need to hold her close to him. "Come here," he lovingly requested, holding out his arms.

Cindy did not hesitate as she scooted over and leaned into

his chest. Vic enveloped her in a protecting and tender hug. Within seconds, Cindy fell into a trembling sob that lasted for several minutes. Finally, pulling away from her father's grasp, she clasped his hand and said, "Mommy couldn't have found a better man to marry."

Choked up, Vic replied with a smile, "You ready to sleep now?"

Concurrent with un-muting the television, she responded, "No, I think I'm going to watch some TV."

■ ■ ■

At about the same time, fifteen miles north in their room at the Garden of the Gods, Patty Jo and Bart were cuddling on the couch.

Patty Jo was finally ready to talk about her ordeal. "It's funny, I don't think I got scared until after I shot the guy coming through the bedroom door. I had no idea what was happening downstairs but I really wasn't concerned; I was confident Joe and Rich could deal with any intruders. After the first explosion, there were numerous gunshots coming from the downstairs. I still assumed Joe and Rich were holding their own. It wasn't until I heard the shots from just outside the bedroom that I realized the bad guys must have gotten past Joe and Rich. Then, after the second concussion rocked the upstairs, everything suddenly went eerily quiet.

"I was trying to envision what might be happening when the bedroom door suddenly blasted open. At that instant everything seemed to go into slow motion. It was weird, I could clearly make out the rage in the intruder's eyes. I watched as he seemed to slowly pan the room with his revolver. Fortunately, he started on the wrong side of the room and before he realized where I was and started to aim in my direction, I pulled the trigger. I swear I could see the mass of pellets leave the muzzle and fly through the air in an ever-expanding pattern. When it hit him, I watched with almost a clinical curiosity as his blood, flesh, and brain matter splattered against the wall. Then, as quickly as time slowed down, it reverted back to normal as the guy crashed to the floor. Amazingly, without thinking, I ejected the spent shell and rammed another into the chamber fully anticipating the next assailant.

"At that point, I figured Tanya was either dead or seriously wounded. You can't believe the relief I felt when I heard her voice just before she stumbled into the room. At first when I saw her clutching her side, I thought she had been shot in the stomach. When I noticed the blood on her face, my heart dropped. I wondered if she had been hit in the face, too. Without thinking, I let go of the shotgun and ran toward her shouting, 'Where are you shot?' She laughed but grimaced as she replied, 'Nowhere, the bastard just kicked me a couple of times.'

"I asked her, 'Where are they?'

"She said, 'I don't know, but I think there is only one of them left and he bolted after I shot him in the arm.'

"She joined me behind the bed, and the two of us kept our guns aimed at the doorway until we heard the police calling from downstairs."

"I almost can't believe how calm you must have been poised behind the bed waiting for them to crash into the room, guns blazing."

"So was I, initially . . . then I realized I had been preparing for something like this for years. Not only did John and I live with the prospect of getting caught up in some Mafia vendetta; you and I were on the run from Al's hit men for almost two years. I can't even count how many sleepless nights John and I had in anticipation of some Mafia hit team barging in. That's why, when we moved to Phoenix, John got us into trap shooting and, just like you, always kept a shotgun in the bedroom closet. Occasionally, when John was off at some doctor's convention, I'd hear a noise in the middle of the night and dash to the closet for the gun. I never told John this, but a couple of times I actually loaded it then crouched behind the bed waiting for an assassin to burst in.

"One of the first things I did after Tanya and I arrived here with the kids was to check the closet for your shotgun and ammunition. Since yours was different from the trap guns John and I used to use, I made sure I knew how to load it and whether there was a trigger lock. Once I had the children locked in the bathroom, it was almost an involuntary reaction for me to get the shotgun. Pulling the trigger was pretty much an automatic thing, too. I never even thought about it; I just did it."

"Remind me never to piss you off," Bart injected with a laugh as he put his arm over her shoulder and, pulling her close, kissed her on the forehead. They sat there silently with Bart softly rubbing her back and shoulders until his cell phone rang. "Damn," he muttered, "Cell phones are such mood breakers."

"Answer it, Romeo," Patty Jo ordered. "You weren't going to get any further with me now anyway."

While Bart was reaching for his phone on the coffee table, she added, "Maybe later, if I get a back rub."

While flashing his infamous lecherous grin, Bart took a quick peek at his phone, announcing, "It's just David."

"So answer it." Patty Jo said, smiling.

"Hey, David, just get in?"

"Yup, you guys up for drinks?"

"I'll ask Patty Jo, but she might just want to hit the sack. It's been a long day for her."

Patty Jo didn't even wait for Bart to pose the question to her. "I sure could go for a stiff drink. Why don't you go down and meet him. Even though I don't have any fresh clothes to put on, I think I'd like to take a quick shower. I'll join you in about a half-hour."

"Did you hear that, David?"

"Sure did, I'll meet you in the bar in ten minutes. Bruce should also be there waiting for us by then."

CHAPTER 40

Bart was surprised and delighted when he walked into the hotel bar and found both David and his wife, Sarah, waiting for him, but no Bruce. After they gave each other an affectionate embrace, Bart leaned back and said to Sarah, "You don't know how glad I am you came along with David. I think Patty Jo needs another female to talk to."

"I figured that might be the case," she responded, then started to add something. But, whatever it was, she repressed it.

Bart picked up on her indecision. "What? You were afraid I'd make it worse like I used to do with Gina?"

"I wasn't thinking that at all."

"Well, maybe you weren't, but your husband probably is."

David raised both his hands in a defensive posture. "Whoa . . . don't get me in the middle of this." Then he added with a hint of sarcasm, "I have nothing but confidence in your ability to relate to your women."

Bart cocked his head to the side, scrunched up his nose while at the same time squinting, and skewed his lips before he slowly and methodically declared, "Sssince when?" followed up by a devious chuckle.

David and Sarah responded with smiles before Sarah got serious. "Really, how's she doing?"

"Well, assuming I've read her correctly, she seems to be

fine, although I'm not sure she's let herself reflect on just how close they all came to being massacred." Bart didn't wait for a response. "Originally, I was thinking she might have trouble coming to terms with the fact she killed another human being, but now, based upon what she just told me, I believe that won't be an issue. For years, John had them preparing for the possibility of his brother's enemies staging an attack on him in order to get even with Al. That's why John insisted they become such accomplished trap shooters. Just like me, he always kept a shotgun in the bedroom closet. So, Patty Jo was prepared for a middle of the night attack. The only thing I suspect surprised her was how easy it was for her to blow away another human being."

"Okay, I'll try to have a heart-to-heart with her. Should I go up to your room and see if she wants to talk privately?"

"Nah, I don't think she's up to it tonight."

"Okay, I can respect that. What are you and David up to tomorrow?" Sarah asked.

Bart glanced at David, looking for some help.

David took the cue. "We hadn't talked about it yet; however, if you're looking for some quiet time alone with Patty Jo, Bart and I could go up to Evergreen and figure out what needs to be done at the house."

"That's good," Sarah replied. "You and Bart can do that while Patty Jo and I hang out here."

■ ■ ■

Despite her rumpled clothes, Patty Jo looked refreshed and at ease when she arrived in the bar fifteen minutes later. She broke into a broad smile when she saw both the Tanners.

David stood and moved in her direction. After they embraced and she kissed him on the cheek, David said, "I understand you and Tanya are being touted on the news as two modern-day Annie Oakleys."

"You're kidding, right?" Patty Jo asked, looking concerned.

"Yeah, just joking. The FBI and local law enforcement officials have only said it was a deadly home invasion, and according to Director Sardo, he's convinced the media not to release any further details or pictures for now. Since you rent the house from one of my companies, you don't have to worry about any personal stuff getting out. On the other hand, one way or another, your names and perhaps even your driver's license pictures will leak out. This whole thing has already made it on the national news. You never know if there still might be one of Al's henchmen out there who thinks the two of you should be whacked, bounty or no bounty. It would be smart for you to disappear again. I'm sure Sardo will agree and provide you with new identities."

"Well, one thing is for sure, I'm never going to be able to walk back in to that house again. As far as disappearing, I just got used to signing my checks Patty Jo Rock. On that note, why don't one of you gentleman order me a dry double martini while I give Sarah a big hug?"

The two friends embraced for a long moment, and Bart noticed tears well up in Patty Jo's eyes as she said to Sarah, "Thanks for coming. You and David seem to always be there when I need you."

Sarah, equally choked up, responded, "Well, just ask; you and Bart are like family."

"Maybe tomorrow we can talk. Right now I just need to have a drink and if at all possible, a few laughs."

Bart motioned for the waitress who hustled over to their table. "Another round for everyone and a dry martini for my darling wife."

While they waited for the waitress to return with their drinks, Patty Jo said to Sarah, "After we go shopping tomorrow morning to get me some new clothes, you've got to meet Tanya. She is one hell of a woman."

"Good, I was hoping I would get to see her. How is she doing?"

"I called over just before I came down here. She answered the phone herself and, in spite of her injuries, she seemed quite chipper. Because of the swelling, it's hard to understand everything she says, but I think she indicated she expected to be released tomorrow. The Air Force arranged visiting officer's quarters for the whole family right on Fort Carson. She suggested I call in the late morning; hopefully by then she'll know when they're going to discharge her. She ended by thanking me for protecting her children. Her last words were, 'I'd go to war with you anytime.'"

"Well, from everything I heard from Bruce this afternoon, apparently both of you performed fearlessly," David said with admiration.

"Speaking of Bruce," Sarah said with the slightest hint of a mother's concern, "shouldn't he have been here by now?"

"Yes," David replied, reaching for his cell phone, "I think I'll give him a call to find out what's keeping him."

Punching *2 on his phone, David waited for Bruce to pick up. After seven rings, voice mail kicked in. "You've reached the voice mail of Bruce Tanner. Leave a message."

Exhibiting a shrug for Sarah's benefit, he replied, "It's your father. Where are you?"

Ten minutes later, David's phone played its old-fashioned ring tone. "Hello, what's up?" he answered.

"Sorry, Dad . . . Sardo waylaid me. If I'm not done in a half-hour, I'll call you back as soon as I can."

■ ■ ■

"How is Tanya doing?" Director Sardo asked Bruce with genuine concern in his voice.

"She's in a lot of pain and being stubborn about not taking pain killers. It was obvious to me the broken ribs and facial swelling make it difficult for her to breathe. Right now, I think Rich and Joe's murders are really weighing heavily on her. Before I had a chance to tell her the state police had caught up with the two that got away, she angrily said to Vic and me, 'You two are going to get the rest of those bastards, aren't you?' Then when I informed her the state police had caught up to the two that escaped and they were critically injured, she managed a brief smile but wasn't satisfied. Looking intently at Vic, she said, 'I meant all of them, especially whoever was behind this whole thing.'"

Sardo had a smirk on his face as he said, "Interesting woman." He paused for a brief second while he seemed to be pondering something, then continued, "What about the children? How are they bearing up now that it's over?"

"I'm not sure. They seemed okay while I was there. It's hard to tell with their father in the room for protection. He'll probably get a better indication of their mental state when he tries to put them to sleep tonight."

"You're probably right. I'd be amazed if they don't have some emotional issues."

Bruce quickly changed the subject. "All right, Director; let's get to the real reason you sent a car to bring me here to the Denver FBI office."

Director Sardo took a deep breath before his whole demeanor changed from casual to strictly business. "Remember when we were talking to Dana this afternoon and she mentioned the DEA had not yet told the Mexican authorities about the drug smuggling connection or the submarine because they were waiting for me?"

"Yeah, I thought that was peculiar at the time. I would have expected they'd be anxious to organize a joint operation to strike at the heart of the Mexican cartel and seize the submarine."

"Actually, that was their intention, but CIA and State threw DEA a curve ball. That's where you and I come in. Since you've previously done some work for the FBI, the director of Homeland Security suggested I be the one to run a proposal by you." Sardo paused to gauge Bruce's reaction. When all Bruce's facial expression seemed to reveal was a mild curiosity, the director continued, "After your old buddy at McLean, Bob Hoffman, located the sub base he felt obligated to inform his superiors. Who, incidentally, are extremely grateful to you for the tip. I don't have to tell you how convoluted this stuff can become. Anyway, one thing led to another and before you know it, the DOD started to balk at the prospect of the Mexicans getting their hands on a submarine, even if it is obsolete technology. That was quickly followed by the State Department requesting we do a favor for the Bulgarians."

"Yeah . . . ," Bruce said uneasily, anticipating the punch line.

It didn't take the director long to satisfy Bruce's expectations. "Short version is, we would like you to commandeer Captain Marinov and his submarine before the DEA and Mexican authorities descend on the Tijuana cartel."

Speechless, Bruce just stared at the director for a long time.

In order to break the uneasy silence, Sardo finally added, "We have some ideas how to do it and can make resources available to you, but it can never be revealed the U.S. government sanctioned the operation."

"Who'll be running the show?"

"It's a joint task force with CIA, DOD, DEA, and FBI."

"You avoided answering my question. In the end, who's calling the shots?"

Sardo's eyes hardened and his jaw tightened before he too emphatically said, "The director of Homeland Security."

"And when will I meet her?" Bruce asked.

"Probably never. You'll work with the task force."

"Plausible deniability, huh?"

Sardo's facial expression looked like he never even heard Bruce's comment. After a few pregnant seconds, Bruce continued, "Who's on the task force?"

"At CIA, besides your buddy Hoffman, there's his counterpart for Eastern Europe, Al Juravich; at DOD it's your old boss Admiral Noon. Dana will be the representative for the FBI and Homeland, but DEA will be also represented by their Southwest Border Initiative leader, Ron Geck."

"Sounds like a real clusterfuck . . . so, why are the Bulgarians anxious to get Marinov back?"

"Two reasons. First; he stole their sub about a year ago from its dry dock on the Black Sea. Second, because they see him as a way to get at his uncle and put a big dent in their country's internal corruption."

"Okay, Director, don't bullshit me; how much meddling and second guessing am I likely to get?"

"None, as long as you follow a few straightforward principles for which I was able to gain agreement at the highest levels."

"I suppose you're not willing to reveal who the highest levels are?"

"As far as you are concerned, it's me."

Bruce's subtle smile exhibited cynical insight before he replied, "So if I fuck up, it's your ass, too."

Again, the director's expression did not reveal that he heard Bruce's assessment. Not expecting a reply, Bruce just continued, "So what are these principles?"

"First, your primary objective is to get Captain Marinov and his sub out of Mexican waters. Second, if you or any of your team is apprehended by Mexican authorities, your cover is that you are on a personal vendetta to apprehend Marinov and his crew for the kidnapping and murder of Allie Reynolds."

"That's it? Nobody cares who I use or what methods I employ to pull this off and you'll provide me with whatever resources I need?"

"That about sums it up, except you need to pull this off as soon as possible because with the Boyers' distribution network currently being dismantled, Don Felix is likely to peddle the sub to another cartel serving the Caribbean or perhaps even to a terrorist organization in the Middle East."

"How much time do you think we have?"

"A week, maybe ten days."

"Does this under-the-table contract pay well?"

Sardo erupted into a hearty laugh lasting for a long time. When he finally was able to suppress his hilarity, he solemnly replied, "If you're successful, you can write your own check." After a slight pause he added, "Deal?"

Bruce grinned. "Deal."

CHAPTER 41

Patty Jo finally seemed to be back to normal. She had David and Sarah laughing their heads off at some of the convoluted measures Bart used to prevent any of their former brother-in-law's would-be assassins from tracking them down and collecting on the standing contracts Al had out on both of them. She was in the process of telling them about the time in Cadiz, Bart, using fake passports, paid off the captain of a rusty old freighter to provide them passage to Dubrovnik, Croatia. She was just describing in vivid detail their nightmarish, stomach-turning passage through thirty-foot seas and torrential rains when David's phone rang.

"It's Bruce," he announced, glancing at the screen.

"Hey, Dad," Bruce Tanner responded when his father answered his cell phone, "I'm not going to be make it over there for drinks with you guys. In fact, I need to use your plane this evening to fly back to DC. I've just hooked up with Dana here in the FBI offices, and we have an early morning conference at McLean tomorrow."

"What's up, son?"

"I've been contracted to clean up a few loose ends related to this Boyer thing."

His father didn't reply immediately while he considered Bruce's sketchy details. After several seconds of dead air, he asked, "Anything I can do to help?"

"Don't know yet, but I'm guessing I'll need to borrow Azzan and Eitan again."

"You want them to meet you in DC?"

"No, but it might expedite things if they'd make their way to San Diego in the next day or so. We'll probably need as much muscle as we can find. They should bring along any of the crew from Eureka who may be interested in a follow-up assignment."

■ ■ ■

Bob Hoffman had just finished briefing the attendees on all the satellite and drone photographs of Don Felix's ranch, his new cliff house in La Bufadora, and the sub base fifteen miles down the coast. Besides Bruce, Dana, and Bob, sitting around the conference table was Bob's counterpart for Eastern Europe, Al Juravich, Admiral Noon from DOD, the DEA's Ron Geck, head of the Southwest Border Initiative, and several analysts and planners from CIA and SWBI.

Bruce turned in Ron Geck's direction. "And you guys didn't have a clue Felix had constructed the sub base?"

"None," Ron replied, a little embarrassed. "We did have reports of some Bulgarians hanging around the bars and whorehouses in La Bufadora and Ensenada. Until Bob showed us the satellite photos a couple of days ago, we didn't have a clue. As soon as we knew what to look for, our undercover agents reported back that Don Felix recently completed construction on a huge cliff house. Fortunately, we've been able to locate an engineer who worked on both projects and is willing to talk to us. We're hoping he can provide us with some additional details; perhaps even blueprints. I expect a report sometime today."

Dana, shaking her head in concern, injected, "Getting inside the sub base is probably doable, but snatching Captain Marinov along with his sub won't be easy."

"Actually," Bob replied, "there is an idea we've been kicking around. We were thinking, going on the theory Don Felix might be interested in renting out or even selling the sub, perhaps Marinov would be willing to go along with it. Rumor has it Don Felix is already shopping it around."

Bruce and Dana, sitting next to each other, responded with dubious looks.

Bob smiled at them before continuing, "You both look skeptical. Let me ask you this, what would you do if you had a couple of million dollars tied up in this submarine operation and your primary means of recouping your investment is suddenly cut off?" Bob hesitated but did not wait for either to answer. "I'll tell you what you'd do; you'd figure out another way to recoup your money either by selling or renting it out. Imagine how many other drug cartels, terrorist organizations, or weapons smugglers would love to get their hands on that capability." This time Bob paused a little longer, letting his assumption ferment before he added with a devious smile, "Suppose we get into the bidding?"

"Just like that," Bruce immediately responded cynically. "What, we send him an email saying we heard about his difficulties and would like to come to his aid? Or better yet, we walk into his hacienda with a suitcase full of money and tell him we are interested in renting his submarine and crew."

Bob rolled his eyes. "Something like that, oh ye of little faith. Tell him your idea, Al."

"We believe we have somebody with the right credentials who can get you a face-to-face with the don." Al Juravich nodded to the analyst who had previously displayed the photos of the sub base on the screen. She instantly started keying into her computer. When she finished, a man's image appeared on the screen. Bruce and Dana recognized the man as Boris Kozlov, JVS Technika's former chief accountant in the Middle East.

"I thought Boris along with General Nikitin had already been executed by the Yemenis for the murder of one of Bruce's father's kidnappers," Dana alleged curiously.

"You're correct about Nikitin, but we convinced the Yemenis to turn Boris over to us. We've been babysitting him for years in a Croatian safe house. He's been very cooperative and has agreed to contact Captain Marinov's uncle to put a good word in with Don Felix for the purpose of arranging a meeting between the don and a prospective Middle East buyer."

Puzzled, Bruce asked, "Are you telling me the word is not out that the Yemenis executed both Nikitin and Kozlov?"

Grinning, Al Juravich replied, "Oh, the word's out on Nikitin, but the big-time weapons smugglers think Boris somehow escaped. Although he no longer is a dealer himself, he's been functioning as a matchmaker of sorts between the buyers and sellers."

"How is it possible he survived without us hearing about it?" Dana asked incredulously.

Grinning like a Cheshire Cat, Juravich replied, "Do you remember a couple of years ago there was a notorious prison escape of twenty-three al-Qaida terrorists from the Yemeni capital, Saana?"

"Sure," Bruce responded, "that happened shortly after we apprehended Nikitin and Kozlov."

"Well, in actuality, they did execute Nikitin; but before they did, we convinced the Yemenis to temporarily turn Boris over to us. We used the prison escape event to put the word out that, in the confusion surrounding the assault on the prison, both Russians managed to escape. However, during the firefight that facilitated the escape, Nikitin was wounded and eventually was found dead less than twenty kilometers from the prison. On the other hand, we put the word out Boris disappeared. In order to foster the idea he got away, we convinced Interpol to quietly put out an international fugitive warrant on Boris. The warrant even went as far as to suggest he was last seen in Istanbul, where he again eluded authorities. At the time we didn't make a big deal out of his escape but let the news find its way back to the smuggling community. If anyone checked, they'd discover the warrant. Meanwhile we had Boris hidden away, attempting to squeeze as much information out of him as we could.

"Being a sly old fox, initially he only gave us stuff we already knew. It took about two years and us finally threatening to give him back to the Yemenis before he actually revealed something useful."

"So, Nikitin is really dead?" Bruce attempted to confirm.

"Quietly beheaded shortly after the prison break," Bob confirmed before continuing. "Anyway, about two years ago we concluded Boris had been out of the game too long to provide us with any further useful information. We were trying to decide what to do with him when he actually proposed we allow him to get back into the game, where he could be a very valuable double agent.

"We concluded his suggestion was brilliant and doable. Given his reputation, it wouldn't take much for us to set him up as a weapons smuggler. However, we didn't actually want him peddling weapons to terrorists. Again, he had the solution. Using his incredible international contacts, he was able to carve out a niche as the premier expeditor of the underworld. For an exorbitant fee he will locate a buyer or seller for everything on the black market. In return for allowing him to live in licentious luxury in a fifteenth-century castle overlooking the Adriatic Sea, we get real time information on what's going down in the smuggling world. How long he can continue to survive as a double agent is the question, but for now, we can use his contacts to get us an audience with Don Felix."

"Okay, I get the concept, sounds plausible. So, who is going to be our buyer?"

"We were thinking you could do it, Bruce. After all, you do speak seven languages, don't you?" Bob replied.

"Nine," Bruce responded. "I don't think I'm the best we can come up with. Don't you think we need a more surly character? Perhaps even someone who could pass for a terrorist?"

"Sure, that would be great," Bob answered. "You have somebody in mind?"

"Yeah . . . Isma'il Hassanat," Bruce answered extemporaneously.

"You mean the Bedouin they call the Desert Wind, the one who helped save your father when he was kidnapped in Israel?" Bob Hoffman exclaimed.

"That's him, the infamous Khamsin. As a notorious arms smuggler in the Middle East, he wouldn't have to do too much acting to fit the part and besides, he and Boris have a long-standing relationship."

"He's been off the radar for almost eight years," Bob Hoffman injected. "First, we don't know how to locate him, and second, why would he agree to come out of hiding?"

His enthusiasm somewhat throttled, Bruce somberly replied, "You're correct in wondering if he'd be willing to reveal himself after all this time."

"We don't have a lot of time here," Admiral Noon injected.

"I may have a way to locate him," Bruce responded. "If I do, I'll convince him to come along. I'm pretty sure I know what might motivate him."

The admiral, nodding, responded, "Okay, you see if you can find him. Let's set a deadline for reaching a decision on Hassanat . . . say the day after tomorrow. Anybody have any objections to this scenario?"

Everybody in the room agreed, whereupon Bruce felt compelled to restate his position. "I want to reiterate, I still believe it would be a bad idea for me to go in there as the primary buyer. Just in case we can't get Isma'il, I'd feel more comfortable if we started to identify another buyer."

"Okay, your reluctance is noted," the admiral said. "While your contact is working on finding him, we'll kick around some more names in case the Bedouin doesn't pan out."

CHAPTER 42

"Who are you calling?" Dana asked while she and Bruce were driving to the three-bedroom condo they shared in the Courthouse Hill neighborhood of Arlington, Virginia.

"My father; I'm guessing he knows how to get in touch with Monsignor Alfano. If anyone can contact Hassanat, it's him."

David Tanner, still in Colorado, picked up on the third ring. "Done with your meeting already?" his father asked as soon as he answered.

"Good morning to you, too, Dad."

"Yeah, sorry, I'm just anxious about how our friends in DC want you to risk your life this time."

"Hey, I picked this profession; they didn't force me into it."

"True . . . sadly true, my son. So what's up?"

"I need to get in touch with a good mediator. You wouldn't still happen to have Monsignor Alfano's contact information?"

"I think I know how to get in touch with him, but it may take some time. One can only guess where he might be rescuing some needy souls. Tell you what, I'll try to reach him and have him call you on your cell phone. Does that work for you?"

"That's fine, but there is a sense of urgency in this. So, if he can't get back to me in a day or two, I'll have to seek someone else's counsel."

"I'll see what I can do, Bruce. You want to tell me what this is all about? Maybe I can help."

Bruce chuckled. "Can you pass as an Arab?"

"Not likely," his father replied.

"Then I just need to find out if the monsignor still knows how to get in touch with your Bedouin friends."

"Oh . . . I'm getting a vague picture here. You're right; Alfano is your best bet. I'll get right on it."

"Thanks, Pop. By the way, how is everything going out there?"

"Tanya is coming along well enough to tell Vic he should be part of any attempt to go after whoever sent those murderers after her and the kids. As far as the children are concerned, it seems they have really taken to Bart and Patty Jo, and the feeling seems to be mutual. It wouldn't surprise me if their next safe house is close to the McCoys."

"How's that coming anyway? Have they gotten new identities yet?"

"Not yet, but Director Sardo pulled some strings and arranged for them to temporarily move into visiting officer's quarters on Fort Carson right next to Vic and his family."

"How long do you think that's for?"

"According to Sardo, a couple of weeks or until the media loses interest in the story. By the way, as best we can tell, no media outlet has linked the Boyer stuff in Humboldt County to the incident in Evergreen. Again, according to Director Sardo, there is no reason for anyone to make the connection. In case you haven't heard, the last two Mexican gunmen succumbed to their injuries so there is no need for any court proceedings in Colorado. FBI and local law enforcement officials are still calling it a violent home invasion. In Humboldt County there is plenty of hard, stand-alone evidence to prosecute the Boyer case on its own merits."

"Well, that's good. Incidentally, if Vic is really interested in being part of the mop-up operation, why don't you suggest he get in touch with Azzan and Eitan in San Diego? We could certainly use someone with his skills."

"Why don't you call him and ask him yourself?"

"I could but then he'd feel obligated to say yes. In spite of

Tanya's urging him to get involved, he does have a family to worry about. Frankly, I'd prefer if he'd volunteer."

Snickering, David offered, "Talking about volunteering, Bart wanted to know if you need him for any mop-up operation."

"He's kidding, right?"

"No, I think he was serious."

"Well, thank him for offering, but I don't think so. The way I see this playing out, it appears it will require the skills of much younger and more physical players. Besides, assuming Vic is coming with me, Tanya will need his assistance. Incidentally, how is Patty Jo coping with her experience?"

"She still seemed to be fine yesterday evening, but Bart quietly told me she woke up in the middle of the night in a cold sweat dreaming about intruders coming after her and her late husband. Who knows if that was a one-time thing or whether it will continue to haunt her? Bart believes she has been able to rationalize the killing of another human being for the sake of the children's lives."

"That impresses me, Dad."

"Why's that?"

"Because I've known many seasoned warriors who have been unable to make that rationalization."

There was silence on the line for several seconds before David injected, "By the way, Tanya has been placed on medical leave and her Middle East orders have been put on hold pending a decision on surgery. I'm guessing, since you don't need Bart's assistance, he and Patty Jo will probably go back to California and stay at the Slaughter place. Bart will help Miles tend to the businesses until Vic returns."

"Well, that's good news. When will they make a determination whether Tanya requires surgery?"

"That decision is still a couple of weeks away, but it would be a surprise if some kind of surgery wasn't necessary. Hey, I'm at the Evergreen house waiting for an assistant U.S. attorney to arrive to discuss how soon they might be able to release it as a crime scene. But before he arrives, I'd better get cracking on locating the monsignor."

As soon as Bruce hung up, he turned his head in Dana's direction. Smiling in his mischievous way, he left no doubt in Dana's mind what he was implying when he said, "Okay, with that in motion, do you think we could have some quality time together when we get home?"

With her best coquettish inflection, Dana replied, "Gee, I thought you might want to eat first."

"No chance," Bruce said as he put his hand on her thigh and gently squeezed.

Dana leaned across the center console and kissed him on the cheek, whispering, "Are you at least going to ply me with a drink?"

Devilishly Bruce replied, "It's not even noon yet, but I'll do whatever is necessary to get your clothes off, babe."

CHAPTER 43

"I can't believe you answered the first time I called. I don't think that ever happened before," David Tanner responded to Monsignor Anthony Alfano's cheery greeting.

"Well, it just so happens I was summoned to the Vatican the other day and now I'm cooling my heels outside the office of Cardinal Virdone, president of Caritas Internationalis."

"Caritas, isn't that the umbrella name under which all the Catholic Church's regional charities and humanitarian organizations unite?"

"Something like that."

"You don't seem too happy about your invitation."

"I didn't say it was an invitation, it was definitely a summons. I've heard through the Vatican grapevine they think I operate with too much independence."

"And I suppose they want to rein you in."

"Yeah, we'll see . . . Changing the subject, what's up, David?"

"Bruce might have a job for our Bedouin friend. Would you happen to know how to get in touch with him in a time-sensitive situation?"

"Normally, I wouldn't be able to predict his availability, but it just so happens I know he is among the connected world for a few days. Do you want me to ask him to call you?"

"It would be more efficient if he contacted Bruce directly. If that's all right, I'll give you Bruce's number for our friend to call."

"Okay, but I can't promise he'll call."

"Understood. It's 703-555-1212."

"Just one more thing, David . . . there wouldn't happen to be a finder's fee in this for my charity?"

David snickered just loud enough for the monsignor to hear. "I didn't think you'd let me get off so easy. Are you still refusing to take Rome's handouts?"

"How do you think I still operate so independently?"

"If anything, you are persistently stubborn. I'll wire a donation to your charitable trust."

■ ■ ■

"Did you and Dana get a good night's sleep?" Bob Hoffman asked teasingly over the telephone at 7 a.m. the next morning.

Faking annoyance, Bruce responded, "None of your business. Is there a reason you woke us up so early?"

"Yeah, while you two were doing whatever you do together, we've been working through the night compiling a game plan. How'd you like to pop down to McLean and critique it?"

"Fine, we'll be there at 9 o'clock."

■ ■ ■

While weaving in and out of rush-hour traffic on the George Washington Parkway, Dana asked, "What if Isma'il doesn't call or isn't interested in helping?"

"I don't know, babe. I guess I could play one of Boris's intermediaries. Having Boris as a reference certainly should grease the way with both the don and Marinov. My Russian should be convincing enough to pass muster with the Bulgarian captain. I could even manage a little Czech and Polish in order to solidify an Eastern European lineage. It's likely I will be dealing with the don in Spanish or English, anyway. My problem is, fundamentally, I just don't think I come off as a bad guy, much less a ruthless smuggler or terrorist."

"Oh, I think you could pull it off. My biggest worry is how you are going to get your hands on both the sub and the captain without a firefight."

Nodding his head, Bruce replied, "I agree. Let's hope the reason they want us in McLean this morning is to present us with a solid plan."

At that moment "Anchors Away" began playing on Bruce's cell phone. "International caller!" he announced excitedly. "Wonder if it's the monsignor or Isma'il?" he said as he swiped across the green phone image on his cell phone. "Hello."

Instead of identifying himself, the heavily accented Middle Eastern voice asked, "How's your father?"

From the question and the accent, Bruce instantly knew it was the Bedouin. "Fine, he'd love to see you and your father again."

"Is that an invitation?"

"Of course, but that's not why we asked our mutual friend to contact you."

"I didn't think so. Is it something we can discuss over the phone?"

"Partly, but if you're willing and able to make a trip to the States, I have a short-term situation you might be interested in. Of course, if you agree to come, I'll pay all your expenses, but we need you here within forty-eight hours."

"That's doable, but at least give me a hint as to what kind of job."

"Sure, it's temporary, dangerous, and pays *extremely* well."

"Is it legal?"

"That's a good question. Based upon our past working relationships, you probably can figure out who the client is, and for him legality is sometimes a two-headed shark."

Isma'il found Bruce's analogy hilarious. When he was able

to contain his laughing, he replied, "Okay, I can live with that until we meet face-to-face. I'm assuming that's the next step."

"Yeah, where do you want us to pick you up?"

"I'm at the airport right now. Figuring you wouldn't attempt to contact me unless it was urgent, I already booked myself on a flight to JFK leaving in a couple of hours. Do you remember what the Egyptians called me?"

"I do," Bruce replied.

"Good, don't you pick me up. Have a driver waiting just outside Immigration Control with that name on a sign. He should show up around 4 p.m. New York time, but tell him he may have to wait for up to two hours for me to arrive."

"That's sounds like a good, cautious plan."

"I'm impressed," Dana said after Bruce disconnected. "That sounds like a pretty effective way to avoid being tailed when he gets to JFK. He didn't disclose where he was coming from, what time he would arrive, or a name the driver is to use to locate him."

CHAPTER 44

"So, is he in?" Bob Hoffman asked when all the team members were assembled.

With a slight sideways nod of his head and a flip of his open hand, Bruce answered, "Well, it's not definite, but I doubt he'd come all this way and not join us, especially if we can sweeten the pot."

"Like how, asylum in the U.S.?"

"No, he'd never leave the Middle East."

"I'm thinking perhaps we could finance a couple of infra-structure projects for some Bedouin settlements in the Negev."

"The Israelis wouldn't like that," the admiral instantly responded.

"Since when does this administration give a shit about what the Israelis think?" Al Juravich matter-of-factly replied.

Everybody chuckled, but nobody chimed in until Bob said, "Okay, I'll run it up the line and see what kind of response I get. Meanwhile, Ron will fill you in on our latest thinking. Go ahead, Ron."

"Before we start, I can tell you we've identified one of the assailants, who gives us a direct link to our target here, the Tijuana cartel. One of the gunmen killed in Fort Collins turns out to be a nephew of Teodoro Sanchez Felix."

"Even more reason to go in and take these guys out!" Bruce announced with venom cascading from every word.

The leader of the SWBI smiled as his eyes passed around the room. "Here's the thing—" He scanned his listeners one more time. "—in the spirit of cooperation with the Joint Task Force on Drugs and Money Laundering, we are going to provide enough intelligence and support so the Mexicans can take down Don Felix and all his operations. That being said, all does not include Marinov and the sub. That's your mission, Bruce."

Ron watched as Bruce's facial muscles tightened and his eyes narrowed. Guessing what was bothering him, Ron continued, "We know you want to see Don Felix pay for the deaths of your two bodyguards, as do we. However, extradition and a trial in the United States would get complicated. Both Patty Jo and Tanya would probably have to testify. Neither of them needs that kind of exposure or risk. The Mexicans will put him away for a long time on drug charges alone. Besides, who knows what might happen to him when the federales invade his operation."

Ron watched Bruce's expression soften somewhat so he continued, "We now have blueprints of the cliff house, sub holding pen, and the Bulgarian crew's barracks. Marinov doesn't usually stay in the barracks; Don Felix has a room for him at his hacienda closer to Ensenada. We also have confirmation the don has been shopping around for a buyer but has avoided other Mexican cartels for fear of strengthening one of his competitors at his expense."

"How's that?" Dana asked.

"Over the last fifteen years," Ron responded, "his Tijuana cartel had lost considerable power and influence to the other Mexican drug organizations. Two years ago things started turning back in his favor. The U.S.-Mexican Joint Task Force on Drugs and Money Laundering helped their government capture two of their most notorious competitors, Miguel Angel Travaris Morales, the head of Los Jetas, and Joaquin 'El Chapo' Guzman. Their arrests temporarily caused the cartels to go somewhat dormant for a year or so. Felix took advantage of this window of opportunity by strengthening his distribution

in the southwestern U.S. and eventually establishing his relationship with the Boyers in Northern California by obtaining the submarine. When word got out he had a unique new
distribution channel and money-laundering scheme, the other
cartels were almost begging him to distribute their drugs and
launder their money. Now with both his distribution channel
and the money-laundering operations shut down, he doesn't
want to give the advantage back to one of his old adversaries."

Bruce was smiling. "So, we'll be sitting in the catbird seat
when we show up with a Middle Eastern or Eastern European
buyer."

Al Juravich interrupted, "It's definitely going to have to be a
Middle Eastern player. Ever since word has circulated one of
Bulgaria's subs somehow managed to sneak out of the Black
Sea, the Turks have tightened their surveillance in the Dar-
danelles. Everybody knows it would be suicide to attempt a
run back through the strait."

"We were thinking, assuming we could find a credible-
looking and -speaking Persian or Arab, we should play the
Iranian or ISIS card. Either one of them would seem to be
likely candidates to want such a unique vessel capable of either
military or smuggling uses."

"Yeah . . . unless one of them has already been in contact
with Don Felix," Bruce said apprehensively.

"True, Boris has assured us that if anyone else shows interest,
he'll know about it," Al replied unconvincingly.

Bruce gave Dana a vulnerable look before he responded
reluctantly, "Okay, I guess we'll have to proceed with that assumption."

"Good," Admiral Noon said. "Assuming everything we've
said holds up, let me bring you up to speed on some of the lo-
gistics we've been working on. Our idea is for you to convince
the don to let you have Captain Marinov take you for a test ride
in the sub before you sign the papers. Assuming that works,
you'll need to convince the captain to take it out into international waters. He probably thinks his new German-engineered

engines and stealth technology make him invisible to our detection capabilities. Not true. All you have to do is get him to cruise within the proximity of one of our naval task forces, which is conveniently returning to San Diego from duty in the South Pacific, and we'll pick him up. Although it is international waters, we have the permission of the Bulgarian government to stop and seize their stolen submarine."

Smiling, Ron Geck chimed in, "Shortly after you and the captain launch in the sub, the Mexican authorities will descend on Don Felix and all his operations." Suddenly, Ron got real serious. "Just in case everything doesn't go off as planned, we're going to want backup teams and plans in place. And . . . lots of things could go wrong, starting with the possibility we won't know where he is going to want to meet until the last minute. It could be any one of several of his facilities so we'll need to have a flexible backup plan."

"Most obvious," the admiral continued, "is his ranch; for years he's operated from there. It's an eight-hundred-acre property with its own air strip. It is off federal Highway 1 about halfway between the sub base and Ensenada. He could have you land there and meet in the hacienda. On the other hand, his new cliff house in La Bufadora is closer to the sub base.

"For us, either place has its pros and cons, but the ranch poses the most difficulties. Opposition-wise, he keeps a lot of soldiers on the ranch. The only way for our guys to get on the ranch undetected is to parachute in at night. Once on the ground, they would find little cover other than the darkness and a few scrawny bushes. Meanwhile, we are still going to have teams at both the cliff house and the sub base, assuming you'll eventually wind up there for the test drive.

"Logistically, the cliff house and sub base are the easiest places for us to get your backup teams in place. Generally they're only patrolled by a handful of guards. Inbound you could launch the first wave of backup teams at night from one of our subs several miles offshore. It's the quietest way to avoid detection. Anticipating you'll want to split your forces to deploy backup teams at both the house and the sub base, we've identified two separate waiting areas for your people. The down side of these sites is the rugged terrain; response time from their holding areas will be ten minutes or more, whereas at the ranch your guys can respond in less than two minutes. Until we know for sure where Don Felix is going to decide to meet, there's not much more we can do.

"In any case, assuming everything comes off as planned, while you sail off with Marinov on the sub, the teams will quietly pull out in their Zodiacs or, from the ranch, disappear into the hills until we can send helicopters to retrieve them. Our emergency extraction plan, in case of a glitch, includes two Bell 412 helicopters that a petroleum air service is willing to lend you. We'll strip off all the markings at San Diego Naval Air Station and reconfigure them to each hold a maximum of twelve passengers. We can give you the names of several outstanding pilots, but we don't want to be the ones contacting or employing them.

"We think the two helicopters should stage on the north island of Islas de Todos Santos approximately twelve miles offshore. They can be at all three locations in less than five minutes. If we are forced to go to the emergency extraction plan, we'd like your team at the barracks to blow up the sub and its shelter before they bug out. If you can somehow bring Marinov along, the State Department will forever be in your debt . . . well, maybe only temporarily grateful . . . if you can't bring him out, he's expendable."

"So what do you think?" Bob Hoffman asked apprehensively.

Smiling, Bruce answered, "I like the idea of taking the sub for a test drive and just sailing off into the sunset." Then his demeanor turned somber. "The emergency extraction plan from the ranch sounds pretty dicey. What's your take, Dana?"

Ignoring Bruce's query for a second, Dana turned to the DEA's SWBI leader. "Ron, how much firepower does the don readily have at his disposal?"

"He probably has between twenty and twenty-five at the

hacienda and another five at both the cliff house and the sub base. That total doesn't include Marinov's eight or nine sailors."

Dana frowned. "Man, if Bruce's and Isma'il's cover is blown, all hell is going to break loose and our on-shore forces will be fragmented. I realize we can't put too many men on shore without the fear of being detected, but we better pack those helicopters ready to go with as many reinforcements and firepower as they can hold."

"Yeah," Bruce added, "I'm thinking at least four guys at each location to hold off the enemy until the reinforcements can get there. Including me and Isma'il, that's a third of Don Felix's strength. On the other hand, I'll take my handful of our trained professionals against thirty amateur banditos any day. Besides, just having NVGs and continuous communications through the Invisio M4 headsets gives us a distinct advantage at night. I also think we can augment our capability with the right skills and weaponry."

"What kind of stuff are you thinking about?" Ron Geck asked but didn't wait for an answer. "If you make too much of a commotion, I can't promise you how long I can hold back the federales."

"No worry, Ron," Bruce said through a devious smile. "I've included in our team a couple of snipers whose weapons will be suppressed." An approving smirk past over Ron Geck's face.

"Just one more thing," Bruce said. "When are you going to tell the federales about the submarine?"

Ron frowned. "If everything goes according to plan, we're not going to tell them. If we did and your guys have to blow it up, it would be a virtual admission we did it."

Looking around the room somewhat sheepishly, Ron announced, "My greatest fear is that the don has an informant in the federales."

An eerie silence descended on the room.

CHAPTER 45

By the time he had weaved his way through the throng massing at the Immigration Control exit, Isma'il Hassanat spotted the driver holding up a sign for a "Mr. Khamsin." He chuckled when he realized the man appeared to be a recent Middle Eastern émigré to New York.

He himself had made a concerted effort to downplay his ethnicity by getting a shave and a haircut at the airport in Milan. He was dressed in a European banker-style gray, double-breasted, pinstriped suit with a starched white shirt and a royal blue tie. He clicked across the marble floor in black, $800 spit-shined Ferragamo boots. Slung over his shoulder was a tan Bosca leather briefcase. He was pulling a red Rimowa carry-on as he made his way toward his driver.

"I'm Khamsin," he announced when he was a few feet away.

The driver eyed him up and down before he handed his passenger a business card and said in heavily accented English, "Welcome to New York, Mr. Khamsin. Let me take your suitcase . . . it's just a short walk to where I parked."

The two men walked silently to a white Mercedes S550 sedan. The driver opened and shut the rear door for his passenger then put the suitcase in the trunk.

When the driver started to pull away, Isma'il asked, "Do you know where you are to deliver me?"

"Yes, sir," the man replied. "Atlantic Aviation at Teterboro Airport in New Jersey. Is that correct, sir?"

"If that's what they told you, that's where you should take me."

Through his rearview mirror, the driver gave his passenger a curious look but said nothing.

Isma'il leaned forward, speaking to the driver in the Egyptian Arabic dialect of the Sinai, "Tell me when we are ten minutes away from our destination."

The man hesitated, keeping his eyes on the road while he replied in English, "Yes, sir," then continued defensively, "I've been instructed to take you on the scenic route since this is your first visit to New York." He waited for a reply but when his passenger remained silent, he continued, "Right now, we are in the Borough of Queens. In just a few minutes, we'll pass through Brooklyn, then assuming it's okay with you, I'll take you over the Brooklyn Bridge to Manhattan. We'll drive up the east side on FDR Drive past the UN, cut through Central Park, pick up the Henry Hudson Parkway on the west side to get to the George Washington Bridge where we will cross over to New Jersey. Assuming we hit normal traffic, the whole trip should take about an hour and a half, and you will have had a quick tour of the Big Apple."

Reading his driver's name on the business card, Isma'il replied, "Sounds exciting, Sami. Are you going to point out the important sites to me?"

Pleased that the important man in the backseat called him by his name, Sami attempted to make eye contact through the rearview mirror. Sami smiled when their gaze met momentarily, and he jokingly suggested, "You may have to shut me up if I get too detailed."

"Don't worry, my friend, as long as you keep one hand on the steering wheel, your performance will be appreciated."

For the next hour, Isma'il was treated to some of New York's most famous landmarks. Sami must have been very proud of his new country because he almost never was at a loss to point out even the most mundane landmarks while providing little-known facts about each.

It seemed to Isma'il that Sami never stopped talking or even took a breath until after they were on the Jersey side of the George Washington Bridge.

After five minutes of welcome silence Sami announced, "We're about ten minutes from the airport."

"Thanks, Sami," his passenger replied as he took out his cell phone and began punching in a text message to Bruce Tanner.

■ ■ ■

Bruce and his father were sitting on the tarmac in one of Tanner Development Corporation's jets.

"I'll go get him," David Tanner said. "You keep trying to call guys to fill out your team."

Not counting the two helicopter pilots, Bruce now had twenty former elite fighters committed to join the operation. He just needed one more battle-hardened medic to complete the team. Bruce had two more names of former Special Forces medics he wanted to call. Meanwhile, at a rented ranch thirty miles northeast of San Diego, Dana and Ron Geck were already assembling supplies and briefing Vic, Azzan, and Eitan.

The senior Tanner was excited to be reuniting with the man who, eight years earlier, risked his own life orchestrating his escape from Palestinian kidnappers. David was standing in front of the Atlantic Aviation Terminal when a Mercedes pulled up. The passenger was out of the vehicle before the driver had a chance to make his way around to open the door. David was unsure whether this dark handsome man in his midthirties was Isma'il. Having not really given it much thought, he half expected his Bedouin savior to look the same as he did when he disappeared into the desert.

The new arrival dispelled all doubt of who he was by bounding across the concrete toward David Tanner, beaming in a wide smile. "David Tanner . . . I finally get to meet you again, but this time on your turf."

"Khamsin!" David exclaimed, radiating his delight. "I never thought we'd ever meet again."

Joking, Isma'il replied, "That's the only reason I agreed make this hellish journey halfway across the world."

"REALLY?" David responded skeptically.

Isma'il laughed. "Okay, you figured me out. I was intrigued by the sketchy details Bruce gave me. Where is he, anyway?"

"He's on the plane making phone calls. Come on, let's get on board. You two have a lot to discuss; and assuming you actually sign on, the two of you are scheduled for a briefing in Groton, Connecticut, this afternoon."

"What's in Groton . . . I never heard of it."

David chuckled at the thought of this Bedouin, who spent virtually his whole life in the desert, crawling down into a metal cylinder in order to cruise beneath the ocean. "Eh . . . Groton is a U.S. Navy base just a short hop up the coast from here. I think it would be better to let Bruce give you the rest of the details."

Bruce was just finishing up a call when Isma'il and his father ducked their heads to enter the cabin door on the four-passenger Cessna Citation Mustang. Bruce raised his hand, indicating that he would be off the phone shortly; however, several minutes later he was still on the call. Catching his father's attention, he raised his eyebrows then pointed to the cockpit before rotating his index finger around in a circle to indicating to his father to instruct the pilot to prepare for takeoff.

It wasn't until the plane was taxiing down the runway that Bruce was able to end the call and greet Isma'il. "Sorry, about that . . . some guys need more handholding than others. Now at long last, we finally get to meet."

After a few minutes of reminiscing about their combined efforts in securing David's safe release from his Palestinian kidnappers, Isma'il said, "So tell me what this is all about and why I should join you."

Since the flight time and taxiing would take less than an hour, Bruce quickly went through the events starting with the general's murder. When he was finished, Isma'il asked, "Whatever made you think of me or that I would even consider taking part in this? After all, I have no interest in some rich American or in thwarting various far-flung smuggling and money-laundering schemes."

"Well," Bruce's eyes bore into Isma'il's, "my father was some rich American and not all the other victims were rich. Socially and economically, the Native American teenager who was kidnapped and murdered had an awful lot in common with you Bedouins. As for the smuggling and money laundering, I recognize you have some sympathy for those lines of work, but I don't believe you would ever be ruthless enough to go after the innocent family members of your pursuers."

Isma'il caressed his face and chin with his left hand, rubbing them for a few seconds while he stared back into Bruce's eyes. "Okay, I despise the thought of innocent families being caught up in these kinds of violent activities." Then grinning he said, "Count me in, if for no other reason that I've been bored stiff playing a rich Arab for the last eight years. Now, tell me why we're headed for Connecticut when you just told me all the action was going to take place in Mexico?"

"You and I are going to sub school."

"Sub, as in submarine?"

Grinning, Bruce replied, "Yep, a boat that goes under the water."

"Whoa . . . why do I need to go to sub school? I'm just going to play the money man . . . aren't I?"

"What . . . you don't want to come with me on the test drive?"

"Not a chance. I'm a desert nomad, we like nothing but open sky over our heads."

For the first time, David Tanner chimed in, "Hell, you'll be a lot safer in the sub than you were when you plunged into the cavern stream and had to swim underwater through a rocky tunnel for almost a hundred meters without any air."

Isma'il gave David a nasty glare but said nothing.

Hoping to move on, Bruce interjected, "Look, forget going

on the test drive; if you're going to negotiate for the sub, doesn't it make sense you know something about it?"

"Fine, but you need to figure out how I'm getting out of there while you're cruising a hundred meters underwater."

"Well, there's no reason why you couldn't just fly back."

Nodding, Isma'il replied, "There, given that plan, I'm in."

CHAPTER 46

Two days later, Bruce and Isma'il arrived at the ranch outside of San Diego to finalize operational planning with the rest of the team. It wasn't until the end of their second full day that they received an email confirming Boris had arranged a meeting for them with Don Felix. Isma'il's cover would be a Saudi Prince, HH Prince Abdul bint Turki bin Abdul Aziz from one of the nonlineage cadet branches. As part of Boris's recommendations to Don Felix, he claimed the prince was a "disenchanted" and "disenfranchised" member of the royal family living in Lebanon and holding a Moroccan passport by virtue of his Marrakesh-born mother. Boris alluded to the fact that Prince Abdul had been a "favorite" nephew of Osama bin Laden and one of the original financial backers of the Islamic Front in the Syrian Civil War. More recently he had become an ardent supporter of ISIS.

Boris was at his facilitating best, offering to have one of his trusted lieutenants, Dimitri Makshimuskin, accompany the prince and help Don Felix get the best deal possible. Bruce laughed hysterically when he first heard his cover name and joked he might have trouble spelling it.

Bob Hoffman came through with their passports adorned with years of entrance and exit stamps from all over the world. He assured Bruce that even the particular country's state departments would be hard pressed to recognize them as forgeries.

■ ■ ■

Don Felix directed Boris to instruct his two visitors to land at Ensenada's Airport, where a car would be waiting to take them to the meeting. He gave no clue as to where they were headed. The uncertainty as to where their backup would be needed was almost a relief to Bruce. Now, they had to thoroughly plan for all possibilities.

It took a full day of brainstorming between Bruce, Vic, Dana, Ron, Isma'il, and Azzan to reach consensus on an approach. First, the no-brainer; Alpha Team with five men would launch in a Zodiac from a U.S. Navy sub several miles offshore and take up position at the sub base. Bravo Team with eight members would board a U.S. Air Force C-130 at March Air Reserve Base one hour before Bruce and Isma'il were scheduled to land in Ensenada. The plane would circle over the Pacific until it was determined where the meeting was to take place. The team needed to be prepared to jump either into the ocean near the cliff house or onto land on the ranch. The two helicopters, each with another four more heavily armed reinforcements, would be poised on Islas de Todos Santos as originally planned. Their deployment, when needed, would be determined by the situation on the ground. It wasn't a perfect plan, but it allowed for flexibility in both its detail and timing.

When they thought they were comfortable with the plans, Vic spoke up. "I have just two nagging concerns."

"Like what?" Dana asked.

"First is keeping our intelligence info current. So, I was thinking, it might be advantageous to have some eyes on the ground at each potential meeting site a day or so before Bruce and Isma'il actually show up."

"Why; what would that accomplish?" Bruce asked.

"Maybe nothing . . . but what bothers me is we don't know

what we don't know. Suppose he beefs up his security at one of them; that would give us a heads-up as to where the meeting is planned. Or suppose he has another potential buyer show up before you guys; or whatever. Like I said, we don't know what we don't know."

"All right, so what are you suggesting?" Ron Geck asked. "I can't provide that capability without the Mexican authorities finding out and getting suspicious."

"I happen to know a few ex-Air Force guys who are quite skilled at forward reconnaissance. They might be willing to camp out on the Baja Peninsula for a few days."

"Even after what happened to your last two volunteers?" Ron replied in partial disbelief.

"Even more so," Vic spit out with conviction. Then addressing the rest of the team he asked, "What do you guys think?"

Speaking up for the first time, Isma'il was the first to respond. "Well, it can't hurt unless they are detected."

Bruce jumped in. "That won't happen; I've worked with these kinds of guys before, they're ghosts. I say go for it. Anyone opposed?"

When everybody shook their heads no, Dana said, "You mentioned two concerns. What's the second?"

"Okay, don't take this the wrong way, but we never specified who was going to be in charge of our central command and communications."

"You're right, Vic," Bruce immediately responded. "I was going to talk to you privately but I guess this will have to do. It's you."

"Me!"

"Yep, I can't think of anyone who is better qualified than you. I know, you were itching to personally get even with the guy who ordered the attack on your family, but you being the pivot man is really the best way for all of us to assure he gets what's coming to him."

The whole room was silent while everyone stared at Vic,

waiting for his reaction. Finally, after a long moment of reflection, he responded, "This doesn't make me happy but you're right; assessing the situation and our team, I am the best choice."

It took one more day with the entire team walking through the operational plans and blueprints of all three sites before Bruce and Vic believed they were ready to launch.

Finally, one week after first accepting the assignment from Director Sardo, Bruce and his team were ready to launch.

CHAPTER 47

Using their own names, Bruce and Isma'il flew commercial to Vancouver International Airport, arriving slightly after 7 p.m. Waiting for them was a Gulfstream V with a tail code indicating registration in Qatar. It had been chartered in the prince's name out of Amman, Jordan. The boys back in McLean had the plane make one stop in Moscow before arriving in Vancouver, British Columbia. Although upon departing Amman it contained only the three-person crew, the prince's name was on the passenger manifest. During a refueling stop in Moscow, Dimitri Makshimuskin was added. Both men's fictitious passports contained Canadian entry stamps.

They were two hours into the flight from Vancouver to Ensenada when Bruce received an urgent call from Vic. Vic didn't waste any time with greetings as his first words were "We've got a problem!"

"What's up?" Bruce replied apprehensively.

"I just got a call from Al Juravich; Boris is missing."

"What do you mean . . . missing?"

"I mean gone . . . disappeared . . . vanished."

"Do they think somebody kidnapped him?"

"Possibly. The consensus is some old enemy got to him and we'll find his body in a few days, but they haven't ruled out that he skipped out on his own accord."

"Why would Boris do that? He's been living the life of a billionaire in a chateau on the Adriatic for over eight years now. He'd have to be crazy to go AWOL now."

"Yeah, that's what Al thinks, but until they do find him, we can't be 100 percent certain."

"Shit!" Bruce exclaimed. "What are they doing to find him?" When Isma'il heard Boris's name, he perked up. "What's up with Boris?"

Bruce held up one finger indicating for Isma'il to wait for an answer while he listened to Vic's reply. "They have facial recognition software scanning all the footage from every major airport and train station from London to Moscow. If he's running and tries to take public transportation, they'll find him, but if someone kidnapped him, they may never locate him."

"Okay," Bruce replied. "That's an interesting development, but I don't see that impacting our operation . . . do you?"

"No, my three guys are on the ground with parabolic dishes listening to everything going on at all three locations. At the moment, the don is at the cliff house with Marinov. So far, there doesn't appear to be any unusual activity taking place.

"Our operation is on schedule, the C-130 and two helicopters take off for their holding areas in the next half-hour. The sub base team left yesterday from Point Luma on the USS *Hampton*. Everybody should be in position by the time you land in Ensenada."

"Okay, Vic; let's talk one more time before we land."

Bruce wasn't off the phone a second when Isma'il said, "I got the gist of what you and Vic were talking about with Boris. I don't like the fact he's disappeared. He's a greedy bastard by nature; he may have decided it was worth more to him to sell out his new partners in the West than to continue to feed off the scraps from their table."

"Yeah, that could present a problem. So do you want to abort?"

Isma'il hesitated, pursing his lips. "No, we've got a good

backup plan should anything go wrong." Then as an after-thought, he announced, "I think I'll change into my Arabian prince clothes."

■ ■ ■

The pilot of Bruce's and Isma'il's chartered jet had just an-nounced they were beginning their approach to Ensenada Airport when Vic called back. "My guy at the cliff house just watched the don and the captain get in a vehicle with a couple of bodyguards. It looks like they're headed to the ranch."

"Good work. That should give Azzan and his guys an early start on their run."

CHAPTER 48

After landing in Ensenada, Bruce and Isma'il were met by four armed men in a Chevy Suburban. With the window open and the warm night air whistling through the vehicle, they rode in silence from the airport. They were sandwiched in the middle row between a sullen-looking middle-aged guard in the passenger seat and two younger, nastier-looking pistoleros behind them in the third seat.

The vehicle headed a short distance south on Highway 1 before turning east onto a secondary road. A surveillance drone controlled from a secret site east of San Diego shadowed them from two thousand feet above. The vehicle's eastward change of direction was monitored by a U.S. Navy drone operator who was in direct contact with Vic. Now there was no question, the meeting would be at the ranch.

Vic relayed the information to Azzan in the C-130. The aircraft had already begun to get in position by heading south for fifteen minutes then starting a wide turn which would take them inland over desolate mountains and valleys. Soon they would turn north, making their approach over the bleak rolling hills bordering the southeast portion of the ranch. The team would jump from 10,000 feet to a point just inside the fence line. That would put them twenty to thirty minutes by foot from the main house. Ideally, they would be on the ground only minutes after the Suburban reached the ranch.

Moments after the C-130 started its south-to-north run, Vic's forward observer, who was virtually invisible in his ghillie suit 350 yards from the main house, picked up on his parabolic receiver what sounded like an intercom call. "The don's on his way. He says fuel up the plane and have it ready to go as soon as his visitors arrive."

Almost instantly, floodlights burst on from the roof of a small metal building adjacent to the landing strip. Parked nearby were a twin-engine Cessna and a small tanker truck. Within seconds, three men emerged from inside the building; one of the men jumped into the tanker while the other two headed for the plane.

Urgently the observer spoke into his global satellite phone linked into Vic's com package, "Central, this is cowboy, we have a new development. I've picked up a voice communication indicating the don wants his plane ready to take off as soon as the visitors arrive. A crew is fueling a twin-engine plane as we speak. It looks like we may have a new location; suggest the airdrop be delayed until I can confirm."

"Roger that, cowboy. ETA for the prince is ten minutes."

Vic first passed the hold order on to Azzan on the C-130, then he informed Al Juravich in McLean along with Ron Geck and Dana, who were with the Mexican federal police assault team. The assault team was waiting in a secluded staging area equidistant between the ranch and the don's meth lab.

Dana received the news of a possible third location with trepidation. She immediately got on the phone to Mike Musgrave, currently working with Secret Service to continue unraveling the international money-laundering network. After providing Mike with a quick update on events in Mexico, she asked, "Do you recall anything Mulrooney said or have you found anything on the hard drive that would help us locate another possible location for this meeting?"

"Not off the top of my head, but let me quickly go back over my notes. I'll call you back if I come up with something."

With desperation in her voice, Dana replied, "Okay, but hurry, I don't know how much time we've got."

In their few days working together, Mike had developed a real fatherly fondness for Dana and it pained him to hear such distress in her voice. "Don't worry, Dana; if there is anything, you know I'll find it."

Realizing she had let her emotions seep into her inflection, Dana took a deep breath before replying confidently, "I know you will."

■ ■ ■

The forward recon man at the ranch watched and reported in when the don's vehicle arrived. Minutes later, when the vehicle carrying Bruce and Isma'il arrived, he was dismayed by his inability to do anything while they were ushered out of the vehicle at gunpoint.

Illuminated by the floodlights on the maintenance building, the don slowly walked toward his guests. Except for the fact he had a gun pointed at his back, Isma'il looked regal in his ankle-length white thobe and red-and-white checkered gutra secured to his head with a black egal. Ignoring Bruce, Don Felix stopped directly in front of the "prince."

Meanwhile, Bruce was doing a quick evaluation of their situation. Besides the two armed goons behind them, now there were two more nasty-looking gunmen poised ten feet away with AK-47s. It would be suicide for him and Isma'il to try anything right now.

Don Felix stopped five feet in front of them, glaring. Isma'il confidently played his role by calmly addressing the don in his best British accent. "Boris alluded to the fact you were a cautious man, Don Felix, but I question the wisdom of treating a potential customer so rudely."

Like an eclipse, a smirk passed across Don Felix's face. "You can stop the bullshit. Boris told me you're imposters working for the American government."

Suddenly, his smirk disappeared and was replaced with a hair-raising expression of malevolence. He paused for an instant then declared, "Normally, I'd have the two of you executed right here and now, but Boris made me promise I would save you for him. I'm guessing he has some special festivities awaiting your long-overdue reunion, Khamsin." Then turning toward Bruce he demanded, "And who the hell are you?"

Bruce didn't answer immediately so Don Felix shrugged and turned to walk toward the plane. "Don't answer; It doesn't matter. We'll take care of both of you soon enough but right now we've got to get out of here . . . your backup can't be too far behind."

■ ■ ■

"Good news and bad news," Al Juravich announced on a three-way hook-up between McLean, Ron, and Vic. "First, the good news. This morning, a video camera at Madrid International Airport caught an image of Boris boarding a plane for Mexico City. So, he's alive . . . the bad news is, the plane landed in Mexico City before we were able to intercept him. This afternoon, we think we captured a fuzzy video of someone fitting his description leaving passport control. As you are aware, pickup and drop-off areas are extremely well-covered with surveillance cameras yet the subject doesn't appear on any of them. Our best guess is he changed his appearance and identity before boarding a domestic flight."

"Damn!" Vic grumbled. "Are you thinking what I'm thinking?"

"Probably," Al replied. "It can't just be a coincidence he's headed for Mexico. That son-of-a-bitch must have sold you out to the don."

Vic was on the phone with Ron at the same time Dana was talking to Mike Musgrave.

Suddenly, Dana interrupted Ron, "Mike found it! He says that one of the first things Mulrooney did with Boyer's cash hoard was buy a golf course villa in San Jose del Cabo. Mulrooney says Clete Senior and Don Felix sometimes meet there. Mike's guessing the Boyers are holed up there, too."

Vic heard everything Dana said in the background. He instantly exploded with excitement. "Holy shit, that's got to be where they are all going to rendezvous! We've hit the jackpot! Does Mike have an address?"

"He sure does! It's on the ninth fairway of the Gran Mayan Resort and Country Club. The address is 3414 Punta Gorda."

Excitedly, Vic announced, "Listen up, everybody, I need a few minutes to do some checking and make some calculations. I'll get back to you shortly. Al, at this point, do you concur it is highly likely Boris is headed to Cabo, too?"

"Makes sense to me," Al agreed.

"Okay, then while I'm working some things out, could you attempt to narrow down which flight Boris is on and what time it lands in Cabo? Call me back as soon as you've got something."

The first thing Vic did was contact the C-130 and the helicopters idling on Islas de Todos Santos, instructing them to proceed toward Cabo San Lucas. He thought the C-130 might be able to outrun the Cessna, giving Azzan time to prepare a surprise for the unsuspecting don, but first he needed to verify some specifications. If he was right with his "off the top of his head" assessment, Azzan and his team would have nearly an hour to put a plan in motion.

Searching on the Internet, Vic was able to confirm the C-130 had a speed advantage of approximately a hundred miles per hour over the Cessna. Figuring it would take another fifteen minutes for the don and his captives to drive from the airport to the villa, Azzan would have the time he originally estimated to prepare. On the other hand, the two Bell helicopters only had a range of 350 nautical miles. Vic had to really scramble to find out if they were rigged for air refueling and then whether he could get either the Air Force or Navy to provide a tanker in time. The pilots of the Bell helicopters confirmed they were rigged for midair refueling, and Admiral Noon was able to quickly arrange for one of the Navy's air refueling contractors to position a plane along the Baja coast. The only issue was the choppers would require two refills on the way down, delaying their arrival over Cabo by over an hour.

Armed with his newfound window of opportunity, Vic called Bob Hoffman, explaining the situation and requesting as much information and photos of San Jose del Cabo and the Gran Mayan Resort property as he could quickly locate. While he was waiting for Bob to get back to him, Vic and Ron Geck discussed what to tell the Mexican authorities.

Although they were initially disinterested in raiding the Tijuana cartel's operations, a strong push by the U.S. State Department resulted in the Mexican government finally agreeing to lead the assaults. Now, with this latest development, Ron wasn't sure if they should go forward with the raids. Finally, after almost a half-hour of back-and-forth telephone discussion and only after the intervention of Director Sardo with Ron's bosses at DEA, it was agreed that Ron would tell his Mexican counterpart that surveillance on the ranch had detected that Don Felix had suddenly and unexpectedly left in a small plane, destination unknown. Ron then recommended the raid on the ranch be scrapped; however, they should still hit the meth lab. This action would help divert the federales attention away from any action at the sub base. To his surprise, the Mexican authorities agreed.

Originally, the attack on the sub base was scheduled to coincide with the coordinated raids on the ranch and meth lab. With the departure of Captain Marinov, Vic figured it would be easier to just destroy the sub and its protective covering; therefore, he instructed Eitan to blow it all up.

CHAPTER 49

As soon as Ron Geck informed Vic the Mexican federal police had begun their assault on the meth lab, Vic gave the word for Eitan to commence his assault.

Five heavily armed but bored men patrolled the area around the submarine. Three patrolled around the outside of its concrete pen and two were on the inside. On board, performing routine maintenance, were its Bulgarian chief engineer and four of the crew.

From their concealed holding position among the rocks on the beach, Eitan's four-man team could only confirm the three guards patrolling outside. Suspecting there were likely additional patrols inside, he split his force perimeter. He and two former Marines began their swift assault on the exterior force while his fourth man, Hal, a retired Navy SEAL, swam into the pen through its sea entrance. Not surprisingly, Eitan's assault was swift and lethal. Within minutes, Eitan and his two companions slipped through the entrance and toward a set of concrete steps. Before they descended, Eitan attempted to contact his man coming in from the sea; however, all he could hear on his headset was static. This had been one of his tactical concerns, that the tons of reinforced concrete surrounding the pen would inhibit wireless communications. Or was it that his man had been neutralized?

Cautiously, Eitan led his men down the stairs. Halfway

down they began to see the beginning of a floating steel dock. Hugging the wall the rest of the way, Eitan began scanning the dock for guards. To his surprise and relief, when he reached the last step and peered out, all he saw was his man standing on the dock looking in their direction.

Speaking softly over his shoulder he announced to his companions, "We're good. Hal's got it under control. You two go back and get the charges while Hal and I check out the inside of the sub. Apparently, we are out of contact with Vic down here; while you're up top let him know we're inside and getting ready to set the charges."

Joining the dripping wet former SEAL, Eitan commented, "I'm surprised you didn't run into any guards down here."

Hal grinned while he cocked his head toward two expanding red discolorations in the water and replied, "Oh, there were, but they decided to go for a swim. I don't expect them back."

Eitan and Hal cautiously walked across the gangplank. They made a sweep of the entire topside before deciding to investigate an open hatch aft.

Eitan, on his knees, listened through the aft engine room hatch. He could make out distant clanking and muffled conversations. Hal had served on U.S. submarines during SEAL missions, and even though this half-century-old Russian-designed vessel was only half the length and width of modern ones, he thought he might have a mental picture of the inside layout.

The worst part about entering through the hatch was that you had to descend feet first down a ladder. Once you started down, you wouldn't be able to see anything and you would be a sitting duck to anyone waiting below. Standing on the first rung, Hal took a deep breath then, in recognition of his uncertain fate, rolled his eyes at Eitan before hooking his hands and feet on the outside of the ladder's vertical legs and virtually freefalling down into the hull.

Hal landed softly on the metal grate running down the center of the vessel. The barrel of his HK NK5 submachine gun tracked his line of sight as he quickly scanned in both directions. His assessment of his surroundings confirmed he was in the aft engine room. Luckily, there was no one in sight, while the clanking and talking sounded like it was still coming from a good distance forward. After nodding the all-clear to Eitan, he slowly moved forward to the next door leading to the forward engine room.

Eitan joined him seconds later. Verifying that compartment was also clear, the two men cautiously began working their way forward. Hal whispered, "I'm guessing they're working in the control room, which should be three more compartments forward."

Hal guessed correctly; they did not run into anyone in the battery room/crew quarters or mess. Pausing in the mess, they had a clear view of four seamen; one was standing while another was on one knee talking to four legs sticking out from under a control panel. Although they were conversing in Bulgarian, Eitan guessed the one kneeling was giving instructions to the two under the panel. No weapons were visible; so Eitan and Hal entered from behind the Bulgarians.

The one standing was a relatively young seaman in his twenties. Sensing someone's presence he turned. Seeing the two armed black-clad strangers, he nervously tapped the man kneeling on his shoulder. A middle-aged man partially turned and looked up. With a scowl on his face, he calmly demanded in English, "What the fuck is this?"

Eitan sternly replied, "We'll ask the questions and if you value your lives, you'll answer . . . understood?"

The man's eyes went wide when he picked up on Eitan's heavy Israeli accent. He wouldn't have been too unnerved to hear an American. To most Eastern Europeans, Americans were soft, inhibited by some strange moral code that valued life above all else. He could possibly reason with an American; Israelis on the other hand rarely entertained discussions. They had an objective, and weren't easily distracted.

"Easy," the senior seaman replied. "What do you want to know?"

"That's good," Eitan responded. "Tell your two guys under the panel to slide out slowly with their hands visible."

The man said something in Bulgarian and the two seamen squirmed out from under the panel and stood up with their hands in clear view.

"All four of you turn around and face the control panel, then put your hands on the wall above the panel, spread your legs and lean forward." Their leader translated Eitan's command into Bulgarian and the men complied.

Hal frisked each man thoroughly, finding only a couple of screwdrivers and a pocketknife. He gave Eitan the okay nod. Eitan then instructed the men to turn around.

Addressing the apparent leader, Eitan asked, "What's your job on this sub?"

"I'm the chief engineer," the man replied proudly.

Smiling, Eitan then asked, "Is this thing capable of sailing out to sea right now?"

The man hesitated and squinted at Eitan. Eitan prodded him, "You did understand the question; didn't you?"

Ignoring the last question, the chief engineer responded, "It will run."

"Good," Eitan replied. "Are you four capable of driving it?"

Again the chief gave Eitan a funny look before answering, "You don't think the captain drives this boat, do you?"

Eitan chuckled. "So are you're telling me you can navigate this thing running on top and submerged?"

"Me and these three sailors could take it around the world, although I wouldn't want to have to attempt to elude a sub-chaser for too long."

"No worries," Eitan responded. "How much diesel fuel do you have on board?"

"Enough for about a thousand kilometers."

"Okay, start her up and prepare to shove off."

Both the Bulgarian and Hal gave Eitan a quizzical look.

Eitan smiled, addressing Hal, "What? You look surprised. Bruce was supposed to confiscate the sub, not blow it up. What the heck, since we have the opportunity, we might as well revert back to the original plan."

While the four men were readying the sub to sail, Eitan's two other team members came on board. Eitan informed them of the change in plans and instructed them to place their charges inside the pen and set the timers to detonate in an hour.

The submarine was several miles out to sea, cruising topside at fifteen knots in a northwesterly direction, when the sub pen imploded upon itself. Eitan radioed Vic to tell him he wouldn't need the helicopter for extraction since they had confiscated the sub and would rendezvous with the U.S. Navy task force at the previously arranged coordinates.

■ ■ ■

The twin turbo-prop Cessna 421 had leveled off at 24,000 feet and was cruising at 275 miles per hour toward Cabo. Bruce and Isma'il were sitting in the two second-to-last forward-facing seats, wondering whether anyone would be able to track them and put a plan in place in time to save their lives. Their wrists were secured to the armrests with duct tape and their ankles were taped together. Sitting behind each of them was one of the nasty-looking bodyguards who had picked them up at the airport. Directly in front of them, facing each other in club seating, sat Don Felix and Captain Marinov.

As soon as the pilot announced they had leveled off, Captain Marinov began pulling out drawers until he located the ice chest. Lustily he extracted a chilled bottle of Stolichnaya Elit. Don Felix grinned at the captain while he retrieved two crystal whiskey glasses from a side cabinet, placing them on the table. Marinov filled each one halfway then held his up, proclaiming, "Nazdràve!" He waited for Don Felix to respond before tossing it down in one gulp. Don Felix followed the captain's lead, shuddering as it scorched its way down his throat. Marinov immediately refilled their glasses, hoarsely announced "Nazdràve!" again but this time didn't wait for the don to respond before he gulped it down.

Minutes later Don Felix, partly out of curiosity and partly to escape the crude Bulgarian, rose from his seat and headed for the cockpit. He spoke to the two pilots for a short time then turned and, hunched over, shuffled back to where the "prince" and his "Russian" companion were sitting.

"Boris didn't tell me what you did to piss him off, but it must have been pretty serious. He made me promise to keep you alive so he could cut you up in little pieces and flush the parts down the toilet." The don hesitated, studying the "prince." "I'm curious, are you really an Arab?"

"Bedouin," Isma'il replied.

"Bedouin!" the don exclaimed. "Sounds biblical. Speak Bedouin for me."

"Sure." Isma'il, smiling, responded sardonically in Arabic, "Go fuck a camel, you asshole."

"What did you say?" Felix asked.

"He wished you a prolific sex life," Bruce responded.

Impressed, the don nodded his approval. He then turned toward Bruce, who was struggling to control his laughter, commanding, "And you, you're supposed to be one of Boris's countrymen; say something in Russian."

Bruce thought about it for a second then complied by telling the don in Russian, "When you're done with the camel, the pigs are waiting."

Don Felix turned to Captain Marinov. "Was that Russian?"

"Sounded like it but I only could recognize a few words; the whole thing made no sense to me . . . it had something to do with camels and pigs."

Don Felix gave Bruce a strange look then, shaking his head, returned to his seat.

▪ ▪ ▪

While the two planes were hurtling down the Baja Peninsula, Bob Hoffman was frantically coordinating the combined intelligence-gathering efforts of the FBI, CIA, and DOD surrounding San Jose del Cabo, the Gran Mayan Resort, and Clete

Boyer's villa. Shortly before the C-130 cut across the peninsula just south of La Paz, Bob's people had accessed, evaluated, and synthesized enough details that Vic and Azzan were able to put together two possible assault scenarios. The first one called for Azzan and his team intercepting the don's caravan somewhere between the airport and the villa. This scenario potentially afforded the don with the least amount of protection.

However, this option left the recapture of Boris up in the air and would most likely have to come off before the arrival of the extraction helicopters, thus risking local law enforcement having an opportunity to respond to the likely vicious firefight.

The second scenario involved waiting until they were sure everyone was at the villa and allowing time for the helicopters to arrive for the extraction.

CHAPTER 50

Like many hastily built tourist towns in developing countries, San Jose del Cabo had a fragile infrastructure. Being in an upscale tourist market, it was better off than most other towns of similar size, but the guys in McClean quickly found its Achilles heel. Its electrical grid lacked any redundancy. Both the town and the resort were serviced by only one electric distribution substation. By taking out that one facility, Azzan and his team donning their NVGs would command a distinct advantage over Don Felix's men. In addition, most of the area's emergency efforts would be directed at the substation and town center, limiting local law enforcement's ability to quickly respond to a disturbance at the resort.

Unlike their aborted run near Ensenada, this time, in order to make their drop, the C-130 would have to transverse directly through San Jose del Cabo Airport's takeoff and landing pattern. Radioing the air traffic control tower, the C-130 pilot requested permission to land and refuel. Prior to his request, the pilot put the plane in position so, once authorization was granted, his flight plan would take him close to both drop zones. In order to land, taxi, refuel and take off before the electric grid went down, a refueling truck was already waiting, and the plane would only take on as much gas as was need to make it back to San Diego Naval Air Station.

Azzan and his three companions jumped over the pitch-black

golf course at an altitude of 2,000 feet. Seconds later, the last two-man team bailed from less than 1,200 feet, landing undetected four hundred yards from the targeted electric substation. Both man carried a brick of C-4 explosives. Once they cut their way through the substation's steel fence, they attached a brick of C-4 on each transformer. Interrupting the electrical power was critical, yet it presented several dilemmas. Not knowing how much firepower they would be up against, Azzan would need as many of his men as possible at the villa for the assault. Therefore, the men could not wait around to detonate the explosives nor could they determine exactly when to set a manual timer. Both dilemmas were solved on the flight down. One of the team skillfully rigged up a cell phone detonator which would allow the two men to begin their mile jog to the villa as soon as the charges were set, then call in the detonation when Azzan was ready to attack.

Concealed in a fairway bunker two hundred meters from the house, Azzan and his men had a clear view across an infinity edge pool at the back of the two-story villa. The entire rear of the property was bathed in a golden glow from six hanging carriage lamps. In between the pool and the house was a large patio furnished with oversized offset patio umbrellas, cushioned lounge seating, and a round dining table. The villa's lower level was separated by four stone pillars. Between the pillars, folding glass doors provided access to the patio and a panoramic view of the pool, golf course and, off in the distance, the confluence of the Pacific Ocean and the Sea of Cortez. Two of the folding doors opened onto a covered patio. This particular evening, they were swung open, allowing the scent of sage and golf course grasses to wander inside on the cool night breeze. Directly above, a roof-top patio was accessed from the master bedroom.

Patrolling the outside of the property were five heavily armed guards. Bright indoor lighting provided an ideal backlight for the Americans to observe much of the first floor. From the blueprints Bob Hoffman provided, Azzan knew the lower level contained a family room, dining room, and kitchen as well as a small bedroom. From his position, he could observe all of the family room, most of the dining room, and half the kitchen. Although he could not see into the bedroom, the lights were out, indicating it was probably unoccupied.

In a large family room, three men stood around a bar while two others sat on a leather couch watching a soccer game. Through his binoculars, Azzan identified the two men on the couch as Clete Boyer Senior and his youngest son, Ken.

At approximately 11:30 p.m. two of the men from inside and two of the patrolling guards climbed into two GMC Yukons and sped down the street. Minutes later, Azzan's two men completed their jog from the power station. Now fully manned, Azzan took advantage of the reduced perimeter surveillance to position his men. Although all of his team were expert shots, two were also experienced snipers. The two snipers remained positioned in the sand bunker while the other five spread out and painstakingly began their assault. To assist them in monitoring activities inside, they had brought along an eighteen-inch parabolic reflector and microphone. Azzan and the reflector operator set up behind the trunk of a twenty-foot-tall elephant cactus only fifty meters from the infinity pool.

Twenty-five minutes later the two Yukons returned, screeching to a halt on the street in front of the villa. One of Azzan's men reported when Bruce and Isma'il were escorted in the front door by two armed guards.

Azzan watched as the two Boyers rose to greet Don Felix. Over their Invisio M4 headsets the entire team received succinct summaries from the man on the parabolic mic of the dialogue inside the villa. Azzan whispered updates to Vic on key events via a satellite phone. Everything was in place just waiting for the arrival of the last chess piece, Boris.

Bruce and Isma'il were duct-taped to wooden captain's chairs at the front perimeter of the dining room facing their captors, who were all loosely gathered in the family room.

Their wrists were secured to the arms, and tape was wrapped several times around their chests and the back of the chair. Don Felix positioned two armed guards directly behind them. While Ken Boyer acted as bartender, Don Felix filled Clete Senior in on Boris and his revelation.

As the don was explaining how the whole thing transpired, Clete walked over to the two bound prisoners and studied them up close. After a few moments he announced, "The Russian here, he fits the description of the intruder from the sawmill."

Don Felix stroked his jaw a few times before he responded sarcastically, "Hmm, could it be Dimitri isn't a Russian after all but an American CIA agent?" The don paused and broke out in a devious smile before announcing, "No matter, Boris will sort the whole thing out when he gets here." Then looking at his watch, he announced, "His plane should be landing right about now."

Twenty minutes later one of Azzan's guys out front radioed that another vehicle was approaching. The team was poised to act as soon as Azzan gave the word. Three men exited the vehicle, with one of them matching the description of Boris Kozlov.

At this point, the villa was protected by ten of Don Felix's soldiers: six outside and four inside. Besides the guards, the team needed to consider the other four bad guys inside as potential armed combatants. Azzan was not concerned about his fourteen-to-six disadvantage. Unless they were very unlucky and their presence was detected, eight of the enemy would be quickly neutralized before the whole area even went dark. Not satisfied with hearing only summaries of what was transpiring inside, he took control of the parabolic headset himself. While he carefully listened to the conversations inside, he began directing three of his men into positions where they would be ready to start eliminating the outside patrols.

Inside, Boris approached Isma'il. With a look of triumph smeared across his face, he stared at Isma'il for a long moment before he declared, "I suppose, at the time, you never thought you'd hear from me again. Why else would you have the audacity to send that," using the Arabic term for asshole, "*ya khorg* in your place?"

Isma'il did not respond quickly enough so Boris spat out contemptuously, "I'll tell you why, because that American Jew and his government bought you off. How else would the Yemenis know about the *Miranda* or that Nikitin was waiting in the *Anastasia* to rendezvous with it?" Now having worked himself up into a rage, he shouted, "Well, now it's my turn to screw you!"

Isma'il remained stoic, but Bruce injected in Russian, "And you didn't sell out."

Boris turned his head toward Bruce, his face contorted. "Ah, when they asked me to also recommend a second imposter, I wondered who it would be, a real Russian or a CIA imposter?"

Bruce grinned before replying in the Muscovite accent he learned to emulate during his nine-month tour at the U.S. embassy in Moscow, "Don't you remember me? We worked together on that gun deal in Macedonia."

"Like hell we did. Russian or not, you're CIA!" Turning to Clete Senior, he asked, "You wouldn't happen to have a plastic drop cloth? I wouldn't want to soil your beautiful villa."

"I do, but whatever you have in mind, couldn't you do it in the garage?"

"Certainly, but Don Felix, I'm leaving the 'Russian' for you to handle."

"That's fine," Don Felix replied, "we'll feed him to the sharks."

CHAPTER 51

Azzan knew he couldn't wait much longer. Into his headset he said, "Take down the three out front."

One after another he got back the desired reply, "Down."

Taking a deep breath, he announced, "Okay, this is it. When I give the word, we take out the remaining three outside and the two guarding Bruce and Isma'il simultaneously."

Then to his man with the cell phone detonator, he instructed, "Start dialing, as soon as you see the two guarding Bruce and Isma'il go down, blow the power station."

Over the satellite phone, he informed Vic, "We're going in now."

As he did before the start of every action, Azzan rubbed the Star of David hanging around his neck then gave the order, "NOW!"

In rapid succession, the three guards patrolling the back of the villa fell where they stood, each with a double tap in their hearts. Simultaneously, the heads of the two guards standing behind Bruce and Isma'il exploded, sending chunks of pinkish matter spraying into the air behind them. Before anyone inside reacted to the gruesome scene unfolding in front of them, a faint explosion was heard and everything started going black. The outage progressed rapidly from its origin over a mile away, taking only several seconds to reach the villa. Azzan and his men flipped down their night-vision goggles before moving toward the open patio doors.

In the blackened family room, pandemonium ensued. Both Boyers stood dumbfounded, staring into the darkness where they had just seen the heads of two men explode. Don Felix, Captain Marinov, and Boris, more accustomed to gunshots, instantly threw themselves on the floor, scrambling for cover. The don's two remaining soldiers dropped to their knees, firing their Uzis wildly out the open patio doors. Finally realizing bullets were whizzing past him, Ken pushed his father to the floor and herded him on his stomach behind the couch.

Bruce, out of the line of fire, stood, lifting the chair's legs off the floor. Then in one violent backward lunge he rammed the chair's rear legs into the floor. There was a loud cracking sound as parts splintered. He and the collapsing chair crashed heavily onto the tiles. Parts began separating. Both armrests came free from their rear supports. Rolling on his side, he managed to get to his knees. Applying his weight and strength on the chair's right front leg, he snapped it away from the seat and rungs. In a Herculean effort he was able to rip apart the rest of the chair's pieces, leaving him with the arms dangling from his wrists and the back of the chair still strapped to his back. In spite of the constraint, he had surprising maneuverability. Meanwhile, Isma'il's efforts were not as successful. He wound up flopping on the floor, hopelessly entangled in tape and splintered chair parts.

Struggling against his remaining impediments, Bruce began groping in the dark for one of the dead guard's weapons with no success. After several seconds he gave up. Reflecting on his recollection of everyone's position prior to the lights going out and confirmed by the muzzle flashes from behind the bar, Bruce quickly accessed the tactical situation. The two remaining cartel soldiers were holed up behind the bar. One of them was frantically spraying rounds from his Uzi out the back doors. The other had put up enough fire to force two of the rescue team who had breached the front door to seek cover in the bathroom in the entrance hall.

Intermittently, in the momentary flashes of gunfire, Bruce thought he detected the silhouettes of two men huddled behind a couch. That left three men unaccounted for; were they also cowering behind something, were they dead, or had they managed to escape? Then, over the sound of gunshots, he thought he heard a door slam, and it wasn't from the direction of the front door which he had come through. He made a quick assumption someone was attempting to make their escape through a side door. If that was the case, Azzan's men would have that covered; however, if it was to a garage with a waiting vehicle, that was a different scenario. Given the second possibility, Bruce knew they needed to make quick work of these last two soldiers before his villains could escape.

Analyzing the tactical position of the men behind the bar, he realized the chance of Azzan and his men quickly neutralizing these two gunmen was not good. On the other hand, they wouldn't be expecting an attack from the side. However, without a weapon, he'd have to physically overpower both of them at the same time. The arms of the chair still hung from his wrists and parts of the chair's back were taped to his body. Isma'il would be of no help, he was still struggling to free himself and Bruce didn't have time to help him. In order to prevent any bad guys from escaping, he'd have to act now.

He made a bold and dangerous decision. He picked up the lifeless body of one of the guards and shielding himself with it, he bolted across the room toward the two gunmen. The man closest to Bruce heard him coming and was able to squeeze off one wild volley. Only one round hit Bruce's "shield," passing through the dead man's chest and lodging in Bruce's shoulder. His adrenaline pumping, Bruce never even felt the impact as he flung the body at the shooter, landing it squarely on top of him. The man fell backward into the second man. Bruce pounced on both of them before they had a chance to react.

Through his night-vision goggles, Azzan saw Bruce begin his desperate dash across the room and watched in amazement as the two gunmen went sprawling out from behind the bar with Bruce on top of them.

Shouting, "Cease fire," he raced into the room. He shot one man in the leg and kicked the other in the head, rendering him unconscious. Meanwhile, the Boyers remained cowered behind the couch.

The two rescuers in the bathroom rushed out. Quickly assessing that Azzan had the large room under control, one rushed toward the downstairs bedroom and the other headed for the staircase.

Bruce was telling Azzan he suspected at least one of the bad guys was attempting to escape through the garage when there was a loud crash and the whole house vibrated.

"The garage!" Bruce shouted. "They must have smashed out with a vehicle!"

Dashing out the front door, Bruce and Azzan were just in time to watch a dark Hummer's taillights rapidly disappearing down the street. Bruce slammed his fist on the side of the house in frustration while Azzan shouted into his mic, "We've got runners in an SUV headed for the exit!"

Suddenly, from over the golf course, the methodically whop-whop-whop of chopper blades could be heard. Instantly, two brilliant searchlights materialized. It was the extraction helicopters streaking toward them. The lead chopper made a sharp heading diagonally on an intercept course with the fleeing Hummer. They had been monitoring the team's communications and picked up on Azzan's announcement. The second chopper hovered twenty feet above the pool, sending waves cascading over the side and into the desert.

Seconds later, a barrage of automatic weapons fire raked across the front of the fleeing Hummer, tearing up the hood, punching out its headlights, and sending it careening off the road into the sandy desert terrain lining the golf course. It plowed through an adolescent elephant cactus, bounced over basketball-sized rocks before sideswiping a potato-shaped boulder half its size and careening into an arroyo, where it rolled over several times before bursting into flames.

While Bruce and Azzan watched the chopper land and the guys spill out around the burning Hummer, Bruce calmly announced, "I think I've been shot."

Azzan stepped around the front of Bruce to take a look. "There's blood," he said. Then speaking into his mic he said, "I need a medic out front, Bruce has been hit."

Smiling at Bruce, he said, "Wait here for help. I'll go find out if anyone made it out of the Hummer."

While one of the guys injected the newest field dressing of miniature sponges directly into Bruce's bullet wound, the rest of the team finished clearing the residence and securing the Boyers. By the time Azzan returned, all hands were ready to go.

While he and Bruce were walking to the chopper, Azzan revealed, "Two bodies were trapped in the front seat and probably will be burned beyond recognition. I'm guessing they're Don Felix and Boris since we found Captain Marinov sprawled on the ground. Apparently, he was ejected or bailed out before the vehicle rolled over. He has some cuts and scrapes but it doesn't look like there are any serious injuries."

Within minutes the helicopters were airborne, racing for their midair refueling over the Pacific.

■ ■ ■

During the assault Vic anxiously listened to the intense gunfire and garbled communications, but it wasn't until Azzan dispatched the last two defenders in the house that he knew Bruce and Isma'il were safe. Then he got the word from the first chopper they were in pursuit of a fleeing vehicle. The next thing he heard was Bruce declaring he thought he had been wounded. After that, the radio communications were intermittent and confusing until Azzan finally announced both choppers were airborne with all team members and three detainees on board.

Initially he was concerned with Bruce's gunshot wound, but that did not stop him from broadcasting the success to all concerned. Later, after personally talking to the medic on board, he was sufficiently confident to inform Dana of Bruce's shoulder wound.

A lot of the details on the assault were still sketchy, but that would all be sorted out after the choppers landed at San Diego Naval Air Station. However, final word from Eitan and the confiscated sub would have to wait until they rendezvoused with the U.S. Navy task force outside Mexico's territorial waters later in the day.

CHAPTER 52

One month later at the Slaughter Ranch

It was a gorgeous late summer day on the North Coast. The brilliant afternoon sun had warmed the temperature into the mid seventies. Periodic puffs of cumulus clouds lazily drifted inland while beneath hundred-foot-tall redwoods on the Slaughter ranch, a celebration was beginning.

The clean forest air was being overwhelmed by swirling aromas from competing barbeques of roast pig, hamburger, hot dogs, corn, and other fresh vegetables.

In spite of the tragic losses of John Slaughter and Allie Reynolds, those gathered on the front lawn had plenty to be thankful for. All the remaining Boyers had been indicted on numerous offenses, and the family would never threaten the citizens of the North Coast again. Most of the Boyers' assets were in the process of being seized and would eventually be put up for auction. The county sheriff had resigned and was temporarily replaced by the former chief of police of the Yurok Reservation, a distant cousin to the Slaughter family and one of today's guests.

The leaders of the Yurok, Wiyot, and Hoopa tribes were beginning discussions on putting together a consortium to bid on many of the Boyers' assets when the Department of Justice put them up for auction. The tribes' objective was to maintain local ownership of as many profitable businesses as possible, thereby guaranteeing livelihoods for the hundreds of Native Americans in the county.

Events of the last few months had prevented Vic and Tanya from following up on the impromptu reception they received upon arriving at the Slaughter house with a party of their own. So today, almost seventy relatives and friends were invited for a good ol' country barbeque.

Standing next to Tanya and the kids on the front porch, Vic announced with all the volume he could muster, "Can I get your attention, please."

Several of the men supplemented his plea by shouting, "Quiet!"

Everyone's attention was immediately focused on the large man who had come to take over the Slaughter estate. Smiling at the crowd, Vic began, "Tanya and our children may be newcomers to Humboldt County, but from the first day we arrived, you have made us feel like family."

Someone in the audience shouted, "You are family," followed by loud clapping and cheering.

Nodding and holding up his hands, Vic continued, "It has been a memorable couple of months. Tanya and I have talked about it, and we both agree, we probably would have turned around and returned to Florida if it hadn't been for the reception we received from all of you and the timely intervention of some of my uncle's other old friends.

"For those of you who are unaware, six months ago at Uncle John's burial I first met his attorney Bob Rivett. Mr. Rivett then introduced me to two of my uncle's old friends, Bart Rock and David Tanner. Neither of them could be here today, but many of you met Bart prior to my arrival and while he was interim CEO of Slaughter Holdings."

Smiling, Vic continued, "Initially, I was extremely skeptical of how two septuagenarians could be of any help. Well, I quickly found out when David arrived with his son Bruce, Bruce's girlfriend, Dana, and two of his trusted bodyguards, Azzan and Eitan.

"Together we assembled an unbeatable team of professionals who were able to take down the dynasty that ruled this county for almost a hundred years, and in the process, we helped dismantle a huge international smuggling operation. I will forever be in their debt, as will the rest of you North Coasters, for ridding us of a century-old cancer."

Thunderous applause, whistling, and shouting erupted from the guests.

Vic held up his hands; he had one more jubilant announcement to share. It took several seconds for the noise to abate. When it did, smiling broadly, he proclaimed loudly, "Just one more bit of good news . . . Tanya heard through the grapevine last week her orders to the Middle East were going to be cancelled. Just this morning, she received her new orders . . . as soon as she gets off medical leave she is being reassigned as the U.S. Air Force's recruiter for Northern California. She will work out of the Army recruitment office on Broadway in Eureka until she retires next near. So, I guess we really are all here to stay."

Again there was deafening applause and shouting. People began rushing the porch to congratulate Tanya. As Vic stepped back to let the crowd gather around his wife, someone put a hand on his shoulder.

He turned to see Bob Rivett standing behind him. "I have to leave soon; but before I go, there's something I need to talk to you about . . . in private."

"You want to go in the general's old office?"

"You mean your office," Bob corrected.

Vic smiled. "I hope I get used to this soon."

"You will, and maybe what I have to tell you will help."

When they were in the office, Bob closed the door and his demeanor turned unusually serious.

Sensing the change in the attorney's mood Vic asked, "What now?"

"Okay," Bob started, "here it is straight out. I have not been totally honest with you. I wasn't sure you were ready to handle it, and there is nothing legally requiring me to reveal this to you."

He paused looking for Vic's reaction but all he detected was curiosity, so he continued, "You weren't the only beneficiary mentioned in the general's will. There is also a woman in Chicago."

"What, an ex-wife, girlfriend, daughter?"

"None of those."

Vic looked puzzled, but Rivett didn't seem anxious to add anything more. Finally, after enduring Vic's piercing glare he continued, "She calls herself Pricilla Whiterain."

Again he paused, and he watched Vic's eyes first narrow, then go wide. *He's ready,* Bob thought. "That's right, she's your mother."

Vic was speechless, and now that Bob had let the cat out of the bag, he felt obligated to tell Vic everything he knew. "Shortly after you enlisted, your uncle hired a private investigator to try to track your mother down. It took years, but the man was good and finally located her in Chicago. She was a drunk and a drug addict living on the street. He couldn't accept this was his niece's fate so he himself traveled to Chicago. Your mother didn't want anything to do with him, but he was unrelenting. Using his influence as a retired general and a Medal of Honor recipient, he was able to convince a judge to issue a temporary commitment order to have her evaluated. Once inside, the doctors decreed she presented a potential danger to herself and others, thus involuntarily placing her in a rehab facility.

"The general rented an apartment near the hospital and spent several weeks a month there until she was released. By then, they had established a rapport, and she seemed committed to staying sober. He continued to periodically check up on her. Finally, after many months, he reached the conclusion she was a changed person. That's when John offered her the opportunity to return here and live on the ranch. She was grateful but refused. That disappointed him, yet he still set up a trust fund for her to live off of and had her added to his will. "That was around 1990, and every year he went back to Chicago to check on her. By all accounts, she stayed clean but still wasn't ready to fully acknowledge her past life. In fact, she always pleaded with him not to tell you she was still alive.

"As executor of John's estate I had to contact her concerning John's death and the will. I personally went to tell her; she cried when I told her John was dead. Eventually, she composed herself and told me to wait while she went to get something. Minutes later she returned with a scrapbook. In it were pictures and newspaper articles of you John had given her. Then she asked me to give her the latest update about you. You and I had already met in Washington so I was able to provide her with a full account of you and your family. She beamed as I told her; she is so proud of how you turned out given the hell she put you through as a small child." Bob stopped again, unsure if he should continue.

Vic asked, "That's it?"

Bob let out a troubled sigh then stammering said, "Eh . . . eh, there was one more thing she told me. She . . . eh . . . said I was the first person she'd ever told this to."

His eyes tearing up, the attorney cleared his throat. "Hmmm . . ." Sighing again he said in a low voice, "The reason she wouldn't come back to Eureka is because of your father."

"My father!" Vic spat out. "Did she tell you who my father is?"

"She did. Do you really want to know?"

"Don't you think I have the right?"

"Yeah, I guess. Okay, but after I tell you, you'll understand why she kept this to herself for all those years . . . It was Clete Boyer Senior."

"Holy shit! Do you think my uncle knew?"

"Pricilla claimed she didn't tell him. My speculation is, originally, he suspected but he wasn't sure. Then, when you were arrested for assaulting Junior, he bluffed Clete Senior into thinking he knew for sure. When Senior didn't prosecute you and worked out the deal that allowed you to join the Air Force, he knew for sure."

Vic just sat there staring into space for a long time before Rivett asked, "So, what are you going to do now?"

"Hell, I don't know. One part of me is pissed as hell she's alive and never contacted me, but another part feels sorry for her. I just need some time to figure this whole thing out and talk to Tanya."

Bob Rivett stood up and started to leave; then he stopped turned around and said, "You know, she wouldn't have told me if she didn't want you to know."

ACKNOWLEDGMENTS

As I have with all three of my novels, I depend on the patience of early readers to give me a perspective on the story and characters. Their diligence in reading and providing feedback on over 300 pages of unedited and often muddled narrative is invaluable to me. This time I turned to four high school friends, Bill and Carol Sellerberg, Doug Casey, and Ray Zambuto. Don't worry, I won't ask you to do it again.

Equally as critical to finally getting my work acceptable for publishing are the professionals who have been working with me since my first novel, Jan Smith and Sandra Williams. I believe they really can turn a sow's ear into a silk purse.

As I toiled away for over two years on *Slaughter House Chronicles,* Angela, my soul mate, never displayed any jealousy over my latest obsession. I doubt, if the roles were reversed, I would have been so understanding and supportive.

If you enjoyed reading *Slaughter House Chronicles* . . .

A forty-year saga of an Italian-American couple whose lives are caught up and shattered by the wife's insidious family relationship with the New York mob.

FROM CHAPTER 67

Stunned by his brother's-in-law indictment, Al seemed to be in a catatonic stupor for several seconds. Bart watched as blood filled the capillaries in his archenemy's face and the arteries in his neck pulsed.

With clenched fists and spittle propelling from his mouth, Al Nicosia vowed, in a voice loud enough to be heard by everyone in the private dining room, "You son-of-a-bitch; your luck has just run out. This time you're going to wish you never heard of me or my family."

Bart, himself now in a bellicose mood, retaliated, "Are you stupid? I already wish I had never heard of you. As for your family, I'm not sure there is any blood relationship between you, John, and Gina. Given how different you are from them, I wouldn't be surprised if I found out some derelict left you on the Nicosias' doorstep."

That did it . . .

Try F. X. Biasi's other novels!

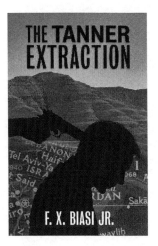

THE TANNER EXTRACTION

F. X. BIASI JR.

The bold political kidnapping of an American in Israel triggers an intense chase across the country while exposing many of the deep-seated political, social, and religious issues confronting the Middle East.

FROM CHAPTER 28

"So, Mr. Tanner, who do you trust to deliver the ransom?"

The caravan had finally stopped for the night at an unrecognized Bedouin village, Wadi El Mashash, just north of Mitzpe Ramon. They had parked the vehicles under a rickety tin-roofed shelter and were waiting in a smelly mud-and-stick shack for the locals to throw together a hastily made dinner for them.

"Look, whatever your name is, I figure I'm a dead man no matter what happens. Before we talk about delivering a ransom, let's talk about how you are going to guarantee I am released safely."

"Have you ever heard of a guarantee in one of these kidnap things . . . don't bother to answer. I know you already realize if you don't pay the ransom, you are dead. So which is it? Don't pay and you are dead, or pay and you might get out of this alive."

"I'm sorry, I was only reacting to something you said earlier: There might be a way of working something out."

"You're right. I did mention something like that. So let's assume I do have a plan; who do you trust to deliver the ransom?"

"Deliver! You don't really want it in cash; that would be 200,000 one-hundred-dollar bills. It would probably weigh 400 pounds, a ton if it's in twenty-dollar bills."

"Did you forget I'm a smuggler? I deliver contraband weighing a lot more than a few hundred pounds. But you're probably right. Although it may be the way your government prefers to make cash payoffs in Iraq, it doesn't make sense for me to tramp across the desert with a skid of hundred-dollar bills. At the moment I still haven't worked out all the details of the exchange, but humor me. Who do you want me to contact about the ransom?"

"My son, Bruce."

"Is he like you, a businessman?"

"No, he's an officer in the U.S. Navy."

"Good, we don't need an amateur involved in this."

ABOUT THE AUTHOR

Born Francis X. Biasi Jr. during the waning days of WWII in Queens, New York, Frank grew up on Long Island and attended Catholic grammar and high schools, where he excelled in football, baseball, and track. He married a "city girl," Angela, in 1966. The couple have four children and six grandchildren. Frank graduated from the University of Maryland and later attended Harvard Business School. From 1966 to 1971 Frank served in the United States Air Force.

Following military service, Frank's business career included positions as a financial and operations executive in the packaging, pharmaceuticals, and electronic industries. Frank retired in 1999 but has remained active as an independent consultant.

During their more-than-four-decades marriage, the Biasis have lived in Amarillo, Texas; Washington, DC; Baltimore, Maryland; Scranton, Pennsylvania; Milwaukee, Wisconsin; Lexington, Kentucky; Danbury Connecticut; Springfied, Massachusetts; and Charlotte, North Carolina.

Frank and Angela moved in 2008 to the Sacramento area, where he was inspired to write his first novel, *The Brother-in-Law*.